MR MUERTE

S.R. STUART

encour
press

EMBRACE THE TOUGH CONVERSATIONS, ENJOY THE OTHERS

Published by: Encour Press.

94b Abercrombie Street, Chippendale, Sydney, NSW, Australia.

ISBN: 978-0-646-89760-8

First Edition: 2025.

Cover & Interior Art by: Clarissa Luk.

For more information visit:
www.encour.co

There is no death, daughter. People die only when we forget them.

– ISABEL ALLENDE

THE CARD

ST. AUGUSTINE - USA - 2002

Four centuries ago, the Nuestra Señora de Atocha sank off the coast of Florida. Spanish gold spilled onto St. Augustine's shores, the tides offering the spoils to the pelicans. But the gold remained on the windswept sands as the sea oats swayed, waiting.

Four centuries later, another treasure washed up on the shores of Anastasia Island. The sea oats stirred, unbothered by time, as the desolate coastline waited once more. Now, only the crabs were impatient as they scuttled closer, skittishly surveying the ocean's new gift.

It was a young man.

Crabs nibbled his toes; the dead skin tastier than fish.

The sheriff stood over the corpse, his deputy by his side. They both stared at the body. The waterlogged jeans, the algae-stained sneakers, the skin crusted with salt.

"You think it's him?" asked the deputy.

"Yup. It's him, alright," the sheriff said with an Alabama drawl.

The crabs darted away as the deputy stepped forward. He reached into one of the dead man's waterlogged pockets. The deputy's face scrunched as his fingers closed around something plastic. Slowly, he pulled it free—a syringe slick with seawater.

"Give it to me," demanded the sheriff as he inspected the thin

1

plastic tube. A small sticker clung to its side, faded and scratched, showing a Spanish galleon.

El Dorado Dust

"Dope?" asked the deputy as he looked around the empty beach, the sand stretching for miles.

"Prob'ly walked out into the ocean high as a kite. Killed himself," said the sheriff matter-of-factly, his boots slowly sinking into the soft sand.

Suddenly, the white water surged forward, the tides skipping a beat as if trying to take the body back. The sheriff shuffled up the sandbank as the white water glazed the dead boy's face in a slick of salty foam. The two officers scanned the beach anxiously, the dense Anastasia Forest pressing close to the sand banks.

"Do you see that?" asked the deputy, pointing to a string of southern pines on the foreshore. The sheriff looked.

"It's called the wind," the sheriff said, turning away.

"I swear I saw a shadow moving in the trees."

The deputy stared into the forest, frozen.

"Prob'ly just another junkie," the sheriff said. "Forest's full of 'em—got a whole camp out there."

"Should we interview them? They might have seen the boy."

The water surged forward again, pushing the sheriff even higher up the sandbank.

"Tide's coming," said the sheriff.

The deputy took out a disposable camera, wound the film with a soft whirr, and clicked the shutter, capturing the boy floating in the whitewash.

"Look," said the deputy, pointing to the boy's forearm. "Injection marks."

"We should ID him and get out of here."

The sheriff waded in the water and reached into the second pocket, pulling out a soggy card.

"What's that?" asked the deputy.

The two men looked at it.

It was the card of death.

THE PARADISE MOTEL

ST. AUGUSTINE - USA - 2004

The parking lot could have been anywhere in America with rows of vacant lots, oversized pickups, and trolleys apathetically abandoned. But this was not anywhere in America. Just beyond the parking lot, gargoyle lions took their century-long sleep, guarding the bridge that crossed the Matanzas River. A stone's throw away stood the Castillo de San Marcos, the enduring seventeenth-century Spanish fort, its coquina walls whispering stories of centuries past. The only sign that the fort had been conquered was the ticket booth attendant, who, for $15, provided a stamp and a recommendation to the Starbucks across the road. In front stood the sign:

St. Augustine: Founded in 1565, it is the oldest continually inhabited city in America. Like Europe, but in Florida!

Lucia was going to miss it. The cobblestone streets, the Baroque buildings, and all their memories immortalized in shoddy souvenirs. She had accepted a scholarship to Stanford on the West Coast to study science and was set to start in the fall—her mother had refused to let her study liberal arts. In the meantime, she was working as a dishwasher at Madre's Tacos to save enough money to rent an apartment close to campus. In her head, she played a game where each guacamole-stained dish she scrubbed equaled one novel she could buy. It was the only way to make it manageable on minimum wage, building an imaginary library of clean dishes.

In her hands was one of the few books she had actually bought in real life.

The Shadow of the Wind

Lucia read the book in the car as she waited for her mother to finish buying groceries. Suddenly, there was a knock on the car door. A man gestured for her to roll down the window. Lucia thought he might be homeless. But despite his face being swollen with lumps, and the wind-encrusted layer of dirt plastered to his skin, his eyes looked gentle. She rolled down the window so there were only a few inches for him to speak through.

"Ma'am you wouldn't appen to aveee a light, would ya?"

Without thinking, she made a big gesture to tap both of her pockets as if they were empty.

"I'm sorry, I don't."

"Not a problem, Ma'am."

Her own words surprised her. She had a lighter nestled in a hidden pocket in her bag. Her response had been so reflexive; she had no power to stop the lie. She watched the man walk away, his slumped shoulders causing a sudden pang of guilt. *He even looked like him.*

"I found it. Here you go." She leaned over to wind down the window completely, her eyes darting around as she searched for her mother.

"Thank you, Ma'am. That's too kind of ya. Always when you be lookin' for something, you…" his voice trailed, as Lucia saw her mother coming out of the bathroom at the far end of the carpark.

"Just keep it," she said as she tossed him the lighter.

Lucia wound up the window as if she were closing a drawbridge and forced a stiff wave goodbye. He walked away from the car as he lit his cigarette, scratching his head. Luckily, her mother didn't see anything.

Mrs. Hernandez strode past the homeless man, her simple white blouse drifting by, indifferent to everything. She was in her usual colors: white, black, and gray, as if the church had its own catalog of approved outfits. Her naturally wavy Hispanic hair was tamed into straight, obedient locks, and the only jewelry she allowed herself was the gold crucifix around her neck.

Her mother slid into the car and turned the key in the ignition.

"You should've smelled that man," her mother said. Lucia didn't reply.

The car lurched forward, and they drove past the Bridge of Lions, its white towers gleaming in the late afternoon sun. Lucia lowered her book, letting herself enjoy the scenery. This was the last month she had in St. Augustine, the last moments with her mother. She wanted to savor them, but it felt like trying to plant seeds in scorched earth. They'd scarcely spoken all year, and now the silence had taken root, choking every fragile sprout of conversation. There was a time when they would talk about the birds. Her mother used to love them, her only pastime pointing out how the swirling thermals lifted ospreys high above the coast. Now, as they drove past Vilano Beach, a great egret waded through the salt marsh. Lucia said nothing, and the silence carried them down Cordova Street.

Eventually, the car rolled to a stop. Lucia scanned around; they were still right in the heart of the city, close enough that the edge of Anastasia Forest couldn't have been more than a five-minute drive away. In front of them, a neon sign flickered like a faltering heart.

The Paradise Motel

"We can stay here before you go to California," said her mother with a hint of disappointment as they looked at the two-story slab building. The pink motel reminded Lucia of a dollhouse owned by a rich kid that didn't much care for it with its faded walls left to crackle and peel in the Florida sun. The rundown motel backed onto scrubby woods. It was unusual to have so many palmetto thickets in the heart of the city without concrete. But the woods seemed to be the last mosquito sanctuary, a patch of green that somehow survived between buildings. Palmetto fronds rustled, hiding whatever lived between their leaves.

Lucia got out of the car. The smell of chlorine, moonshine, and burnt hair curlers welcomed them to the neighborhood. They'd bounced between motels and sketchy rentals in St. Augustine her entire life—anywhere that took cash and didn't ask for ID. Her mother didn't have any papers, even though she'd arrived in America over twenty years ago. It meant Lucia knew how to pack quickly: one suitcase, clothes rolled tight, ready to load into the car at a moment's notice, moving from motel to motel. She learned to enjoy the botched designs of Florida's worst architects—murals of dolphins, neon fla-mingos, and fiberglass tiki statues. However, the Paradise Motel was worse than the rest. At the center was a bean-shaped pool, proudly named Heaven's Spring. Its greenish tint more closely resembled a pond, only a few shades away from spawning frogs.

"We need to check in," said her mother.

Lucia paused; the guilt gnawed at her. She pictured leaving her mother here while she walked the green paths of Stanford, eating apples from campus trees.

"C'mon," said her mother.

Lucia grabbed her bag from the trunk, along with *his*. They made their way to the reception. The room was dimly lit with burnt orange wallpaper and mismatched bathroom tiles. Behind the desk sat a strange-looking man with fresh shaving cuts and gel-slicked hair. His proportions unsettled her—there was something eerie about them, though she couldn't quite name what.

Her eyes flicked to the plastic name tag pinned to his chest: Mick Coates.

"Can I help you?" Mick said, snapping shut a diary.

"I called ahead. You said you have a room at half price?" said her mother softly.

"Yes," he said, as he stared at Lucia with his cursor eyes, clicking. "You need to fill out a waiver." He passed over one of the papers covering his diary.

"Here."

Her mother started to sign while he resumed writing in his diary. At first, Lucia assumed it was something administrative, but then she noticed he was drawing something. She tilted her head slightly, trying to catch the angle of his strokes. It looked like a face. He caught Lucia peering at it.

"Our guests value privacy," he said firmly.

"Please, Lucia, just give me a second," said her mother, treating her like a child again.

After her mother signed, he handed her the keys: *Room 201.*

"Welcome to paradise!" he said. "You're on the second floor, first room on the left as you come up the stairs."

His eyes followed them to the door. They left the reception and made their way toward the stairwell. Something about the way he watched made Lucia's skin prickle, like a crab scuttling over her skin. He even looked like one—peering out of its shell, the way his neck disappeared into his torso.

"I got you a little something before you go to college," said her mother in a serious voice.

"Thanks," Lucia smiled. Her mother never got her presents. Lucia's smile faded—eighteen years together, and now she was leaving her behind. The guilt set in. All her mother had was the church, and their closest thing to a family friend was the pharmacist who dispensed her mother's pills.

As they walked in silence, Lucia's suitcase wheels thudded over the pavement, catching on gum and bottle caps like tiny speed bumps, as they passed the rooms on the bottom floor. Most of the doors were bolted shut, but she couldn't shake the thought of prying eyes pressed against the peepholes. A vending machine jutted into the pavement, forcing them to step around it.

"I could always stay another year and help you with the bills," said Lucia, shifting her weight as she peeled her shoe free from a sticky blot of gum.

"You're going to college," her mother replied firmly.

On their way to the stairwell, they passed a blonde lady, about walking-stick age, sunbathing on a lounger.

"Welcome to paradise," she said sarcastically, with a bottle of bourbon at her feet like a domesticated house cat. She burped, punctuating her sentence.

Lucia smiled.

They finally reached the stairs after passing a dozen or so doors. Lucia's foot hovered on the first step when something caught her eye in the shadowed corner of the stairwell. Nestled among the broken shards of amber glass was a thin glint of metal. She crouched closer. It was a needle, bent slightly at the tip, stained with a dark, tar-like residue. The needle tip prodded her memory. The dark images burst back. Her mother continued up the stairs as Lucia stopped.

Cautiously, Lucia wove through the shards of glass to get a closer look.

Then she saw it.

Stamped on the syringe, beneath a faint smear of grime, were the words she couldn't forget—*El Dorado Dust.*

Her stomach twisted. The Spanish galleon logo stared back at her; the same emblem that had been stamped on the waterlogged syringe found in her brother's pocket.

It was the same dope they said killed him when he walked into the ocean to die.

The crabs nibbling his toes.

Lucia felt a chill creep over her as though a shadow had been stitched into her skin. It had been over a year and a half since she first heard it in the news. St. Augustine police had barely investigated the case before ruling it a suicide. One journalist wrote that it was, "yet another tragedy tied to the city's drug epidemic." After the case was closed, the police returned all his belongings, including the card they had found in his pocket.

"Sorry for your loss."

It all felt so empty when the sheriff first told her, like he was talking about a runaway dog. He never wanted to leave her, Lucia thought. People only left behind things they didn't love. He loved her. *He must have.*

"Are you coming?" called her mother from the top of the stairs.

Lucia left the syringe and hurried up the stairs. Her mother stood at the door, waiting, but Lucia couldn't bring herself to make eye contact. The noise in her head was back—a ceaseless, nagging hum that refused to let her think. The smell of smoke calmed her. She looked up to see an old man perched against the railing in a three-piece suit, a cigar resting between his fingers. He had a warmth in his tobacco-stained smile that made Lucia feel like she knew him. Although she'd never seen someone in a three-piece before, especially not at a motel. The black silk framed his charcoal features, his thick goatee, and heavy-set eyebrows. He puffed rings into the clouds.

Room 201

The keys rattled as the lock refused to open. When the suited man realized where they were staying, he ashed his cigar on the motel railing and shook his head. It was the same look of pity that everyone always gave her.

"Come on," said her mother from inside. Lucia followed, only to be greeted by the smell of mercury vapor, the foul odor highlighting every defect in the room—the cigarette cavities in the cushions, the soda-stained carpet, and the deflated airbag pillows.

"It will do," said her mother. Lucia wondered if constantly wearing glasses had altered her perception of reality. Her mother probably saw a black and white version of a room that was 15 ft by 15 ft with a modest king single, a sofa bed for Lucia, and a kitchenette.

Lucia sat down on her sofa bed. The springs creaked under the weight of her back. She closed her eyes. Suddenly, she could hear Emi's voice. Then she saw him. He was standing right in front of her, his lush mop of brown hair. Everyone always said he could have been a movie star. Especially when he smoked, he looked like those noir detectives with the oversized trench coats. He stood in front of her—solid, real. Then, like a trick of light, he was gone. She rubbed her eyes, only to see the hazy orange wallpaper that must have been the closing credits to another dream.

"Don't you want to see your gift?" said her mother. "I know it's a month away, but…"

"You don't have to, Ma," Lucia replied.

"I wanted you to have something when you are on the other side of the country, to remember him by."

Lucia sat up. *Was she talking about him?* Usually, her mother pretended he never existed. She went to her suitcase, and scrounged around for the gift, and pulled something from the suitcase, no larger than her hand, wrapped in plain white paper.

"I know it's a month before you go, but here it is," she said. "So you don't forget him."

Lucia smiled and carefully tore open the paper, expecting to find a photo of him tucked inside. Instead, she uncovered a plastic necklace with a small oval pendant embossed with the Virgin of Guadalupe.

"I want you to keep this with you," her mother said. Lucia turned the pendant over in her palm.

"It's important you don't forget Christ while you're away. There will be temptations. The Virgin will protect you."

"Thanks," said Lucia, trying to mask her disappointment as she put on the necklace.

Lucia wouldn't forget Emi, even if her mother had.

FAREWELL

In one week, Lucia would say goodbye to St. Augustine forever. In her last three weeks at the motel, she had hardly spoken to her mother. The two had drifted in and out of the room, like the sun and moon, never crossing paths. Her mother worked as a receptionist at the Casa Monica Hotel during the mornings, while Lucia washed dishes at Madre's Tacos in the evenings. The only crossover was when Lucia came home after dark, her shirt stained with sour cream, while her mother lay in bed, smelling of lavender, rereading the same pages of *Isaiah 11*.

That night, Lucia sneaked in later than usual: *12 a.m.*

"Where have you been?" her mother asked, the light still on, clutching her rosary beads.

"Work was busy," said Lucia, dropping her bag at the base of the sofa.

"It closes at 10 p.m."

"I had to close up," said Lucia.

"Don't lie to me." Her mother pointed to the sand on the carpet. "I thought you were done with this." Her voice rose, heavy with the weight of a thousand arguments that always circled back to—him.

"Fine. I was on a date," Lucia lied.

Her mother's grip on the rosary beads slackened; her frown softened as well, though more slowly.

"Well, I suppose that's just part of your age," she said uncertainly. "Where'd you go?"

"We just got ice cream and walked on the beach," Lucia lied again.

"What was his name?"

"I don't want to talk about it."

Her mother looked at her skeptically through the lenses of her reading glasses.

"Are you wearing the necklace I gave you?"

"Yes," said Lucia, shifting her shirt to show the plastic Virgin of Guadalupe.

"Good. Make sure they see that."

Lucia slipped off her sneakers, the soles still dusted with sand from the shores of Anastasia Forest. She'd been back to the beach again, alone. After work, she went to the shore where Emi had washed up, like she'd done a hundred times before. She always sneaked past the homeless camps out there. The police claimed Emi had been out there with them, high as a kite, before walking into the ocean to die. But she didn't believe it. None of them had ever seen Emi—she'd asked. Another dead end.

Now, she avoided their camps in the forest. This time, the moonlight guided her to the shore, unseen.

She couldn't tell her mother that she kept returning to the place where he had died; she'd get angry again.

Tonight, along the sand, hundreds of baby turtles hatched, their tiny flippers rippling as they jerked toward the water. Moonlight gleamed on their shells, and the soft crash of waves called them home. Even the crabs scuttled aside, clearing the path.

Lucia had never seen a turtle migration before. There were hundreds of them going out into the ocean. It made her feel something deep in her stomach, so deep she could feel it pressing against her heart. A yearning to join them, even though she didn't know where they were going, or how to follow.

She missed him so much.

Even as she watched the turtles crawl across his grave, she couldn't help but wish he were there to see it—he would've found the humor in it.

It made her do something that surprised herself. She had carried the card of death—the same waterlogged one they'd found in his pocket. She had impulsively tossed it into the sea, watching as it drifted away on the backs of countless baby turtles. Lucia decided it was the last time she would visit the shore before she left. She wanted to leave with the memory of the turtles and the moon, not the daylight and the crabs.

It was gone. And now she could sleep.

✤

Lucia woke to the soulless sound of the motel alarm clock.

"You need to pack your bag," said her mother, giving her no time to acclimatize to the burden of consciousness. Lucia drowsily rubbed her eyes.

"You need to choose what to take from his bag. I'm not going to carry it around when you're gone," her mother said, pointing to the second suitcase. It was packed with Emi's things. Lucia hadn't brought herself to let go of any of it since he died. She hauled it from one budget motel to the next.

Lucia rolled out of bed; she'd only had a few hours of sleep. Her mother always woke her early, even though she worked the night shifts. Lucia adjusted to the lack of sleep, starting each day with a cold splash of sink water. This time, the motel water tasted of rusted pipes, sharp with fluoride.

She pulled on a pair of jeans and a plain white t-shirt before settling cross-legged on the carpet, sifting through the items in her case to see if there was anything she could throw away.

Her fingers drifted over the soft folds of fabric, then caught on something rough. She paused, tracing the coarse edges before realizing—it was the seashells. She collected a new one each time she went to visit Anastasia Beach. If she pressed the shells to her ear, she swore she could hear him whispering. He would've teased her for saying something like that, labeling her too innocent for the world. He'd probably have called the shells abandoned crab homes and joked that she was curating a crab graveyard.

She slipped the shells back into the suitcase, careful to keep them out of sight, while her mother stood by the stove, stirring a pot of café de olla. She stirred for the hundredth time, eyes fixed on the teacup like it was a sinkhole. She was somewhere else today.

Lucia could tell. Ever since she was little, Lucia had an uncanny ability to sense how other people felt, without them moving a muscle. Once, in Walmart, she saw an old man staring at canned beans with a heaviness in his eyes. When she said hello, he started to cry. Emi called her the Psychic Princess.

"Do you need me to make dinner tonight?" asked Lucia.

"It's okay," she replied, snapping out of her daze. "I'd better get ready for work," she said, pouring the undrunk tea down the drain. It reminded Lucia of those mornings when their mother left for work—how Emi would wait for the door to close before immediately putting on *The Crocodile Hunter*. They'd watch Steve Irwin wrestle crocs, while Emi, cigarette in hand, rattled off every reptilian fact he knew. She wanted to tell Emi that she hadn't watched a single episode since he'd been gone. It would have felt wrong to watch without his commentary. No one else knew every shell's Latin name.

Her mother opened the bathroom door and went to the shower.

Lucia waited for the sound of water, giving her a rare moment of privacy. Then she dug into the deepest part of her suitcase.

There was a scrapbook titled:

Investigation

When Emi died, it felt like Lucia was the only one who didn't believe the police reports. But all she had to go off was the card of death they found in his pocket. The one that was now floating in the sea. Still, she remembered every inch of it. It was too high-quality to be mass-produced with gold foil accents that glistened on its edges, and cardstock that felt like linen under her thumb. She was convinced that it had been handcrafted, because she couldn't find reference to it anywhere.

Mr. Muerte

Lucia knew enough Spanish to understand what it meant: *Mr. Death*. Even though her mother was from Mexico, she hadn't taught Lucia Spanish as a child. But Lucia and Emi had spent years eavesdropping on her hushed bathroom calls, quickly picking up all the serious adult words.

She knew just enough Spanish to listen for the name in films, hoping to catch even the faintest mention of him. She had begged Blockbuster for every foreign film, systematically working her way through a decade of Mexican movies, ears sharp for any trace of Mr. Muerte. But still, nothing. Then she'd resorted to collecting clippings from magazines, comic books, and old card games of anything that vaguely resembled a skeleton. But still, she couldn't find any reference to a character with that name. The closest thing she had seen was *La Santa Muerte*, the saint of death, printed on cheap t-shirts in Florida tourist shops for *Dia de los Muertos*. But when she asked the old woman at the market, the one who sold sugar skulls and candles for the dead, she just crossed herself and vigorously shook her head, denouncing any man of such a name.

Lucia had made one of those collages of newspaper headlines, the kind of cliché thing she'd copied from detective films. The first was about her brother disappearing, followed by the report when they found him washed ashore. She'd added a few other cases—stories of younger girls who were still missing—but no matter how hard she tried, she couldn't find any connections between them.

The only pattern she had was a string of disappearances—young girls with similar-sounding names, all from the city.

Marti Cortez.

Sofia Delgado.

Isabela Ramirez.

All Latin or Spanish names, but that was the only link. There was no mention of the card anywhere.

She picked up the tape recorder that she had used for interviews from the bottom of the suitcase. She must've spoken to a dozen people: her brother's ex-girlfriends, old band friends, even people he had chatted with on internet forums. But every time, it was a dead end. They all said the same: Emi was such a lovable person; he just struggled to love himself. "Self-destructive" was how his ex had described him. They all said he had a problem with heroin and was not acting like himself in the last few months of his life. Always disappearing for long periods of time, looking like he hadn't slept in days. Eternally jittery. No matter how many people told her the same thing, Lucia didn't believe he wanted to die. Emi had promised to watch the finale of *The Crocodile Hunter* with her—he never broke promises.

Someone killed him. She felt it in her bones.

Suddenly, the bathroom door opened, and her mother stepped out, a towel wrapped around her hair, already dressed in her hotel uniform.

"What are you looking at?" her mother said, peering down at the scrapbook on the floor. Her face changed when she realized what it was. "We've talked about this," she said irritably.

"I'm getting rid of it," said Lucia, tossing the investigation book onto the trash pile. She felt guilty instantly. But she didn't have space to take it to Stanford, and there wasn't a single useful piece of information in the notebook. *Maybe it was time to let go.*

"Have you sorted out what stuff of his you are going to take?" her mother said.

"No."

Lucia rummaged through Emi's bag. She once took a psych class where they said a room revealed more about a person than any questionnaire. Emi's suitcase would have defied all laws of classification. He had CDs for punk rock, rap, country, and classical music. His bookshelves were just as diverse, with classic novels, thrillers, and even a copy of *The Bhagavad Gita*. Emi was the most radically open-minded person she had ever known—his curiosity teetered on the edge of a destructive obsession, always chasing the next thing. He never ordered the same fast-food meal twice and was obsessed with opening letters, even the utility bills for his mother. He floated around the world, an amorphous bubble, being carried by the strongest wind. It was what made him so vulnerable to the wrong types of people.

She picked up a hefty book titled *The Tunnels of St. Augustine* with a sticker from the St. Johns County Public Library on its spine. Emi loved borrowing history books about the Spanish Empire and the conquest of Mexico. He was also obsessed with the history of the city, especially the tunnels.

"Where did you get that?" said her mother, pointing to the spine of the book.

"It was Emi's."

"No, it's not. It's the library's. I can't believe he didn't return it."

Her mother marched over and snatched it out of Lucia's hand.

"Well, maybe he was planning on returning it," Lucia said, hopefully.

"He never planned anything," she said. "Just another thing he didn't think about."

Lucia stayed silent. She didn't want to argue again.

"Now I'm going to take this back to the library before I go to work," said her mother angrily.

"I could take it with me to Stanford."

"Steal it?"

"No, I mean… just keep borrowing it," said Lucia, stumbling over her words.

"I didn't raise thieves," snapped her mother.

"Fine, I can take it to the library for you," Lucia said.

"No, I'll do it. It's my responsibility—I need to apologize to the librarian."

"Why are you making such a big deal out of this?" Lucia asked.

"Because stealing is stealing," her mother said firmly. "I don't care if it's a book or a dollar—it's not how I raised you."

Lucia stayed silent. *You didn't raise him,* she thought. Her mother kicked him out long before he died. She was the one who made Emi homeless. He had nowhere else to go, and she knew it. But admitting he was actually on the streets was too much—easier to pretend that he didn't exist at all.

"Okay," Lucia said. She only had to get through one more week. Lucia heard Emi whispering again, his voice soft and distant, like echoes in a shell. She pulled out the birthday letter from the suitcase, the final thing he ever wrote to her.

✦

Dear Lucia,

Happy 17th Birthday! I know it's not a particularly important milestone. It's no longer your sweet sixteen and you're not old enough to die for the motherland. But I wanted to write a longer letter than usual—I've been rather sentimental of late. It's strange that we can only say nice things to each other on birthdays—I really should've said this stuff on the other 364 days of the year. Fuck it. You're the best little sister in the whole wide world. I know everyone says that in birthday cards, but thanks to our father's infidelity, you're probably one in a hundred, kid! You don't need to lie for me. I know I'm not the best older brother. I drag you down like an anchor as Ma would say. I don't know where she gets the nautical imagery from, like she's some old crone from the Elizabethan era. But she's right—I do drag you down. I guess she doesn't see how much fun it is getting shipwrecked together. All my favorite memories are of me as the captain of your moral corruption, like when we swapped all the R-rated VHS tapes for rom-coms. I still laugh thinking about how many first dates we torpedoed by having a slasher flick play when the guy thought he was being smooth with *When Harry Met Sally.* I really suck, don't I?

But I wanted to say thank you for putting up with me. Sometimes it feels like you're the only thing that keeps me here. I'm sorry for putting all that pressure on you. Everything will go back to normal soon—I just have some things I need to work through. Until then, Ma's right—I think that it's best that I don't stay with you. Please don't get angry with Ma for kicking me out, we may have our differences, but she's only trying to look after you. Even if she gets caught up in all that 'pleasure is sinful' Puritan crap. She would have fit right in a hundred years ago with a pitchfork and a frown.

Sorry, this letter really has been a self-indulgent rambling mess. I was always bad at writing essays at school—I guess I'm too distractible. I guess the thesis of this letter is twofold: a) happy birthday, I love you, and b) I promise I'm getting better. I can't wait till Ma lets me see you again and we can explore our favorite parts of the city. I promise I'll take you to visit the Fountain of Youth again, just like we did as kids.

Remember when I dared you to drink from the spring, and Ma cuffed me over the ear? It was probably the filthiest water in America—teeming with tadpoles, typhus, and who knows what else—but you gulped it down without a second thought. You have always been the greatest sidekick. Who knows, maybe the water will make us live forever and we can grow older than the tallest tree in the Anastasia Forest. You may not see me for a while, but trust me, I'll be back as soon as I can. Just remember the world's full of darkness—you have to work to find the light.

Happy birthday little sis. Love you forever and ever.

MOTEL OMENS

It was Lucia's last day in St. Augustine; her flight was booked for 5 a.m. the next morning. She looked at her packed suitcase, waiting for her at the door, stuffed full of shells and socks. The room's fluorescent light flickered, unsteady. In the past month, her eyes had calibrated to the perpetual cloud of smoke drifting through the air vents and the melodic microwave beeping in the early hours of the morning. But she never got used to the view of the thick, anti-ram bars welded to the window. She hoped that her room in California had a view of something green, or at least a rogue ivy creeping through a crack in the wall. She loved nature, but she had rarely experienced it outside of what she saw on TV.

Lucia sat by the window, waiting for her mother to return from work, anticipating their final silent drive to the airport that loomed ahead. She restlessly traced patterns on the glass, trying to figure out if she was making the right decision. It felt like she was finally giving up on him, just so that she could make her mother happy. Emi would've laughed at a school like Stanford. He lasted one semester at St. John's Community College before he quit to self-study. He told her he learned physics from an old Russian at the bus stop and understood people better after haggling for cod with Greek ladies at the Sunday market.

Lucia was giving up.

She felt her chest tighten. Needing air, she pushed the door open. The sun dipped toward the horizon, painting pink streaks across the Florida sky and coating the strip mall across the road in a honeyed glow. For a moment, the light filled in the motel's pink plaster cracks.

Then she heard crying.

"I told you to keep an eye on her," came the crying voice.

"The Gators were playing," said a man defensively.

"I only left her with you for an hour."

"It's your kid."

"Not now, Frank. Not fucking now," she yelled. "Where is she?"

Lucia peered over the balustrade to see where the voices were coming from. A man sheepishly slinked out of the door in his boxer briefs and a pair of flip-flops.

"Alright, fine. I'll ride around 'n see if I can spot her."

He made his way to the parking lot, fumbling with his car keys and Gators can cooler that he had rescued. The lady came into view, pregnant and holding a can of rum. Her mascara-smudged eyes locked onto Lucia.

"You seen my girl? She's six—lil' thing with blonde curls. Ain't seen her nowhere," she yelled from next to the pool.

"No, but I'll come help," Lucia said, hurrying to the stairwell. She took the steps two at a time, dodging a tipped-over trash can before cutting toward the pool, where the pregnant woman stood waiting.

"Where did you last see her?" asked Lucia, panting.

"With my no-good piece'a shit boyfriend," she said, taking a sip of rum.

"What's her name?" Lucia asked, already scanning the dark edges of the parking lot. She tried to keep her voice steady, but something felt wrong.

"Jolene."

"Alright, I'll start asking people if they know anything," said Lucia.

"Preciate it, hon," the pregnant woman said, wiping her nose on the back of her hand, her eyes red from tears.

"I'm real nervous, you see. The other day, my friend said she saw a girl get scooped up in a van down by the Sunoco on Ponce Boulevard. She swears it happened, but she's all strung out, so I don't know if she's talkin' shit or not."

"We'll find her," Lucia said.

Lucia dashed toward the parking lot, hoping Jolene had wandered across the road to the strip mall. In the lot, leaning against the back of the reception building, stood the man in a three-piece suit, watching the world pass by at the pace of his cigar.

"Excuse me, sir, have you seen a little girl called Jolene?" Lucia asked politely.

"What does she look like?" he replied.

"She's six—blonde hair."

"I haven't, sorry. But if someone's looking for a sixty-year-old with black curls, let me know," he said, exhaling smoke with a tired smile.

"She's missing."

The man straightened, planting both feet firmly on the ground as his cigar lowered to his side.

"Have you checked the woods?" he said, concerned, jerking his thumb toward the back of the motel.

"No," Lucia replied.

"Let's look there. My name is Javier by the way."

"I'm Lucia."

Javier marched toward the woods with a sudden urgency that caught her off guard—the moment he heard she was missing, his cool, cigar-smoking demeanor disappeared entirely.

"This way," he said to Lucia.

Lucia had seen kids play there before; some of them swung on low-hanging oak limbs, building forts out of palmetto fronds and fallen pine branches.

"How long has she been gone?" he said in a very serious voice as they stepped off the concrete onto soft, uneven dirt at the edge of the woods.

"I'm not sure—maybe an hour."

With the sun gone, the shadows felt heavier, the damp air clinging to her skin as she thought of the little girl alone. Javier didn't hesitate, even in his suit. He pushed through the dense oaks, little twigs snagging on the silk, mud coating his cotton socks.

"Jolene," Javier yelled.

Lucia followed behind, palmetto fronds scratching at her ankles.

"Jolene," she echoed.

Lucia froze. In the mud ahead, something caught her eye—tracks. Long, wide, uneven grooves cut through the dirt, as if someone had been dragged on their stomach. Javier saw it too, following the trail deeper into the woods.

"We need to find her before it's dark," he said.

Lucia kept her eyes glued for little footprints, but there was just the trail of sludge. The air smelled sour, the kind of rot that clung to places where water pooled too long.

"We found her! We found her!" the lady's voice yelled.

Lucia and Javier froze. They turned to each other, half-smiling in relief—but then their eyes drifted back to the trail in the mud. Javier frowned, nudging the dragged path with the toe of his shoe.

"Could have been a gator," he muttered.

"We should go check on her," Lucia said, thinking of how scared the girl must be. They hurried back to the motel.

When they arrived, the little girl was already grinning, ice cream smudged around her lips as she laughed, clutching her mother's hand like she was being picked up from school. Her mother absentmindedly stroked her hair, her fingers sticky with condensation from the rum can. A few motel guests had gathered at the commotion.

Then Lucia saw him.

The sheriff stood in front of them, a gray goatee, a cowboy hat, and the six-foot swagger of a man who thought he belonged on Mount Rushmore.

"Found her wanderin' down George Street, tryin' to sweet-talk some older kids into buyin' her ice cream," the sheriff said, in his thick Alabama drawl. His gaze flicked to the pregnant woman's rum can. "Ain't illegal, ma'am, but might be best if you set that down."

"I 'preciate ya findin' her an' all, but don't go tellin' me how to live, Sheriff."

"Just a suggestion, that's all," the sheriff said, his tone lighter as he looked down at the girl. "You take care now, alright?"

He turned to leave but stopped when he saw Lucia.

"Lucia? How you doin'?" he asked, his voice slipping into something almost friendly.

"I'm good."

"You stayin' outta trouble?"

"Yeah," she said flatly.

"Glad to hear it. Don't want you runnin' with the wrong crowd. Your brother had so much—"

Lucia stopped listening. The sheriff's voice faded, as the memory started to play. She could see it—Emi locked in the cell.

After he got kicked out, he drifted through the city, sleeping wherever he could. One night, he curled up under the palms in the gardens of the Casa Monica Hotel. The sheriff found him there and threw him behind bars for two nights. She still remembered the call: Emi's voice, scratchy through the static.

"I'm okay. Don't tell Mom."

When Emi died, the sheriff brushed it off—another troublemaker, nothing more. He didn't look twice at the card of death, just chalked it up to some Mexican gambling. She wouldn't forget how he handled her brother's case, no matter how much Southern hospitality he feigned.

During her conversation with the sheriff, Javier stood at the vending machine, punching in the code for a Coca-Cola. As the can dropped, he grabbed it, popped it open with a hiss, and strolled over, carbonation still fizzing.

"Sheriff," said Javier.

The sheriff's swagger changed when he saw him.

"I best be leaving. Sorry if I caused any trouble," he said, talking to the floor before nervously scuttling off. Javier took an indulgent sip of his Coca-Cola, then let out a slow, satisfied exhale.

"What happened with you two?" asked Lucia.

"I should ask the same to you?" said Javier. "Seems like you two aren't the greatest friends."

"Yeah. We have history," Lucia said.

"Same," said Javier.

"What happened?" asked Lucia.

"It's not a nice story," Javier said, gazing pensively at the water.

"That's okay," said Lucia. "I can listen to sad stories too."

Javier cleared his throat and pointed to the pool.

"Someone died there, a mother and her children. She was my friend, Maya."

"What did he have to do with it?"

"He called it a suicide. They barely even looked for evidence in her room."

Lucia froze. It was just like Emi.

"Come to think of it, I think you are staying in her room," Javier said.

Room 201

"Thanks for your help today. I need to pack my bag," said Lucia, shuffling up to the room, disturbed by what Javier had said.

⚜

Her mother arrived late that night; Lucia was tucked in bed, ready for her flight the next morning. Her mother commenced her usual nightly ritual, taking out the Gideon Bible from the motel drawer. She had her bedside light on as she flicked through the pages to find her place. Then something made her pause.

"Lucia," her mother said firmly.

Lucia looked up, her eyes heavy with sleep.

"Yes?"

"Why did you put Emi's card in here?" she said angrily. To Lucia's surprise, her mother lifted the card of death. It was in perfect condition, the skull glistening in the low light, with gold foil accents sparkling. *But she threw the card into the ocean.*

"Where did you find that?" Lucia asked.

"It slipped out of the pages," her mother replied.

"I'm sorry, I must've misplaced it," Lucia lied, coming to take the card from her mother. This card was new. The texture was unmistakable—the same linen grain beneath her thumb.

It was the card of death.

Lucia's eyes flicked to her suitcase. Her flight was in the morning—one last step, and it would all be behind her. But after a year of nothing, just as she was ready to move on, a clue had dropped straight into her lap. If she left now, she'd always wonder. Lucia exhaled sharply, pressing her thumb against the gold-foil skull.

She had already made up her mind.

THE STORYTELLER

The alarm clock crowed in the half-light. It was time. Lucia pressed her face into the pillow as her mother rolled out of bed.

"Come on, let's go. We don't want to be late," her mother said, grabbing her keys from the bedside table, where the Gideon Bible lay open from the night before.

Lucia hesitated, then sighed. "I checked before bed—the flight is canceled."

Her mother frowned, fishing the granules of sleep sand out of her eyes. "What? Since when?"

"Last night, I called the airline. Something about a mechanical issue." Lucia sat up, keeping her voice steady. "They said they'll rebook me."

Her mother blinked hard, still waking up. "Why didn't you tell me?"

"I figured there was no point waking you up over it."

Her mother anxiously rubbed her arm. "But you could get kicked out of the course if you don't make it to orientation day?"

"I can miss a few days; it's fine. I'll call later and see what flights they have this week."

Her mother exhaled sharply, eyeing her. "Fine. But you better actually rebook, Lucia. You're not putting this off."

Lucia nodded. Her mother rolled back into the bed, pulling the sheets over her head. Lucia sat on the edge of the sofa, turning the card of death over in her hands, its gold foil catching the dim morning light. *She had thrown it into the ocean.* She was sure of that. Yet here it was at her fingertips again, crisp, untouched—not like the warped, salt-stained card of before.

It was new.

Same printing. Same name. *Mr. Muerte.*

But who was it for?

She thought about what Javier said—the woman and her children who had died in the pool. The police labeled it a murder-suicide, but something didn't add up. The card of death had appeared twice now—first in her brother's pocket, and now tucked so innocuously into the motel Bible. She thought of that night on the beach, watching the baby turtles crawl toward the sea. Yet here it was again, as if it had ridden the tide back to her. The card was trying to tell her something—something that might lead back to Emi. She needed to find out more about what happened to that woman—what was her name, *Maya?*

She pulled on her hoodie and stepped outside into the crisp morning air, heading for Javier's room. From memory, he lived two doors down. She didn't know his sleep schedule because the curtains were perpetually closed. She walked outside. Skittish eyes peeped from the neighboring curtains before they scuttled back behind the pinch pleats.

She knocked on his door. The smell of freshly burned incense drifted into her nose as the spices danced their way up to her brain, creating an image of a cozy carved treehouse. Javier peered out of the door.

"Ah Lucia. To what do I owe the pleasure?" A thin slither of orange light, the same color as the last minute of a sunset, crept out from behind the door. The soft, warm glow was a stark contrast to the harsh fluorescent lights illuminating the other rooms.

"Why does your room look so different?" asked Lucia curiously.

"Because a room is a reflection of a mind. And I refuse to ruin the quality of my thinking by the unfortunate design of this place."

As he spoke, the door drifted open a fraction, allowing Lucia to peer inside. He had completely refurbished his room. Instead of the basic bedside table, there was an oriental cabinet with dragon carvings on the panels. A bronze water jug sat on top, beads of condensation dripping down its sides, freshly filled.

"Wow, I didn't know you could bring your own furniture," Lucia said, momentarily forgetting why she had come to his door.

"Neither did management. But sometimes it's just easier to not say anything."

Then she remembered the card in her pocket. Lucia hesitated; people usually treated her like she was delusional when she mentioned something as mercurial as the card of death. Especially a stranger that she barely knew. But Javier knew things about the woman.

"I need to ask you something. Is it okay if I come in?" asked Lucia.

Javier exhaled through his nose, glancing at the floor.

"I'm a perfect stranger. I'd feel uncomfortable having you in my room… unless, of course, your mother knew about it."

"That's the problem," said Lucia, scanning the corridor. "My mother can't know I'm speaking to you." Her mother would never forgive her if she knew she had missed her plane to talk to strangers about tarot cards.

"That sounds conspiratorial. I do love a good conspiracy, but I don't know if it's quite appropriate," he said, shutting the door a smidgen.

"Please. I need to ask you something, it's important," Lucia said. "It's about your friend who died in the pool: Maya."

Javier's resistance softened, injured a little by the name. He opened the door again.

"Fine, come in," he said. Lucia stepped inside.

The degree of refurbishment was far greater than she realized. He had swapped the sofa for a mahogany coffee table with two plush red chairs that looked like they were borrowed from Buckingham Palace. There was a bookshelf stacked high with leather-bound books, with old maps stuck on the wall. Next to it was a framed picture of the Virgin of Guadalupe, the same as Lucia's necklace.

"Would you like some coffee?" asked Javier as he made his way to the kitchenette. "Please feel free to take a seat."

Lucia sank into one of the plush chairs as Javier disappeared into the kitchenette.

"Black coffee?"

"Thanks," replied Lucia.

"I like your decorations," said Lucia, pointing to the maps on the wall. She noticed that in contrast to the Paradise Motel's dull wall art, the maps were thoughtfully picked. Each one was an old Spanish chart showing trade routes and colonial territories.

"Maps tell stories that history books often miss," said Javier, measuring coffee into a brass filter. "The Spanish were artists as much as explorers. Look at those sea monsters in the corners—they knew the ocean held more mysteries than we could chart."

The rich scent of coffee filled the room as he poured water in slow, careful circles. His movements were precise, ritualistic.

"You seem to know a lot about history," Lucia said, watching him pour, confused by the enigmatic old man.

"It was my first love, before coffee." He smiled, the wrinkles around his eyes deepening. "In Mexico City, where I grew up, every street corner held a story. You'd find Aztec ruins under colonial churches under modern shops. Layer upon layer of history."

He brought over two delicate cups, the coffee inside dark as ink.

Lucia noticed how his suit remained perfectly pressed even as he bent to serve, not a thread out of place.

"You must also be from Mexico," he said.

"My mother is," Lucia said, idly tracing the rim of her untouched coffee. She looked up. "How did you know?"

"Your necklace," he said, pointing to the Virgin of Guadalupe around her neck. "It's a very *Mexican* saint."

Lucia touched the pendant. "It's from my mother. She thinks it will protect me from boys."

Javier smiled, a gentle understanding in his eyes. "Well, you're a good daughter for wearing it then."

"I wear it to make her happy. She's... very traditional with her faith."

"Ah." Javier settled into his chair. "Many mothers are. My own mother was the same way. Mass every Sunday, *novenas* for every occasion. She even kept these dried marigolds in her kitchen and whispered to them so she could talk to the dead." His eyes crinkled with fondness. "The old ways have a way of surviving."

"My mother doesn't believe in all that. Our priest says the dead only talk to God," Lucia said, remembering the countless sermons that she and Emi had been dragged to.

"Well, I'm afraid your mother gave you the wrong necklace," Javier replied.

"What do you mean?" asked Lucia.

"The Virgin is a folk saint. When the Spanish conquered Mexico, they were very clever. They didn't destroy our gods—they transformed them." He gestured to his own Virgin on the wall. "They built their churches on our temples, painted saints with Indian faces. But underneath..." He smiled, setting down his cup. "My grandmother used to say the old gods still live in the cracks between the stones."

"You mean they combined gods?"

"Precisely," said Javier. "The Christian God just inherited the power of all the gods before him. And their darkness too."

Lucia sipped her coffee.

"But don't tell your mother I said all that. I don't want to corrupt a good Christian," Javier said. "But I don't suppose you came to me for a history lesson. What is it that you wanted to talk about?"

"I wanted to know about what happened to the woman who lived in my room."

Javier paused, shifting back in his seat, mulling over the question as if it were tobacco between his teeth.

"What would you like to know?"

"Everything," Lucia said.

Javier took a slow sip of his black coffee, his gaze distant.

"It's a sad story."

"I need to hear it."

He exhaled, setting the cup down.

"Alright. I'll tell you."

THE MAYOR AND MAYA

Evil was set in motion long before us and will continue long after we're gone.

"All we can do is watch its ripples spread through time. Nothing is more satisfying than watching the dominoes fall one by one until they end in tragedy. That's why we read books, watch movies, and listen to stories about evil things. We package our darkness into neat boxes and ship them to others with a nice bow of explainable events. Gift-wrapped causality. It allows us to isolate the first moment that went wrong, then we can dispose of it like a piss-stained sock, with our own conscience as clean as cotton. If we understand where our character went wrong, we can avoid their mistakes and escape their fate.

"After all, it is the rule known by all storytellers. Bad people are punished, and the good are rewarded. Everyone knows the age-old tale of the unfaithful lover. The cheating husband shot by his wife. We act disgusted but deep down we are satisfied. Our souls nod in silence, as if we respect the work of fate, yet are too 'civilized' to ever voice our approval. For thousands of years, our species has used stories to define right and wrong—every good story carries a moral message if you look closely enough. But what about the stories that don't? Where evil is as random as the wind. Now this is the type of story that we never hear. It's impossible to understand. There are no moral lessons. It's just pure chance that hangs around our neck as we wait for the day that the gallows drop from beneath our feet. This is why the story I am about to tell is so uncomfortable.

"Truth doesn't care for neatness. In this story, death came as quietly as a fox stealing a hen in the night. Why it chose Maya, we will never know—but I won't try to force it into some neat conclusion for you. I will merely tell it as it was.

"Maya was a single mother who moved here a few years ago with her two children: Carl and Jasmine. Aged five and six. They were the only kids in the motel who let their elders go down the stairs first, but I always insisted they go before me, not out of any illusion that I am a young man. Carl would always say 'fanx,' and Jasmine rounded it off with a 'Mister.' 'Fanx, Mister.'

"It made me smile every time. That's what happens to children when they have an English teacher for a mother; grammar and manners are bundled together. Maya taught in Beaufort, Georgia, and was as dedicated to her students as she was to her children.

Even though she worked in one of the most illiterate districts in the country, she had her students acting out Steinbeck's *Of Mice and Men* and maxing out their library cards. At first, the librarian suspected students were stealing the books to make paper planes. Only when the librarian read in the local news about the success of the English department did she realize it was Maya's doing. It turns out her husband also had ambitions for being in the paper, albeit not the *Beaufort Tribunal.* He left them to double down on a fledgling music career in California—but not before swindling all the kid's college savings for the plane ticket. She never wanted them to be jaded, to carry the baggage of a walkout father like she had, so she gave them the gift of an honorable one. Maya told the kids that their father had joined the army and was stationed in Japan. An invention that ensured she could never voice her anger about him leaving them behind. She had to get out of Beaufort. So she left. And what better place than the Sunshine State?

"From the moment she checked into the Paradise Motel, she attracted a lot of attention. If you saw a photo, you might understand why. Maya was one of the most gorgeous women anyone had seen. Black skin, long curly hair, and eyes that lulled you into a sober daze, but it wasn't just her looks that fizzled men like insects around a flame.

"She didn't drink. Didn't smoke. Didn't have men over. It made all the lowlifes want her more, as if she possessed the serum to save them from their self-destruction. She attracted some precarious people. There was Mr. Coates, the receptionist, who used to collect her gum wrappers from the bin. Whenever she was by the pool, he would lurk, following her around like an inseverable shadow. One time, I even saw him in the laundry sniffing her underwear; he even had the audacity to crumple them in his pocket and take them as a souvenir, right in front of me. There were other less obsessive types, but equally dangerous. The type of drunk too delirious to take a hint. They would constantly try to court her by offering her sips of the bottle; she would always decline in a way that was firm but polite.

"A sip of summin spicy Maya?"

"I'm no good with spice, but thank you."

"That was her demeanor. She treated everyone with respect, even those who didn't deserve it. When I asked her why she never report- ed Mr. Coates to management, she said that her priority was her children; she couldn't risk getting kicked out of the one place that she could afford. So she kept going, without complaint. I never once heard her talk badly about this place. But make no mistake, she was dogged about getting out of here. Suppose that's what I admired the most about her: she didn't make you feel inferior while she aspired for more. A lot of people tell themselves they are better than their circumstance and by extension the people in it. Everything's one big Band-Aid that they can't wait to rip off the moment things start to get better. But not Maya. She didn't think she was better than anyone, even though she was better than us all.

"After work, no matter how tired she was, she would read stories to the kids by the pool. She even wrapped their school books in plastic sleeves so the pages wouldn't get wet. She heard somewhere that a child's future vocabulary was a function of their parents' vocabulary. Seeing as Carl and Jasmine would hear half as many words without a dad, she took to speaking to them in a verbose way.

"Carl, don't make me *reprimand* you."

"But unlike many parents who had such high ideals that would crumble when the first thing went wrong, Maya was persistent. She would speak to them like this even when Jasmine stubbed her toe while Maya juggled Carl in her other hand.

"Now, now, sweetie. Pain is *transitory*. Just a moment, and I will patch it up for you."

"She loved those children. Some people will tell you differently, but they're just trying to push over dominoes that never existed. They forget the way things were. But Maya did struggle to provide. She always tried, despite how difficult it was on just her teacher's salary. Some in her position might have sought a wealthy man—it would have been easy with her looks. But Maya never went on dates, nor was she receptive to the advances of opportunistic men. Her life's purpose was her children, and she did not want to subject them to *transitory* men, in and out of their lives like all the others she had known. It was easier to keep that door closed. Besides, there was no money for a nanny and no trust for a friend. There was just family, the three of them, nestled into their small room as perilously as a bird's nest on power lines. But things were about to change for Maya, and what she never looked for, found her. It all started when the mayor of St. Augustine decided to knock on her door.

"Knock, knock?"

"Who's there?"

"The end of your life."

"Death enters our lives unnoticed, slipping into the places we never think to look—on our lover's lips, or resting quietly at our own fingertips. That's what makes it so insidious. It learns our habits, when we wake up, what we eat and only when we feel most at peace, does it take us away. We get lost somewhere very dark, our old life, a faint pulse of light that we can scarcely see before complete nothingness. Then we are lost forever.

"But before Maya met death, she met love.

"His name was Rami Garcia, the mayor of St. Augustine. A big man, six feet tall, who shook hands with the force of a bear and hugged with the warmth of his mother, a Cuban lady, whom he still visited once a week. His family lived in a nice house on the beach with photo frames of them in matching white outfits. The worst thing he had done in his life was consume a six-pack in his senior year of college, nine months before he was 21. But he never vomited. He made that clear in the papers. He was steadfastly resolute on becoming the President of the United States and anyone who met him for more than a second could tell. While there was great warmth to him, there were many things that were simply too rehearsed to be natural. Like the way he knew the names of the little towns in Florida, and when someone in a gas station told him they were from Palatka, he would smile and say, "Great place, I love the key lime pie from Wendy's." It was impossible to know whether he had ever tasted the pie or whether a staffer had practiced with him what he needed to say. But everyone here liked him as much as you could like a politician.

"The first time I saw Garcia, he was doing the rounds, knocking on motel doors to cajole the 'downtrodden.' Mr. Taylor, a Vietnam vet four doors down, kept insisting he wanted everything 'back to the way it was in the good old days.' Garcia teased him, "If you go back to the good old days, the Spanish owned this place."

"He knocked, listened, and smiled his way through each floor. Floating from door to door until he stopped outside Maya's room. He knocked. She opened. Nowadays we live in a world that thinks it is too wise to believe in the magical. In an older time, this infatuation would have been blamed on a curse. But in this country, the most that we are allowed to say is that it was 'love at first sight.' A reluctant acceptance that something can pass through the air and disarm all reason, causing people to act in inexplicable ways. But like so many things, it is wrong. A man as ambitious as Garcia does not give up his life's dream because of something as ill-defined as love. And a woman as devoted to her children does not forgo everything for something as feeble as a feeling. There was a force more powerful than gravity that drew those two together. One they fought hard to resist. While no one heard the contents of their first conversation, people who saw them said it was over in a few seconds. Maya shut the door in the politest way possible. I can only imagine her pressed against the back of the door frame as she prayed to God that she would never see that man again. But fate doesn't care for our prayers. And as the story goes, one day Garcia was having dinner with his beautiful wife and children in their sprawling home, and as he bit into his wife's famous chicken roast, a macabre taste spread on the tip of his tongue. Each bite got more acidic until he had to rush to the trash to regurgitate the pulped chicken.

"What's wrong, honey? I knew it was too dry."

"No, I just bit off more than I could chew," he said.

"Soon more and more things in his life started to feel wrong. His shoes felt two sizes too small, his wedding ring two ounces heavier, and a bird shat on his car almost daily. At first he thought he was going crazy. There was no one to confide in about these strange occurrences, no checklist for his symptoms. But then he realized there was a pattern. Whatever was happening to him, it had all begun the day he first met Maya. That was when everything started to go wrong. Now all this is what he told a handful of journalists after the fact. Many have labeled them as excuses, trying to align the mystical to distance himself from what happened. But I am inclined to believe the man, as he fears the wrath of his mother more than God, and only curses can make boys go against the wishes of their *madre*.

"One day, he and his wife were smiling for a photo to be shared in the *Orlando Sentinel*. He wore his usual charismatic grin, paired with her New Hampshire smile, perfected by decades of orthodontics. She never once questioned his dream. On their first date, he told her he was going to be President of the United States, and she had smiled at him the same way she smiled for the camera. Every family compromise they made, she did without complaining as if it were her dream too. He loved her so much for that, for so many things.

"Sir, can you tell us more about what your wife means to you?"

"She means everything to me. I wouldn't be here without her."

"But Garcia was not there. He described it as if he were outside of his body, standing with the journalists as he watched the other version of himself embrace his wife for the photo. At first, he thought maybe he had become his shadow, but that was impossible, the sun was shining from the other direction. When he inspected his arms, he saw that blood coursed through his own veins. It's a rather dramatic telling of something we have all felt before. A feeling of dissociation from our bodies. But Garcia was adamant that he felt like a different version of himself.

"Soon he was a hundred yards away from everyone, already in a car, heading toward the Paradise Motel. When he arrived at the motel, he went straight to Maya's door. Mr. Taylor thought he was back to talk politics.

"Mr. Mayor, you know these motels really should be forced to clean more. Yesterday I saw a rat larger than a rabbit. There should be a law about that."

"Garcia, a patient man, not known to ignore anybody, walked right past him without so much as a nod.

"You're just like all the other politicians. Good for nothing."

"Garcia knocked on her door. No one answered. It was the middle of the day and in his stupor he had failed to consider that she might be at work. So he sat by the pool in his suit like an executive unable to relax. For the first time in his life he experienced self-doubt. What if she did not want him? What should he say to her? What if she had gone? A few vagrants offered him a sip from the brown paper bag thinking he had just been let go from a sales job. But his persistence had not faded. He waited for five long hours, accompanied only by the persistent percussion of doors.

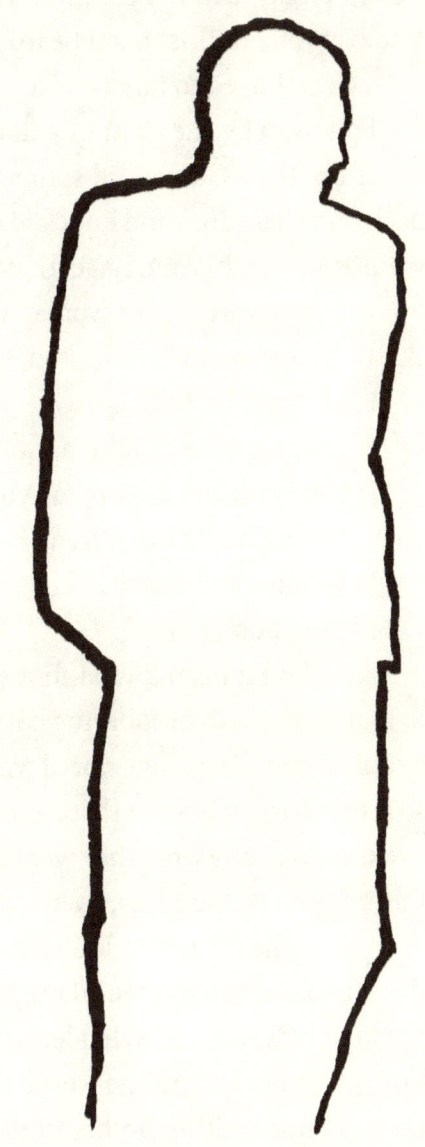

"Finally, Maya arrived. She glanced at the mayor before she put her head down and hurried toward her room. Maya never ignored people; it was not in her nature. Yet there must've been something in Garcia's eyes that made her run away. Now you may think this is just a story told by a lonely old man with a penchant for embellishment. But everyone in this motel heard it.

"Maya, I need to talk to you."

"Followed by the slam of a door. It was something Maya would never do; then Garcia did something he would never do. He went back up to her room and knocked again. Now no self-respecting man would blow up his marriage for a woman with whom he exchanged less than ten words. For a woman who slammed a door on him twice. But this time when he knocked, words answered.

"Hello."

"It's me. Can we chat for a moment?"

"If you want me to vote for you, I will. But I don't have time to chat. I'm feeding the children."

"What about tomorrow?"

"I'm too busy. Sorry."

"Now had it been love at first sight, our story would have ended here with a splash of sobering cold water to the face. But sometimes people share a language not of words, but of energy, where they are so attuned to each other that all they need is the intonation of a word to express exactly what they want to say. As if it were obvious to them but imperceptible to us. When he heard her say 'sorry,' he knew everything he needed to know, so he returned the next day, and the day after that, and then the day after that. Each time communicating through a drawn-out syllable, an elongated vowel, and the way his knuckles knocked on the wood. Eventually, no one looked twice at the mayor knocking on her door. He did this for weeks. Until his persistent knocks hollowed out her resistance.

"I would like to talk with you. But I cannot talk to a married man."

"I understand."

"The mayor left. When he arrived home, he calmly laid the divorce papers on the table as if it were the utility bill. His wife was distraught; their dream was over. The children couldn't understand how a piece of paper could make their mother cry. Even so, they felt obliged to cry too. A different Mr. Garcia might have thought about the repercussions. A family man, the darling of this city, leaving his wife and children for a black single mother from Beaufort, Georgia. A blue state may forgive him, but a red one would not.

"Something had taken hold of Mr. Garcia's soul. Something he had lost the moment he first looked at Maya. Maybe the only way to get it back was to fall deeply into the eyes that stole it. I can only assume that Maya felt it too, that she had lost something. Maybe it was the shield she had spent so many years building. Of course I cannot read minds, but everyone noticed a change in her behavior. When she read to the children at the pool, she would no longer change her intonation for the climax like she was lost in another story.

"Mom, this is the important part! Something is about to happen to the *BFG* and Sophie!"

"Everyone remembered her being more distant, and vague, which was the opposite of a woman who marked children's haircuts on the calendar. Steven claims she finally had a sip of his spiced rum, but Steven claims lots of things. Although everyone agrees: she'd changed. Then one fateful day, Mr. Garcia arrived at the Paradise Motel and knocked on the door for the umpteenth time.

"I'd like to take you somewhere."

"Without knowing where Maya stepped out of the room.

"I'd like that."

"She asked me to look after the children. Yet even amid the magic, she didn't lose her sensibilities and insisted they go to a diner nearby in case we needed anything. It was the start of something great.

"There were months when that couple was the most beautiful thing in this entire city. They reminded me of what it was like to be young and in love—when time feels eternal, and we feel immortal. But what brought me more joy was seeing that the children had a dad again. They were too young to ask questions about the new man in their life. Too innocent to harbor resentment. How could they not like someone who would get them all the sweets that their mom was too strict to buy? Soon Garcia spent all his time with his new family in the Paradise Motel. Garcia became accustomed to a different type of life. He learned the ways of the coin machine where you would have to keep the exact amount of change to do two loads for the family. He learned the intricate lending system where everyone kept a mental ledger, and you never wanted to be too many coins in debt; otherwise, your goodwill would dry up like it had been lost in the dryer. He learned to love washing. This place taught him a language of love that was more powerful than any he had known before. Instead of promising the world to his wife and sacrificing himself to get it, he gave Maya his life and forgot about the world. Maya didn't want to be the first lady; she just wanted someone who would show up for her family. Washing and all.

"Love was a blanket that wrapped them both in their own private world, turning this place into a fleeting paradise.

"The last time I saw Maya was around 11 p.m. the night before she died. She passed me without so much as saying hello. It was most unusual—she almost always greeted me as a friend. She was carrying a piece of paper and went straight to her room, slamming the door behind her.

"It is the biggest regret of my life that I didn't go into that room and sit with her through the early hours of the morning. I remember the day after—15th January.

Javier stopped speaking. He nestled his head into his palms. Lucia wasn't sure if he was crying.

"Are you okay?" Lucia asked as she stood up to get the box of tissues from his bedside table.

He lifted his head, his eyes heavy, but with a nod, he steadied himself, his entire demeanor softening.

"It is a difficult memory."

"It's okay. You don't have to keep telling it," Lucia said softly.

"We can't forget her," said Javier, taking the tissue and gently dabbing the corners of his eyes. "Death doesn't make someone disappear, even if it's easier if they do."

Lucia felt it now; the corners of her eyes wobbled too. Without needing to say a single word, she understood how Javier felt. Every time she thought about Emi, it hurt, but the idea of forgetting him hurt even more. She felt like she was the only one carrying the candle of his memory, and if she gave up, his soul would be extinguished forever. It was easier for everyone else to forget. Maya and her children must have meant something to Javier too.

"What happened next?" asked Lucia.

"Normally, I rise early but that morning I couldn't. It was so cold, I clung to my blankets and tucked myself under the covers like I did as a child. At 7 a.m., I heard a scream. I got changed and went to the balcony. That is where I saw Maya, Carl, and Jasmine. Floating face down in the pool. Jasmine in a little white dress, Carl in a button-up shirt, and Maya dressed in pink. I remember the way they floated in the water. Their bodies bobbed at the surface while their arms dangled toward the pool floor like they were reaching for something. I've never seen something float like that; they were sinking and gliding at the same time. But soon an ambulance came, the bodies were fished out like driftwood. They had such confused expressions. I wonder whether the water had frozen their last moment in time, letting us see the last thing they saw in their eyes. Whether it was fear or love. Cops came not long after. They shook their heads, sipped coffee, and scribbled on clipboards. I remember the sheriff's face. His cowboy hat was tilted to the ground, he couldn't stop looking at the floor. He barely spoke to any witnesses, convinced that Maya was just some jealous woman who sought to punish a powerful man for leaving her. A few weeks later they would confirm—murder-suicide. The autopsy determined that the kids were drowned. Water clogged their lungs, big gulps that pointed to signs of resistance. They must have tried to fight back, but they were barely sixty pounds each. What chance did they have? As for Maya, they found the syringe marks on her wrist. She shot up with enough heroin to put herself to sleep forever. No one could imagine where she bought it from; she was the purest soul in this sordid place.

"I tried to get the sheriff to keep looking, but he only cares about public perception. Most were content with the story of a drug-addicted single mother who took her life after a powerful man left her. But that wasn't the woman I knew.

"It didn't matter. The sheriff closed the case. The problem is you can't close the memories. I still see it in my sleep, in some sick way it all reminds me of a painting—*The Birth of Venus*. Their bodies were Botticelli white, glazed in chlorine. Lifeless. It was one of those rare moments where no one in the motel said anything, not even the junkies. They just sipped silently. The next day the pool was cleaned but no one swam. Everyone stood outside their balcony waiting for something to happen like there had to be more. But there wasn't.

"A barrage of journalists arrived, eager to secure the front-page exclusive on what happened to Garcia's girlfriend. They loitered outside the hotel like flies, some even booked rooms so they could stay among the residents to ask questions. Then, everyone had something to say—something they saw, something they knew.

"Garcia said he left the motel at around 11 p.m. the night before Maya and the children died. There was security camera footage of the pool at that time, and there were no bodies. Apparently, the lights short-circuited around midnight, so the security camera couldn't capture what unfolded after that.

"Naturally with these things, people always jump to conclusions about the lover, but Garcia's mother was quick to stand up for her son. That night of Maya's death, she was convinced someone had tried to break into her house, pried open the window with a crowbar. She called the police, and they confirmed the attempted break-in. The second person she called was her son. The poor lady was terrified, she didn't want to sleep alone, so Garcia stayed the night at hers. The paper ran photos of the moment he heard the news—walking out of his mother's home in a rumpled suit jacket. You can't fake that look of devastation. The man could hardly speak. The great orator he once was had also died. His trademark charisma and warmth had evaporated and all that was left to remind you of his former self was his towering stature that his soul was now too small to stand in.

"His old wife let him move back, she put him in a spare bedroom caring for him like a sickly child. The newspapers ravaged her, but I think she still clung to the idea that she could build him back up to be president, that all her sacrifice wasn't wasted. Rumor has it the couple moved to California, though no one in town has seen Garcia since. It was big news for a long time, but like everything in this country, nothing lasts. The collective attention shifted onto the next tragedy, and then onto the next. After a while, only those who saw the chlorine-coated corpses remembered it all. By spring, people swam in the pool again.

LA LOTERIA

Lucia stood up. Her knees buckled after sitting down for so long. In Javier's room, the lamp's amber glow blurred the edges of time. There was a decorative globe perched on a stool that seemed to spin on its own axis. But it wasn't the globe that was spinning—her head was. Everything was too similar to Emi. The way everyone dismissed them both as overdoses, finding their bodies conveniently washed up in the water.

"Is everything okay? You're going red," said Javier. The anxious thoughts left her head all at once giving her a moment of complete clarity. Now she could see every freckle on Javier's face, every wrinkle, the sadness in his eyes.

"I'm sorry, I should've never told you that story. It's far too dark a tale," he said, as he filled a glass of water and offered it to Lucia. "Please drink something, I was afraid you were going to faint."

Lucia took the glass reluctantly. Long shadows cast off the plush red chairs, obscuring the dragon carvings on the cabinet. She sipped the water slowly, scanning the room again. In the corner, a piano sat tucked away, topped with a brass lyre-shaped ornament to hold sheets of squiggles that Lucia couldn't read. There was a small shrine next to it with candles, photos, and marigold flowers. The scent of melted wax drifted into her nostrils. She looked at Javier in his suit. She felt like she was inside a museum, not a budget motel. *Who was he?*

She couldn't make sense of him, but she felt like a fish caught on the hook of a question mark.

"What's that?" Lucia said, pointing to the marigold petals.

Javier wandered over to the shrine.

"My daughter," he said softly. He picked up a photo frame and showed it to Lucia.

"What happened?" asked Lucia softly.

"She died," Javier said, taking out a Zippo to light one of the candles.

"I'm sorry," said Lucia.

"It's okay." Javier paused. "We were on the way to her graduation, she just finished high school. I went to get her *tamales* from the metro station. Car blew up. Mechanic said it was caused by a faulty fuel line."

Lucia didn't say anything, she knew there was nothing she could say.

"She was set to receive an award from the school. She loved words—she wanted to be a writer. She would eat her morning cereal and try to write better slogans than what was on the box. I had to usher her out of the door sometimes, because she would have a hundred taglines for her *Estrellitas*."

"What award was she going to get?" asked Lucia with a gentle smile, trying to bring back the warmer memories.

"She was the Dux of the school. I used to only wear shorts and a Hawaiian shirt back then, Mexico City is a desert in the summertime. But my daughter had an imagination like no other, she insisted her father wear a three-piece suit to the ceremony. She didn't want me to embarrass her on her big day. When I came back to the car, there was nothing left."

Lucia looked at Javier's three-piece.

"We all have different ways of honoring those we love," he said with a soft smile as he walked away from the shrine.

"What was her name?" asked Lucia.

"Nachi."

"I won't forget her," she said. "My brother died too. His name was Emi."

The two of them said nothing. The silence felt natural, unbroken by the usual rush to fill it with awkward, rambling words about nothing. Javier had the same look in his eyes, the one he had when he spoke of Maya and her children. He dabbed the corner of his eye with a tissue.

"You don't believe it," said Lucia.

"What?" said Javier, taken aback.

"You don't believe Maya killed her children."

Javier paused deeply, watching the ripples in his glass settle into stillness.

"You're right," he said after a pause. "She couldn't have killed her children. She loved them." His words were so perfectly placed; he put his finger on the best evidence of all.

"Someone killed her. Didn't they?" Lucia probed.

Javier frowned.

"I mean... What evidence do we have other than rumors?" replied Javier.

Immediately, Lucia thought of the card of death she had found in the Bible. The one she thought was the same as her brother's. Maybe it was left in that room for Maya, not her.

"I need to show you something," Lucia said. "I found it hidden in Maya's room, wedged into the Bible pages." She reached into her pocket and withdrew the card. She slid it over the coffee table, so it sat squarely in front of him. Javier squinted at it. Then he went silent, seeing its illustration of a skull.

"Have you shown this to anyone else?"

"No."

"Interesting," he said. "It's a Loteria card," he said after a long pause.

"What's that?"

"They're from Mexico. You're bringing back old memories. I used to play it with my Tio. There's a deck of cards, each with a different symbol. It's like Bingo."

"What are the other symbols?" asked Lucia.

"You're talking to an old man—I left Mexico a long time ago." He paused. His expression shifted to a nostalgic glaze. "Everyone's a poet in Mexico. Everything has a symbol. There's the El Nopal card, the cactus, which represents resilience. My Tio was so obsessed with it that when he proposed to his wife he gave her a cactus instead of a bouquet of flowers. He said all the other Don Juans who gave roses would be gone before the first petal wilted. Not him. He may've been a prickly bastard, but their marriage would endure like the most stubborn desert cactus. He was with his wife for forty years before he died. I guess there must've been some truth to it."

"Did your Tio ever tell you what this card means?"

"It represents death," Javier replied while looking at the card on the coffee table. "But in Mexico, death is not something that is feared, it is celebrated. Nothing so morbid as in America. It's a rare card. It doesn't usually come in most Loteria decks, collectors would pay a small fortune for it."

"Why would Maya have a Loteria card?" asked Lucia.

"That I can't tell you. Maya was a very secretive woman. It goes hand in hand with being humble, people like that are so quick to deflect questions that soon you realize you know nothing about them. Even if they're your friend." He lingered on his last words.

"What if someone gave it to her… before they killed her?" Lucia said.

"You mean, like a calling card?"

"Yes," replied Lucia. He started to laugh but was stopped by her frown.

"Isn't that a bit far-fetched? Wouldn't there have to be more than just one case of it?"

"What if there was more than one card?" Lucia said.

"That'd be very strange indeed," Javier said, reexamining the card. He read the name aloud: "Mr. Muerte. A man who calls himself Death?"

"Yes."

WASHING WHISPERS

The Paradise Motel came with a Paradise Laundry, a misleading name for the cramped, airless laundromat where the scent of detergent never quite masked the damp. The room was no wider than a corridor, with three industrial washing machines wedged into a crevice in the wall. Three dryers were precariously stacked atop the washing machines, rattling as if held together by a single loose bolt. The room was empty as Lucia made her way to the last available washer with her laundry bag. It had been a few days since she learned of the story of Garcia and Maya. She had become obsessed with learning about the deaths at the motel. Her mind paced through all the parallels with Emi's death—the card, the needle marks, the drowning.

She checked the dates Javier told her: Maya and her kids had died a few months after Emi washed up ashore.

The rattle of the dryer brought her back to the powdery reality of Paradise Laundry. Lucia looked over her shoulder, then slipped in a coin as the machine whirled to life. She imagined Garcia doing the same, while Maya waited for him upstairs, the children laughing as they read books from their plastic sleeves. There was a time when Lucia's mother still did that, protecting them from peanut butter smudged fingers. That was when she still had enough energy to care. After a while, she gave up on trying to look after Emi, instead making up imaginary rules for him—like saying please and thank you—even if he ignored all the others.

Something caught her eye in the machine next to hers. A racy red corset tumbled around as it got tangled with leopard-print lingerie. There were fifteen minutes left on the cycle. Suddenly, the laundry door burst open, and a woman froze in place, as if for dramatic effect. Then, with a huff, she marched to the other machine—a young blonde with tattoos spilling down her waist and acrylic nails sharp enough to gouge out an eye. She came over to inspect the machine next to Lucia.

"Ugh, seriously?" she sighed, eyeing the timer. She turned to Lucia.

"Any chance you can give me a hand?"

"What do you need?" said Lucia.

"You must be old enough to have a spare pair of lingerie."

"What?' said Lucia.

"Oh, don't play dumb. Some prepubescent boy probably bought you a pair once."

"I don't have any, sorry," Lucia said, awkwardly staring at the ground.

"Shit. I need a dry pair in the next ten minutes."

"Why's that?" asked Lucia.

The lady chewed her bubblegum like it was the soundtrack to her thoughts. There was a manic energy that surrounded her every move, as she paced back and forth in the narrow corridor.

"You're the new kid, huh? Moved into her old room."

Lucia nodded, adjusting her grip on her laundry bag. "Yeah."

"Couldn't pay me to move there."

The machine shook violently. Lucia pressed a hand on top to steady it.

"Did you know her?" asked Lucia, prying for details.

"Yeah, I knew her," said the blonde, her acrylic nails tapping the steel like she was playing piano keys. "She's one of those goody-two-shoes types. Not my people."

Lucia went silent. People probably thought the same about her. Emi did. He was always trying to shield her from everything he did, like she couldn't handle people making mistakes. He'd lie, saying he stayed at some hotel, but the dust marks on the side of his face told the truth—she knew he'd been sleeping on the street.

"But don't get me wrong, I'm sad for her and all," said the blonde, filling the silence left by Lucia. "Jealousy's a bitch."

Lucia put down the laundry bag and frowned.

"Who was jealous?" Lucia said, confused.

"You know if there's one thing I've learned in my line of work, it's that men are not to be trusted. But the second rule is: God have mercy on a jealous woman, for there has never been a fiercer creature."

"And what line of work's that?"

"I'm an actress," she said before reaching for a cigarette from her purse. She lit a cigarette inside, the scent of laundry detergent bullied away by the tobacco. She looked again at the timer on the machine.

"Shit. I'll wait another two minutes."

"And you think that Maya was jealous?" said Lucia, trying to listen to the lady without any judgment.

"Maya? God no. The woman scored the jackpot—rich lover boy with his own beachside mansion."

"His ex-wife?" said Lucia.

"Bingo. I mean you wouldn't believe the stories I've heard," said the blonde.

It felt wrong to be gossiping about Maya. It reminded Lucia of the internet forums about her brother and all the theories that surfaced when he went missing—like his ex-girlfriend from seventh grade, who suddenly claimed to know his every motive. But Maya and

Garcia were her only leads on Emi; there was an invisible thread between them.

"What did you hear about her?" asked Lucia.

"I mean all the normal stuff. Raging political sociopath who couldn't fathom her husband left her for a younger woman. Apparently, she'd picked out the exact outfit she was going to wear when she became first lady, she'd show anyone who would pay attention. These will be my shoes... My necklace... You know that's when people do crazy shit—when they sell themselves a story. I think she had sold herself a life, and the only person who got in the way of it was Maya and her children."

"But why would Garcia move back in with his ex-wife if she was a murderer?"

"You heard of Swedish syndrome?"

"Stockholm syndrome?" Lucia asked.

"Whichever. The man was probably scared shitless, someone savage enough to kill someone else's kids is not someone you want to anger, especially when she's the mother of your own children."

Lucia looked at the red corset as it spun around in dizzying circles.

"Did anyone ever see Mrs. Garcia around the motel or anything like that?" asked Lucia.

"I saw her a few times. She'd park her Mercedes on the street, the engine still running. She treated the whole thing like she was picking up her kids from Hampton summer camp, not her rogue ex-husband. Maybe she was a voyeur or something. I know a few of those."

At this point, another lady walked in. She was the old blonde that Lucia had seen when she first arrived. She walked to the dryer at the far end of the laundry.

"I've met politicians before, trust me. They have this smile where they look really nice, but they also want to bite your face off. Garcia wasn't the politician, his wife was, she had the smile. She was the one pulling all the puppet strings, accumulating power in the background, until one day little Mr. Pinocchio got a hard-on for old Maya and set himself free. The best way to get your power back isn't to eliminate your star performer, it's to cut off the thing that distracted him."

She started to tap the timer on the machine, there were five minutes left.

"Ah fuck it. I need to run." She hit the stop button, sticking her hands into the machine's sopping wet stomach to pull out her lingerie. It dripped all over the tiles.

"Lovely to chat, darling. I really must be going." The young blonde disappeared through the door, her presence as sharp and quick as a gust of wind. At that point, the older blonde at the far end of the laundry turned to Lucia. Her crocodile skin bore each wrinkle as a testament to time, with big shades hiding her eyes. Unlike the younger woman's hurried energy, she was in no rush.

"That's the last person in the world I would trust," said the older blonde as she slowly put her coin into the machine.

"Why's that?" asked Lucia.

"She's a compulsive liar."

"She's an actress," said Lucia innocently.

"She's a stripper."

"Oh..."

"Sounds about right," the old lady chuckled. "Sara thinks everything's a conspiracy. Hard not to when you work in a place where all the powerful men drop by—just with their pants down."

"I guess you heard our conversation."

"Anyone who's lived here has heard it all a thousand times before. When you get to my age, you become a cynic. I've lived long enough to see the same patterns play out, not everything's one big mystery. I guess you got the ex-wife iteration but believe me there are a lot more theories than just that."

"Such as?"

"A few of the drunks like to peddle that it was Maya's old boy-friend." The lady started to violently stuff her overflowing clothes into the washer. A tangle of scarves fell on the floor.

"I thought he was in California," said Lucia, remembering Javier's story.

"Drunks see things," she said, picking up the scarves off the floor and jamming them in.

"Like what?"

"I don't want to spoil their tales. It's about the only thing they can talk about. They'll tell you they saw a man loitering in the shadows as black as night."

"How could they know it was her ex-boyfriend then?"

"Exactly. How could they? They were probably in withdrawal."

Lucia caught a glimpse of the luxury silks and cashmere trims of her laundry. The clothes radiated wealth, and judging by the size of the ring on her finger, she must have been the richest person at the motel.

"You ever seen a Jesus in a box of Lucky Charms?" asked the lady.

"What?" said Lucia, snapping out of her snooping.

"You know the cereal?"

"Yeah."

"Well, the type of people that saw a shadow are the same type that claim to see Jesus in their breakfast cereal. When you want to see something, your brain can mold reality to serve you what you want."

"But maybe they did."

"See Jesus?"

"Yeah. Maybe someone at the factory thought it would be funny to put Jesus in a bowl of cereal, so they secretly snuck it into the production line," Lucia said defensively, thinking of all the times people had been dismissive about Emi's stories.

"Oh God. Don't tell me you're another one of them."

Emi would tell Lucia all types of wild stories like that. He once told her that he saw a black swan in their neighbor's kiddie pool, and that he was sure it was the only one that existed in America. She believed him. He saw so many things, some of them must've been real.

"Well what do you think happened then? If you don't believe in any of the stories."

"I think that Maya was depressed."

"But she loved her kids," said Lucia immediately.

"I'm sorry to say but people kill their kids, darling. Look at history."

"That's not true," Lucia replied, thinking of all the nature documentaries where elephants cried when their calves died.

"The Spartans used to carry babies with defects to the forest and leave them there to die. They may have loved them, but they still left them for the wolves."

"Maya wasn't a Spartan. She was an English teacher."

"And you think English teachers don't have a proclivity for tragedy? Do you know how Sylvia Plath died? She put herself in an oven."

"But not her children," interjected Lucia.

"Fine. Maybe it's less common than one would think. But how can you know what it's like to be depressed and have to care for two children? Maybe she couldn't bear the idea of the children suffering without her. It was the easy option for them to all tap out together."

"You're wrong," Lucia said.

The old lady laughed dryly.

"You've been here for a few weeks and now you know more than me? Come back to me after a divorce. See how hard life gets then."

"I need to go."

"Welcome to paradise!"

THE CRAB'S EYE

"Lucia, it's been a week. When is your flight to Stanford?" said her mother. Lucia snapped shut her book.

"I could only get one for this Tuesday," Lucia replied.

"But you've missed the entire first week. They will fail you," said her mother.

"Don't worry, I called them. It's okay."

Her mother gripped the newspaper so tightly it tore in two.

"Well, I'm sick of seeing you lounge around doing nothing, I didn't work so hard to raise my daughter as a bum."

Lucia took a deep breath. That was her mother's highest degree of insult.

"It's Saturday. I worked all week."

"I don't care. You should be studying now. Your classmates will be studying," said her mother from the bed.

"I need some air," Lucia said, stepping out of the cramped motel room, leaving behind the welded bars on the window. She looked out to Heaven's Spring. It was midday, and there were troves of guests outside. Next to the pool, someone had parked their smashed-up Honda with a boombox in the trunk, playing the punk rock that Emi had loved.

Lucia canvassed the other guests. She wondered how many of them had seen Maya and her children floating face down in the water. Yet Lucia was no closer to a lead to follow other than murmurs of a woman who wore leopard-print lingerie.

Everyone seemed remarkably at ease with their situation as they sunbathed on loungers crusted with dried bird droppings. It reminded Lucia of a pond that collected all the stormwater with no drains for the dregs to be flushed out. The last stop before the streets.

Lucia blinked hard. She was seeing things again. Maya's body was floating in the water, her two children side by side. No one else seemed to notice. She got stuck in a daze before the image was shattered by a ginger boy cannonballing into the pool. A mushroom cloud of water surged into the air, hanging momentarily before slapping back down like a pancake. Suddenly, she was seeing the same water-soaked reality as everyone else.

"Control your fucking kid!" snapped a six-foot man with a long trident tattooed on his chest.

"It's a free country," burped his father in between gulps of a Bud Light. He sported a big belly, unevenly smeared with sunscreen. The tattooed man walked over to him and snatched the can out of his hand, crinkling the aluminum in his palm.

"Don't talk to me about freedom," said the tattooed man towering over the kid's father, blocking the sun with his heavy-set shoulders.

"Tucker, say sorry to the man," stammered the kid's father as he sprang up from his lounger. The boy must've sensed the impending belt buckle on his bum because he heaved himself out of the pool with remarkable agility.

"I'm sorry, sir," he said with water gushing from his cling-wrap tight rash guard.

"Don't say sorry. Just don't do it again." The six-foot man walked back to his lounger and flipped open a hunting magazine. Everyone waited for him to flick the first page before they resumed talking. Seconds later, the crab-like receptionist scuttled over to the pool and placed a sign that read:

NO DIVING

Once he dropped the sign, he disappeared back into the shadows. Lucia didn't understand how he emerged so quickly. It was as if he could see through walls and knew the boy was going to jump before he splashed everyone. But then she saw it. Mounted in the corner of the motel was a rusted security camera. A pigeon stood shamelessly atop it, with its droppings staining the casing. The lens was intact, fixated directly on the pool. The receptionist watched everything. Then it clicked. The camera must've been there when Maya and her children died, if she could find the footage, then maybe she could see what happened on the night of Maya's death. The sheriff would've looked at it, but she trusted him as much as she did the pigeon for spotting details. To him, everything was a solved case.

Lucia slunk toward the reception. She needed to create a diversion so that she could sneak into the staff room and check out the old VHS tapes. In the entire time she had been at the motel, there had not been a change of staff. The crab never left reception; he even slept there. Lucia had seen him stumble out of the small door behind the desk one morning, yawning and bleary-eyed. Her only hope was to make a diversion during the day, so she could sneak in and find the old tapes. She didn't want to break someone's window, but she needed to cause enough of a stir to get the crab out of hiding. It was the type of mission that she had apprenticed for her entire life with a brother like Emi. She'd watched him pull off every scheme, scam, and score in the books. He could use a paperclip to pick locks and knew how to scream 'fire' in ten languages. His entire arsenal of tricks was designed for diverting attention.

"The key to magic is misdirection," Emi would say.

Lucia had an idea. She hurried a few blocks to the nearest Piggly Wiggly, darting between the aisles until she found what she needed—a bottle of bright red food dye. It wasn't elegant, but it would work.

Before long, she was back at the motel, the bottle tucked into her pocket. She made her way to the pool, hugging the shadows of the building. The man spotted Lucia standing in the shadows. He looked ex-military. It was as if he were waiting for her to hurl a grenade so that he could catch it with his teeth. Lucia took another step forward; his eyes followed. No one else seemed to notice her except for him. She pretended to tie her shoelace; it was enough to dislodge his gaze. While she crouched down, she unscrewed the lid of the red dye. The nozzle was coated in a wispy blood red that nicked her fingertips. It stained. She took a deep breath and positioned herself in front of the vending machine.

She couldn't afford to be seen. If they got kicked out of the motel, her mother would have nowhere else to go. She hesitated, clutching the bottle in her hand. But then the tapes would stay hidden, and she'd never know. Her grip tightened. This was the only way to find the truth.

From a crouch, she lobbed the little bottle toward the pool. It flew in the air, gliding over the loungers, sputtering red ink like a steam engine, until it finally landed in the water.

"What the hell was that?" someone yelled with red droplets on their towel. Lucia spun around, pretending to press buttons on the machine. She hoped the dye would be spreading in the water, co-alescing into a murky crimson mess. There was a long pause. There was too much confusion for panic. Her heart raced as she thought of the tattooed man's eyes crawling on her back, at any second he would tap her on the shoulder and tell her he knew what she did. Then the shouting started.

"Someone's bleeding!"

"Jesus—is there a shark in there?"

"Who swam without a Band-Aid?"

It was working. The dye was spreading. Any second now the receptionist would see and come crawling out of his room. Lucia hurried toward the reception, keeping her eyes glued to the concrete. On cue, the crab came sprinting out with a medical kit as the two of them passed without an exchange. It worked. Lucia felt a rush as if she were the conductor of chaos, wielding misdirection at will. She slipped into the reception. Behind the counter with the crab's computer there was a door.

STAFF ONLY

The room he slept in. Carefully, Lucia snuck into the room. It was dark. It felt like being in a submarine cruising the ocean floor, the white walls about to implode from the pressure of an entire ocean pushing against them. His smell lingered in the air, trapped with no windows to escape. A thin layer of sweat glazed every surface. In the corner, a mattress lay with an immaculately made bed. At the center of the room, an old monitor sat like a submarine's dashboard, broadcasting security camera footage. Now she could see him. He had a pool cleaner in his hand and was fishing for the bottle of dye. The footage was grainy, but she was sure it was him.

There was no turning back now. Lucia took a deep belly breath and then scanned the room.

There were shelves stacked with VHS tapes. Clearly they archived all their footage. Each had masking tape along with the date it was recorded. She remembered the date Javier told her. January 15, 2003. Her eyes nervously darted between the monitor and the shelf to make sure that the crab wasn't coming back. Then she saw it: January 15, 2003. She snatched it.

Now, she held the final moments of Maya's life in her hands. Lucia nervously looked back at the monitor; she could see that the crab had finally fished out the bottle of dye onto the pool ledge. Now that he knew it wasn't blood, he would be coming back any second.

Her room only had a DVD player—this was the only place with an old VHS player still hooked up. The problem was that as soon as she played the VHS tape she would lose sight of the pool and the crab's movements. Lucia gulped. Her only hope was that he would try to clean the water. She jammed the VHS into the player. He disappeared from the screen.

She was trapped now.

The footage was terrible; the frame rate was so slow it appeared more like a series of grainy photographs cobbled together. It was black and white, but judging by the amount of people outside, it must have been daytime. She watched the pool knowing that in twelve hours Maya and her children would be floating face down. A few figures came and went. Using the remote, she fast-forwarded to get to nighttime. Then she saw Javier. It was impossible to miss his three-piece suit as a cloud of smoke billowed from his face. She stopped the footage, looking at the timestamp in the corner. It was 10:55 p.m. Javier was alone standing on the balcony. She fast-forwarded the footage. 11:15 p.m.

Suddenly, a woman came running past. It appeared like a gust of wind as opposed to a human being. It was just like Javier had said, that a woman brushed past him so fast that she nearly knocked out his cigar. Lucia rewound the tape and then paused. It took her a few attempts to perfectly capture the lady in frame. Finally, she got it. Even with the paucity of pixels, her beauty was unmistakable—black skin, flowing black hair cascading past her shoulders. It was Maya. She wore a dress, but what caught Lucia's eye was the stiff piece of cardboard clutched to her chest—too rigid to be ordinary paper, yet held close, as if it carried some significance.

Lucia hit play.

She fast-forwarded so that she could get into the early hours of the morning. After a few seconds, the time stamp reached midnight. Everyone was gone now, including Javier, and the pool weakly reflected moonlight, idly waiting for the inevitable. But then something else happened.

A lady in a wheelchair rolled into view, but the angle made it difficult to see her face. Long, flowing hair spilled over her shoulders, nearly tangling in the wheels. She wore a shawl draped over her torso, its distinctive floral pattern woven with rosebuds and scattered lilacs. She was searching for something. Her wheelchair stopped at the base of the stairs. Even in black and white, Lucia could see her mangled legs. To her horror, the lady thrust herself off her wheelchair onto the concrete stairs and began to crawl.

12:05 a.m.

It took her a few minutes to get to the top. Lucia had never seen someone ascend a flight of stairs so stubbornly, her elbows grazing against the grimy concrete. Finally, she stopped in front of Room 201. The same room as Lucia's—Maya's room. Then she started to knock. She was so close to the ground that she was practically tapping at the base of the door. Nothing. 12:10 a.m. Suddenly, the lights went out. Lucia thought that maybe the tape was scratched but she could see that it was still playing. There was a dim glow from a distant streetlight that twinkled in the corner of the screen. The VHS tape still worked but Lucia couldn't see anything. The screen was black.

She pressed the remote, fast-forwarding to the early hours of the morning, but the screen remained black. Behind that darkness, their bodies would already be floating in the pool, the killer vanishing into the night.

Suddenly, a bell rang. Lucia jumped. Someone was waiting at reception. She rushed to eject the VHS tape, quickly placing it back in the spot she found it. She looked over at the monitor and could see that the crab was no longer by the pool. Her heart dropped.

She sneaked out of the staff room, expecting to see him behind the counter. Instead, it was a young boy. He looked at her confused. Lucia put her finger to her lips. The boy shuffled away, then darted out of the reception. Lucia's eyes shifted to the crab's desk. She needed to figure out who had stayed at the motel that night—someone in a wheelchair wouldn't have gone unnoticed. If the woman in the footage had been a guest, she'd have stayed on the bottom floor, likely near the entrance. That narrowed things down.

Lucia scanned the desk—a lone piece of sashimi sat on a plate, alongside hefty Russian novels and a few motel waivers scattered haphazardly. They were the same ones that her mother had to sign when they arrived. Then she remembered when they first came, the crab had been sketching in a diary. *Maybe he kept his own record?*

Everything about the space suggested he was a man of order. The pens were perfectly aligned with the edge of the desk, and the papers were folded into precise angles. But one thing stood out—the trash can. It was a chaotic mess, cereal boxes crammed in, and paper balls spilling over the sides. It felt almost artificially chaotic, like a neat freak's attempt to mimic a messy person. She began sifting through the trash, the smell of stale milk and discarded wrappers making her nose wrinkle. Then she found it. Wedged at the very bottom, hidden beneath the clutter, was the diary.

She snatched it and ran upstairs to her room.

THE CRAB'S DIARY

4th September 2002

Garcia arrived today. I saw him while I was cleaning the pool, at first I didn't recognize him. There were disgusting specks of lint on his suit jacket and the lapels were stitched by someone with arthritis. People don't understand good tailorship anymore, it's unnerving. Garcia was knocking on doors, going room to room. At first, I thought he was another Jehovah's Witness, but the guests were far too chatty with him for that. I only recognized him when he smiled—it was that big greasy grin, the type he always does in the papers when he makes those vacuous speeches. I've never seen such a professional puppet; a bottle of Dom Perignon is all it takes for a new road to magically appear in your district. Everyone knows that. When I asked why he was here, he claimed that it was a part of his 'community outreach' program. I didn't buy it, so I kept an eye on him all day. There's a lot one can learn from such a slippery schmooze or what society calls a 'people person.' He matches the speed of his nod to the anger in their voice. It's quite incredible actually. You can use a nod to pretend that you care even when you are thinking of how much you hate someone. I tried it on Barbara from Room 209.

"My toilet is broken. Fix it! I paid good money for this room."

You paid nothing, you bitch. Your toilet's clogged because of the deficit of fiber in your highly-processed diet. Unclogged toilet. Restocked vending machine. Reordered pens.

5th September 2002

Mr. Crenshaw's son nearly died today. The fat ginger boy. Fat people lack discipline in every aspect of their lives —they always have the worst smelling rooms. The higher body fat equates to more bed sweat, more dead skin and more candy wrappers on the floor. I'm not like them, I have discipline. I eat to a state of 75% fullness which is 5% less than the Japanese proverb advises. Self-control is a muscle and one that I must work out regularly. Being fat means you have fat thinking, fat feelings, and fat choices. Mr. Crenshaw's son is full of fat thoughts. The boy was toasting bread, but he decided he couldn't wait for the toast to pop out. Instead, he jammed his Nutella-coated knife into the toaster. Electrocuted himself. The boy handled the whole thing as you would expect. Crying and wailing, refusing to take any responsibility for his actions. The first step of self-improvement is acknowledging our weaknesses. Cleaned pool. Fixed washing machine. Washed stains.

6th September 2002

Maya was reading to her children again. She wrapped their books in little plastic sleeves to keep them from getting wet. My mother never did that. She poured bourbon on my copy of *Crime and Punishment* when she saw the Russian name on the cover.

"Get rid of that communist trash," she said.

My mother was weak; the gulags would have done her a world of good. I suppose imprisonment would have been the only way to curb her promiscuity. Throughout my childhood, she brought men to our trailer—the kind of men who mocked a boy for reading, the kind who made sure you knew what they were doing with your mother. They would always come bustling through the caravan door, some lumbering oaf lunging for her neck as her cheap Cotton Blossom scent woke me up. She never had the class for an upmarket scent, nor did the men. They stunk of beer and tire fluid. The worst part was they never stopped when I looked up—they just kept going. When I was little, I thought I could protect her. I believed if I hit the man hard enough, he'd leave her alone. I didn't understand that having your neck kissed was supposed to feel good. That was all she cared about, feeling good. I wish she had read to me. Cleaned pool. Cut room keys. Printed brochures.

7th September 2002

The police came by today. Some self-loathing imbecile put a deodorant can in Mike's microwave. It exploded. It would have set fire to the whole motel if his gas heater had been on. Police took names, asked for the security footage. Some kids running down the corridor, laughing, incapable of the sentience required to understand their stupidity.

They will be punished.

Cops asked me if I've seen some missing girl. Mexican name. They seemed more interested in her than the extensive damage to the kitchenette. Management will not be happy. No one sees the work I do. I'm holding this entire place together, soon management will see how important I am. Soon they will be forced to reassign me. I know what they do. Cleaned pool. Swept parking lot. Took out trash.

8th September 2002

Nothing to report. The drunks were drinking, and the junkies were junking, I mean that quite literally. They were sifting through the trash to find old electronics to pawn. They reminded me of seagulls fighting over a French fry. Pathetic. I had to clean up their mess in the parking lot.

There is no excuse for the drug addicts of this city. I was born in a trailer park, yet ascended my circumstance with raw intelligence. I suppose my genetics worked in my favor. My mother always claimed she conned the sperm bank into giving her a 'premium donor'—the kind who was pitch-perfect and spoke five languages. She had a way with semen.

I inherited nothing from that woman. I'm certain I am almost entirely my father's composition, though I've never had the chance to meet him. If I had, I'm sure he would find me a formidable son. I hope I can meet the man one day, to say thanks. But I have inherit other baggage, other impulses which seem to have the hallmarks of hereditary.

⚜

Lucia flipped through the entries, most covering the usual banalities, until she arrived at something interesting.

1st October 2002

Garcia was back. It's been a few weeks since I last saw him, the man looked even more disheveled. No greasy smiles or nodding this time. Instead, he sat on a lounger the entire day; it must have been longer than six hours. No book. No newspaper. Nothing. He had the composure of a drunk, mumbling to himself, rolling his head in the palms of his hands. But he kept turning down a sip of the bottle from all the usual losers who loiter around the pool. It seemed like he was having withdrawals. It reminded me of the story of Odysseus, where he had himself tied to the mast of his ship to resist the call of the sirens—enchanting mermaids whose voices were said to drive sailors mad with lust. The sailors would eagerly jump into the water, only for the mirage of mermaids to disappear. To avoid drowning, the sailors would block their ears with wax. However, Odysseus had other plans. Instead of blocking his ears like the others, Odysseus wanted to hear the tempting calls while he was chained to the mast of the ship. Only that way could he truly resist them. It would appear that Garcia chose the Paradise Motel to beat his addiction. The fool.

It was in the afternoon that I discovered the source of his addiction: Maya. When she arrived, she hardly looked at him. She rejected him: coldly, methodically, perfectly. The door closed. She always closes her door at the same time every day—4:45 p.m. Initially, it didn't make sense to me. She works at Matanzas Bay School which is only a 12-minute walk, and all schools in the state finish before 4 p.m. After some field work, I learned that she takes a detour past the Hidden Lantern bookshop each day. That's why she's always late. Cleaned pool. Restocked vending machine. Double-checked Maya's lock. Secure.

2nd October 2002

Garcia was back. I had to tell management. They were happy with me—they finally realize the value I can contribute to the organization. Now I have more important work to do. I've been told to keep an eye on him so I can report back my findings. Maya didn't open her door for him, she kept it bolted shut no matter how many times he knocked. Cleaned pool. Restocked coffee room. Unclogged toilet.

7th October 2002

I see him through the camera. I know the way he moves, every bone of his body. One might think he's an athletic man with a frame like that but he's actually flat-footed. That greasy smile hides his gangliness, if people could see him run he would probably lose half his votes, especially because he coasted on the idea he was a quasi-jock. Even his knock is weak.

I can only imagine her on the other side of the frame, pressed against the door, wanting to be saved. After he left today, Maya sat by the pool staring at the water for hours. It troubles her. She was writing in her diary, tearing and scrunching five whole pages before she finally finished her daily entry. I wish I could read those pages, to be inside her head with her. We are both so similar. Creatures of silent reflection, pond-gazers, page-turners, library-lovers, tea-drinkers. We would never run out of things to talk about. Garcia doesn't exist outside of a two-minute conversation, he is but a string of prepared talking points. He would never be right for a woman like Maya, someone who reads Kafka and Dostoevsky. Someone of that caliber needs a fellow intellect to discuss the finer things of life—the shades of gray in a Hopper painting or the cadence of a Bach composition.

He's been knocking on her door every day for over a week now. Management is asking more questions—they have taken a keen interest in what is unfolding. My power is expanding. I can feel it. Cleaned pool. Swept floors. Took out trash.

12th October 2002

He has been coming for nearly two weeks now. Every time it is the same. He comes in the late afternoon and fruitlessly knocks on her door. Not once has the door handle so much as budged. Maya continues to impress me. Her chastity is more commendable than I could've ever imagined—she is commensurate to the Virgin Mary herself, even with the devil knocking at her door, she has the power to keep it closed. As for the devil himself, I have grown a sick appreciation for him too. Make no mistake—I hate the man. But there is something that I cannot help but respect, in part because I see myself in him. His persistence. His plan. It feels like we can both see some big mosaic that others can't, and each day we are filling in the tiny pieces. Tile by tile. I can see it now. Cleaned pool. Restocked coffee room. Fixed dryer.

13th October 2002

Maya opened the door today. I couldn't believe it. I thought the monitor was glitching, so I ran outside to see it with my own eyes. It was strange, I had watched him for so long from the screen that it felt like I was entering a film set. In color, everything was so much more disorienting, all my plans disappeared with the glare of his high-definition eyes. But Garcia didn't even see me. He looked straight through me. I felt like I did as a child when my mother pretended I wasn't there, as our Tampa trailer rocked in the early hours of the morning. That stupid look on her face when she poured me cornflakes the next day.

I stood there as lifelessly as a pool noodle and waited. The two of them had a hushed conversation. Then they strolled right past me without as much as a nod, like I didn't exist. It didn't make any sense. There was simply no way she could've had any feelings for him. Even as they walked together, it seemed like they were business partners, not lovers. I wanted to be patient, but I slipped up. Soon I found myself using the master key to break into her room. My usual poise was replaced by a franticness as I tried to find her diary. I looked under the pillows, in the cupboards, and even in the flush valve of the toilet. There must've been some explanation for why she finally accepted the date after weeks of saying no, I thought I would find it in her room. But I couldn't find it anywhere. Someone saw me. It was Javier, the old man who always wears a suit.

"Why are you in Maya's room?"

I know how to lie. Broken AC. I need to be more careful. People talk. When I saw him in the doorway, he had Carl and Jasmine holding his hands. Maya must've trusted him because she left the kids with him, she could have asked me to do that, I would've helped. Maya made some bad choices today but it's okay. We all make mistakes—I have made many. Cleaned pool. Cleaned security camera. Made preparations.

27th October 2002

Maya's moral degradation continues. In the last few weeks, it appears that she has fallen head over heels for the slimy politician. They have the disgusting smugness of all new couples, that unrestrained giggling at life's banalities. Somehow I'm meant to believe that there is something funny about having ice cream on each other's faces. It's disgusting. I don't know how much longer I can continue to watch it all. Part of me never wants to work here again, but I'm reminded that I have no choice. I cannot leave—such is a pact with the devil. Cleaned pool. Restocked coffee room. Unclogged toilet.

1st November 2002

Maya is making a mistake. Not all mistakes can be forgiven. After all, no one forgives me for mine. No—they exploit it for their gain, constantly reminding me of my options. Why can't I do the same? Why can't I make her regret the decision that she's made? She was meant to be pure, but she's as tainted as all the others. Cleaned pool. Fixed dryer. Archived tapes.

26th November 2002

Management has told me a secret. They have finally let me into their world, one that they guard like the gates of the underworld itself. Now the three-headed dog bows to me. I know the secret too. I always knew that Garcia was hiding something, you can never trust a man in a suit, let alone an oversized one. My operation has changed, my work continues to increase in importance. I have been tasked with following Garcia while he stays at the motel. Mostly, I watch him through the cameras, but sometimes, I follow him at night when he goes for a walk. He doesn't see me—I blend in with the shadows. I know how to move like a cat tracking prey. It's all in the eyes, you need to focus on their neck, constantly maneuvering to angles of darkness that would give you a clean pounce. Of course I never do. I wait. I've started to follow him into the laundry too, he takes phone calls from here. He never notices me. I use that to my advantage, pretending to look busy while I eavesdrop. I relay every single phone call. Management is impressed, they often comment on how sharp my memory is. I always knew I was destined for pro-fessional greatness, when I was young I was certain I'd become a nuclear physicist. I suppose I was only thoughtlessly mimicking Dr. Manhattan from the Watchmen comics. How foolish! No im-portant physics work has been done for decades—my talents would be wasted. Every epoch has a defining career. In the sixties, I'd be an astronaut. In the eighties, I'd be a banker. But now, I am exactly where I belong. An espionage agent of the highest level. Cleaned pool. Buried dog shit. Chased away dog.

2nd December 2002

My work is taking a toll on me. The two of them are inseparable, Garcia has practically moved into her room. She is putting herself in danger. I want to warn her, to tell her of the consequences of being associated with such a man. There is darkness in this world that she could never know, she is too pure a soul. But angels can fall. It was Lucifer cast from the kingdom of heaven, his name in Hebrew was the 'light-bringer' which is ironic for the devil himself. There will be no light for Maya if she continues down this path, soon she will find herself face to face with Lucifer. Not the biblical version, but the one that lives and breathes, who brings darkness upon everything he touches. The one that only goes by the name of death. I have heard only mentions of him, whispers. But I have seen his work. I know the way he wields death like the wind, to blow out the flame of life, without anyone noticing a thing. Maya is not safe. I cannot save her. I answer only to them. Cleaned pool. Swept parking. Took out trash.

10th December 2002

Things are happening. Big things. In truth, I don't know if I can stop them, it feels as if the universe has set things into motion that are predestined. Garcia's fate is sealed. Yet part of me hopes that Maya's is not. Maybe she will come to her senses in the next few weeks, but I fear not. I have tried to detach myself from her, as my previous affections will only stunt my professional growth. I have been given an opportunity to get a clean slate, to advance in this world. Cleaned pool.

14th January 2003

Today is the day. Tomorrow I'll be a free man. I've finally been given the signal. Lucifer will arrive—darkness will be all around us. Cleaned pool. Restocked coffee room. Cut the lights.

15th January 2003

The cripple was here last night. She was knocking on her door at midnight. Then, tragedy...

✦

There were no more entries after that. Instead, the diary degenerated into a series of gestural sketches. Flipping through, Lucia found dozens of portraits of guests from the motel. She stopped when she saw one that looked exactly like her.

He had drawn it the day she arrived.

Lucia closed the notebook, her mind racing. She couldn't ignore it—the receptionist had mentioned a man who goes by the name of death. But for now, she had something concrete. The lady in the wheelchair. She may have been the last person to see Maya alive.

Lucia exhaled slowly. She took his diary and wedged it to the bottom of her suitcase; she would hide it for now. First things first: she had to find the lady in the wheelchair.

THE PAGEANT QUEEN

The sun was setting as Lucia approached the phone booth opposite the Plaza de la Constitución. Depending on the wind, the air carried the salt of the Matanzas River or the aroma of fried fish from the restaurants on St. George Street. But today, the wind was still, and the earthy scent of damp soil lingered as the oaks stirred, their Spanish moss casting dappled shadows over the leafy square. Surrounding the plaza were the imposing stucco walls of the Governor's House and the towering spire of the Basilica of St. Augustine. Lucia used to come to the square with Emi when they were little. He loved teaching her things; he'd point at the white obelisk in the plaza and tell her about the times pirates nearly burned the city to the ground, but the Spanish stood as defiantly as the stone itself.

The phone booth had been there for as long as she could remember, even in those days, with some shadowy figure thumbing through the Yellow Pages. Now it was her turn. The glass panels were scratched with graffiti, and its metal frame rusted red. Inside, there was a payphone unit with a bulky handset chained to the wall.

25c for 3 minutes

Emi used to call her from phone booths like this when he lived out on the streets, it was the only way they could talk. She wondered if he had used this one before.

In front of her, there was a thick Yellow Pages book, its spine barely holding together the tattered, dog-eared pages. Lucia didn't even have a name. All she had was the grainy footage of the lady crawling up the stairs in her floral shawl with her hair down to her waist.

She had a plan. She would search for wheelchair repair shops, physical therapy clinics, and disability groups in the city.

She started her laborious search, painstakingly reading each column for a business name that matched. She flipped through dozens of pages before she found one that she could call.

Chair to There: Wheelchair Repair & Mobility Solutions

She slid the coin into the slot, and the machine whirred as the number began to dial.

"Hello, how can I help?" came a disinterested female voice from the other end.

"Hi, my name is Lucia."

"You got a popped tire?" said the lady, cutting her off.

"Um, no."

"Snapped armrest?"

"No."

"What happened then, hun? That's 90% of problems usually."

"Um, I was actually wondering if you remember a middle-aged woman coming into your store—she had really long hair, almost down to her wheelchair wheels, and wore a floral shawl?"

"Who's asking?"

"A friend," Lucia said.

"Some friend you are—don't even know her name."

The line went dead with a sharp click. Lucia's heart sank.

She took a deep breath as she stood alone in the booth. The long list of names loomed large in front of her. She needed to keep searching; it was her only option. This time she sifted through at least two dozen names before she found something.

Momentum Physical Therapy

"Hello, this is Sally speaking. How can I help you?"

"Hey there, I was wondering if you help clients with wheelchairs, like some recovery type of thing?" asked Lucia optimistically.

"Of course, sweetie. Honestly, most of our clients are in wheelchairs. The insurance companies don't argue much when you get hit by a car."

"Have you ever had anyone without legs?"

"Of course, we help all kinds of people," the lady said cheerfully. "One case stuck with me, though—this poor girl, maybe eight or nine. Her dad didn't see her hiding under his car during hide-and-seek. He ran over her legs." She let out a breath. "They had to amputate, both of them."

Lucia swallowed. "That's awful."

"Yeah, but you know what? She was tough. Put everything into rehab, built up her arms like a machine. She ended up making the national wheelchair basketball team. Strongest kid I ever met."

"Wow. Have you ever worked with someone older—middle-aged, with long blonde hair?"

"Gee, you're really pushing me now. I wouldn't remember if we did. But how about you come into the clinic sometime? We can get you recovered in no time."

"Thanks. That would be nice."

"Would you like to make a booking?"

Lucia hung up. Guilt hit her the moment the line went dead—the woman had been so kind, but she'd just freaked out when she wanted to make an appointment. Lucia sighed. The sun was slowly disappearing outside the booth as she clutched the thick book in her hand and realized she was no closer to finding her.

Still, it was the only clue she had to follow. Someone in the city must have encountered the woman before—there had to be a way to narrow it down. Lucia thought back to her floral shawl. It wasn't something you'd find just anywhere. It wasn't from a chain store; it had to be from a boutique. St. Augustine wasn't a big city—there couldn't be too many places like that.

She shifted her strategy, focusing her calls on any shop with "boutique" or "handmade" in the name. Lucia worked through a list, dialing one number after another as her pile of quarters steadily shrank. Every few calls, she dashed across the street to exchange more bills for coins. When she called, some shop owners chuckled at her description, others dismissed her outright, claiming they had no idea what she was talking about.

Then, finally, someone answered who didn't hang up.

"Hello, *St. Augustine Artisanal Cloth*, speaking."

"Hi there, I was wondering—has a lady in a wheelchair ever bought anything from your store?"

"Well, that can only be one person."

"What do you mean?"

"She's my best customer, Mary. And honestly, the only one in a wheelchair."

"Thank you so much. Wow. Thank you," said Lucia ecstatically.

"Is everything okay?" the lady said, confused.

Lucia took a few seconds to compose herself. "Yes. She left her medication outside your store, and I was trying to return it. Do you know where she lives?"

The shopkeeper hesitated. "Well, she doesn't have a fixed address, if that's what you're asking."

Lucia's heart sank. "Oh…"

"But I see her all the time. She usually sits outside the Pizza Hut on King Street, it's on the same strip mall as our shop. She likes to hang out there in the afternoons."

"Thank you," Lucia said, trying to process the new information.

The Paradise Motel was on King Street too. Mary had been so close this whole time and never even realized it.

"Sure. I'd try there first—she's hard to miss with her bright shawls. But… be gentle with her, okay? She's been through a lot."

✦

Lucia arrived at the strip mall in the dark. She was surprised she hadn't ever seen her; the strip mall was just across the road from the motel. Then again, the night shifts over the past few weeks had kept her world small—just the motel, sleep, and neon-light-infused dreams.

A few storefronts were bolted shut repelling the faint glow of the mall's flickering fluorescent tubes. She passed *Kyle's Taekwondo Dojo*. It had a large, laminated sticker of a white man in a karate gi mounted on top of an Asian teenager. The poorly drawn Asian man grimaced in pain while the man she presumed to be Kyle, the egotistical owner of the store, looked like a film star as his black belt flailed in the imaginary wind. Then she saw the artisanal store that she had called earlier. Its shopfront had a mosaic of bright, bold shawls, scarves, and skirts.

Lucia kept walking down the strip mall until the familiar glow of the Pizza Hut logo came into view. Then she saw her—the woman in the wheelchair.

She had never seen a homeless person so glamorous. Freshly applied red lipstick, peroxide-blonde hair styled into a Christina Aguilera do. She could have belonged on a stage—if not for the scabs on her skin and the mangled puppet legs. Lucia couldn't fathom how the woman had hauled herself up the concrete stairs using only her arms.

She approached cautiously.

"Any spare change?" the woman asked.

Lucia frowned, glancing at the woman's bright red lipstick and curled lashes. Too perfect for someone living on the streets.

"I'm sorry, I don't have any change."

"You can give me a slice of your pizza. I don't do Hawaiian."

Lucia walked into the store and handed over the note. She needed to build trust before she could start asking questions. It was just like Emi told her—patience is how you coax a cat out from under the porch.

"Chicken please."

Ten minutes later, she walked over to the wheelchair lady with the greasy box pressed into her white shirt.

"Here you go," Lucia said, handing her the slice with the most pieces of chicken. It felt like feeding a lion through the bars—she wasn't sure if she would bite her hand off. This was, after all, the last person to see Maya—standing outside her door at midnight, knocking.

"Thanks, darling. Sorry for being so fussy and all; it's just that pineapple doesn't go down well, and this thing isn't exactly a toilet bowl." She motioned to the frame of her wheelchair that looked like it had never been repaired in its tortured existence.

In three bites, the lady wolfed it down, coating the chicken in red lipstick. The lady wiped the sauce from her mouth with her blue scarf. Lucia masked her disgust by biting down on her lip.

"Let me get us some hot sauce."

The lady rolled her wheelchair over to a small box of her belongings.

"Do you always beg around here?" asked Lucia.

"Beg?" the lady scoffed. "Darling, I don't beg, I manifest. And the world always delivers."

"Do you usually manifest right here?" Lucia asked, nodding

toward the Paradise Motel.

The strip mall sat directly across from the pool, its neon signs flickering against the pavement. From where they stood, Lucia had a clear view of the motel's second-story balcony—straight to Maya's room.

"A warm pizza makes people more generous."

"How long have you manifested here?"

"A long time, darling. A lot longer than you've been around," she said, waving Lucia off.

Lucia hesitated. She needed to build rapport fast. Pushing wouldn't work, but maybe a story would.

"I like your sign," she said, nodding toward the cardboard propped beside her. "My brother and I used to make ones like that when we hitchhiked together. Once, he scribbled, 'Not kidnappers, just kids.'"

The lady's lips twitched, the first crack in her guarded demeanor.

"Your brother sounds like my kind of person."

"You would have liked him. He could get along with anyone."

The pageant queen hesitated, studying Lucia. "You say that like he's gone."

"He is," said Lucia softly.

"I'm sorry, darling, it gets us all," said the wheelchair lady, her eyes softening. "Life's tough out here."

"You want another pizza?" asked Lucia. "I mean I'm not saying that you look like you want one, but only I could..." Lucia trailed off into an awkward string of sentences.

The wheelchair lady chuckled.

"You remind me a lot of me when I was younger."

So often the face thought before the brain and Lucia didn't have time to suppress her frown as she looked at her alleged doppelganger. The lady was so large that she spilled over her wheelchair, and despite the concerted effort on her outfit, the makeup couldn't hide the decades of wear and tear.

"Oh, relax. I never said that you look like me. Only that I once looked like you. There's a big difference, sweetie. There's about thirty years of the best kinda living between us."

"No I didn't mean that. Here, have another piece." The lady mitted the pizza as the toppings squished inside her palm.

"Now that's generosity," she said, smirking. "I like you. You know how to treat a lady."

Lucia forced a smile, watching as the woman reached into her bag, pulling out a small, dented flask. She unscrewed the cap with her teeth and took a sharp swig.

"Want some?" she asked.

"I'm good."

"Suit yourself." She tipped the flask back again. "I was young and pretty once." The pageant queen chuckled darkly. "You get dealt a bad hand, you play the cards, or you fold." She took another swig in quick succession, the alcohol taking a sharp effect.

Lucia didn't say anything. The pageant queen snapped her head toward her.

"You don't believe me, do you?"

In a matter of seconds she had already reached into her pocket for an old, grainy Polaroid. The speed of withdrawal suggested that Lucia wasn't the first person to have seen the photograph.

"That's me when I was eighteen. About your age."

The lady in the photo was Princess beautiful. Her roots were butter blonde, and her eyes were bluer than the ocean in the background. She looked too innocent to know curse words, and too polite to get pizza stuck between her teeth.

"Wow, you were beautiful."

"What do you mean *were*?"

"No I mean you're still pretty now…" The lady cut Lucia off with a howling laugh.

"I'm just messing with you. I'm 'bout as pretty now as a scarecrow made of potato sacks. There was a time when I was the most beautiful girl in Kansas. I'd walk past a construction site and they wouldn't even whistle because their jaws were on the floor collecting dust. But I just wanted you to know that you can't judge a book by its cover or in my case, the last page. For the first few chapters, it looked like I was going to be Queen of the universe."

Lucia watched as the woman took another long sip, then another—her guard slipping with each swig. She studied her face. It was difficult to read. Despite her situation, she didn't seem sad. If anything, she was surprisingly cheerful, almost carefree. The alcohol had softened her edges, made her words looser, her laughter fuller.

Lucia had expected to feel wary, but instead, she felt something stranger—an unexpected sense of trust. Maybe it was the honesty in her voice, the way she spoke about her past without flinching. Still, she couldn't forget why she was here. She needed information.

"Where did you grow up?" asked Lucia.

"Kansas, darling. Me and my daddy," she said, leaning into her chair.

"My daddy never got to have a son you see, and the last thing in the world he wanted was a beautiful daughter. Treated me like a slut since the day I was born. Apparently, hillbilly logic is that it was my fault that men looked at me like that, even though the old perv looked at everyone else's daughter in the same way. He wouldn't let me wear dresses until he realized there was money to be made for being pretty. The pageant industry sure ain't as bad as rearing chickens. So he carted me around and dropped me off at shows across the state. It was only a matter of time before I won the Kansas State Little Miss Pageant. He spent the prize money on a new tractor and gave me the rest for a dress so I could enter the competition again the next year. Some gentleman. My daddy started studying all the fashion magazines like they were sports stats. Skinny ass is in fashion, he would say. I became so thin, I'd slip down the grate of a drain. Now you're probably wondering where it all goes to shit? No spoilers here. You're the one feeding me pizza. Well one day we were driving to meet for a big role in one of the magazines."

She reached under her chair and pulled out the latest cover of *Vogue*. As she did, she took a quick, hard swig from her flask—not for the taste, but for something else. Lucia caught the slight tremor in her hand but said nothing. The memories had their own aftertaste.

"This is the one. It's tough to teach an old cow new tricks. This is the magazine cover I was meant to be on. I can't help myself—I buy every new edition even if it costs me a meal. Don't know what I am looking for to tell you the truth. Maybe a new girl who looked like I did back then."

Her usual jolliness faded, and she looked like she was about to tear up. But then in a second she snapped out of it.

"But this ain't no pity party. Anyways, daddy was taking me to chat about being the cover of *Vogue*. I was 21 and as beautiful as I would ever be. No one ever tells you the day that you reach your peak but sure as the sun goes up, we all have one. Think about it. There's your last day of being young, but no one ever tells you when. I suppose my fate was cruel because I'll never forget my last day of being beautiful. We was driving to an office in the city. It wasn't an audition or anything, it was a done deal, a handshake promise. They just wanted to chat about the contract before they took me for the photoshoot. Anyways, as we were driving, there was a big billboard across the road. *Miss Universe. International Pageant.* The lady on the poster was beautiful and even more beautiful than that, she was holding a check for one hundred thousand dollars. My daddy saw the poster and couldn't stop looking. In fact, he didn't stop looking until he died. Got T-boned by a truck that smashed into the driver's side and killed him instantly. Broke both of my legs and now I have these T-rex arms for legs."

She motioned to her legs in the wheelchair. Lucia stared at them for the first time. They were so skinny they could have belonged to a child and it looked like they were missing the bones, just a bit of flesh dangling from her torso.

"What happened after that?" asked Lucia.

"A whole lot of life happened. Life's not like a story. It's not as basic as the parentless, crippled pageant queen who ended up on the street the next day. The end. The best years of my life were with these fleshy stumps. I did hand modeling for a while—you know all those ads where people open crisp packets and lather on hand soap? Yep that was all these puppies," she said, showing off her now calloused hands. "Paid great for a while, even got them insured in case something happened to them. But the best part of it was that I still felt beautiful, that people wanted me, not all of me but at least a part of me. My ex-husband was obsessed with my hands. But try being a hand model past forty when your veins pop more than your knuckles. That doesn't pan out well and I didn't have a dollar to my name. All I knew how to do was sit and look pretty, so I guess you could say it served me well for this line of work. Everyone's always apologizing to me, saying how sorry they are that my luck turned out this way. It ain't no tragedy. It's a sign I had a damn good life. I made sure that I spent every single penny on the good times. Drank more than I should've, stayed with deadbeat men and got my life savings swindled twice, but to hell with it, I don't regret a thing."

"Whoa, what a story," Lucia said.

"I bet you think I do that all the time," said the lady with a sigh.

"What do you mean?"

"Tell my whole damn life story. Like some drunk who doesn't

know when to stop talking," she said. "I promise you, it's the first time I've ever shared all that. I honestly don't know why I did."

Lucia held the silence.

"There's something about you. You have this way about you, no judgment in your eyes, just a pure little thing."

"Thanks," Lucia said, but she still couldn't shake the feeling that the pageant queen was hiding something. She'd loosened up, sure—but not enough. There was still something she wasn't saying.

"I have one question," Lucia said.

The woman blinked slowly, swaying slightly in her chair. "Shoot, although you practically know my whole damn life." She let out a lazy laugh, her words slurring just a little at the edges.

"Do you wish you could have done anything differently?"

The pageant queen grinned, lifting what was left of her flask in a sloppy toast. "Not one damn thing."

Lucia hesitated, then leaned in slightly. "Was there ever a time you let someone else get hurt?" She kept her voice steady, inching the conversation toward Maya.

The pageant queen's smile faltered. A beat passed before she tilted her head, eyes sharpening beneath the alcohol haze.

"What exactly are you angling at, girl?" Her words weren't slurred anymore.

"I mean, was there ever a time when you knew something but didn't say anything—and someone got hurt?"

She didn't answer right away. Instead, she grabbed another slice of pizza and took a deliberate, heavy bite.

"Careful, girl. You didn't buy me enough pizza to run your mouth like that."

Lucia paused.

"Did you know Maya?"

The woman's grip tightened around the crust. The moment Lucia said the name, something in her changed. The loose warmth from the booze was gone.

"You're exactly like the cops. Try to pin everything on a bum."

"I never said you did anything," Lucia said quickly. "To tell you the truth, I trust you, but I just need to know what happened."

"Bullshit." The pageant queen wheeled back, creating space between them. Lucia took a careful step forward.

"Why were you knocking on her door?" The motel footage played on a loop in her head.

The pageant queen's eyes flashed. "How do you know about that?"

"I saw the footage."

"They showed you that too?" she said, her voice lower now. She huffed a bitter laugh. "And don't you think it's strange that the footage cuts right when I knock?"

"Yeah," Lucia admitted. "That's why I wanted to talk to you."

The pageant queen exhaled hard, shaking her head. "How the hell do you think I drowned two children and a grown adult? I can't even stand on my own two feet."

"I don't think you did. I just want to know why you were there." Lucia's voice softened, testing the space between them. "I was a friend of Maya's. I'm not looking to get you in trouble."

The pageant queen sighed heavily, tilting her head back against the chair.

"I tried to tell people," she muttered. "How come the only person who cares in this entire city is you?"

Lucia's pulse kicked up. "What happened?"

The woman stared at her for a long time.

Then, finally—her voice came back colder.

"That's the story of the moonlight wedding."

MOONLIGHT WEDDING

It was the night before they died.

"Now I remember where I was, because I remember where I was every night. Right here in front of that damn motel, waiting at Pizza Hut. I sit outside this store three hundred sixty-five days a year. I may as well have a PhD in people from studying what happens across the road in that cesspit. The night she died, the moon was out, there are always more donations on a full moon, people get all skittish, so coins start dropping like Skittles. It was a cold night, but I had to stay out late because that's when my clientele buys pizza. I managed to find some plane socks in the trash that just about severed my legs, they were so tight. So imagine me shivering my ass off, reading *Vogue* for the four hundredth time while all these cover girls are practically naked in the Caribbean. Torture. There was the usual flow of cars into the motel—nothing out of the ordinary. A couple coming back from dinner, some young punks in a beat out Ford and the odd drifter trying to snag a free parking spot for the night. But then an all-black car with tinted windows pulled up.

"Now I should tell you that I live quite close to the motel. I sleep in the woods directly behind it. So I take a keen interest in anyone who pulls up on my doorstep. People are always chucking their shit into the curb. I would complain but it makes a nice hardware store. I got Pawn Store Mike to build me a hut made from two abandoned whisky barrels and a broken motel door. The door's my roof, not my door. Anyways where were we? Ah yes. So the car parks at my doorstep but no one gets out. They were waiting. If there's one thing about me, it's that I'm as stubborn as a broken gear stick and my bladder could outlast their gas tank. I wasn't moving until I saw who got out. So I stayed where I was for the next thirty minutes outside the Pizza Hut. Still nothing. It was getting late now, must've been around 10 p.m. By that time on a Sunday, the motel's completely dead. I could only see their car with the faint flicker of the streetlight, but I promise they were watching me from those tinted windows, waiting for me to fall asleep. So I wrapped the blanket over my head and slouched to the side. Dead as a log. But what they didn't know was that I had a tiny peeping hole. About two minutes later the door opened. I couldn't see much, but two men got out. They hurried into the woods behind the motel, heading for my home. Now at this point I don't know if it was curiosity or good old-fashioned American pride, but I wasn't going to let strangers take my shit. So I threw off the blanket and wheeled myself across the street. Now obviously I know what you're thinking—how does a pageant queen get into the woods in a wheelchair? I wish I could tell you there was some magic carpet, but the answer is far simpler than that. I leave my chair hidden in a little hole that I dug at the edge of the woods and then I crawl face down into the mud like a fucking GI Joe. Every morning. Every night. On the streets, you must fight for a place to sleep. Underpasses are all taken. Parks are too dangerous for women, even me. The only place left for a cripple is the woods. So I hid my chair and started to crawl. You're the same level as the rabbits. From that height, a pebble is a boulder. I crawled for twenty yards until I found my little clearing. It's about the size of a small car with my home smack bang in the middle.

"Lo and behold, they'd decided to use my roof as the altar for their

fucked-up moonlight wedding. Now at the time you must understand that I was angry as hell. They were tromping around on all my
stuff but when I saw the priest.

"I was too curious to blow my cover. He was wearing his Sunday
robes, white as children's chalk, even though he had just clambered
through the trees. The priest was young, and he had a real serious
look on his face. He stood behind the altar, reading his Bible. A
young couple stood in front of him. It was Maya and that Garcia. She
was in a pink dress with a veil that covered her face like a morning

mist. He wore a suit that fit him perfectly without a speck of lint. They could have been on a magazine cover, the two of them. At first, the priest spoke softly, as if each word was a loose rock that he stepped on toward his next sentence. But then he found his footing, firing off wild, fiery sermons that gave me goosebumps in the mud. He couldn't look at the young couple. It felt like a scene from those low-budget movies, the type they broadcast in the early hours of the morning when you're too high to know what genre it is. Garcia lifted the veil of the bride, and the priest said, "Do you, Mr. Garcia, take Maya to be your lawfully wedded wife, to have and to hold, from this day forward, for better, for worse, for richer, for poorer, in sickness and in health, to love and to cherish, till death do you part?"

"I do," said Garcia firmly.

Then instead of doing the normal vows, he spoke off-the-cuff.

"I'm sorry I knocked on your door. We both know that I have caused more trouble than you could've ever expected, you were justified in keeping it closed for so long. But even after everything, I would still knock again. Thank you for coming on this journey with me. You have done so much good already."

Maya didn't break eye contact.

"Till death do us part," she said.

Then the priest withdrew a certificate from somewhere beneath
the tangle of his robes.

"It is official, you are now legally recognized as husband and wife.
All I have to do is sign this," said the priest. He pulled out a pen and
signed the certificate.

"I'll take it," said Maya. She grabbed the certificate and looked at Garcia. The two of them stood, holding each other's arms as the night breeze ruffled the priest's robes.

"I have one last thing to do," said Garcia.

"And like that, Garcia left his own wedding in the cover of darkness. The priest following behind him, leaving Maya alone in the woods. I sensed she didn't want to leave—she lingered behind the altar looking up at the moon as if it could talk. There was someone else out there in the woods. I could feel it. When you live alone for long enough, you develop a sixth sense for being watched. I scanned the trees to find them, but before I could, Maya started to move, so I hid behind the bush. When the coast was clear, whatever was watching us had also vanished. I took stock of all my possessions. They didn't touch my magazine collection, but they'd painted my pillow with their shoes. So that was all the thanks I got for hosting their moonlight wedding."

The pageant queen stopped. Lucia waited in silence for her to finish. But the pageant queen leaned back in her chair, chewing on her fingers as if they were the last kernels of popcorn left.

"But why did you go back to her room after the wedding?" asked Lucia.

The question halted her fidgeting immediately. She looked at Lucia cautiously.

"A photograph," she stammered.

"A photograph," replied Lucia, confused.

"Yes, a photograph."

"What was the photograph?"

"It was of the couple," said the pageant queen. "A photograph is a personal thing. Now most people would have probably tossed it in the trash, but I am a visual creature, and the thought of a displaced picture hurts me. It could have been the only copy in the world. I would kill for some of my Polaroids from when I had both my legs."

"Okay," said Lucia skeptically. "What happened next?"

"I decided it was only right that I return it. So I got on my wheelchair and made my way back to the motel at midnight. The lights were on, and I remembered that I'd seen Garcia a few times on the second floor, knocking on the first door to the left. It must've been Maya's room. Now there are few things in this world that get me more enraged than politics, but a concrete staircase is one of them. I couldn't wheel up, so I had to climb the damn thing. It took me a while, but eventually I got there. The plan was simple—return the photograph to Maya and then leave. I knocked. No one answered. Seeing as I'd made the effort to go up the stairs, I wasn't going to give up as easily as the mailman. I must've knocked for five straight minutes. Maya was in there all right. But for some reason, she wouldn't come to the door. Eventually, I just slipped it under the door.

"Then all of a sudden the lights went off. At first I couldn't see shit, but slowly my eyes adjusted, and the moonlight guided me back down the stairs. When I got to my wheelchair, that's when I felt the eyes watching me again. There was someone there in the shadows. It was a man. I couldn't make out any details other than his silhouette, but there was a dark energy to it. Now, I'm not the type to believe in backwoods saints, but there was something about him. I'm telling you. It felt like he had sucked all the light from the motel, his soul a black hole feasting on stars. To tell you the truth, it scared me so much, I rolled straight back to the woods. But I could've never known that it would turn out the way it did. I would've stayed all night long outside her room if I had known what was about to happen, those poor kids floating face down in the pool. After I heard the news, I was in disbelief. If it weren't for the grazes on my knees, I would have thought it was all a dream.

"But there was something I didn't understand: Garcia never mentioned the wedding in the news. I thought that he would say something so that the police would widen their search, maybe they could find that shadow in the woods. But he said nothing. Instead, the only person they questioned was me. I was the only lead they had. I told them about all the crazy stuff I saw in the woods, but no one believed me. They didn't understand why two of the most respected members of the community would lie about something like that. They didn't want me near the motel for a while. I couldn't manifest outside the motel for months, had to lay low at some shitty Spanish statue getting donations from tourist buses.

"Eventually, they stopped asking questions. The coroner was confident that it was a suicide, there were just no other leads for it to be anything else. I thought surely the priest would come forward, but he never did. I tried to track him down. I wheeled from church to church, begging at the end of each Sunday mass. Everyone's pockets were empty because they said they had already donated, like I would understand that the church needed the money more than me. Until one day, I found him. He was at the Basilica of St. Augustine. Obviously he didn't know who I was. So at first, he treated me with great compassion, me being the whole leper type.

"Hello, sister. Here is some bread that we can spare you. May God help you find shelter."

"He spoke in Bible verses and the only reason he gave me bread was probably because that was something Jesus did. He was a strange man. Always seemed very nervous but then whenever he was in front of a crowd, he transformed into a man possessed by the power of his own self-belief. I heard the way people talked about him when they left his church.

"Father Roderick should have been a battle commander."

"Yes. He turns the Bible into a movie. It's electric."

But when I asked him about the moonlight wedding, he played dumb.

"What in good heavens are you talking about?"

"I saw you with Garcia and Maya in the woods. The night before she died."

No more offers for bread after that, he shifted gears like he went from fifth to first on the highway.

"It's tragic what happens when one lives without shelter for too long. I know many institutions which may be able to help."

"I've been around long enough to know a threat when I hear one. I wheeled away from the man as fast as I could. I haven't spoken about Maya since, but I still hear her though. It's like her words are muffled, gargled almost as if she is trying to speak to me from underwater. I guess it's the price we pay for having done nothing, but I can't get those vows out of my head.

Till death do us part.

ROMEO AND JULIET

Since missing her flight to Stanford, Lucia had spent the past week deflecting her mother's questions about rebooking. She told her mother there was a housing issue—some mix-up with dorm assignments—and that Stanford was sorting it out before she could book her flight.

"No point flying out with nowhere to sleep," she'd say, before slipping out the door.

Now, leaving St. Augustine wasn't an option—not after learning about the moonlight wedding on the eve of Maya's death. She wasn't ready to walk away, not yet. But telling her mother she wasn't going to California? That was a conversation she still couldn't face. Lucia's acceptance into Stanford was the only thing her mother talked about at church, boasting between the pews, as she invented scholarship names and courses.

"My daughter is in the pre-med stream."

Some of the ladies from church would feign sympathy—but it always came with a barb, just sharp enough to deflate her bragging.

"It's such a shame that Emi couldn't be there to see her."

Her mother would go quiet then, the pride draining from her face. Mrs. Johnson didn't care about Emi—she just wanted to remind her mother that she had lost one child already. Now Lucia carried the weight of being the other one, the one who was supposed to make it all okay. Here she was, about to let her mother down too.

To hide her new line of investigation, Lucia had also converted an exercise book—its cover once casually titled *A Freshman's Guide to Scientific Inquiry*—into her investigation notebook about the case of Maya and Garcia. That way she could pretend to be doing pre-work while she populated it with her learnings from the past week.

The sun blazed off the white paper, making her squint. Though she hadn't uncovered much about Emi's final days, the pattern was undeniable: two people in St. Augustine, both marked before drowning. The person who left Maya's card had to be the same one who slipped it into her brother's pocket.

Yet the connection was strange; Emi had lived on the streets while Garcia was the mayor of St. Augustine. Lucia didn't understand how the two stories could intertwine.

Since she had heard the story, she was starting to wonder whether it was Mr. Muerte himself who had hid in the shadows while the lights went out at the motel. Maybe it was the receptionist, the crab scuttling out of his hiding hole in the dark. All his diary entries suggested he was obsessed with her. Yet still, it didn't make sense. Leaving behind the card wasn't the work of a jealous creep. It was something more sinister, more thoughtful. But she still didn't understand why Garcia and the priest had lied about the wedding. It would've helped the police assign a motive for a murder. They could have proved that the receptionist witnessed the secret wedding in the woods, then in a jealous rage, drowned Maya and her children.

I'm sorry I knocked on your door.

It was as if Maya already knew her fate—she was cursed to die.

Suddenly, a door slammed upstairs. Lucia turned from the lounger to see a giant of a man at Javier's door. He was so tall his head nearly brushed the ceiling, his bald skull reflecting the sun. Then she saw it. There was a tattoo on the back of his head, an eye nestled in an open palm, its inked pupil staring straight through her.

Javier opened the door.

The man spoke to Javier in Spanish, but he was too far away for Lucia to hear what he said. Javier's shoulders tensed as he gestured to the stairs, but the giant didn't move. He towered over Javier, blocking the exit with his bulk, and in that long pause, Lucia saw how small Javier looked beneath his shadow. She thought the giant was going to swat him into the sky with a single swoop. Instead, after a minute, the giant nodded and walked away. Javier quickly shut the door behind him.

The encounter left Lucia's mind racing. Javier—she'd almost forgotten about him. A memory flickered: the night of her murder, when Maya brushed past him on the balcony, the ember of his cigarette glowing in the darkness. She hadn't thought much of Maya's friendship with him before, but now she wondered if he knew about their wedding in the woods.

Lucia walked to the stairwell.

When she reached the base, the giant was descending the stairs. Now she could see his face. He had teardrop tattoos beneath his eye and a wife-beater that exposed sunburnt muscles, worm-like veins burrowing just beneath his skin. He scowled at Lucia and kept walking.

She raced up the stairs with her investigations book and knocked on Javier's door. It opened a few seconds later.

"Ah, Lucia, I wasn't expecting you," he said. Instead of stepping forward to greet her as he had in the past, Javier stayed back, several feet inside his room.

"Who was that man?" Lucia asked.

"Oh, him. That's a long story… The short version is I want nothing to do with him."

"Lucia turned, watching the man climb into his car—his tattooed eye dissolving into the distance. Javier followed her gaze.

"Well, I suppose I do owe you more details about my life, I appreciate it is hard to make sense of a man who has maps stuck to a motel wall. My work has introduced me to all sorts of characters," Javier said.

"You worked with him?" said Lucia, confused.

"In another life, I used to work as a detective in Mexico City. I was a young man, back when there were no computers and the only way to make sense of a crime was with a paper and pen. You learn to track rumors through the things around you—half-drunk bottles of mezcal, library borrowing lists, or waitstaff eager to trade secrets. I got quite good at it. Too good. Reported the wrong people who were high up in the city and then…"

Javier stared at the carpet. Without looking away, he reached into his trousers for his Zippo and lit a cigarette. His hands steadied after the first puff.

"Then I had to leave the country, start life afresh here. The only skill I had was figuring things out. So I started out as a private detective in Florida about thirty years ago. I'll spare you the details, but you learn all manner of things about people's private lives. That's how I met Jonny the Giant."

"His name's Jonny?"

"I know it doesn't suit him, but how could his parents have known he'd turn out like that," said Javier. "He hired me to see if his wife was cheating on him, paid double my normal rate, all in cash."

"So, was she?"

"Of course. She was cheating on him with a local pianist. I had to drop him as a client—he would have broken the poor pianist's fingers if he had found out."

Lucia paused.

"You really were a detective?"

"You don't believe me? Look, let me teach you something." Javier stepped outside and let the door swing shut behind him. The latch clicked firmly into place.

Javier smirked, then slipped a hand into his suit pocket, pulling out something small and metallic. Lucia squinted at the strange, thin tool glinting in his palm. It wasn't a key.

"What is that?" she asked.

"A shortcut."

He knelt by the lock, pulling out a second tool—a narrow, curved piece of metal. He slid one into the keyhole and began to wiggle it, his fingers barely moving. Lucia watched, confused.

"You can't just—"

The lock gave a soft click. The door swung open.

Lucia took a step back. "What?"

Javier flicked away the bit of ash clinging to his cigarette. "*Voilà.*"

Lucia gawked. "Did you just—?"

"You can do it without the wrench, too." He pulled the tool free and showed her how he twisted it slightly before raking the pins.

"Okay I believe you," Lucia said, staring at the open door. "Well, I have been doing some investigating of my own, and I have something I need to ask you about."

"You should come inside," Javier said. He ushered her into the rose-lit room, gesturing toward one of the plush chairs. Then, he scanned the corridor for eavesdroppers before stepping in himself.

"So what's your big breakthrough?" Javier asked, as he took a seat.

"Did you know that Maya was married?"

"What?" he said, his eyebrows rising high on his forehead.

"The night before she died, she got married in the woods behind the motel."

He stared at the floor for a long time. "I can't believe it." His fingers drummed against the chair. "She never mentioned anything to me."

"I thought you were friends?" said Lucia.

"I was her closest friend here, but she never said a word about getting married. Nor did I ever see a ring on her finger," he said. "But then again, you must understand that Maya was an exceedingly humble woman. To her the idea of flaunting Garcia's wealth would have been morally inconceivable. It does make sense that she would want some secret ceremony."

Lucia frowned. Her modesty still didn't explain the secrecy of the priest and Garcia.

She leaned back into the red pillows. "But why would Garcia lie about the wedding? Why would he say it never happened?"

"Well, it's the first I've heard of all this, but if he is lying, I would assume it's because he has something to hide. That's the first thing you learn in the trade: people have a million reasons to lie."

"Exactly," Lucia said. "There's something else that I didn't tell you. When they got married, I heard that he apologized for taking her down this path. She didn't get upset, though; she seemed almost resigned to her fate, like she knew something was going to happen."

"Hmm, there is one thing she told me," Javier said, lighting himself another cigarette. "Now that you mention it, it seems more important than I realized."

"Go on," said Lucia.

"Well, I'm sure it wouldn't hold any weight in a court of law, those legal types aren't amenable to the world of fiction, but Maya was reading an interesting book."

"Yes?" said Lucia, hanging on every word, each one drifting between Javier's slow, deliberate puffs.

"Well, she was reading Shakespeare's *Romeo and Juliet*. She had bought the play for her class at school, and she had developed somewhat of an obsession with it."

Lucia blushed. She had never read Shakespeare. She loved reading, but Emi always said only pretentious kids pretended to like it to sound smart. So, in quiet protest, she had avoided it altogether—even though it often felt like a requirement for anyone who loved books.

"I'm sorry, I haven't read it."

"I don't blame you. Shakespeare was a thief, one of the greatest, stealing every story ever told and making it his own." He took a slow draw of his cigar, exhaling as his gaze darkened. "Which is relevant because—there was a secret wedding."

"What?" Lucia said in disbelief.

"They had a secret wedding to avoid an arranged marriage. Juliet pretends to poison herself. When Romeo arrives, he kills himself because he thinks that she is actually dead. So when Juliet awakens, she kills herself too," Javier said. "Thus, with a kiss I die."

Lucia stared at Javier reciting the plot in shock. It was strangely similar.

"For never was a story of more woe, than this of Juliet and her Romeo," Javier said, in a British accent. "Those are the final lines of the play."

"Did Maya say anything about it? Maybe her thoughts?" pressed Lucia.

Javier paused to think.

"You must forgive me, my memory is like a trash can. I must be careful with what I choose to stuff it with." His hand sifted through his charcoal-black hair.

"Well did she say anything about love? About why Romeo and Juliet got married?"

"Now that I think about it, there was one thing that, in hindsight, was quite strange… Yes, that's right—Maya was wrestling with the dilemma of whether we owe a moral duty to our families, even if it means forgoing the pursuit of our own hearts. In the play, the young lovers choose a self-destructive path, believing it to be the right one.

But for what? The play doesn't show the years after—the passion faded, their youth gone, their families growing old without them. That, in itself, is the real tragedy," Javier said.

"So you think that she wasn't sure whether to follow her heart or not?" asked Lucia.

"I think she was grappling with the price she was willing to pay—whether to protect her family or follow her heart," he said.

For several moments, the only movement in the room was Javier's cigar smoke, curling in ugly ringlets toward the ceiling.

"Isn't it strange how closely related it all is?" said Lucia. "I mean she was reading this book, and then she had her own secret wedding in the woods."

"You might be surprised. As both a lover of fiction and a practitioner of justice, I suppose I'm uniquely positioned to comment. The stories of the human condition are few, and yet they echo through time, repeating themselves in countless lives," Javier said, staring out at the vast ocean on his map, pinned to the wall.

"What do you mean?"

"Don't mind me, I'm being a lousy poet again, that's all. I mean to say that to us every story is completely new, revelatory in its novelty. But if you could speak to the oldest tree or even the oldest whale, it would laugh and tell you of the hundred times it has watched the same story unfold in us sad humans. We are less original than we believe—most tales circle back to the same themes."

"You think something like this has happened before?" Lucia asked.

"Have you heard of the myth of La Llorona?"

"Yeah," she said. "My mom used to threaten that she would come if my brother and I didn't wash our plates."

"Of course, it's a myth that's been co-opted by parents all over Mexico. But the story is much deeper than a warning for little children. As the story goes, a beautiful indigenous woman fell in love with a wealthy Spanish nobleman—a romance that crossed class barriers. She bore his children, and for a time, they were happy. But soon, he left her for a woman of high society. In her madness and jealousy, she took her children to the river and drowned them before taking her own life. Now she wanders the waterways, weeping for what she destroyed."

"That also sounds similar to Maya," she said, surprised.

"Myths shape life, just as life shapes myths. They have for thousands of years. The only predictable things are our own fallibilities. Our fault lines of jealousy and greed cause the same events to replay, over and over, in the cosmic timeline."

The cryptic remark unsettled Lucia.

"When you were talking earlier about Maya's reading—did she ever keep a diary? Write down names, thoughts?"

"She did. But I'm sure the police took it for evidence, even though their investigation was so poorly done," Javier replied.

Lucia sank back in her seat.

"What about her other stuff—was there anything else she left behind?" Lucia asked.

"Well, she had no family members—I believe she donated a box of her stuff to the Basilica," Javier said. "I think that's what happens when there are no family members to give it to, just collects dust in the church's basement."

"How do you know that?" asked Lucia.

Javier hesitated.

"I'm fairly sure I saw a priest come around to pick something up a few days after she died," he said. "The one from the Basilica."

Lucia shivered, picturing the priest's white robes shifting in the moonlit woods, the wind stirring through the trees. The shadow.

THE BASILICA OF ST. AUGUSTINE

Lucia stood in front of the Cathedral Basilica of St. Augustine as rain droplets rolled down Mother Mary's face like tears. The bell tower got lost in the clouds, while the mist painted the building bone white. It was one of the oldest churches in America. The parking lot was full of luxury black vehicles with windows tinted darker than the stormy clouds on the horizon. Something was happening inside.

Lucia needed to find Maya's box of stuff that had been donated to the church, collecting dust in the basement. She pushed the lumbering orange doors that towered over her like the greatest oak in the Anastasia Forest. The cold slipped in behind her. She shut the door as she clung to the walls, avoiding the aisle. Every time she entered she felt like a tiny candle inside of a paper lantern because of the roof's orange glow. Yet she had never been to a place with so little natural light. Darkness sat in the rows of pews amongst the hordes of well-dressed people. She couldn't make out any individual features as everyone merged into one anonymous black blob. The crowd was staring at the candle lit sanctuary, where a golden crucifix hung suspended from the Basilica ceiling. Below it, there was a woman in a flowing white dress that spilled onto the carpet. Her face was covered by a veil, yet Lucia knew she was beautiful from her side profile alone. She had slender arms, sun-kissed skin, and auburn hair that ran down to her waist. The groom was a greasy-looking man whose bottom button was about to pop, with a face built for spitting out olive seeds.

The priest stood behind them. He was too engrossed with his reading to notice Lucia slink into an empty pew at the back of the church. For the first time, she saw the priest's face—paler than his robe, his round cheeks giving him the eerie look of a full moon. His thinning hair was painstakingly combed over his bald patches. As she took her seat, some guests glanced at her with smile frowns.

"We are gathered here today for the wedding of Kelly and Santi Stuart."

The priest smiled warmly to the bride and groom. He drew out the pauses as if he was enjoying himself too much to rush it. All she could think about was the priest standing in the woods, shaking as he presided over the moonlight wedding. Reading the same verses that he was now, too scared to smile. "Do you, Santi, take Kelly to be your lawfully wedded wife?"

"I do."

The priest continued, "And do you, Kelly, take Santi to be your lawfully wedded husband?"

"I do."

"You may now kiss the bride."

The man lifted the veil; they kissed, causing the pews to explode in applause. The lady in front of Lucia whispered to the man by her side.

"Let's see how long this one lasts." The man didn't say anything, but the sly smirk was enough to egg her on. "It's his fourth in fifteen years. Not bad."

"The perks of being a millionaire," whispered the man. The applause died down and the priest continued with his sermon. Lucia surveyed the hall trying to find a door that could lead to the basement where they could be storing Maya's stuff. There were too many people to snoop around. She had to wait. The more the priest spoke, the more her heart raced as the church acoustics made everything sound ominous.

"Please remain with us to celebrate this joyous occasion with a reception right here in the Basilica."

The ceremony was over. Before she had time to process her next move, everyone stood up. People started to mingle in small groups as Lucia awkwardly lingered at the back. She had never crashed a wedding before—she had no idea what to say if someone asked who she was.

She rose cautiously, skirting around the edges of the pews, and nervously scanning the crowd. She sensed the eyes following her as she moved self-consciously in the shadows. Even the paintings tracked her. She hugged the wall as she hurried along the aisle looking for a door. The chatter was getting louder as all the conversations merged into one rising hum. The invisible conductor geared up for her anxiety crescendo. Then she saw the door. It looked older than the Basilica itself, but it probably led to the basement that Javier was talking about. She rushed toward it but then something caught her eye in the crowd.

The giant's bald head rose above the crowd, and there was that eye again—inked into his skull, staring at her through the darkness.

She never thought he was the type of man who was invited to weddings, yet the other guests looked comfortable around him. Next to him, there was a large circle forming around the married couple as people eagerly shoved to get to the front. Everyone was showering the man with praise, while the woman waited by his side like an afterthought. The woman glanced over and saw Lucia in the shadows. They held eye contact. Lucia's heart dropped. She was waiting for her to point at the uninvited girl, to frown at the intruder.

Fish out of water.

Instead the bride smiled. It was so gentle, she felt like she knew her. The women turned away, and the cold draft of the passage reminded Lucia she had work to do. The priest must've been lurking somewhere.

She headed for the door. It had an iron-rung for a handle, the kind you'd find on an old cellar. The rusty hinges groaned as she pushed it open. She slipped into the gap and yanked it shut behind her, sealing herself in complete darkness. Taking a cautious step forward, her foot landed on something small and round. It rolled beneath her weight, throwing her off balance. She gasped as her ankle twisted, and before she could steady herself, her body pitched forward. The cobblestone edges smashed into her ribcage enough times for her to realize she was falling down a flight of stairs. The pain rag-dolled her body. Everything hurt as her eyes watered, and her mouth welled with warm blood. She whimpered. Finally, the staircase spat her out at the end like a washed-up whale on the shoreline. Lucia bit into her tongue to check that she had all her teeth. A pain was pulsing in her spine where it felt like the stairs had pushed out her vertebrae like a Jenga piece. She lay flat on her back, groaning.

She gave herself a minute to breathe. All she wanted to do was go to sleep. But she thought of her brother, how lucky she was to feel anything in her limbs, even if it hurt. She cut her rest short and forced herself to stand. Her legs wobbled beneath her. Reaching up, she touched her face—her fingertips came away smeared with blood. A sharp sting flared across her cheek; she must've cut it on the way down.

With her left hand she grasped blindly in the air, trying to find something to hold onto. Her fingernails scraped mossy cobblestone. She used the wall to prop herself up as she hobbled along. The wall was slightly curved toward the top, it must have been an old tunnel that the Spanish built hundreds of years ago. She was too sore to be curious. Her entire focus collapsed to a single solitary mission.

Lucia couldn't remember being this motivated when she arrived at the Basilica. She kept hobbling as she plunged deeper into the tunnel, the never-ending labyrinth of twists and turns. Her hand traced against the mossy wall to guide her, as her fingers bumped against the rivets between the stone. But then she felt something unnatural. Something plastic. It was a switch. She flicked it. A dim light illuminated the passage. It must have been a single bulb because there was just enough to see her body. Her wrists were slashed, blood seeped through her jeans in patchy ink blots. It made the pain worse to see her cuts. But it didn't matter, she needed to find Maya's stuff. At the end of the tunnel was another door. She stumbled toward it. Someone had replaced the old keyhole with a new lock. She reached for a hairclip and bent it into a fishing hook, then jimmied it inside the lock pin, just like Javier had shown her. Lucia pressed her ear against the door to hear it click. The pressure made the blood gush out even faster. She tried to be still so her hands could work.

After a while she heard the mechanism click. The door buckled open as stale air rushed into her mouth all at once. She wheezed, coughing up blood and dust. It was the storage room. Shelves were stacked high with cardboard boxes labeled by masking tape. She scanned the labels. *Gift from the Umbridges, U14 Communion, Project: Fountain of Youth, Church Archives.* Then she saw it. It was tucked away on the bottom shelf. The masking tape had a single word inscribed upon it.

Maya.

Lucia took it out. Things had been hastily shoved into it; her entire life reduced to a cardboard box. On the top, there were children's clothes. The outfits didn't need to be folded to fit. She picked up a pair of Carl's cargo shorts. Her heart dropped at the little pants that the boy would never wear again. He was much smaller than she had thought. She imagined him floating in the pool with the same waterlogged pockets as her brother.

There were echoes in the tunnel. Two men.

"Why are the lights on?"

"Who cares."

"Look. There's blood on the floor."

"Fuck. They would never do it here."

"No. We'll have to speak to Father Roderick."

"Do you have the key?"

"Yep."

Lucia panicked. She placed Maya's box back where she found it, scanning the room for a place to hide. There was a large wardrobe in the corner. It would have to do. She clambered into it as the priest's robes brushed against her cheeks. Sweat and stale wine rushed up her nostrils. She closed the doors from inside, waiting.

"Why's the door open?"

"I don't want to know. Better to not ask questions."

"Place scares the shit out of me."

"Can you find it?"

"Yep, got it. Let's go."

There were ruffles from the shelves. A moment later the door slammed shut. The voices trailed off as she jumped out of the cupboard. The room felt even smaller with the door closed. She knew the priest would be coming any minute, but she still hadn't found anything useful from Maya's box. She threw away the clothes to get to the bottom. There was a pile of books. She picked up the first one she saw. It had a marble statue of a man with curly hair, and an even curlier beard that looked like the rock had been chiseled into a dozen snail shells.

Meditations by Marcus Aurelius.

She put it down and kept looking for the diary. It wasn't there. But then she saw *Romeo and Juliet*. It was the last play Maya studied—the one she discussed with Javier. Lucia flicked through the pages. The dust in the cobblestone storage room triggered a fit of coughing. She wheezed into her arm, desperate to muffle the sound—if the other men heard her, it could be over.

The glossy paper Maya had once held now prickled at Lucia's fingertips, sending tiny shocks of unease up her arm. Her breath caught as she flicked to the final page. And then she saw it—blood, smeared in jagged streaks across the bottom of the page. Three stick figures stared back at her, crude and childlike, each marked with a small, sharp arrow with their names.

Carl

Jasmine

Maya

Lucia's skin tingled. The stick figures looked like they had been finger-painted. The red streaks turned salmon at the end of each stroke. She wet her finger in her mouth, then rubbed the saliva onto the smallest stick figure. Slowly, Carl disappeared. The tingles rippled on her arm.

It was blood.

She looked up from the book to the four stone walls, and the confinement of her discovery. Lucia felt so dizzy she could barely think. Someone had drawn Maya and her children in blood. Now the book was buried deep in the basement of the Basilica, along with all of Maya's belongings, conveniently donated to the church for storage.

She turned to the text next to the drawings on the final page. Shakespeare's last sonnet.

Some shall be pardon'd, and some punished:

For never was a story of more woe,

Than this of Juliet and her Romeo.

Then she saw that extra lines had been added in black ink. The font was different. It wasn't Maya's handwriting. This person was in a rush. It read:

Be careful with the secrets that you sow,
Speak of Emi, and you shall go.
Mr. Muerte.

The book shook in her hands. All the pieces shifted—there was Emi's name. Maya and her brother, both tied to Mr. Muerte, both dragged into something dark enough to kill them.

Someone had left this as a warning to Maya, a threat wrapped in blood.

Suddenly, the door opened. Lucia still had the book in her hands.

"What on earth are you doing, girl."

The priest stood in the archway blocking her escape. He looked at Lucia like she was some incarnation of the devil. The fall had clearly left its mark on her.

"I'm just reading," she said innocently with dried blood in the corner of her mouth.

"How'd you get in here?"

"The door was open."

"That's impossible. I locked it," the priest stammered.

"You mustn't be in here."

"Sorry."

Lucia stood up, preparing to make a dash for the exit if he gave her the opening. The priest saw what she was reading. He snatched the book out of her hands.

"It is a grave sin to steal the possessions of the living, let alone the dead," he said in a troubled voice.

He looked down at the final page, he saw the blood too.

"You have no idea what you've done, child."

Lucia hated it when people called her child. She couldn't help but snarl at him after all he'd done. The priest no longer looked angry. His demeanor shifted suddenly. His hands were shaking, he couldn't stop tapping his foot. He didn't even notice Lucia. It was the same million-mile stare that her mother had whenever she wanted to be somewhere else. He dropped his head into his hands, trembling along the lines of his palms. Then he clutched the cross around his neck, murmuring prayers to himself.

"Please God forgive me. I tried. You know I did. I can still fix things," he continued to babble senselessly until Lucia couldn't understand him. Now he was on his knees with his head pressed against the cobblestone in prayer. She slipped out of the room and ran out of the tunnel. The priest started to cry.

THE CASA MONICA HOTEL

Lucia stood in front of the Casa Monica Hotel—her face bloodied with cuts from her fall in the Basilica. Rain slid down her cheeks, cleansing the blood from her face. Across the road, just beyond the plaza, the church stood solemnly during the storm. She thought of the priest, dry in his robes, crying in the tunnel while he clutched a book holding Emi's name. Lucia had to tell her mother—Emi didn't leave them behind. Her Stanford acceptance letter weighed on her mind as she thought of the deadline she was about to break. She couldn't choose to live her mother's dreams if it meant giving up on Emi, his truth sealed in the cobblestone. She had to uncover it. For Maya too. For her children.

She looked up at the hotel where her mother worked—a place she had never stepped foot inside. As a child, she had seen it once on a walking tour, the guide's voice drifting into the background as she studied its towering façade. Tourists were easily deceived by its turrets, towers, and Spanish Baroque flourishes. But beneath the illusion of history, there was no true Spain in its terracotta tiles or stucco walls—only the vision of an American oil tycoon who built it in 1887. Yet, time had wrapped the hotel in the weight of its own myth, lending it an air of antiquity as if it had shaped the very history of St. Augustine. Rainwater streamed from the edges of its red-tiled roof, spilling over the wrought-iron balconies. At the front of the building, a conquistador statue loomed over an overflowing fountain, his sword raised to the heavens, rivulets of water running down his face like melting gold.

Emi always hated it; he said you shouldn't play games with history like that. But it was the only fancy place in town that didn't ask for papers, so her mother got a job instantly.

Lucia shuffled through the hotel's revolving doors. The doors spat her out into a beautifully dry lobby, as her jeans dripped onto the polished tiles. Luxury had a scent Lucia had never quite gotten used to. Sometimes, she caught traces of it on the street—wafting from a bakery, lingering in a rich woman's handbag. Always the same: new leather, warm croissants, fresh flowers—the smell of a world just beyond reach.

"Can I help you?" came a man's voice.

She turned to see a doorman with a large top hat and a three-piece suit.

"I'm looking for my mother."

"She's a guest?" he said disapprovingly, as he surveyed her cuts and sopping wet clothes.

"No, she works here," Lucia replied.

"Oh. Of course," replied the doorman. "Yes, just wait in the lobby and I'll get her for you. What was her name?"

"Mrs. Hernandez."

"Oh, she works at reception," he said. "But I must remind you that unauthorized people are not permitted past the lobby."

"Sure," replied Lucia, looking over to see her mother behind the counter serving a guest.

"You can wait here."

He gestured for Lucia to take a seat on a red recliner that unfurled onto a Persian rug. Lucia sat down. Her mother was checking in a couple who had a furless cat in their carry-on bag. The lady was feeding the cat little bits of chicken breast from a small glass container. Her mother ignored the cat completely, even when the lady took out a bottle of baby milk. She was good at pretending things weren't there. Meanwhile, on the opposite recliner to Lucia, an overweight man was smoking a cigar. His eyes were hidden behind black aviators, even though he was inside. Lucia remembered seeing men like that at Daytona beach, they were always the ones who sat right behind the ladies in bikinis. It seemed the only rule of the place was that non-guests couldn't go past the lobby, everything else was allowed.

After the couple her mother had been serving left for the elevator, Lucia rushed up to the counter.

"Lucia? What are you doing here?" her mother said, adjusting the collar of her uniform, masking her shock with forced politeness. "What happened to your face?"

Lucia forgot that she was still bleeding from the fall as she rubbed her cheek with her sleeves.

"I need to tell you something."

"Can't we talk about this at home?" her mother whispered, glancing around while the other receptionist checked in the man wearing black aviators.

"It's about Emi," Lucia said. "I found something."

"No," her mother whispered, shaking her head. "I can't talk about this now."

"I found his name in a bloodied book—it's at the Basilica. *Romeo and Juliet*," Lucia said, her voice rising with urgency as the other receptionist shot a glance at them.

"Lucia, please," her mother murmured, her brows lifting in a silent plea for quiet.

"It all has something to do with the card in his pocket. I found another one at the motel. A lady drowned in the pool, just like the myth of La Llorona," Lucia said, her words tumbling out in a single breath.

"You need to stop making up stories," her mother said, eyes darting around the marble counter.

Something cracked inside Lucia. The accusation—that she was fabricating this—set off a festering rage within her. For the first time, she could not stay silent to her mother's apathy.

"All you care about is what people think," Lucia shot back, loud enough that the man in aviators turned his head. "You don't care about him at all."

Her mother leaned forward across the counter, her voice dropping to the same whisper she used with difficult guests. "Your brother was a dopehead, and I will not let my daughter become one too."

Water dripped from Lucia's jeans, pooling at her feet. "He was a good person," she said.

"Is that why the police locked him up?" Her mother's hands were trembling as she compulsively straightened a stack of key cards.

"How do you know about that?" Lucia said, remembering Emi's staticky call from the cell.

"The sheriff told me." Her mother wouldn't meet her eyes, focusing instead on wiping an invisible mark from the counter; the mindless cleaning seemed to be the only thing holding her together.

"Well, did the sheriff also tell you that all Emi did was sleep on private property?"

Her mother's composure finally broke. She gripped the edge of the counter, knuckles white against the marble. "No. He was having a psychosis, running around screaming that there were evil spirits in the hotel. He nearly knocked over a pregnant lady—it took three officers to hold him down." She looked up at Lucia, and for the first time, Lucia saw real fear in her eyes. "You don't understand. He was unwell. He was seeing things that didn't exist. And I won't—" her voice caught, "I won't have my daughter doing the same thing."

For a moment, Lucia felt the ground shift beneath her feet. Was she seeing things that weren't there? The bloody book, the death cards, the priest's tears—they seemed to waver like a mirage in her mind. But no. She'd touched them, held them. Her mother was doing what she always did: burying the truth under convenient lies. The certainty hardened in her chest.

"I'm not going to Stanford," Lucia's voice shook. "Everyone's happy to lie about what happened to Emi, but I won't."

Her mother didn't blink, her eyes glowed like hot embers in their sockets, searing the air with a silent rage. She stared at Lucia for what felt like minutes.

Then, the tension snapped as a man in a cowboy hat stepped out from the manager's office behind the counter. He strolled over to her mother, placing his hand on her shoulder. Lucia watched her mother straighten, all trace of their fight vanishing beneath her perfect receptionist smile, just like she did whenever somebody asked about Emi.

"What's going on here?" he said, his squinty farmer eyes gliding over Lucia's body like she was a glaring cornfield.

"Nothing," said her mother quickly.

"Are you a guest with us, darling?" the man asked, though his disdain made it clear he already knew the answer.

"No, she's not," said her mother, stepping back from the marble counter. In that single movement, Lucia felt eighteen years of shared microwave meals in motels reduced to cold nothingness—just to appease a stranger.

"Well, as the manager, I'm obliged to ask—how can I help?"

"It's okay, she's leaving," said her mother.

"And who is she?" he said, staring at Lucia.

"I don't know, she just walked in from the streets," said her mother, turning her back to Lucia. The perfect mask of her mother's politeness didn't crack—it never had. She had spent her life burying shame beneath practiced smiles, pretending her family wasn't broken, even if that meant breaking her children to keep the illusion alive.

"Well, you better walk on, we have some very important people about to arrive," the manager said to Lucia.

The grand lobby had never felt so empty. She rushed to the exit, rage spewing like molten lava until grief cooled it into icy volcanic glass. As she pushed through the revolving doors, the low hum of an approaching engine cut her swirling thoughts.

A sleek black limousine glided to a stop at the entrance, its polished bonnet reflecting the hotel's lights. The back door opened and out stepped the millionaire property mogul from the wedding at the Basilica—this time, alone. He caught Lucia's eye and smiled—that same practiced politeness her mother had perfected.

"I didn't know you gave such a warm welcome," he said, winking at Lucia. His eyes lingered on the cut. "Things get rough?"

The doorman walked over to him and whispered something in his ear. Suddenly, the man frowned.

"Oh. Wrong person," he said, before hastily walking away. The millionaire disappeared into the revolving doors, swallowed by the hotel's gleaming facade.

Lucia was all alone.

❧

Lucia arrived back at the motel room and sat by herself on the carpet. She felt like a seal stranded on a sheet of ice that was slowly melting. In nature documentaries, there was always a happy ending, the comfort of a silky-smooth narrator guiding the seal to safety. Emi used to tell her those documentaries were as fake as fiction—they spliced in shots of captive animals to get the storyline they wanted. Reality was lonelier than that. No reassuring voice to guide her. Every single person in her life had left her. But she couldn't give up on Emi, on Maya and her children. Something had happened to them that only she could see, and she had to keep looking, even if it pushed her further out to sea.

What if her mother was right about Emi? What if she was following the same path into madness? But it didn't make sense. None of the people she'd talked to had mentioned anything about him seeing things, or him losing his grip on reality.

Maybe the answers were there in the old tapes she'd taken.

She pulled out the recordings of the people he'd lived with on the streets. She'd listened to them so many times before, when all she wanted was to understand who gave him the card. The search hadn't been fruitful: most people just talked about how smart he was or how kind he had been. But now, knowing about Maya and the church, the recordings might hold clues she'd missed.

She pressed play while she sat cross-legged on the carpet, waiting.

"I used to crash with him. Emi never stayed put long—you know the type? Like, one week he scored this prime spot beachside, hidden in the palmetto bushes near the bay. Most of us would kill for a hideout like that, but he just hands it to me one day. Says he's got places to be, just like that."

Lucia fast-forwarded, scrubbing through static, voices dissolving into white noise. The rhythm of the city bled through—the wail of sirens, the shuffle of footsteps, laughter clipped short. Hours blurred together, voices overlapping, one memory slipping into the next. She sifted through them all, listening for something—anything—that hadn't mattered before but does now.

"That was your brother? Damn, sorry. Yeah, he had his demons like the rest of us. But that boy was sharp—sharpest I've seen out here. Once, he talked his way into some restaurant, convinced them their dumpsters were attracting rats. Walked out with three days' worth of paella. Fed half the people under the Bridge of Lions that night."

She pressed play on the next recording, waiting for anything useful.

"I'd always give him a bite of my burger for a story. Kid loved history, y'know? Always ramblin' 'bout them tunnels under the city. Swore they been there since the Spanish, runnin' under all of us. Said if you knew where to look, you could get damn near anywhere. Helluva a place to hide things."

Lucia pressed pause, the icy memory of the Basilica tunnels snaking up her spine. She hit play, as the man kept rambling.

"Told me 'bout some big-ass fire, way back. Burned the whole damn place to the ground. So they built the city outta seashells so it wouldn't go up in smoke again. If you look close, you can see the beach in all them old walls. Kinda poetic, ain't it?"

Emi always told her that. It's why she collected the shells—they were the most indestructible material she knew, the best way to remember him by. She pressed play again, sifting through the rest of the tapes to see if there was any more mention of the tunnels.

"Man, that kid was different. Always posted up under the streetlights on St. George, nose in a book. Half the time, high as hell. Then, outta nowhere, he'd snap to, dead serious, and hit you with, 'Thus with a kiss I die.' Like he was some big-shot actor. Said it was from some fancy play he was reading at..." His voice drifted, then came back sharp. "Ain't never seen nobody eat up words like that."

Lucia froze. She replayed the tape.

"Thus with a kiss, I die."

It was Shakespeare.

Lucia had interviewed so many people in the year after her

brother's death that she couldn't match the voice to a face. All she knew was that he was homeless. His accent was strange, he had a lisp that teetered on spitting, making him sound British. She rewound to where he mentioned St. George Street. Then she realized. The pageant queen manifested by the old monument there. She would have known every other hustler and homeless from that part of town. If Lucia played her the recording, maybe that distinctive lisp would stir a memory.

She slipped outside to cross the road, as rain spilled from the bathtub in the clouds. It washed Lucia's cuts, masking the blobs of blood in her jeans. She used her sweater as an improvised umbrella as she ran toward the strip mall. The pageant queen was underneath a bright pink umbrella, the umbrella's diameter formed a perfect circle of dryness around her wheelchair. She didn't even notice the rain as she thumbed the magazine with her spare hand. Lucia bolted across the road without checking for cars.

"Darling, you look like a drowned rat. What happened to you?"

"You were right about everything," Lucia blurted out, realizing that she was the only person in the world who might believe her.

"Well, of course I am. Take this—you're going to wash away." She unsheathed a matching pink umbrella from a concealed compartment in her wheelchair.

"There are great sales in the summer," she said like an esteemed catalogue peruser not a trash forager. Lucia unfurled the umbrella as the two of them spoke under the cover of the bright pink canopies in the middle of the storm.

"The priest is hiding something in the Basilica. He has all of Maya's things locked up," Lucia said in one breath. The pageant queen looked out at the clouds.

"There's something about the weather in this godforsaken state. Whenever it's sunny, everyone's all sunshine and roses. But the second we get a storm, everything changes. Some nice-looking women asked me if I sold crack. Can you believe it? It starts raining and some strait-laced doll thinks she should try crack."

"I need your help," Lucia cut her off, with the tape recorder wrapped under her shirt to keep it dry.

"What you got under there? Don't tell me you're also looking for crack?"

Lucia pulled out the tape recorder.

"Do you know who this is?"

She pressed play, his lisp was barely audible over the pattering of rain. The pageant queen moved her head a few inches away from the recorder.

Half the time, high as hell. Then, outta nowhere, he'd snap to, dead serious, and hit you with, 'Thus with a kiss I die.'

The pageant queen laughed.

"I know that lisp a mile away. That's Pawn Store Mike."

"Where is he?" asked Lucia, as a puddle slowly formed a few inches away from her feet. The rain was getting heavier.

"He used to set up shop in St. George Street. But he kept getting robbed. He's a trader, sells parts to others who live on the streets. You give him a twinkie and he can get you a blow dryer. He's that type of guy. But be careful, he's a real hustler, will bleed you bone dry if you don't have your wits about you."

"I need to find him. Have you seen him recently?"

"You could try the underpass at Interstate 95. I heard he moved there for a while."

"Thanks," said Lucia, preparing to run through the rain.

"Hey—be careful, it's dangerous over there."

THE UNDERPASS

Lucia stopped at the edge of the underpass, hesitating before stepping forward. The pillars closest to the street were covered in the usual graffiti—cartoonish tags, neon-colored swirls—but where the highway's shadow swallowed the concrete, the paint abruptly stopped. As if even the vandals hadn't dared to go further. The deeper recesses of the underpass looked like a hollowed-out cave, cut off by a sagging wire fence that stretched between the support columns.

A crude symbol had been spray-painted just before the darkness—a jagged, black eye. Its lines dripped like ink bleeding down the wall, a warning rather than art.

Lucia's pulse quickened. This was the kind of place people disappeared.

A wire-cut hole had been ripped into the mesh fence like some warped urban take on *Alice in Wonderland.*

Lucia stepped through, her jeans caught on an exposed steel wire, snagging a thread of denim. She let it tear.

She moved into the darkness, each step drawing her deeper into the concrete cave. The shadows shifted between the skeletal remains of burned-out shopping carts and piles of sodden blankets. The air was thick with the stale tang of gasoline, urine, and something rotting. She covered her mouth with her sleeve, trying not to gag.

She thought of Emi sleeping in a place like this, but before she could feel pity, a cough cut through the air. Low, wet—human. Someone was here. The person who had sliced open the fence. She dropped into a crouch, scanning the shadows. At the far end, where the light barely reached, a bundle of blankets stirred against the abutment. Lucia exhaled slowly, steadying herself. A sleeping bag shifted, wriggling like a worm trapped inside.

She approached cautiously, her steps light, her pulse heavy. She couldn't remember Mike's face; she needed to hear him speak.

A sudden jolt.

The sleeping bag jerked upright, and a man sat up, brandishing a long bread knife, its serrated edge glinting in the low light.

"What do you want?" the voice growled.

Lucia stopped. Other bodies stirred sluggishly, the sound of shifting fabric.

"I'm a friend," Lucia pleaded.

The knife didn't lower. "We don't have any friends."

Lucia swallowed, forcing herself to hold her ground. His face was nearly lost in his beard, the gray follicles dangling like icicles in a sea cave.

"I'm looking for Pawn Store Mike?" Lucia said, remembering the strange name the pageant queen had told her.

Slowly, he lowered the bread knife.

"So—you know Darlene." Behind him, bodies sluggishly shifted inside their sleeping bags.

Lucia looked confused. "The lady in the wheelchair?"

"She has a lot of names."

Slowly, the others sat up in their sleeping bags. They were all men, although their grime-encrusted skin made it impossible to tell their ages.

"That's Mike," said the man with the knife, pointing to a lump in a sleeping bag. Mike had a garbage bag wrapped around his head to block the light while he slept. "Only Darlene calls him that. I'm Butcher."

"I'm Taylor," said a boy next to him, his voice thin but oddly polite. Unlike the others, his face was still soft—hunger hadn't carved it hollow. Couldn't have been much older than Emi was.

"Don't get so cozy boy, she'll swindle us for all we got," said another.

The others exchanged suspicious glances.

One of the men snapped open a blade, his hand twitching.

"She's a decoy," he said, his eyes darting wildly. "They're using her to bait us."

Lucia froze. For the first time, she wondered if she'd just walked herself into a trap.

"Calm down. She's just a girl," Butcher said. The other man jitterily scratched his wrists, as he closed his eyes, as if it were too noisy for him.

Mike stirred in his sleeping bag, then tossed the garbage bag eye mask from his face as he pushed himself upright and yawned. Now she remembered him. Long blonde hair past his shoulders, matted, curling into unruly locks at its tips.

"So what do you want to trade?" asked Mike with his familiar lisp. He stood up.

"Wait, I've met you before," he said, slowly curling a strand of his hair. "You're the sister of that kid who washed up dead."

Lucia nodded silently, taking the tape recorder out of her pocket.

"That's me," she said.

"I remember that tape recorder too. Could fetch a pretty penny if you traded it," he said, his eyes narrowing in on it.

"Man, that's a week's worth of burgers," one of the men muttered, eyeing it greedily as he shifted in his sleeping bag. Lucia quickly put the recorder back in her pocket. She could feel their eyes all over her body.

"I don't want any trouble," she said. "I just want to ask some questions."

"You're Emi's sister?" asked Taylor, as he sat up from his sleeping bag.

"Shut up Taylor," said Mike. "Stop getting so friendly."

"You knew him?" asked Lucia, desperately. Mike stepped in between her and the boy.

"Questions will cost you," Mike said. "We never make a free trade." He stood staring at her, his bare feet blackened by soot. The rainfall grew heavier behind Lucia.

"But I don't have anything to trade," Lucia replied.

"You always got something to trade," said the man with the bread knife, its serrated edge twinkling below his chin.

Mike looked at Lucia up and down.

"Maybe we'll start talking if you give us the tape recorder."

"I can't. It has evidence on here," said Lucia, gripping it even tighter in her pockets.

Mike scoffed, shifting his weight. "You got something else then?"

"But we could help her," said Taylor.

"Shut up boy. We're not in a position to be giving freebies."

Lucia reached for the recorder in her pocket and pressed play. The sound of Mike's lisp filled the air.

"Half the time, high as hell. Then, outta nowhere, he'd snap to, dead serious, and hit you with, 'Thus with a kiss I die.'"

"Do you recognize this?" Lucia said. "Why was he quoting *Romeo and Juliet*?"

Mike squinted at her, then snorted. "What the hell even is that? The boy was crazy."

"I know why," Taylor muttered.

Mike's head snapped toward him. "I told you to stay quiet."

Before Taylor could react, Mike's barefoot caught him in the ribs. He folded over with a sharp gasp, clutching his side, his breath coming in short, pained bursts.

No one moved to help him. One of the men circled behind her. Fear coiled tight in her chest, but she forced herself to hold steady. She took a step forward. "Leave him alone." Her grip tightened around the recorder. "You can have it. Just promise me you'll leave him alone. I just want to speak with him."

He just stood there, rolling the thought around like a coin between his teeth. Lucia's grip on the recorder tightened. The man behind her hadn't moved away.

"Fine. That's a deal," Mike replied. Lucia hesitated, then tossed the tape recorder. He snatched it out of the air with wide-stretched hands, shoving it deep into his pockets.

"Are you okay?" Lucia said to Taylor who was still wincing on his side.

"Yes," he said between big breaths. "I need to show you something." Taylor jumped up from his sleeping bag, his left hand still nursing his ribcage. He led Lucia to the back of their camp, where a rusted shopping cart sat wedged against a concrete slab. It was a makeshift pawn shop of salvaged junk: tangled cables, old remote controls with missing buttons, dented radios, and scraps of metal overflowing from the cart. There was even an old tube TV teetering on top, the kind Lucia remembered from school when substitutes rolled it in on rainy days.

Taylor dug through the cart, shifting layers of electronics, sending loose screws and batteries clattering to the concrete.

"Hey! Quit handing out the goods and just answer her damn questions," Mike snapped.

"I'm just showing her something."

Taylor's entire arm vanished into the cart, the metal frame digging into his bruise. He winced but kept going, fishing for something buried deep. His fingers found it, and with a sharp yank, he pulled it free, sending the mound of junk shifting on its tectonic plates of plastic.

"Here it is." He handed the book to Lucia. The crimson cover, gold font, and icy-faced lovers.

Romeo and Juliet

It was the same edition as the one she had found in the Basilica. The hard-bound book turned to lead in her hands at the weight of the discovery. Emi and Maya were reading the same book.

"Your brother was quoting this," Taylor said. "This is my copy."

"How did you get it?" Lucia muttered in disbelief.

"I met your brother, only very briefly," he said. "The Basilica runs a soup kitchen for the homeless. That's where I first met him. He gave me his piece of bread because mine had been nibbled by a rat. He was real smart and all, talked a bunch of big words."

Lucia smiled. "He was too smart, made him think too much about everything."

"Yeah, I could tell he was real deep, not like most people—they just kept whining about the chunky carrots in the soup."

Lucia checked over her shoulder—the others were shadows in sleeping bags, cigarette tips glowing. She turned back to Taylor.

"Where'd you get the book?" she whispered so Mike didn't snatch it away.

"He took me to a church thing for reading. Said it'd help with spelling, writing, and making CVs. I needed a job, so I went. A teacher there helped fix up my CV real good—I got a job on the phones after that. Your brother liked it more than me. He was real into the reading, talking a lot with the teacher. They did Romeo and Juliet, but I didn't get much of it. I just needed to sound better on calls, so I stopped going."

Lucia paused to think.

"You said this was at the Basilica?"

"Yep."

"Was the teacher's name Maya?" asked Lucia.

"That's the one," Taylor said. "Saw her in the papers. Died a few months after Emi, real strange. Both of 'em so nice, y'know? Everyone thought they was happy. Then they both went and drowned themselves."

Lucia's heart fluttered. She thought of the card of death, the way their bodies both floated in the water. For the first time, it was as if the water had stopped rippling, and she could see their faces clearly.

"Did you ever hear anything else about it?" Lucia asked.

"Nah, sorry, I only went to a couple. Don't really like school much, and it just felt like another classroom—'cept I wasn't gettin' paid to be there."

"Was there anyone else there that you can remember?"

"There were lots. People always coming and going in these parts. Difficult to keep track of people out here. Now that I think about it, your brother was with a girl once. Real pretty thing. But I don't know what happened to them."

Lucia kept her voice hushed so Mike couldn't hear the desperation.

"What happened to the girl?"

"I dunno. Ain't nobody keep track of folks out here. Seen plenty just up and vanish, like they was never here. 'Specially the Mexican ones."

Lucia paused to think, she remembered the names of people she'd seen go missing.

"Do you remember the girl's name?"

"I think it was Marti. But tough to say. Lots of people passed through. Everyone got a free book if they went, most probably threw it away," Taylor said. "Here: you can have mine. Just don't tell him about it," Taylor whispered. He passed Lucia the book.

She flipped to the last pages to see if the same words were written in blood.

Some shall be pardon'd, and some punished:
For never was a story of more woe,
Than this of Juliet and her Romeo.

But there was no message this time. Just a small sticker, pressed neatly into the corner of the page.

Thanks for buying local!
Where the book finds you.
The Hidden Lantern.

It was the bookstore across from the Paradise Motel, the crab had mentioned it in his diary—where Maya must have begun this trail of breadcrumbs.

"Thanks Taylor."

She tucked the book under her arm and hurried back toward the motel, the streets were quieter than before, the air thick and restless. The letterboxes rattled with a kinetic angst. A gust of wind kicked up a newspaper, sending it tumbling across the sidewalk. It snagged against a lamppost, its front-page stark against the darkening sky.

STORM WARNING: HURRICANE WATCH ISSUED

Something was coming.

THE HIDDEN LANTERN

The next day, Lucia stood in front of the Hidden Lantern. The storm was still a day away but the wind howled like a wounded wolf as the streetlights blinked in and out of consciousness, preparing for the long night ahead. Lucia had walked past the Hidden Lantern before, but she never knew what it sold. It could have sold any antiquity: crockery sets, dolls, candles, typewriters or pickles in glass jars. There was even a porch in the front where the sloped roof met two stout wooden columns. Lucia imagined it to be from a time where people came into town on horses, letting them graze while they talked about books. There was a graveyard next to the Hidden Lantern that appeared to be the garden of the old property. It looked even more historic. The names blurred into the tombstones, fading each year like chalk on a blackboard. The dates etched into rock were more visible: 1770, 1780, 1780. The rest of the bookstore was surrounded by the woods that separated it from the Paradise Motel.

She approached the door more cautiously than the last time she had done so in the Basilica. She stepped inside, her foot landing on the rock-solid floorboards. The store felt infinitely bigger compared to what it looked like outside. The bookshelves lined the walls straight up to the ceiling with most out of Lucia's reach. Fairy lights illuminated the shelves, playing games with her sense of depth. There was no clear structure to how the books were organized, it appeared that the order was only known to a bookkeeper with a memory that must have been amassed over decades. Soon enough, Lucia spotted the bookkeepers. They were an old couple, diametrically opposed in appearance. Both looked in their seventies. The old man was dressed formally in a tweed suit jacket with double-stitched cotton trousers and gray-rimmed spectacles. His gaze was sharp, almost academic, but his smile held a quiet warmth. The old lady wore a blouse splashed with rainbow fractals, her bright red hair damp and slightly mussed, as if she'd just stepped out of the rain.

Another customer stood at the counter as Lucia eavesdropped on the conversation, pretending to peruse through the books.

"I am looking for something light-hearted and fun to read. Something like *The Curious Ape*," said the man.

"With all due respect, Sir, that is not how this bookstore works. At the Hidden Lantern, we believe that the book must find you," said the lady.

"Okay—well, can you help me then?" said the man skeptically.

"Of course. We've been matchmakers for fifty years," the old man said, his words polished from decades of repetition. There was a natural rhythm to their exchange, and it was clear the couple enjoyed the small theater of their trade, their eyes lighting up as they leaned into the familiar routine.

"But first you must tell us about yourself," continued the lady. The young man stood uncomfortably in front of the counter with his hands buried in his pockets.

"Fine then. I'm thirty-six years old and I am a lawyer for a construction company, the one that owns the Casa Monica Hotel."

The lady looked at her husband with a cheeky grin and then turned back to the insurance lawyer.

"I'm afraid I haven't the faintest idea about who you are. Professions tell us less about a person than the color of their hair. Although

I can recommend a Blockbuster down the road which has a fine selection of films." It made the thirty-six-year-old insurance lawyer only want the currently non-existent book even more.

"Look, I don't know what's going on in this little store of yours, but I promise you that I read books. I have been reading since I was twelve."

"Gee, that's a lot of books, isn't it darling?" said the old man with a cheeky grin.

"I suppose we have no new ones to sell," said the lady. The insurance lawyer exhaled sharply, his hands tugging at the cuffs of his sleeves. Lucia stopped looking. She pretended to reread the same blurb for the fifth time.

"Fine. You want to know more about my life so I can buy one of your precious little books? I'm an insurance lawyer. So every time someone dies building a new hotel or office, guess who's the first person that gets called? I'll give you a clue. It's not the kids who just lost their dad. It's not their wives who now have to worry about how they are going to pay all their bills. It's me. And you know what my job is? I have to go through every little detail to find one tiny instance of them breaking the rules. Maybe they took off their hard hat for a smoke. Or maybe they forgot to sign in to work that day. And then I get paid to find a way to void the family's insurance claim. That's my job. So yes, when I come to a bookstore I just want an easy read, not to be psychoanalyzed at the door."

"Thanks for sharing. That was brave of you," said the old lady in a sarcastic voice.

"Now we can help you," said the old man cheerfully.

"Exactly! Now that we know you, we're able to provide the book that you need."

The insurance lawyer exhaled like a broken AC machine spewing hot, bothered air. He towered over the old couple, who seemed unfazed by his anger, as they were safely nestled behind the maple countertop. There was no till on the counter, only a little silver bell. Lucia wondered how they made money, or why they needed a bell when the two of them were always there.

"Let me guess: I need some pseudoscience self-help shit."

"Don't think so lowly of us, Sir. We don't stock self-help books here," she said.

"And even if we did, that's not what you need," said the old man.

"Now my husband and I have been known to disagree, but I have a hunch that in your case the answer will be quite straightforward. We won't be a moment."

With that, the old couple left the counter in search of the lawyer's book. They split up, tracking the shelves with the intensity of a blow hunter scanning the canopies. The old lady approached Lucia and reached directly into the shelf in front of her.

"We'll be quick, my love. Your turn is next," she winked. Lucia gulped. While she was listening she had been trying to find anything written by Shakespeare. An old bound book, or anything from that period—but the bookshop was too much of a labyrinth. She was going to have to play their game.

The old couple returned to the counter, and both slammed down separate books. Each was the size of a small shoebox.

"Do you have something shorter?"

"But Sir, that seems to be the only thing my husband and I agree on. You need a book of this length."

"I don't have time to read something that long."

"Understood. As my wife said, for a shorter attention span there are many ninety-minute run times at the Blockbuster."

"Fine. I'll play along. What book did you think I need?" he said in a half-mocking tone, thinly veiling his growing curiosity

"Darling, would you like to go first?"

"Of course. You see, despite my appearance, I am a classicist. I come from a long line of frontier women. My great-great-grandfather was one of the first folk to arrive in Kentucky. He came with a rifle, a book of Whitman poems, and a hoard of children. Always believed that a man, and a woman for that matter, needed to be able to shoot a pistol from the hip and recite a poem from the heart. And so I have a soft spot for great American literature."

The insurance lawyer looked puzzled by the redhead in the colorful dress talking about the frontier. Sensing his confusion, she changed her tune.

"Don't worry sweetie, I'll get to the point. It's just important you understand my mission. In many ways I feel I'm no different to my great-great-grandmother. Both of us holding the fort in a strange state, doing our best to spread the power of words. In your case, I think you will need a lot of them. And a very strong strain." She edged forward the book on the counter.

"Steinbeck's best work. *East of Eden*. Now it is not my business to say why you need it. You will know the answer to that once you are finished." The old lady smiled proudly as the lawyer skeptically inspected the book.

"My wife's got an eye for things, I'll give her that. But I'm not from a frontier family. Been in cities since the day I was born. She says it makes me soft, curdles my taste in books. But I believe this is what you need." He edged his book forward so that it was in line with *East of Eden*.

"*Game of Thrones*. It came out a few years ago. Not very popular but an excellent fantasy read." The man inspected both of the books.

"It'll take me 100 years."

"We never said you had to buy them," smiled the old man. There was a long pause. It seemed to not bother the old couple whether they sold a single book.

"Fine. I'll take them both," said the man, pressured by the silence.

"We'll sell them to you only if you promise to come back once you've finished."

"Alright. But I can't promise that I'll finish. But if I do, I'll come back."

The man paid for the books and then he left the store. Lucia wondered whether it was an old trick of the trade to always recommend the opposite to her husband.

"Hello, sweetie. I suppose you know the drill. Care to tell us about yourself?" said the lady. Lucia stared at the floor, anxiously. The old man spoke again, his tone softer now—gentler, as though he were trying to put her at ease.

"Don't be nervous, sweetie. My wife and I get carried away with performances sometimes—we don't get many guests."

For a brief second, they seemed to break character, looking at each other with heavy faces.

"It can be lonely here all day with just each other. I guess we get overexcited with customers," said the lady, before snapping back into character. "So, tell us about yourself."

"I've lived in St. Augustine my whole life. Mom and I move from motel to motel. So I've always liked stories about castles and long family sagas where no one leaves for generations. I suppose after packing my suitcase so many times, I started romanticizing the idea of staying put."

"Interesting," the old lady mused. "You're the perfect breed to be a writer. I have the book for you."

Lucia shifted her weight, searching for a way to steer the conversation.

"But that was when I was little. Now I like stories about love. Sad ones. Happy endings are boring because I can always see them coming."

"And how old are you, darling?" said the woman. Her eyes crawled over Lucia's body like an inquisitive spider. Her gaze settled on Lucia's cuts and bruises.

"I'm eighteen."

"Okay, how wonderful to have a young reader in our store. There is still hope for the young ones," she said in an overly cheerful way to mask the pity. The old man tried to smile but couldn't. He also saw the cuts.

"Let's get you something then, darling."

"I like old stories, tales about love that are hundreds of years old. Ones that explore whether you should follow your heart."

"Noted," said the old man.

The couple slipped out of the counter, going into separate nooks of the store. After a few minutes, they both returned to counter with a book each.

"I think this will be an excellent choice for you." She pushed forward a thick paperback. *One Hundred Years of Solitude.*

"But darling it's such a long read."

"You were the one who recommended that book about being a cockroach to a fourteen-year-old," she quipped.

"But that boy needed to be saved. He was already talking about personal finances," the old man said.

"The girl is a born writer. I can sense it. She needs to see how stories can bend time, how rules can be rewritten. What's real and what's not."

The old man turned to face Lucia. "My taste can get me in trouble sometimes. But I think that this book will be more in line with what you want."

He pushed forward a thin paperback on the maple counter. The crimson cover, gold font, and icy-faced lovers made it clear—it was *Romeo and Juliet*. Lucia shuddered. The exact same edition had been in Maya's box. Without thinking, Lucia snatched it, frantically flicking to the last page.

For never was a story of more woe,

Than this of Juliet and her Romeo.

There were no more words after that. No blood-stained pages. Her heart raced as she thought of the book hidden in the vault of the Basilica, the words ringing out like church bells on the morning of a funeral.

Be careful with the secrets that you sow,

Speak of Emi, and you shall go.

Mr. Muerte.

"Is everything okay sweetie?" Lucia had completely forgotten about the bookkeepers as she frantically flipped through the pages searching for another mention of Mr. Muerte.

"It looks like she has not eaten words her entire life," said the lady.

"Poor girl. Starved of sonnets and soliloquies," said the man.

"Can I ask you a question?" asked Lucia.

"Why of course sweetie."

"Do many people buy this book?"

The couple looked at each other.

"A book doesn't need to be popular to be worth reading," said the lady.

"Oh, I never thought I'd see the day you say that," said her husband.

"Classics are different from blockbusters honey."

"I don't see the difference."

"Did Maya ever buy this book from your store?" said Lucia, cutting them off. They both gasped in shock as the old man wiped his spectacles to take a fresh look at Lucia.

"Young girl, if this is some cruel practical joke, then I must ask you to get out of the store right now." The old lady pulled the book off the counter. "You and your friends can run off now." Lucia looked at the old lady, dumbfounded.

"It's not a joke. I just wanted to know."

"Let me guess: you're the daughter of a cop and you and your friends want to make fun of the crazy old couple who see things."

"I don't have a dad," said Lucia. "And I don't have very many friends."

The old man's pupils pinned her against the wall. He studied her face.

"There's something about her that makes me think she is telling the truth," said the old man.

"Don't be deceived so easily, darling. You'll end up like *Don Quixote*, chasing illusions."

"How could you possibly know what books Maya did or didn't buy?" asked his wife.

"I moved into the same room as Maya at the Paradise Motel. I went to find her box of stuff at the church." The old couple looked even more disturbed. Lucia sensed they knew something but didn't trust her. "I found things in her copy of *Romeo and Juliet*," said Lucia. The couple's ears pricked up as they leaned forward.

"What things?"

"Someone had drawn three stick figures of Maya, Carl, and Jasmine. In blood."

"Do you have it with you?" muttered the old lady.

"No. It's in a vault at the church."

"Darling."

"Yes my love?" replied the old man.

"For once you are right. She is telling the truth." The old couple leaned over the counter, as if extending an invitation to be on their team. Who they were against, she did not know.

"So did she buy the book?" asked Lucia.

"Yes," said the old lady in a hushed voice. "It was us who recommended it to her."

"Why?"

"For that we must begin before the beginning," replied the old man.

"You see, darling, we know a lot more about this town than people might think," said the lady.

"Many think that it's the doctor who knows the most about a town. Some think it's the lawyer. But no one ever says it's the bookseller. We have the luxury of knowing exactly what people are reading at any given moment. We know who people let into their beds to sleep beside them. I'm talking about ideas, of course—the ones that fester in their brains in the early hours of the morning until the first sip of coffee breathes life into plans hatched in their dreams. It is for this reason that when we sell a book, in a way, it gives us the ability to read the future, to shape it."

"We know when teenagers will rebel before their parents do," interjected the old man. "I suppose sometimes we help it along."

"You certainly do. But you know what power we have over the town doctor? We know more about introverts. They don't speak about their problems to doctors and lawyers. But they read books, lots of them. And that's how we first met Maya. She came into our store, and we asked our usual question: 'Tell us about yourself.'

"All she told us was that she was an English teacher who had moved from Georgia that loved books but struggled to find the time to read fiction anymore. Other than that she said absolutely nothing about her private life. But over the course of many months, we got to know her very well from all the books she read. As with so many introverts, when they feel they aren't being judged, they often have far more to say than us extroverts—who have already run out of words. We got to know a side of that woman that no one in this town ever knew."

"Did you know both of them?" asked Lucia.

"I presume you are talking about Garcia?"

"Yes."

"We did. Unfortunately, we also got to see a side of Garcia that no one else did."

"But darling, you are getting sidetracked. First, you must tell her about Maya," said the old man.

"Yes, of course. We must start with Maya. There are many different types of readers, but broadly speaking, they fall into two categories: those who read to know and those who read to feel. The ones who read to know are carnivorous animals, devouring information and sucking the marrow from every bite. Naturally, they only buy non-fiction—hell, they even buy books on how to read books faster. For them, it's about quantity. They compile must-read lists, power through them, and wear their book tally like a badge of honor. They have page goals. Wish lists. Yet for all their attempts to know, their mindless pursuit of knowledge leaves them dumber than when they started.

"Now, you might think that I am about to compliment those who read to feel. But they are equally guilty. They may think they read widely but in reality it's always the same. Romance and drama. They are searching to feel something, anything. They'll read slop as long as it follows the same formula: a nice emotional resolution where everyone lives happily ever after. They'll be in the store the next day to find some other mindless thing to replace the hole in their hearts. I tell you all this so you can understand our method for assigning a reader a book. When Maya first came to us, I made the mistake of thinking she was the first type of reader. It was because she almost exclusively read books on parenting or books for her students at school."

"Of course we gave her a special price," said the old man.

"When she first came to us, we indulged her love of practical reading. We gave her the psychology books, the science ones too, but eventually I sensed my opening to push her deeper. I saw the way she talked about parenting books, critiquing authors for concepts far more abstract than the optimal bedtime. She read them like philosophy books. Arguing with the central premise of what it means to be a responsible citizen. At first, I used memoir as the gateway drug to fiction. I gave her the classics: Anne Frank, Maya Angelou, and even Marianne Williamson. Each time she returned she stayed in the store slightly longer than before. Now I must admit that my husband and I both come from fancy colleges where the study of books is bastardized by theoretical frameworks, but Maya's literary education finished in a one-story shed in Georgia. So every comment she had about books was free from snobbish interference, yet she could dismantle a literary movement with a single question. Soon she was reading the entire canon. The Romantics, the Russians, and of course the American greats."

"I snuck in some comic books too," said the old man with a grin.

"She fell in love with reading again. And she became the elusive third type of reader that every bookkeeper in the world tries to foster. Someone who reads to think. For the first few months, we never talked about anything other than books. I don't mean to be presumptuous, but I think this place was a sort of refuge for her. She never said anything disparaging about the people in the motel, but it was obvious that they were not her crowd.

"But when did you first meet Garcia?" interrupted Lucia.

"Up to that point, Maya had never mentioned Garcia. It wasn't until he walked into our store that we realized they were a couple. I'll never forget the day he first walked through our door. When we asked him to tell us about himself, he had no difficulty. No doubt he had done it many times before."

"My parents are from Cuba. My mother raised me to believe that the only thing more important than hard work is the value of family. I come from a household of brothers where to be heard you had to be good with words, so quickly I learned how to speak so people would listen. When I was a boy, I loved reading old books with great political speeches, I practiced them in the mirror to perfect my English. Sadly these days, I don't get much time to read fiction. But I have always wanted to read more, especially the Great American novels that our nation has produced."

"Now I'll admit, I did have a soft spot for him. He spoke like a politician, yes, but there was something about him that was undeniably sincere. You knew exactly what type of person he was when he spoke. He was not one of those lab-grown politicians from Boston who came out of the womb in a cardigan and spent their first birthday in a golf club. There was a flair to him that made me feel he was the only politician who could dance. Make no mistake: he was a hustler with a sizable chip on his shoulder, but he was warm. At first, we both liked him as much as anyone did around here. The two complemented each other. He would do most of the talking, she would do most of the listening. But whenever she spoke, he would listen as if she were saying the most important thing in the world. It was foreign to me—my husband hardly speaks."

"I slip a word in every now and then. But there's not much point when I'm married to such a wordsmith," joked the old man. The old lady didn't laugh; she stared into the abyss of books with a frown.

"Then everything started to change around the last few months of her life. Maya became fearful. It was as if she believed someone was following her, constantly checking over her shoulder. Of course, she would never say anything was wrong, but I couldn't help but feel like there was some dark cloud that hung over her. It was around the time we gave her *Romeo and Juliet*. She became obsessed with it. She spent hours discussing it with me, analyzing it from every angle, I feared telling her it was only a work of fiction. The question she couldn't shake was whether the moral choice was for *Romeo and Juliet* to live quiet lives of unhappiness to spare their families pain, or to follow their hearts, knowing it would destroy them.

"This single question consumed her. It seemed to be all she could think about, but I was certain that her problems extended to something greater than a literary discussion. If there is one thing I am certain about that woman, it is that her children were the most important thing in the world. She was as devout as any nun I'd ever known, and whatever was weighing on her mind had to be tied to her kids.

"Around the same time, Garcia started to visit our store alone. The bubbly man we had first met was gone, replaced by a weary pilgrim. You could see it in his clothes. He stopped doing up his top button. But it was not only his appearance, his requests for books were equally strange. He had the same voracity for reading as Maya. Garcia asked us to order anything that we could find about the tunnel system underneath St. Augustine. Apparently, the Spanish had built a maze of underground tunnels connecting many of the early buildings, so they could flee from their forts and churches in case of invasion."

"Like the tunnels of the Basilica?" Lucia interjected, her mind flashing to the cold draft of the mossy cobblestone, where her blood had seeped into the cracks after her fall. It was the same obsession that Emi had with the tunnels of St. Augustine, the book in his suitcase that he left behind when he died.

"Yes, precisely. There is a tunnel network in St. Augustine that connects the Basilica and a few other places together. He was very interested in that. It was difficult to track down the books, so we ordered them from the Florida Historical Society; many were first editions that fetched such a price tag we had to request payment in advance. Price didn't seem to worry Garcia. He would spend thousands, not even flinching when we told him prices that would cause the average Joe to squirm in their boots. At first, we dismissed his keen architectural interest as something related to city planning. We gave him the benefit of the doubt and assumed that there was some new infrastructure project that he was researching. But then his research took a darker turn. He asked if we had access to newspaper archives, any bookkeeper worth their salt should be able to source newspapers. So we did. Admittedly, our professional pride caused us to see the whole thing as a challenge of our ability, and we overlooked such suspicious behavior. How could we have known? He gave us a long list of dates, each was very specific, spread over a period of nearly twenty years. Being naturally curious, we started to comb through the papers to see if we could glean the reason for his request. Perhaps there were some major government announcements about new property developments. But there were none. The only commonality of all the papers was tragedy. It was a combination of missing people, tragic deaths, and gang violence. In one of the papers, the front cover was of a young boy who washed up on the shore."

"His name was Emi Hernandez."

Lucia experienced a sudden vertigo, as if her heart were free-falling inside of her stomach. Mayor Garcia knew her brother. The old lady's voice faded into the background as Lucia's thoughts spun wildly, the realization ricocheting through her mind. She was getting closer to the truth.

"Darling?"

"Darling?"

"Are you okay?" said the old lady.

"Sorry, please go on," Lucia said quickly, her voice steadying despite the rush of anticipation. She was close now—she could feel it.

"Now I am not a forensic psychologist, but it is my professional opinion as a bookkeeper that he had developed a strange obsession with death. It's hardly a hunch, but a statement of fact. His third line of inquiry shifted to that exact topic. He asked for anything we could find on the philosophy of death, especially Mexican, and religious iconography. This was more difficult to source. We had to pull favors with friends to be able to locate anything of use. We contacted professors from far-flung universities with department names that were even vaguely tangential. The only one we had any luck with was UT Austin's Center for Mesoamerican Philosophy and Thought. When we told him that the book would take two weeks to arrive, he snapped. Garcia stood in our store, yelling at us, berating our professional ability. The rage was so sudden that we were completely flabbergasted. The smooth-talking politician that we had seen on the TV became a deluded crackpot hurling obscenities that belonged only on a sailor's tongue. That was when we first learned of his darker side."

The old lady paused.

"Did you ever see a symbol that looked like the saint of death in that book?" asked Lucia.

The old lady dropped her head.

"I saw it."

"Where?"

"The tunnels," she said. "Under the city."

"What happened?" asked Lucia.

She cleared her throat.

LA SANTA MUERTE

I will never forget this memory for as long as I live.

It happened one week before Maya died. Garcia made another one of his solo visits to the store, dressed in his wrinkled blazer, but this time he had a bouquet of roses. I remember the smell of those dew-kissed petals, the stalks freshly cut. After a marriage of nearly fifty years, roses become a distant memory of the early chapters of courtship. They play games on an old girl's heart as you remember how you felt falling in love for the first time. And so I was too enchanted to remember one important detail when he walked into the store.

"Those are such beautiful flowers," I said.

"Yes, I bought them for Maya."

But as soon as the words left his mouth, the smell of fresh petals turned rotten, and I couldn't hide my frown. The emotion must've come before the realization because I didn't know why for the life of me I was scowling at such lovely flowers. My husband interjected to diffuse the tension.

"She's a lucky woman. You're making me feel bad, it's been a long time since I did that for my wife."

He placed his hand on my shoulder, offering a convenient rationale for my frown. But he was wrong. I didn't care for roses—they are a cheap trick for when love is easily bought. So often flowers are used to bandage a wound that words inflicted. After enough disagreements, you learn that without change, flowers mean nothing. And my husband had compromised for fifty years, he didn't need to buy a bouquet to make me love him.

"We had a fight today," said Garcia.

"It happens," said my husband.

Then it hit me. They didn't have a fight, and those flowers weren't for Maya. Maya was with the children in Orlando taking them to Disney Land. She'd spoken about it to us for weeks and it was hard not to notice when she hadn't been to the bookstore for more than two days. So I let him lie.

"How sweet," I said, waiting for my opportunity to figure out the true recipient of the flowers. Then Garcia pestered us about the status of the *Mexican Symbols of Death* book. We told him it still hadn't arrived, and he left the store in a huff. Now this is the point in the story where I did something that I have since come to regret. I regret it not because of a moral transgression but because it burdened me with a truth that I wish I could rid myself of. That is the cost of curiosity I suppose. My strain borders on obsession, it's the reason I finish books in a single night. I simply need to know what happens next. And I felt stirred by this righteous anger on Maya's behalf, if she had been betrayed, if she had suffered for someone else's lies, I had to know.

So, I decided to follow him. Thankfully, it was nighttime, darkness provided a cloak of invisibility. Still, I kept a few hundred yards between us, wrapping a scarf around my red hair—it's not exactly the most covert color in the rainbow.

We walked for thirty minutes, straight past the Paradise Motel, past the Basilica, and toward the outskirts of the city. A few times, he looked over his shoulder, but from that distance I was no more than a blurry Babushka on her nightly stroll. He was paranoid enough that he avoided any major roads and clung to the shadows of the sidewalk. He knew what he was doing. The further we got from the center of the city, the more confused I became. All the nice restaurants are near the Historic District or Vilano Beach. I couldn't figure out what other woman would get a bouquet of roses so far from the city. The mystery intensified as he took a turn down a dark gravel road. I couldn't believe it. I had been expecting him to arrive at some other lady's house—yet there he was, sneaking into the woods. My skin chilled as the streetlight faded away, replaced only by the dim glow of the moon. Garcia pulled out a flashlight, so I stayed off the road in case he shone it behind him. I kept following.

Soon we arrived at the Nombre de Dios Cemetery. I recognized the cemetery from the marble entrance, even though moss covered the lettering. Garcia's flashlight flickered across the graves, as though he feared what lay beneath. He had broken into such a brisk walk that I could hardly keep up with my cramped calves. I followed his beam of light as he went deeper into the cemetery. It felt wrong to be there at night, like an intrusion. I tried not to trip over the tombstones as I trailed behind him, the cold touch of moss spreading to all the surfaces of my body. It felt like caterpillars were crawling over my pores, and maybe they were, I could barely see.

Then he stopped in front of a grave. It was a small tombstone, unlike many of the larger ones. He stood in front of the grave and placed the flowers at its feet. I watched, hidden behind a tombstone. Garcia stood still for a few minutes, then hastily pressed forward. I waited for a few minutes before I trailed to see the flowers he had placed at the grave. It was difficult to see in the dark, but I traced my fingers on the shallow engraving.

Emi Hernandez.

It was the same name from the one I saw in the paper. The one Garcia had requested about the boy who washed up on the shore. I never remembered him having any other children outside of his marriage or anything like that. I didn't know for the life of me why he was paying respect to the dead. Then I thought of all those strange books he was reading, the ones about death, the symbols.

Just as I thought he was going to turn around and leave, he pressed on. He made his way to the woods that backed onto the cemetery. The deeper he went, the denser the trees became, and the fewer the graves appeared. The beam of light was so far ahead that he must've been in the woods. The woods near the Nombre de Dios Cemetery are overrun by Spanish moss, it's like walking through a maze of cotton curtains. Garcia led me deeper into the woods. Then he stopped. I jumped behind an oak tree. A few seconds later his beam of light cut past me as it scanned the trees next to me. He would've spotted me had I not been hiding by the oak. I closed my eyes and took a deep breath. There I was all alone with him in the woods, no one to hear my screams. I waited for the light to go away and then poked my head out. Garcia was shining his light on a tall tree about fifty yards in front of me. Then the light disappeared. The woods went completely dark. My heart popped out of my chest, it was beating so hard. There was complete silence, not even the sound of ruffling leaves or crackling twigs. At that moment, I was convinced that Garcia had evaporated into thin air. I would've heard something if he had moved. I thought he was waiting for me. So I stood motionless for nearly twenty minutes, without as much as raising a finger. My gamble paid off. Around twenty minutes later, the flashlight flickered back to life. He was still there, and now the flashlight was aimed at my tree. I carefully rotated behind the trunk, using its shadow to stay out of sight. He was getting closer. Twenty yards. Then ten. Now he was so close to me that I could smell his cheap hair gel. Yet somehow he didn't see me. He motored right past me, guided by the beam of light as if he was under some strange spell. I waited for him to disappear back to the cemetery. I should have left but I simply needed to see what he had been doing. So I made my way over to where he had been standing.

When I arrived at the tree, I noticed a dim glow of light coming from the ground. It was as if there were fireflies in the perfect configuration of a circle.

I looked closer.

It was a hatch covered by leaves and sticks. I opened up the manhole and descended down an iron-rung ladder. It had the smell of a ship's hull, the rusty iron dripping droplets of a week-old rain. When I got to the bottom, I realized I was in an old tunnel. There were torches mounted to the walls that must've been recently lit. The flames flickered, guiding me under the low-hanging ceiling as I made my way to the end of the tunnel. Toward the end, the space widened into a cavernous room. A few gnarled tree roots dangled from the ceiling, winding through cracks in the rock as if searching for something below. They pointed toward the end of the room.

That was where I first saw it.

A lady.

A skeleton statue stood on an elevated stone platform. Her hollow eye sockets watched me, as her rusted scythe rested in her bony grip. A tattered veil draped over her skull, shrouding it like a mournful bride. Surrounding it were candles flickering in uneven rows, their wax pooling like blood. Above it all, in jagged red letters smeared across the wall, it read:

LA SANTA MUERTE

The saint of death.

I'd never seen anything like it before. Someone had built an entire shrine for her in the abandoned Spanish tunnel. I wanted to scream. I couldn't shake the feeling that this was just the beginning of something far worse. Then I saw that there were offerings placed at the saint's feet. There were dozens of candles, wilted flowers, and even gold coins.

I imagined Garcia kneeling before it, uttering prayers to the skeleton saint. Instantly, I felt a strong sense of guilt, as if I were an accomplice in some scheme I didn't fully understand. We had sourced all the books about the tunnels in the city for Garcia, and it was our words that must've led him to the shrine. It was us who had radicalized him on the ideas of death as he spent his evenings sneaking into such evil places.

The saint knew it too. She looked down on me from her elevated platform with such piteous eyes. The old lady stupid enough to find her way into such a dark place. Even looking at her, I felt a strange compulsion to give her something. I am not a superstitious lady, but there was an energy in that room that seemed to demand it. I picked up a coin from the floor, my hands went numb, and the coin slipped out of my fingers as it ricocheted off the cobblestone. It echoed so loudly I thought it would turn the statue to life.

I sprinted for the exit, not stopping until I was home. I spent that entire night awake, staring at the ceiling as if I couldn't escape that tunnel. All I wanted was to warn Maya. Something was wrong with Garcia. Deeply wrong. I waited for her at the bookstore, ready to tell her about what I saw in the woods. But Maya never came. And then, a week later, Maya and the children were dead.

My husband and I were besieged by guilt. We couldn't have known it would end like this. His obsession with tunnels, death, and symbols—the shrine. I mean, I thought he was crazy, but evil? That was something I couldn't have foreseen.

After Maya and the children died, we called the police straight away. Only in hindsight do all the signs align, mocking us for not seeing them before. Maybe we could've stopped the whole thing if we had said something earlier. They sent some new kid from Memphis, like it was his rite of passage to deal with the crazies. We told them about his borrowing history, all the random newspapers, the Spanish symbols, and the shrine in the woods. Clearly, the kid hadn't picked up a book since high school, and words held no weight in his jaded worldview. He asked us if we had any actual evidence that put Garcia in the place of the crime, or if we could pinpoint the location of the shrine. I told him it was too dark to remember exactly where it was, but it was somewhere near the cemetery. He laughed. He told me I reminded him of his old English teacher. He said he'd have a look, but we never heard anything back from him. No one believed us."

Lucia stared in horror—Garcia had gone from her brother's tombstone to the shrine of death.

NOMBRE DE DIOS CEMETERY

The supermarket shelves were ransacked of cans as locals hoarded everything they could. Trees were preemptively cut near powerlines and the sandbags started to pile up in people's porches. Electricity crackled in the air before a big storm tore through the city, a jitteriness that zapped at the end of people's fingertips. The Paradise Motel was making its own preparations. Management had requested that each guest put a lounger in their room to prevent it from flying away. People begrudgingly dragged them inside, as the crab crawled out to inspect the pool. He stood with his hand on his lips, a smile on his face, as if the prospect of the storm excited him while he bunkered down in his submarine hatch.

Lucia snuck past him as she returned to her room after her visit to the Hidden Lantern. She hadn't seen him for so long, but she'd felt his presence the entire time: the mechanical blinking of the security camera.

"Hey! You need to take a lounger to your room," he yelled at Lucia.

She froze. For a second, it felt like she had finally been caught after weeks of snooping. His cursor eyes tracking her every move. But then she remembered, he couldn't have known anything, she'd stolen his diary in secret.

"Sure," Lucia said, as she took a lounger. The receptionist continued staring at her with eerie eyes, and Lucia felt something deep inside him. It was as if she could hear his stream of consciousness, his restless thoughts spilling from the diary pages into her mind.

Lucifer will arrive, darkness will be all around us.

She didn't trust him. Yet he seemed too weak to be capable of evil. He was a creature of habit, returning to his quarters like a house cat—his feline lurking through the night, an opportunist at best.

"What are you looking at?"

Still, there was a darkness to his soul, she could feel it.

"Nothing," Lucia replied as she hauled the lounger to her room. He stared at her before he scuttled back to his bunker. He was hiding things about Maya. She was sure of it.

Lucia heaved the lounger up the stairs, feeling the same animosity for concrete that the pageant queen must've felt when she crawled up to Maya's room. She looked out at the clouds as they sagged on the horizon, waiting to unleash their pent-up wrath. The storm was getting closer.

Her mother was still at work; Lucia hadn't seen her for days, not since everything fell apart. Their relationship had reached rock bottom since she told her she wasn't going to Stanford, and now Lucia was just another thing to pretend didn't exist, another failed child that her mother had to hide in conversation.

"You need to move out, to pay your own way," her mother had said.

She was getting kicked out, just like Emi.

Lucia remembered the day her mother told him he had to leave. She had folded the corners of his bed tight, ironed every shirt, and packed them into a neat little suitcase that she placed at the door.

"What's this?" Emi had asked.

"I ironed your clothes."

"But what for?"

"For your next place," her mother had said, pretending he was off to college, knowing full well there was nowhere else for him to go. She was sending him to the streets with pressed collars and Sunday school pants, as if dignity would save him. She was probably petrified of a churchgoer seeing him in a crumpled shirt; even if he had slept in the underpass, God could turn a blind eye to that.

Lucia opened the door, placing the lounger in front of the window. She saw her book open on the sofa, its pages teleporting her to the Hidden Lantern. She felt a chill as she thought of the bookkeeper's story about Garcia and her brother. The shrine of death in the woods.

She needed to visit the Nombre de Dios Cemetery—she had to find the shrine near Emi's grave. Everything was starting to come together—her brother studying the same play as Maya in their Basilica's English classes, the wedding, the strange obsession with Mexican symbols, the card of death. Then—there were the tunnels. All the books that Garcia was borrowing were strangely familiar to Emi's books. His obsession with the history of the city, the tunnel network underneath St. Augustine.

She sifted through Emi's suitcase. She found the book, the same one that Garcia had borrowed, *The Tunnels of St. Augustine*. Its leather-bound cover was worn, the pages smooth as velvet beneath her fingers. It had the strange allure of fiction yet carried the weight of history. She flicked it open and scanned the brief blurb at the beginning:

There are dozens of tunnels beneath the city of St. Augustine, originally built by the Spanish. This intricate network of coquina passages once connected the city's oldest buildings and served as an escape route to the fort during sieges. While the government has since sealed most tunnels for public safety, several entry points remain accessible from the Basilica, the old fort, the Casa Monica Hotel and the St. George Tavern.

There was a map that marked tunnel entry points in the opening pages. However, an accompanying warning was issued:

Be warned, the precise entry points to the tunnels are unknown. It is believed the Spanish created secret exit routes into the surrounding woods, allowing women and children to escape while the men defended the fort. Centuries of neglect and clerical oversight have obscured their exact locations. However, historical records suggest they were built on higher ground, sheltered by large trees to prevent flooding and erosion.

Beneath the blurb was a map of the city. She traced the small markings of the exit points—then stopped. One was near the Nombre de Dios Cemetery, buried deep in the woods, exactly where the shrine of death was said to stand.

Lucia scooped the shells from her suitcase—she had to go before the hurricane arrived.

✧

Over the centuries, the Nombre de Dios Cemetery had fallen into disrepair. Moss suffocated the tombstones, hurricanes chipped away at the granite blocks, toppling angel statues. The roots of the oak bulged from the topsoil.

Now, as the storm closed in, the cemetery seemed to brace itself. Wind whipped through the trees, rattling branches like brittle bones. The ancient oak groaned, its roots gripping tighter, as if anchoring itself to the coffins below.

Lucia walked through the rows of tombstones with the shells clanking in her pocket. The Spanish moss lashed in the wind, tearing loose at the strands as her hair tangled alongside it. She stopped at Emi's tombstone.

Emi Hernandez
1982 - 2002

Let his pain be replaced by peace

A small candle she had put down last time had been blown away by the wind—so too had any flower petals. Lucia took the shells from her pocket, rolling them in her palm, their edges smooth from the ocean. When they were kids, she and Emi would collect them before a storm, racing the tide as it churned up the sand. He had always said nature had a way of returning things—the way the birds followed the wind home, or weeds swallowed abandoned cottages in the woods.

She crouched by his tombstone, pressing the shells into the damp earth at its base. She remembered how they tossed the common shells back into the water, believing the tides would carry their messages across the world.

The storm was coming fast, the air thick with salt, but she stayed a moment longer, securing the shells deep into the topsoil. She had to find the shrine. She looked up to the woods—they were a few hundred yards in the distance like the bookkeeper had described.

"Lucia?"

She turned around, startled.

There was Javier, dressed in his suit, his hands covered in dirt.

"Javier? What are you doing?" she said as the wind howled around them.

"Someone has to look after the dead before a storm," he said, dusting the dirt off his hands. "The last storm wrecked the cemetery—tombstones knocked over—the ground flooded when an old pipe burst. They lost a little girl's plaque from a few hundred years ago, but there was no family to pay for a new one."

"You came out here all by yourself?" asked Lucia, confused.

"Yes, even if my efforts are futile, someone has to try. I pack extra soil around the tombstones and try to keep them steady." His gaze drifted to the shells she was burying in the dirt. "What about you? What are you doing out here?" Javier caught himself on his last word as he saw the name etched into the tombstone.

"Your brother?" he asked.

Lucia nodded.

"Do you still talk to him?" Javier asked softly. The wind died down for a moment.

"I hear him sometimes," Lucia said. "A whisper—but I don't know where. I don't know if he's waiting or already gone."

"I can hear my daughter too," Javier said. "She's with me," he smiled softly.

Lucia smiled, feeling something shift inside her. For the first time, she wasn't alone.

"Do you think she really is there?" asked Lucia, thinking of all the times her mother couldn't hear Emi's whispers.

"Of course," Javier said. "In Mexico, the dead are alive. But here, they treat death like it's contagious. Put it in hospitals, behind white walls, take it away in long black cars by serious men who dig very deep holes. They try to keep it as far away as they can. People talk about the dead in hushed voices, they speak of them so reverently that we forget they were humans too. In Mexico, we know better. Death sits at our table. We feed it bread, tell it jokes. Death is not something that we fear, it is something we celebrate. It is the moment we are finally at one with the universe."

"You can talk to the dead?" asked Lucia, as the wind howled in response.

"Of course. People have been for thousands of years. But this country is so obsessed with purity that it hides its soul in the shadows of its cities. The older gods understood humans better—they knew our flaws and welcomed death to sit at our tables, rather than letting it sneak around in graveyards."

Lucia paused.

"My mother says that we go to heaven or hell as soon as we die,"

Lucia said. "She says that you can't talk to someone in hell, the only way is if you join them."

"Your mother has spent too much time with American priests," Javier replied. "What do you believe?"

"I don't know," Lucia said slowly. "Even though I can hear him, he's not really here. It's like... like a faded version of him. But I'm afraid if I stop listening to him, then he'll just disappear completely. I think we die twice—once when we're buried, and again when we're forgotten."

"The dead can't die," Javier said with a soft smile.

"But maybe they stop talking to us," said Lucia, thinking about all the sermons she'd listened to about hell. "I think Emi went to heaven—he was a good person." She hesitated, twisting a shell between her fingers. "Good people go to heaven, right? That's how it works. You get to be with the people you love. I don't want him lost in nothing, unable to talk to us forever."

She looked at Javier, her brow furrowed.

Javier traced his fingers over the granite as the first droplets of rain started to patter down from the skies. "When my daughter died," he said quietly, "the priest told me she was in heaven because she was pure and good."

He looked up at the storm clouds, their edges tinged black.

"But how could I ever join her? No one goes through life without mistakes. A place that pure—it's not meant for sixty-year-olds."

"But you're a good person—" Lucia said in a reassuring voice.

"No one's good once they've lived long enough. That's when I realized I didn't believe in all this Catholic stuff. It's too binary, hell or heaven, the only two options for six billion different types of people. The ancients knew that spirits are like the wind—sometimes gentle, sometimes fierce. My daughter's spirit," Javier continued, "isn't trapped in some distant paradise. She's like these storms that come in from the sea—moving between places we can see and places we can't. Sometimes helping, sometimes testing us, but always part of the great cycle."

The rain was falling steadily now, and in the distance, lightning illuminated the tree line. "The old gods knew that death was just as messy as life. Nothing is right or wrong. Even down to the atoms in our body, everything exists in a cloud, a state of flux shifting between universes, constantly changing. Nothing can ever be only one thing."

It started to bucket down with rain.

"We better go," Javier said.

"It's okay, I need to do something first."

Javier looked at her, confused.

"Are you sure?"

"Yes," Lucia said. "By the way, I have a question."

"Yes?"

"Did you know Maya volunteered at the Basilica?"

"Yes, I think she did some work there for Father Roderick."

"Did she ever say anything about it to you? Any of the kids there?"

"No," said Javier. "She was a very private person. Why? What's the matter?"

"A lot of people from that class seem to have disappeared or died."

Javier's expression tightened. "Others? You mean this has happened before?"

The rain poured down even heavier as if floodgates had finally burst open.

"I need to go," said Lucia as she dashed for the woods. Lucia pushed through the rain-soaked trees, her shoes sinking into the wet earth as she searched for the manhole. Water dripped from the moss hanging in long strands from the oak branches, pooling in the hollows of fallen logs. Frogs called from the flooded patches of grass, their croaks like little warnings that she was getting closer.

She scanned the ground, moving past saw palmettos and patches of prickly pear, but the shrine was nowhere to be found.

She searched for what felt like hours, circling back over the same ground, brushing away layers of wet leaves, pressing her palms into the mud where she thought it should be. A sharp crack split the air as a branch came crashing down a few feet away. The wind had picked up, shaking the trees. It wasn't safe to stay. Shivering, she exhaled, turned back, and started the long walk home.

The shrine of death was nowhere to be seen.

THE LIAR'S DEN

The rain was bucketing down as Lucia sprinted through the backstreets. The water gushed through the cobblestone gutters, forming a violent stream, sweeping along Coke bottles and crumpled fastfood wrappers. Lucia had been running through the rain for at least thirty minutes. She wanted nothing more than to crawl into a drying machine and swirl around in a warm womb of clothes, leaving the outside world alone.

By the time she reached the motel, she was soaked to the bone. The storm had only grown fiercer. She looked across the road, realizing that the pageant queen had nowhere safe to shelter in the storm. The woods would be a sludge fest, with branches whipped into projectiles by the wind.

Lucia turned her gaze back to the motel, drawn by the warm pull of her own bed. Surely the pageant queen had found somewhere else to stay? *It wasn't her responsibility.* She needed to get home—her mother would already be furious. She didn't have time to wander into the woods during a hurricane for a stranger she barely knew. As she stepped closer to the motel, her foot splashed into a low-lying puddle, the guilt seeped into her socks. Suddenly, she could feel it—feel him. Emi, sleeping outside for all those nights she clutched her warm blankets, pretending he was somewhere sunny.

Lucia couldn't leave her alone—her hut would be decimated. She ran toward the woods, following the mud trail from the pageant queen's squelching torso squirming through the sludge. Unlike the Anastasia Forest, these woods were thick. The trees groaned under pressure, sounding like they'd splinter at any second. She needed to find her—the hurricane was close.

Soon she found the clearing. There were two whiskey barrels with a door for a roof just like she had described. A tarp had been flimsily secured to the barrels for privacy but was about to blow off. She approached cautiously.

"Hello?" said Lucia.

"Who the fuck's there? I've got a knife."

"It's me. Lucia."

"What're you doing here?' she growled. The voice was still hostile, but it was the same southern drawl as the pageant queen.

"I wanted to help. You can't stay out here," Lucia said.

"Go away. I didn't ask for help."

"But you'll get blown away."

"Leave me alone," she yelled.

The wind howled, pummeling the tarp like a storm-tossed sail.

"You can stay with me."

Just as Lucia said it, the tarp ripped open and flew away into the woods like a stage curtain violently yanked open. The pageant queen lay crumpled on the floor. Without her wheelchair and make-up, she looked like some wild creature that emerged from mud-holes. She was lying on a mountain of crocodile-skin handbags, as she frantically tried to secure them from the gale.

"Look what you've done!" she screamed as a candy-red bag flew away.

"Grab it."

Lucia chased after the handbag, snatching it from a snagged tree stump. When she inspected it, she saw there was still a price tag. It was brand new, worth nearly $1,000. The pageant queen lived on the streets, yet she had a stack of handbags worth a small fortune.

"Give it to me," she yelled from the ground.

Lucia walked over and dropped the bag behind one of the barrels. Then she saw it. The pageant queen had clawed two human-sized holes into the dirt, chunks of gravel still lodged beneath her polished nails. Overflowing from the holes were stuffed patent leather heels, a pair of scuffed white sneakers, gold watches, and crumpled clothes—faded jeans, a sequined blouse, and a torn windbreaker. There was even a faded pageant sash, its glittering letters peeling away, *Miss Universe.*

"Where'd you get all of this?" asked Lucia.

"Get the tarp back on. I'll lose everything. Please," she begged. A second later, a stray shoe was whipped up by the wind, the heel slamming hard against a tree trunk. Lucia turned around and saw that the tarp had caught on a cluster of brambles. She bolted toward it, then dragged the tarp back to the shelter.

"Tie the rope to the corners," yelled the pageant queen.

Lucia wrangled the rope as the tail of the tarp tried to take flight. Finally, she secured it to the corners. Then, she crawled through the flap, tucking herself beneath the shelter, shielded from the wind. It felt like being in a tin can tossed about by raging waves. The pageant queen wouldn't look at her as she mumbled something.

"Thanks."

"Where did you get all this stuff?" asked Lucia again.

"I bought it," she said over the roaring wind, using her torso to jam the high heels into the hole.

"But I thought you didn't have any money?" continued Lucia.

"Well, I guess I do." The pageant queen stopped moving. She stared at Lucia. "You wouldn't know what it's like."

"I wouldn't know what?" replied Lucia.

"To be ugly." The lady started to sob. She was clutching one of the handbags tightly to her chest.

Lucia looked around the mud hut for tissues. There were none. She cleared her throat.

"I think you're pretty," said Lucia.

"I'm ugly inside and out," she replied, her movement slowing as if she had given up trying to save her handbags. Then Lucia saw something at her feet. It was wrapped in a tablecloth, but the needle glistened in the low light. Its metallic edge was a sharp contrast to the globs of mud that dulled the leather handbags.

"What are those?" Lucia said, pointing to the needles.

For the first time, the pageant queen looked up at Lucia, her eyes puffy with tears.

"I don't want you to see me like this," she said.

"I just want to help."

"I don't deserve help."

"Why?" asked Lucia.

The pageant queen sat up for the first time. Pockets of air snuck into the shelter, rattling the tarp like a war drum.

"I haven't been honest with you."

Lucia yanked the tablecloth. It wasn't just needles—it was syringes. Dozens of them. Her heart raced as she picked one up, her hands trembling. That's when she saw it

The sticker.

The same old Spanish galleon: *El Dorado Dust*.

Her chest tightened as the realization hit. It was the exact same type they'd found in her brother's pocket when he washed ashore. The same one Maya had when she died.

"Be careful. You're too pure to be touching that," said the pageant queen.

"Where'd you get this?" said Lucia in a trembling voice. She couldn't look at the pageant queen the same way. Now she remembered the grainy footage of her torso, knocking on the door the night of her death, before the screen cut to black. Lucia shuffled away to make space between them.

"I promise I didn't hurt her," she said, rubbing the tears from her eyes. "Please trust me."

"How can I?" said Lucia.

"I'll tell you everything."

The tarp flapped wildly above them, the thin rope tied to the barrels the only thing keeping the shelter from collapsing. Lucia felt like she was sinking into the muddy floor, trapped in the dilapidated box in the woods.

"That's how I make my money," said the pageant queen. "The dope."

"What?" replied Lucia in shock.

"I told you I'm no good inside. I have a problem. I can't help buying things. It's the reason I live on the streets, the bills come quicker than the paycheck."

"You buy heroin?"

"No, I just sell it. I'm an oniomaniac. It's what the docs call someone who has a compulsive buying problem. You don't understand what it's like," she said softly. "It's this urge deep within you, a bottomless hunger. I go into a store, and I'll empty every last cent buying ten of the same handbags even though I know rent's due the next day. It got so bad that the only way I could keep pace with my buying is if I started selling dope."

"But people die from that."

"I told you I'm fucked up. Don't make me feel bad about it," she said. The tears were gone now, and her expression was almost relieved as she unburdened herself. Lucia thought of the woman she first met, the seemingly honest lady with pizza sauce around her lips.

Lucia felt the anger swell up inside of her.

"I trusted you," Lucia said bitterly. All she could think about was Maya and Emi.

"I never lied to you," pleaded the pageant queen. "I promise everything I told you is the truth."

"You didn't tell me about this," said Lucia. "You visited Maya the night before she died, and then you're the one who sold her the heroin." Lucia raised her voice, nearly shouting to be heard over the howling wind.

"I didn't sell it to Maya," she replied.

"What?" said Lucia, confused.

"I sold it to Garcia."

Lucia's heart dropped. *Garcia?* She thought of the *La Santa Muerte* statue, the moonlight wedding. There was something evil going on that she still couldn't understand. It was as if there were some curse that the church was trying to hide.

Suddenly, the wind ripped the tarp off again. Now the handbags flew everywhere as the pageant queen screamed.

"They're all gone!"

"What happened?" yelled Lucia. The wind was too loud to hear one another.

"I get this brand from my supplier," she yelled, pointing to the little sticker of the Spanish galleon. "Dope's got different strains. *El Dorado Dust* is the purest stuff on the market. So strong it can make you feel the touch of God."

When she said it one of the syringes was snatched by the wind, the murky liquid sprayed into the air as the droplets scattered into the raging storm. The pageant queen seemed to track every droplet with her frenzied eyes.

"Get it. Please. I'm dead if we don't get it."

"It's gone," said Lucia.

"No, it can't be. They'll come for me."

"Tell me about Garcia."

"We have to save it," she rambled manically.

The pageant queen scrambled to gather the syringes, hastily wrapping them in a spare shirt before shoving them deep into her pockets.

"Get on my back," ordered Lucia. The pageant queen stared at her in shock, but even in her daze, she grabbed hold of Lucia's shoulders. With a grunt, Lucia hauled her onto her back. She was lighter than she looked. The storm roared around them, louder than the engine of a plane, as Lucia carried her out of the woods.

"Garcia knew I sold. He'd seen me outside the motel selling before. A week before Maya and the children died, he approached me," she said directly into Lucia's ear, the snap of a tree branch echoing around them.

"He was all over the place—he could hardly look me in the eyes. Said he wanted to buy dope. I offered him the cheap stuff—it's such low grade that it'll only give you a light buzz."

Lucia nearly tripped over a stick as she readjusted the pageant queen on her back.

"I don't like giving new timers strong stuff, increases my risk that they'll OD. But he insisted he only wanted *El Dorado Dust*, the strongest stuff I had."

Lucia reached the end of the woods. She found the pageant queen's wheelchair and propped her onto it.

"I'll take you to my room. Keep talking," yelled Lucia over the storm as she pushed the wheelchair along the waterlogged pavement.

"He asked me a million questions. Where I got it from, how much I had, where he could buy from my supplier. I told him straight, I'm not a fucking tour guide and if he didn't want to buy, he could scram. So he bought one. Ran off with it really quick after that."

"So you lied about all that to the police?" asked Lucia, swerving to miss a crater-sized puddle.

"Of course I did. You think I'm going to confess to being a drug dealer to the cops? It's called self-preservation, sweetheart."

"But why'd you have to lie about it to me?"

"I didn't know you."

"Well, you told me about the moonlight wedding."

"Yeah—because that story doesn't involve me committing a felony, does it?"

"Is there anything else you didn't tell me?" Lucia asked, as they got closer to the entrance of the motel. The rubber handles on the chair were so slippery that Lucia had to grab onto the steel frame.

"There's one thing."

"What?" asked Lucia desperately.

"The reason I spent so long knocking on her door that night wasn't because of the photo, it's because I was worried. I knew Garcia had the dope, and after I saw them in the woods like that, I just got a bad feeling. The whole thing felt wrong."

"So you wanted to check if she was okay?" asked Lucia.

"Yes. I wish I had broken down the door," she replied.

Now it all made sense. She didn't crawl up concrete stairs, grazing her hands for some photograph. She was trying to save Maya; she sensed something was wrong.

Finally, after what felt like an eternity, they reached the motel. Lucia wheeled her past reception, looking through the window. The crab wasn't there. She wheeled her to the stairwell where they were sheltered from the wind.

"I'm sorry," said the pageant queen. "It's weighed on me for a while, even though I am such a piece of shit, I still have a heart you know. I guess I hoped by telling you all that stuff about their secret little wedding you would figure it out. I never trusted Garcia and that priest. When I heard what happened, I knew they had something to do with it. *El Dorado Dust* is strong, it's easily enough to kill someone, especially if they've never done dope before. Game over for someone Maya's size. All it would take is someone to inject her while she is sleeping, and she would be dead by the hour."

"You think he killed her?"

"Must of."

"But why?" asked Lucia.

"Your guess is as good as mine."

Lucia remembered the church vault.

Be careful with the secrets that you sow,

Speak of Emi, and you shall go.

Mr. Muerte.

Maybe she was exposing some dark secret hidden by Garcia, hidden by the church. Maybe she knew about the shrine in the woods, the card of death—Emi.

"I'll stay here, darling," said the pageant queen from her hiding spot in the stairwell. The area was shielded from the wind by concrete.

"No, you can stay in our room," Lucia said.

"I don't think that's a good idea. I'll knock if I need something. Besides, this stairwell is probably the safest place in Florida right now," she said with a smile.

"Be careful."

HURRICANE SEASON

Lucia twisted the handle; the motel door creaked open, releasing the stale scent of week-old water. Her mother sat on the edge of the bed with the Gideon Bible in her hands.

"Where have you been?"

"I'm sorry. I've been busy."

"I called the police," she said, the Bible shaking in her hands, she always read Isaiah 41 when she was nervous. "Why didn't you let me know you'd be out in the middle of a storm?"

"Sorry. I had to help at the bookstore. They were putting shutters on the windows," Lucia said, looking at the floor.

"So they're using you to carry things now?" her mother said accusingly, as Lucia self-consciously hid her slender arms.

"Yes."

"I've barely seen you for the last few days and now you tell me you're boarding up the bookstore. Don't lie to me." It seemed the storm's electric charge had flowed into her mother's body, now her voice surged with an emotion that Lucia hadn't seen for years. She knew her mother would only get angrier if she told her what she had discovered about Emi.

"I'm not. I was reading books," she said, half-lying as she thought of the book she found in the Basilica.

"You can't keep your head in the clouds."

"I'm not," Lucia snapped. "Why can't you just be happy for me living my own life? Why does everyone have to be miserable in the real world just like you are?"

Her mother stiffened. For a moment, Lucia thought she'd lash out, but instead, she let out a slow breath and set the Bible down on the table.

"It's not that," she said. "I don't want you to make the same mistakes as me." She looked at the ceiling, as if the mistakes were threaded into the cobwebbed corners of the roof. The dishes in the sink looked old, and the air felt stuffy with flecks of dust lazily floating in the air. Her mother had been alone by herself for a while. Now, something shifted in her gaze—like the morning mist had finally lifted from her pupils, letting her see clearly.

"What do you mean?" replied Lucia.

Her mother sat on the edge of the bed.

"When I was a girl, I thought I'd be a poet." Her mother paused, softening.

"My dad used to work in a mine. He'd come home every week with a new book for me to read. We read *Piedra De Sol* by Octavio Paz, and other books I had no business reading. My father never complained about working fourteen hours a day. He managed to read to me in the gentlest voice even though his hands were hardened by rock. He told me I could be anything I dreamed of, to follow my heart. I was convinced I'd be a poet, that I would write lines that other dads could read to their daughters. And for a moment, it felt like I would—I won a small prize, had my work published in a local paper. I believed it was the start of something. Then I met your father in Puerto Escondido. He convinced me to run off to America. So I followed my heart. It was the only impulsive choice of my life, and the consequences stayed far longer than your father ever did. I had no degree in a country where I could not speak the language with two babies. No one cares if you can quote lines of poetry —in the wrong language—when you work in a hotel. My manager only cared that I didn't put the wrong soap in the shower. In this country you need a degree, it's the only way it will respect you."

Her mother paused. Lucia had never seen her say so many words.

"I never saw my father again. I couldn't stomach writing a letter to him. I think if he knew that I'd followed my heart and it ruined my life, everything he'd sacrificed would be for nothing. I like to think that he still keeps buying books, checking the author each day with the hope that one day he will find my name on them. I didn't want to rob him of that. The man killed himself in those mines. And for what? I guess I'm not even good enough to work at a hotel."

"What do you mean?" asked Lucia.

"I got fired." Her mother stared blankly at the lifeless TV.

"What?"

"The Casa Monica Hotel 'didn't require my services anymore.'"

"Did they say why?"

"No. The manager came up to me after my shift and made me sign some document that said I legally couldn't mention them again. Then they gave me a $100 severance check."

Her mother put her head in her hands. Lucia rushed over and put an arm around her shoulder.

"I will help to pay the bills too."

"No. I didn't give up being a poet for you to fluff pillows."

The two of them sat at the edge of the bed, the room eerily quiet as the storm raged outside. For a second, Lucia forgot all about her investigation. All she wanted to do was to hug her mother. It'd been so long since she'd had an excuse to. Lucia wrapped both arms around her and squeezed. For a moment, everything felt okay. After a few seconds, her mother pulled away.

"We'll be okay," said her mother softly.

Lucia smiled. Before she could truly savor the moment, her mother had snapped back into her sensible self, pacing forward to the TV.

"We should monitor the storm. I don't know if we have enough cans for three days without electricity," said her mother. She pressed the remote; the TV sputtered to life. A news anchor stood in front of Vilano Beach. His rain jacket was pulled taut by the wind, as the gusts nearly doubled him over.

"The hurricane is intensifying as it moves up from a low-pressure system in the south…"

Clutching the microphone with both hands, the anchor steadied himself as the camera shook, filming the salty spray dousing the coastline with enraged seawater. Suddenly, the hood of his rain jacket blew back, and his hat flew off, instantly snatched by the wind.

"We need to go back to you in the studio," said the anchor.

The footage cut to the studio. A female presenter sat with her mug of coffee in front of a green screen.

"Oh, my—thanks, Mark… looks like the hurricane has arrived. I look forward to giving you a cup of warm coffee when you're safe and sound in the studio. I hope that all of our listeners are safely hunkered down inside. You can expect wind gusts of up to 100 miles an hour. Citizens of St. Augustine are urged to go inside and secure any loose fixtures to avoid projectiles as the storm picks up. I've been notified that our meteorologists believe there's a chance we may only get clipped by the weather system, with the worst hitting the Carolinas. However, you are advised to stay inside for the next 24 hours before we have more information. Across St. Augustine, emergency crews have set up flood defenses to protect historical sites and businesses. The fire department has sandbagged most storefronts along Avenida Menendez. Many of the old buildings have been repurposed for emergency evacuation centers, and the Basilica of St. Augustine opened its doors to the homeless displaced by the hurricane. We'll now cut to our reporter inside of the Basilica."

The TV cut to the inside of the church. It was completely different to the last time Lucia saw it. The pews had been pushed to the sides, even the altar had been moved to make way for hundreds of sleeping bags. Volunteers walked around providing cans of food to the homeless. A reporter stood in the center of the frame, standing next to a robed man. It was the priest from the moonlight wedding. The one who cried when he saw Maya's book.

"So, Father, can you tell us how the church managed to respond so quickly to the current crisis?"

The priest spoke as if he were delivering one of his sermons.

"As soon as we heard about the hurricane, we knew we had to help. We do a lot of volunteer work with the homeless and we knew their encampments wouldn't survive the storm."

"Where do most of these people come from? Many of our viewers wouldn't have known that the homeless crisis was so bad in the city."

"Many are settled in the Anastasia Forest. Their camp is ground zero for the storm, which is why we knew we needed to act so quickly."

"That's very kind of you, Father. I hope God is with us all. Back to the studio."

The priest smiled at the camera, and Lucia's whole soul shivered. It felt like he was staring at her straight through the TV, a hand away from yanking her through the screen. Lucia switched off the remote.

"What are you doing?" said her mother.

"Why does the church know about the Anastasia Forest?" asked Lucia.

Her mother looked annoyed.

"They provide a meal service for people who live out there."

"What do they get out of it?" asked Lucia bitterly, thinking of the church program that Emi went to.

"They're just trying to help."

"They're liars," said Lucia.

"What?"

"They're hiding stuff."

"I'm not in the mood for this."

"Emi was looking for something out there. Maybe he found something, and the church was trying to cover it up."

"Don't do this."

"Do what?" retorted Lucia.

"You need to accept things."

"That's the problem. You accept everything," said Lucia, her voice rising in anger.

"You don't know how I feel."

"You forgot all about him the second you kicked him out." There was silence after Lucia's words left her mouth.

"I kicked him out because he stole your college money."

"What?"

"I didn't want to be the one to tell you. He stole the money that I was saving for you to go to college. There was nearly $5,000 in there."

"You're lying."

"I'm sorry, Lucia. Not everyone is lying. I know how much you loved your brother, and I didn't want to take that away from you. But you need to realize that the church is just trying to help. The Anastasia Forest is home to people living hard lives—drug addicts, criminals. For many of them, the church is a last resort, the only ones who still care."

Lucia wanted to run away but there was nowhere to go. She sat alone on her bed. Her brother would never steal from her. A tear slipped down her cheek, then another.

"He was killed," she whispered, barely hearing her own voice.

"No. They were the only ones who didn't give up on him. I loved

Emi. But sometimes people go to a place where they are so sick that they can't love you back. It's a sickness that strangles their soul like vines wrapping around a tree, until no sunlight can reach them."

"You gave up on him," Lucia repeated.

"I chose you."

"What does that mean?" Lucia snapped back.

"I couldn't let you go down that path. I couldn't lose another child, even if it meant I needed to cut him out of our lives."

"So you left him."

"No. I left him to make his own choice. If there was any part of him, deep down, that still wanted to set himself free, he could have."

"He was trying. His letter said that he was trying."

"He just wanted me to give him more money. I gave him loans that you didn't know about, he's my son. I still loved him. But he was just trying to make it look like he was okay so he could get more money."

"Why do you never believe him, but you believe everything that the church says?"

"God was the only one who didn't give up on Emi, he gave up on himself."

"God's full of shit," yelled Lucia.

"Don't you dare say that in my house," said her mother.

"It's not your house. We live in a goddamn motel."

"Watch your tongue."

"If you cared as much about swear words as you did in real life, maybe none of this would've happened."

"You need to see Father. I'm worried you're becoming just like your brother."

"Don't take me there."

"They can help you."

"No."

Lucia walked over to her sofa bed and pulled the covers over her head. Her mother couldn't see what was happening. Lucia closed her eyes—it would be easier to sleep. For a second, she forgot about everything. Then a large thud erupted as something hit the window. The hurricane was here.

DEATH RETURNS

For decades, lovers fastened locks to the Bridge of Lions, hoping their love would be as enduring as the bridge itself. Hundreds of locks clung tightly to its steel frame. Yet with every storm the rusted locks rattled with the wind, clattering against the steel like a tortured tambourine. After each storm, more locks would break loose, tumbling into the sea. Nothing stood untested: every fractured window, every mangled streetlight, and every trembling roof in the city had earned its place through sheer endurance. The Paradise Motel was no exception. While the pool was clogged with debris—loose planks, buckets, and chairs—the building remained remarkably intact.

The news that day suggested the worst of the storm had passed, the system having surged up the coast toward the Carolinas. Wind maps showed its spiraling arms stretching northward, dragging bands of rain and thunder away from Florida.

Guests emerged cautiously, like moles leaving their burrows after a predator passed. People surveyed the damage, inspecting the motel. A mockingbird had splattered into someone's window, and now they were trying to scrape it off with a toothbrush. Onlookers checked their own windows for damage—most were cracked or coated in a veneer of mud paste from the swamp banks.

Lucia watched from the balcony as Javier stepped out of his room. His suit looked even more out of place against the backdrop of hurricane carnage, with not a single thread of cotton straying from its stitching. He smiled when he saw her.

"How did you sleep?" he said as if they were chatting over warm eggs and coffee.

"I couldn't. Every time the wind howled I thought the windows would shatter."

"Ah, you mustn't worry—the windows are laminated glass. They can withstand a brick to the face."

"It sounded like they were eating bricks all night."

Javier smiled. Then someone screamed.

"What was that?" said Lucia.

"It came from downstairs," replied Javier, his smile replaced by a cautious frown. Lucia bolted for the stairwell as Javier jogged behind her. When she got to the bottom, she saw a group of guests congregating around something. She wove through the crowd, passing the two blonde women from the laundry and the large ginger boy with his father. When she got to the front, she saw her. She was sagging in the wheelchair, her chin sank into her collarbone, eyes motionless.

Lucia knelt in front of her wheelchair and held both of her limp hands. She tried to shake her to life, but nothing happened. Her arms felt heavier than when she carried her through the woods. She kept shaking her arms, hoping to jolt her back to life. The pageant queen was dead.

"Step back, girl," said the voice of a lady. Lucia turned around. It was the young blonde from the laundry, the one with the racy lingerie. "The coroner won't want you to touch her, it will leave fingerprints on the body."

"Oh who cares. The writing is on the wall—she overdosed on dope. Don't need a coroner to tell you that," piped the cynical older blonde.

"Well, it's always best not to touch a dead body, isn't it, Sharon?"

Lucia's eyes raced to the syringes. There was a pile of them still on her lap. On her arm, there were two entry points like she had been bitten by a snake. They were the ones the pageant queen had tried to salvage from the storm.

"God. I need to get out of this place," said Sharon, gawking at the emerging scene.

"Of course you make everything about yourself," said the younger blonde. "Even in the midst of tragedy."

"She couldn't handle it."

"You cold bitch."

"Like she was a saint. We all know she supplied just about everyone here."

The crowd stared at the wheelchair, as though waiting for her body to spring up like a grotesque circus act. But as soon as Lucia touched her hands, she knew. There was a coldness to her body that could not be faked, the blood in her veins no longer ran red. Sadness settled in Lucia's chest, before guilt took hold. She felt strangely responsible. Everyone in her life always left because of her.

"We should check her ID—maybe she has some family," Javier suggested.

"I'll do it." Lucia's voice was firm. "She was my friend."

Lucia reached into her handbag—one of the designer bags from the woods. She rummaged through it, feeling a pack of cigarettes before her fingers closed around a leather purse. She grabbed it. She opened the purse to find a stack of cards inside. Most were free food vouchers or advertisements for a handyman. Lucia sighed. The pageant queen probably just wanted to feel like her purse was full of credit cards, like the queen she always wanted to be. Lucia kept combing through the cards, looking for anything that resembled an ID. Then she saw it.

It was the card of death. Wedged between a free Subway voucher and a Costco coupon. She nearly dropped it, shock hitting all at once. Her mind emptied, every thought replaced by a single instinct. *Run*. She looked around at the crowd of onlookers; none would understand what it meant, none except Javier.

"Did you find it?" said Javier.

Yes," Lucia murmured, shaking as she held the card in her hands. Her eyes swept over the handbag, searching for an ID. But the pageant queen was nameless, faceless in death—no license, no trace, no identity. She remembered the story of her dad being T-boned by the truck. She wondered if anyone would care if she died.

"I will," Lucia whispered to herself.

"Let's call the family," Javier said. "Show me the ID." Lucia reached into her pocket and secretly shielded the card from view.

"This is her name," she said.

Javier looked at the card. He nodded. "Let's use my phone to make the call."

Now they both knew. It was Mr. Muerte.

✦

Lucia sank into the plush chair in Javier's room, still trembling as he shut the door behind him.

"Is the door locked?" she asked, her voice unsteady.

"I'll double-lock it," he said, sliding the flimsy metal chain into place. It rattled against the wood, too weak to feel reassuring. "Are you okay?"

Lucia caught her reflection in the polished bronze of the water jug—her cheeks were flushed, her breathing was uneven. She barely recognized herself.

"I don't know," she murmured. "It feels like it follows me. No matter where I go."

Javier frowned. "What does?"

Lucia stared up at the ceiling. "Death."

Javier exhaled slowly, folding his hands in his lap. "How can that be your fault? Death follows all of us. His voice softened. "When a tree dies, it feeds the soil beneath it. Its decay gives life to a hundred new saplings. That's how it's always been—death isn't an ending—it's part of the cycle."

"Well, nothing new seems to grow in my life," Lucia replied. "Just more death."

"Me too," Javier admitted, his voice quieter now. "It's the same card, isn't it?"

"Yes." Lucia gripped the arms of the chair, her nails pressing into the suede. "She told me Garcia was buying dope off her. The same strain they found in Maya's body." She paused. "Twelve hours later, she was dead." She swallowed hard, her chest tightening. Javier said nothing at first. Then, finally, he leaned forward.

"We need to be careful. If Mr. Muerte is here, then it's likely he already knows that you are close to figuring out who he is. You won't be safe."

Suddenly, there was a knock at the door.

They both exchanged worried looks.

"I'll open it," Javier said.

"No. Wait. Let me see who it is first," Lucia replied. She raced to the door, then peered through the peephole.

"It's the receptionist," she whispered. The crab was holding a clipboard and pen, tapping his foot nervously on the concrete. His hair remained stubbornly slicked back despite the rain. Lucia put her finger to her lips, signaling for Javier to be quiet. He knocked again. For a moment, his gaze met the peephole, but even the glass was too much for him, as he slunk away, disappearing out of view.

"I've never trusted him," said Javier, breaking the silence.

"He cut the lights the night Maya died," said Lucia. "It was as if he knew she was going to die, he kept mentioning bad things that were about to happen to her in his diary. Like he knew the exact hour."

"I've heard things about him," Javier said. "After Maya died, I did some digging into the colorful characters of this place."

"What'd you hear?"

Javier leaned back. "Well, I gave a lady in a trailer a case of Bud Light and a week's worth of cigarettes. That was enough to get her talking about her old neighbor. She said he used to live with his mom in some rundown Tampa trailer park. They got a discount because their lot was right next to the port-a-loos." He smirked. "She said he was a strange kid, made her skin crawl. While the other boys played basketball, he'd sit off to the side, making anatomical drawings of raccoons."

"Did she ask who you were?" Lucia said.

"People in Florida don't do that," Javier said. "She probably thought I was a cop. That's the advantage of being a retired detective—you figure out how to be just familiar enough to be forgettable. Anyway, when we got talking, I asked if anything weird ever happened when he was growing up. None of the usual dead-rats-under-the-pillow or lizard-in-a-glass-jar kind of stuff. But there was one thing." He exhaled.

"She said his mother had this boyfriend once. Covered in tattoos, a big dragon on his back. Used to shake the trailer when they were indulging themselves—everyone in the park knew about it. The boy would sit outside, reading a book, with little bits of tissue stuffed in his ears. She said it was a regular thing—the boyfriend coming and going, always in and out. And then, one day, he was gone." Javier tapped his fingers against the table. "The kid was happy after that. He even started playing basketball with the others. A few years later, she read in the paper that they found someone buried in a ditch in the woods. Shot through the head. Exactly the same dragon tattoo on his back."

Lucia frowned. "You're saying he killed him?"

"Just trailer park rumors. But maybe the lady's right. Maybe he had it in him."

Lucia shook her head. "I don't think he killed Maya. The police would have checked all the tapes, taken his fingerprints, and everything. He's too obvious a suspect, like someone wants us to think it's him."

Javier sighed. "You know how the sheriff operates. He doesn't chase the truth—he settles for what's convenient. The easiest option, the least paperwork, the choice that keeps the right people happy."

"But it doesn't make sense. It doesn't explain everything about the priest and Garcia. When Maya was reading the play, you said she had a debate about following the right path even if it was self-destructive. Garcia apologized for ruining her life when they got married. It's like she knew her fate too," Lucia hesitated, chewing on her lip. "There's something I haven't told you."

Javier straightened. "Yes?"

"Garcia visited my brother's grave," Lucia said. "When my brother died, he had the card of death in his pocket too."

Javier went still. His brow furrowed. "I'm sorry, I didn't know."

"It's okay," said Lucia. "After Garcia visited my brother's grave, he went to some shrine of death."

"Where?"

"In the back of the woods, near where we were in the Nombre de Dios Cemetery."

"Did you say that Garcia was praying to the saint of death?"

"I'm not sure," said Lucia. "But I think there's something underneath the city that people are trying to hide. Something that my brother was trying to find."

"What makes you think that?" Javier said.

"My brother was obsessed with the tunnels under the city, always trying to map out where they were. There's apparently an entry point into the Basilica. Maybe he found something in the church while he was there. Something he wasn't meant to see. All the books Garcia borrowed seemed to be about the same thing. The symbols, the focus on these strange saints."

"Interesting," he said. "I should show you something." Javier stood up, wandering over to his motel library, where leather-bound books lined a cedarwood shelf. He picked up a book titled:

Mexican Symbols of Death

It was the exact same one that Garcia had ordered at the Hidden Lantern, there were only a few copies worldwide.

"Do you know the history of your mother's country?" asked Javier.

"No," replied Lucia, slightly embarrassed. "My mother only talked about American history, she idolized John Adams."

"Each to their own," said Javier. "But the story of Mexico is far more interesting than that of any corn farmer in Virginia."

He opened the book.

"There was a time when people on this continent knelt before gods whose names were feared, not spoken—gods who demanded more than just silent devotion. They demanded your soul. These were the old gods, the ones the ancients worshiped for millennia, praying for the sun's return and the harvest to endure.

"The ancients knew that all things have a price. Prosperity is not guaranteed by words alone, and only the blood of man can establish the order that allows others to live in peace. So for thousands of years, the Mixtecs offered their sacrifices to the underworld. They understood that death must be fed for life to grow, loyally offering up their brothers and sisters to feed their gods. There was *Mictecacihuatl*—The Aztec Lady of the Dead, ruler of Mictlán, the underworld. They honored her with feasts, but soon realized she had an insatiable hunger. Cows were slaughtered before tournaments, virgins sacrificed for the harvest, and warriors offered for the summer solstice. Death was worshiped. It became the highest of honors to die for your people.

"When the Spanish arrived in Mexico, they were disgusted. They slaughtered dissenters, burned temples, and forced their own God upon the land. But belief isn't so easily buried. Thousands of years of blood sacrifice had already seeped into this continent, tilled into the soil itself. So the old gods didn't die. They had a metamorphosis.

"The indigenous Gods merged with Catholic saints, reshaping themselves in the shadows. People began to pray at the feet of *La Santa Muerte*, her skeletal face an eerie echo of Mictecacihuatl. She took root in the mountains, in the villages, the humble folk who still saw death every day and knew it wise to honor her with sacrifice, secretly slaughtering a goat to appease the old gods.

"And then, people began to disappear. Not just the natives—Spanish soldiers, too. They'd find their bodies at the old temple grounds, stripped down, their hearts..." He paused, glancing at the door, his voice barely a whisper. "Well. The Church called it resistance. Pagans refusing conversion. But there were whispers—whispers that some of the priests had seen something in those rituals. That they knew death was hungry, and it needed to be fed."

Javier paused.

"These are the tales of Mexico, I grew up on these folk stories. My parents were corn farmers."

"You think some people still believe all that?" asked Lucia. "In sacrifice..."

"Maybe they still do?" Javier said. "The church has had darker secrets before. If someone wanted people to disappear, the literacy program would be the perfect place to find them. No one keeps track of the homeless. No one asks questions when they're gone."

A chill ran through Lucia as the memory of the wedding in the woods crept back.

Thus with a kiss, I die.

She had to find out who else had vanished.

THE SHERIFF

Lucia hurried down the stairs. She rushed past the pageant queen's body, not daring to look. Then, she made her way to the parking lot. She needed that list of Maya's English students from the Basilica—somewhere, someone knew something.

As she ran across the lot, she spotted a branch that had shattered a car's windshield; shards of glass glistened on the passenger seat. Someone had already looted the glove compartment with the car manual torn to shreds. As she went to leave, a police car skirted into the parking lot with the sirens whooping. It screeched to a stop, blocking the exit. The driver's door flung open. A shoe stomped onto the concrete, planting itself like a flag on conquered soil. It was the sheriff, his goatee meticulously trimmed, showing the lines of his clenched jaw.

"Lucia, you'd best come with me now."

"What?"

"We got a few questions 'bout the death of Miss Jo George."

"Who's that?" replied Lucia.

"I reckon she's gone by a few names, but you'd prob'ly know her as the lady in the wheelchair."

"Oh. Sure. I'm sorry I shouldn't have touched her body. She was a friend. Kinda."

"Ain't no trouble, we just need to ask a few things, that's all. You got my word."

The sheriff reminded her of her old PE teacher—the kind who made the heavier kids climb the rope in front of everyone, just to watch them struggle.

"Should I tell someone I'm going with you?"

"You got every right to, no doubt 'bout that. But I reckon we can sort this out ourselves. What d'you say?"

"I think I should probably speak to someone first," she said, peering back at the pool, unsure if there was anyone who would even care.

"Sure can. But shame if you felt like you couldn't trust me. I know some things 'bout that brother of yours—you might wanna hear 'em."

Lucia stared at him in disbelief. He was withholding things about Emi.

"You should get in the car."

+

The interrogation room was dimly lit, a single bulb suspended from the ceiling, dangling like an anglerfish's lure. The light cast an aqua green glow over the tiles, as if the room were a drained fish tank. Lucia sat in a stiff wooden chair, as the sheriff sat opposite her in a leather one that had been dragged into the room by another officer. Lucia stared at the sheriff, waiting for him to talk.

"Need some water?"

"I'm okay."

"What 'bout snacks? Police vending machines got the good stuff."

"I'm okay."

Lucia's foot tapped restlessly, her gaze flicking over the tiles, measuring the distance to the door.

"Relax, now. You ain't in any trouble."

Lucia's gaze flicked to his sheriff's badge. He noticed.

"Florida Sheriff of the Year," he said, tapping the medal pinned above his badge. "You don't earn that by treatin' folks bad."

Lucia said nothing.

"Ain't about how much you shine your boots—it's about how much folks trust you. That's the key. When someone trusts you, they'll tell you everything you need to know. And make no mistake—we're in the business of knowing."

He stood and began pacing.

"I need you to trust me, Lucia. Need you to see we're on the same side."

"What do you know about my brother?" she interrupted.

The sheriff smirked. "That ain't how trust works. Trust's 'bout give and take. I learn 'bout you, you learn 'bout me, and together we land somewhere in the middle—call that compromise. Just like they did in the old days."

He leaned back in his chair, getting comfortable.

"See, I come from a long line of lawmen. Granddaddies been sheriffs longer than I can remember. They'd tell me stories 'bout ridin' two days just to reach the next town. Ain't no backup, no reinforcements, nothin'. To keep law in a place like that, you gotta make deals. Sometimes you turn a blind eye to the town drunk so you can catch the real outlaw." He leaned forward, locking eyes with Lucia. "Miss Jo George? She was that kind of person."

"What do you mean?"

"I need to know what she told you."

Lucia felt a strange sense of loyalty to her.

"I barely spoke to her," she replied.

The sheriff tilted his head. "That how you wanna start buildin' trust between us?"

"It's true. I only spoke to her once outside of the Pizza Hut."

"That's all?" He raised an eyebrow. "No other times?"

"That's all."

"Well, then we got a problem, 'cause I got an eyewitness who saw you carryin' her outta the woods the day she died. Said she had somethin' in her pouch that looked an awful lot like the syringes we found in her arm." He let the words hang. "Now that? That puts you in a tough place."

Lucia froze. She felt the stiff wooden slats pressing into her spine. The room smelled of stale soda, with syrup sticking to the table.

"I was helping her."

"So you lied to me?"

"I was worried about her in the hurricane. I thought she needed somewhere to stay."

"That right?" the sheriff said, watching her. "Then why couldn't you just tell me the truth?"

Lucia went quiet again.

The sheriff sighed. "Ain't no reason to lie if you was just helpin' her."

"Can I get some water?" Lucia's voice was hoarse as she cleared her throat.

"It's my turn to be real with you." The sheriff leaned over the table, his two forearms taking all his weight. Lucia could smell the barbecue on his breath. "Ain't sayin' you did nothin' wrong, but I need to know what she told you. Everythin'," he said, placing his palms flat on the table. "Make this easy on yourself, now. I give you my word—it'll go a whole lot smoother that way."

Lucia looked at her feet. There was nowhere to go.

"Lemme get you that water," said the sheriff in a lighter tone, hauling his body off the table. He stood up and slipped out the door. The lights throbbed to the same slow beat as the neon sign at the

Paradise Motel. Lucia closed her eyes and imagined she was floating in the sea. She focused on breathing, picturing herself being carried away on the backs of the baby turtles. But then the image in her head soured; suddenly she was struggling to breathe underwater.

A glass slammed onto the table. Lucia opened her eyes. The water in the cup was as still as the surface of a koi pond. She reached for it and took a sip, half-expecting it to taste of poison.

"Now, you ready to talk?"

"You promised to tell me about my brother."

The sheriff held up a hand. "Gave you my word, didn't I? Our word's all we got."

Lucia swallowed. Her gaze flicked to the door, then back to the sheriff. "Fine," she muttered. "She told me her story—how she was a pageant queen from Kansas and how her dad died."

"She told you that?"

"Yeah."

"That's real interestin'," he said, sitting back in his leather chair. "She go into the details?"

"He got T-boned by a truck?"

The sheriff chuckled. "T-boned, huh? Well, that's new." He sat back, stretching his legs. "Ain't no truck. She drove into a pole. Killed her daddy instantly. Some folks said it was like she turned into it on purpose—cut the car clean in half."

"But the crash crushed her legs?" said Lucia.

The sheriff snorted. "Crash? Naw. She walked away with nothin' but a scratch on her ankle. You wanna know what happened? She let that scratch get infected. Let it fester till it turned to cellulitis, till they had no choice but to amputate. Right 'round the time of her manslaughter trial. Pretty convenient, don't you think?"

Lucia thought of the stories about her dad, him forcing her to all the pageant shows.

The sheriff shook his head. "She played the game. Figured a jury'd feel bad 'bout puttin' a crippled woman behind bars. And wouldn't you know it—worked like a charm."

"She was a model," Lucia said. "She needed her legs."

The sheriff let out a short laugh. "A model? What else she tell ya?"

"Not much," said Lucia. The sheriff frowned again. He reached for his glass of water and took a big, long sip, as if he were slurping up a pond in the desert.

"Gon' need more than that if you wanna hear 'bout your brother."

Lucia tensed.

"Why do you wanna know?" she asked. "You think someone killed her?"

The sheriff leaned back in his chair, his arms relaxed on the armrests.

"That ain't how this works. I ask, you talk."

Lucia exhaled.

"She told me she dealt dope to fund her shopping habits. Apparently, she sold some to Garcia a week before Maya died. It was the same syringe they found with Maya."

The sheriff leaned in, eyes sharpening. "Now we're gettin' somewhere. She mention where she got it? Some kind of supplier?"

"No."

"Are you sure? She didn't mention any names?"

"No. That was it. The only thing I remembered was that she called it *El Dorado Dust*."

"Bloody dope." The sheriff shook his head. "That whole mess with Maya and her kids… damn shame. I was the one who handled it. What that woman did… ain't got words for it."

Lucia stayed silent. The sheriff leaned back, arms stretching behind his head, irritated by the lack of response.

"I handle all the big cases in town—the higher-ups made sure I was assigned to them. They didn't want anyone else."

Lucia pushed the water aside.

"How come you didn't check the security footage?"

"'Course we did. That's how we saw your friend Miss George knockin' on Maya's door. But let's not kid ourselves—a woman with no legs didn't take out three people on her own."

"What about the receptionist?"

"That freak? Naw, impossible. Burned his damn hand fixin' the breaker box. Went straight to the ER 'round midnight. Nurses had him there all night."

Lucia clenched her jaw. "Then why didn't you investigate Garcia?"

The sheriff's smile tightened. "Easy now. Told you—I'm the one askin' questions here."

Lucia's frown morphed into a snarl.

"You real sure Miss George didn't drop any names? No clients, no suppliers—nothin'?"

"Positive," Lucia said. The sheriff smiled.

"Well thank you for your time, Lucia. You've been most helpful." The sheriff stood up from his chair and made his way to the door.

"And my brother…" Lucia said. She hadn't moved from the chair.

"That boy gave me more headaches than I can count."

"He wasn't a boy. He was 21."

"Well, he was old enough to be a paying customer of our dearly departed Miss George. Regular, too."

Lucia stared at him in shock. The sheriff smirked.

"Sorry to bust up the picture you had of him. But your brother wasn't no saint—he was a junkie, same as the rest. Picked up whatever he could get. And Miss George? She sold cheap." He leaned back in his chair. "Could read you his whole rap sheet, but hell, we'd be here all night. Last time I saw him, we were slappin' cuffs on him for breaking into the Casa Monica. Boy thought he could crawl through the tunnels."

"He was probably looking for somewhere to sleep, he didn't have anywhere to stay," said Lucia defensively.

The sheriff cocked his head. "That so? Then why'd he need to sleep with a gun?"

Lucia stiffened. *Emi hated violence.* He was a sworn pacifist—he wouldn't even kill spiders.

"That's not true."

"Ain't what it looked like. Security caught him tryin' to bust into the Basilica tunnels. Busted the damn door right off the hinges."

Lucia's breath hitched. *The Basilica?*

"Claimed he was onto some big secret, rootin' around for a hidden entrance. Know what I call that?" The sheriff leaned forward. "A run-of-the-mill thief."

Lucia clenched her fists. "He was looking for something."

"That what you tell yourself?" The sheriff let the words hang.

Lucia swallowed the anger rising in her throat. "Can I go?" she asked, barely keeping the bitterness from her voice.

The sheriff didn't move at first, just studied her like a man who already knew what she was going to do next. Then, he leaned back, exhaling through his nose.

"One more thing. As a friend, I should warn you—some things aren't worth digging into." His voice dipped, the smirk fading. "I've seen what happens to folk who don't back off. Never ends well."

"What?" said Lucia with a look of confusion. The sheriff was standing at the door, with his hands behind his back. Had she heard him right? Something about his Southern drawl made everything sound sweet—like iced tea with cyanide cubes melting in the glass.

"Just trying to help," he faked a smile.

"With what?"

"Best not get yourself tangled up in this Garcia and Maya

business." He lingered on the last words, then twisted the door handle. "You're free to go." He smiled. Her investigation had been secret. *How did he know?* She kept her eyes fixed on the sheriff as she walked toward the exit. He didn't take his eyes off her either.

As soon as she left the interrogation room, she wanted to run out of the police station. The corridor was dark—and the vending machines were stocked to the brim. As she turned, her gaze flicked to a cluttered desk near the vending machines—a taser had been left unattended. She hesitated only for a second. Then, she slipped it into her pocket in one fluid motion. She needed to go to the Basilica.

Restless, she scanned for an exit. Pinned against the walls were missing person posters. Each had the face of a young girl, mostly Hispanic. Lucia stared into each girl's eyes as she made her way to the door. She stopped. One of the posters read:

Marti Cortez

She'd heard her name before.

"Can we help you?"

Lucia looked up. A female officer stepped in front of her.

"No. Sorry. I was just leaving."

"I'll walk you out," said the officer.

Lucia walked out of the police station.

She knew that name: Marti Cortez. She'd been in Emi's English class at the Basilica.

THE CONFESSIONAL

After the storm, the Basilica remained unscathed as it had for centuries. Flags were hoisted once more, bells ready to chime, and the stained-glass windows polished to a gleam. The only reminder of the storm's rage was a few missing terracotta tiles, knocked loose by the wind. The Basilica's towering presence made Lucia feel as inconsequential as a candle flickering in a cathedral's draft.

Lucia recalled Javier's cryptic mentions of *La Santa Muerte*: the blood sacrifices that the saint silently demanded. She looked up to the crucifix atop the church's spire, Christ still standing at the building's highest peak, surviving the wind. She thought of everything she had seen. There was a pattern—something Father Roderick, Garcia, and the sheriff were desperate to keep buried. She needed to find whatever Emi had been searching for in the Basilica—whether it was the tunnel entrance, or something hidden in the storage room she had overlooked the first time.

Lucia wasn't imagining it anymore. Someone was tracking her. The wind cut sharply against her neck. The plaza was empty, but something lurked just out of sight. She could sense a shadow that was not her own. The sun was setting as the light slowly retreated from the skyline.

Lucia looked back at the Basilica. The doors creaked, inviting her in, while the taser pressed cold against her skin, hidden snugly at her side. She had also brought Emi's pocketknife in case she needed to open any locks.

She slipped inside. The pews were full, churchgoers fixated on Father Roderick as his sermon echoed through the vaulted stone walls. His chalice sat on the lectern, a smear of his papery lips pressed against the copper rim. Lucia exhaled. The sound caught the attention of a baby perched over its mother's shoulder. Its blue eyes—wide, unblinking.

She averted her gaze, shuffling into the back pew.

If she hadn't seen the news, she'd never have known the homeless had taken refuge in the church during the storm, everything was perfectly arranged. There weren't even skid marks on the Spanish marble floor, not a single fleck to hint that a hundred homeless from the Anastasia Forest had slept there the night before.

"Thank you all for being here today. We were lucky—the hurricane only clipped us—but it still wiped out homeless shelters across the city. Our helpers will now pass around the donation bags to support those left with nothing," said Father Roderick from the lectern, prompting two altar boys to shuffle down the aisle, their purple velvet bags outstretched like fishing nets.

Everyone stood and stretched, their rustling clothes masking Lucia's approach to the heavy oak door, its iron-rung handle the last barrier to the tunnels.

"I will now offer the chance for those seeking absolution to come to the confessional." Father Roderick still hadn't noticed Lucia as he stepped down from the altar, making his way toward the confessional hidden in the shadowed wings of the Basilica. The confessional booth was made of aged walnut, so dark it looked like a gothic dollhouse carved into the trunk of a dead tree. The twin doors each had small windows, veiled by a mesh grille that reduced anyone inside the booth to a mere shadow.

A small line of about six churchgoers had formed in front of the booth. Lucia figured it would give her enough time to snoop unnoticed. In the pews, a gaze met hers—an eye, not human, but inked into the bare skin of a bald head. It was Jonny the Giant. His tattooed eye sat unblinking at the center of an ink-black hand; fingers splayed like a ritual sigil across his scalp. He was lining up for confession. Lucia swallowed.

Before she second-guessed herself, she heaved open the door, careful to feel her step before descending the stairs. She flicked the light switch, illuminating the cobblestone passage. A spider scuttled into the sediment-filled gaps between the stones, and stale air seeped out. Everything felt different this time as she scanned the tunnel for offshoots she might have missed. According to Emi's book, this was one of the entry points to a vast network of old Spanish tunnels hidden beneath the city. But last time she was here, there had been no sign of it—just a dead-end corridor leading to a locked storage room.

She pressed deeper into the passage, passing a series of alcoves repurposed for storing broken pews and discarded lecterns.

Finally, she reached the locked door at the end of the tunnel, where the passage abruptly stopped. The rock at the tunnel's end didn't sit flush with the wall—there was a rivet, a break in the stone. The newer cobblestone was a chalky yellow, its cracks free of sediment, unlike the older, weathered blocks lining the passage.

Lucia pushed the stone, but it was immovable. *Emi couldn't have come this way.*

She turned to the storage room, trying to pry open the lock, but her usual tricks failed. Father Roderick must have changed it since her last break-in. Gritting her teeth, Lucia pulled out the pocketknife, recalling the other method Javier had taught her. She angled the blade like his wrench and worked it into the mechanism, hoping for the same luck.

After a few minutes of fiddling, it popped open.

Dust motes swirled like a swarm of restless fireflies, disturbed by her unwanted intrusion. She smothered a cough into her sleeve, then stepped inside. The wardrobe of the priest's robes loomed in the corner, its door slightly ajar. Maya's box sat untouched, wedged between towering stacks of cardboard that pressed in too tightly. Something had changed since her last visit—the shadows were pooling in corners where they hadn't been before. The space felt tighter, the air heavier, as if the room itself were holding its breath.

Emi had been here.

She scanned the stacks, noting the masking tape peeling from the older boxes at the bottom. Most were archives—communion records for the wealthier kids from the east side of the city. She wasn't sure how they would have labeled Maya's special English class, or if it was even here.

Before she could find out, another box caught her eye.

Donations – Confidential

She slid out the box, its weight immediately pulling it hard to the ground. Inside were heavy, paper-bound ledgers. Flipping through the pages, she searched for the date of Emi and Maya's deaths. Most entries listed donations of around $10,000, accompanied by words like "bequeathed" or "trust."

But a few months before Maya died, the numbers shifted. A string of $250,000 donations appeared, each marked with little more than a title: "Project: Fountain of Youth."

Signed by Rami Garcia.

The indulgent cursive scribble could only belong to a self-aggrandizing man like him. The other entries were mainly signed off by Father Roderick. But there was another difference too; they listed bank details, while Garcia's had none, implying they were paid in cash.

Lucia looked toward the door, listening for any sounds in the tunnel. A slow, deliberate drip echoed, slithering through stone and feeding the moss between the cracks. She felt it on her skin as her goosebumps pricked at the thought of what was hiding in the tunnels.

She scanned the other labels on the boxes. Then she saw it.

Project: Fountain of Youth

The sagging cardboard box bulged under the weight of its contents, its seams on the verge of splitting. Lucia rose onto her toes, carefully sliding it from its place. Inside, the box was a mess of random items. There were a few tattered copies of *Romeo and Juliet* as well as *Macbeth*, their spines cracked. Scattered résumés, printed on cheap paper, some creased, others smudged with fingerprints.

Then, beneath the clutter, a folded newspaper clipping caught her eye.

✦

Mayor Pledges Funding for Basilica Literacy Program

Mayor Garcia has announced a new city initiative to invest in a literacy program managed by the Basilica. The program purports to provide homeless individuals with 'essential reading and writing skills' to help them secure and maintain employment. This masthead is the first to support a literary education, but many are questioning how it will help to clean up the streets. The mayor was quoted in a recent speech:

"Our homeless people have enormous potential, but they have been neglected by a system that penalizes those who lack basic literacy skills. How can we expect them to apply for jobs or create CVs when they don't have the tools to do so? Literacy remains one of the greatest barriers to meaningful employment."

The mayor has made cleaning up the streets one of his campaign promises, spending big to solve the homeless crisis. Many have criticized the program, labeling it as a 'book club for bums' and demanding more tangible reform to solve the underlying issues. However, Father Roderick has applauded the work of the mayor, saying that these types of programs will have an immensely positive effect, especially for the younger people living on the streets.

✢

Lucia put down the article. Something felt wrong about the flimsy cardboard box that was all that remained of a program that spent nearly a million dollars on a bundle of Shakespeare books.

At the end of the article, there was a photo of Garcia standing with the priest. The two men were smiling together. Maya was in the photo as well. There were a bunch of boys and girls in front of them. All smiling.

Her heart stopped.

Garcia was in the program alongside Father Roderick. They would have met her brother. She scanned the faded newspaper picture for Emi, but his hopeful smile was nowhere to be seen. She set the newspaper back in the box, sifting through the contents to find anything else.

There were a few other newspaper clippings. Someone had cut pages from the paper, collecting headlines the same way she had in her scrapbook. She flipped through them—missing persons, other tragedies—until she saw it.

Emi.

His disappearance. Then the article from when his body washed ashore at Anastasia Beach. Her grip tightened as she scanned the rest—a string of other names, mostly girls. She studied their faces, holding them up to group photos from Maya's English class. A few were exact matches. At least three were identical. Then she picked up one with a face she recognized.

✦

Authorities Seek Information on Missing Teen, Marti Cortez

Authorities are searching for 15-year-old Marti Cortez, who has been missing for over two months. Cortez, described as Hispanic in appearance with a tattoo above her thigh and a birthmark on her left ear.

Her parents, undocumented immigrants who arrived in the U.S. a year ago, hesitated to report her missing. They were employed picking fruit, where they worked long hours in difficult conditions in Louisiana. Believing Marti had found work washing dishes at a friend's restaurant in Florida, and staying at a nearby motel, they only realized she was missing after weeks passed without contact.

However, the restaurant has no record of her employment, and staff do not recall anyone matching her description. She was last seen reading *Macbeth* outside of the St. George Tavern. Authorities urge anyone with information to come forward.

✦

She was the missing girl from the police station, the one who was last seen with Emi.

She studied the faces of the girls in the newspaper clippings, comparing them to the photo of Maya's English class. A pattern emerged—all between 15 and 22 years old, mostly Hispanic. Their names were Mexican, just like Lucia's. Just like Emi's.

✠

Father Roderick seemed to orchestrate everything from the shadows—inviting the homeless into the Basilica, accepting Garcia's donations for the program in secret while he hid Maya's bloody book in the basement. She remembered the way he cried, there was a deep shame that seemed to permeate through him, overflowing as tears. There was a paper trail of money from Garcia to the Basilica. Her brother had tried to break in before he was put in a jail cell.

She slipped the boxes back, closing the door as she made her way to the confessional booth. Images of the saint of death swirled in her mind as the shadows contorted into silhouettes at the edge of her vision. The church program would make a perfect pipeline—misplaced Social Security numbers, vanished records, lives that no one would trace.

She raced up the stairs, the taser in her pocket. The line for the confessional had halved. Jonny the Giant sat in the pew, staring vacantly at the walnut confessional booth.

He locked eyes onto Lucia.

His eyes flashed briefly before fading back to emptiness. Intermittently, she looked over her shoulder as Jonny's eyes drooped in and out of sleep. He was waiting for something.

An old man wandered into the booth but stepped out only moments later, his expression somber yet serene.

Lucia moved forward with the line, glancing at the flickering votive candles, at the carved wooden pews—anywhere but behind her. Still, the image lingered—Garcia and Father Roderick in the photo, their smiles steady, unreadable.

Then it was her turn. The Basilica had emptied, leaving only Jonny the Giant and her.

She stepped inside the booth. A a thin grille separated them. All she could see was his shadow, but his scent seeped through the tiny holes in the grille. She recognized the sweat drenched cotton from when she hid in the wardrobe. It was him.

"May the Lord be in your heart and help you to confess your sins with true sorrow. What is it that you wish to confess today?" asked Father Roderick.

"I have nothing to confess," Lucia said, her words faltering as she struggled to push past the fear.

"I beg your pardon." There was a long pause. "This is a confessional. You have come to be absolved of your sins."

Lucia hesitated, then straightened. She let the silence settle before she spoke.

"What about you?" she asked, her voice quiet but steady now, the anger beneath it controlled.

Lucia saw his shadow shift.

"It's you," he said softly, the grille masking any subtle expressions on his face.

Lucia leaned in. "Why are you hiding things?"

"You don't understand," he murmured. "I have no choice."

"No choice," she repeated, quieter this time, like the words tasted wrong. "Then explain the photos in the basement. Explain the disappearances."

She could hear him wheezing for breath, the shallow inhales filled the booth with warm, wine laced air.

"You are mistaken." His voice was paralyzed by fear. Father Roderick had the same tinge of shame that her mother had when speaking about Emi.

"What happened to Marti? To my brother? To all the people the world pretends don't exist—like they were never here at all?"

Father Roderick coughed violently. He tapped his chest. "We cannot speak of that."

His breath warmed the grille between them. "They are here."

Lucia's grip tightened on the taser in her pocket.

"What do you do to them?" she pressed. "Is this some perverted sacrifice? Some death cult."

"Please," he whispered urgently. "Be quiet."

"Who?"

"Shhh!"

A long, ragged exhale.

"You don't know the weight I bear," he murmured, his voice so soft she had to lean forward to hear it. "If I speak, others will be punished."

Lucia's pulse pounded. "How convenient," she said, voice dripping with venom. "A vow of silence makes a good shield, doesn't it?"

"I was friends with your brother."

"That's a lie."

"He loved you," the priest murmured. "He used to talk about watching *The Crocodile Hunter* with you. Said that's why he wanted to get better. Even after everything else."

The priest hesitated.

"You need to leave," he said finally. "You're not safe."

A shadow passed outside the booth.

Father Roderick's voice rose, shifting into something performative, something loud enough for the outsider to hear.

"It is okay, child," he said, his tone a warm, pastoral mask. "Doubt is part of faith. We all struggle with temptation."

Lucia stiffened.

"What are you doing?" she whispered.

His voice dropped, barely reaching her ears. "I told you. I cannot say."

Then, louder—pointedly—for the person outside: "Tell me about the last time you sinned."

"Is it the man outside?" Lucia whispered.

The priest went silent.

"Is Garcia here?" Lucia asked. "The liar."

Then, something cracked in his voice, something desperate.

"Why do you think Garcia has stayed silent?" he rasped. "Why do you think we lied about the wedding in the woods? His children aren't safe. That's why I had to lock Maya's book away—where no one else can see it."

Maya's book.

Lucia's heart pounded.

"What happened to Marti?" she pressed.

Father Roderick suddenly raised his voice, his tone taking on the cadence of a sermon, words chosen as much for the person outside as for Lucia.

"Some people have no value for life. No beauty in the eyes of a newborn. They see death as a butcher sees a lamb—no soul, just blood to be washed away with the entrails. I have met them. Their hearts beat with thick, black blood, slowing their pulses to a dull thud."

He took a breath. Then, quieter, just for her.

"They worship the saint of death."

Then, suddenly—movement. A sharp sound outside.

Lucia barely registered the priest shifting. A thin slit opened between them in the booth. A piece of paper passed through.

She took it, fingers trembling. The priest scrawled something in hurried, uneven letters.

Go to the Anastasia forest. The Spanish used to keep their gold in a tunnel near Anastasia Beach. Here you will find Marti. Your brother was last there.

Lucia's mind flashed to Emi's book. The page with the tunnel, the historian's note: *Sealed 1962. Deemed hazardous.*

A sharp knock on the confessional door.

"They're here," Father Roderick breathed, so faintly it was almost swallowed by the silence.

Lucia went still.

"Stay quiet." His voice was barely a whisper—just the shape of words slipping through his breath.

"How do you know?" she whispered.

"They've been watching you since you entered." His shadow shifted. "Listen carefully—behind the panel to your left, there's a latch, it will open to my private passage."

Lucia's fingers traced the wood, feeling for the seam.

"Go," he said, his voice barely more than air. "Now."

RETURN TO THE FOREST

The forest groaned, timber creaking under the weight of the wind. Lucia stood at its edge, the night closing in around her. She had slipped out of the Basilica through a private passage Father Roderick used between sermons. Now, the cold clung to her skin as she thought of the tattooed men on her trail.

Past the parking lot, the last streetlights bled into the shadows between the oaks. She'd walked this path countless times, tracing the familiar route to the shore to collect shells. But now, everything felt warped—distorted by what she knew. The tunnel beneath the homeless camp. The money Garcia had poured into a project no one seemed to know about. Emi had been taken there. Now Marti.

Lucia flipped the taser prongs forward and pressed the button, her grip tightening. She didn't know who to trust. The electric charge crackled to life with all the force of a million insects being fried to death. For a second, she considered turning back. But then she glanced at the empty parking lot, where a few stray mutts feasted on an upturned trash can. They growled when she looked at their food.

She took her first step into the tree line. Instantly, the cold welcomed her back, the soft sand an old friend underfoot. The streetlights disappeared from view as she ventured deeper. Moonlight doused the forest in a purple mist, where the trees stood like trench-coated men and the ground and sky blurred into one. She remembered Emi reading her *Grimms' Fairy Tales*, the way he spoke about forests as if they were alive, watching. Now, she could see it—the branches shifted like shadow puppets, their crooked twig fingers inviting her deeper. She focused only on each step as she scurried between the oaks for cover.

Soon she was surrounded by the dark woods on all sides. She scanned the silhouettes, searching for the dim glow of embers or the dull sheen of a tent. Something that marked the edge of the homeless camp, where the tunnel entrance lay hidden beneath. The tunnel couldn't be too close to the shore; the sand was too loose. It had to be deeper inland, where the oak roots held the earth firm. Lucia traced them into the densest part of the forest.

Then she heard it—something distant, unnatural. It wasn't constant like the breeze or sporadic like the chirp of a tree frog. It came in muffled bursts, rising and falling every few minutes.

Sobbing.

She followed the sound as her compass bearing, her finger hovering over the taser, ready to zap the shadows. The soft sand gave way to packed earth, knotted with roots that caught at her steps.

The sobbing was getting louder.

She quickened her pace, imagining Emi walking this same path. In the distance, a tent came into view. There was a small break in the brush, just wide enough for a single tent. The shoreline was somewhere beyond the trees, but she couldn't tell how far—only that the salt in the air thickened with each gust of wind.

The sobbing came from the tent.

Lucia edged closer, each step slow and deliberate. The tent's cords were tightly secured to two trees, its blue canvas flapping helplessly in the wind.

She whispered, "Marti?"

No reply.

She tightened her grip on the taser, forcing herself not to think about what else might be lurking in the shadows. She was close enough now to touch the fabric. She dropped to all fours, reaching for the zipper. The metal was ice against her fingers.

Breathe.

The sobbing was loud. Her heart pounded.

In one swift motion, she unzipped the tent flap. The screech of the zipper rattled her bones. Inside, a pair of eyes met hers. The girl didn't move. They locked eyes like two animals in the dark, unsure which was predator and which was prey.

"It's okay. I'm a friend," Lucia said.

The girl clambered under the blankets, her voice quivering.

"Don't hurt me. Please. Please. Let me live."

"I'm not here to hurt you," Lucia said, raising her hands.

A flashlight beam hit Lucia's eyes, blinding her.

"What do you want?" the girl demanded. The harsh light made Lucia shield her face with her forearm.

"Can you lower that? I can't see."

Neither of them moved. Slowly, the girl lowered the flashlight, its harsh beam shrinking to reveal the shadows of her face.

'Marti?' The girl flinched. It was her.

She looked nothing like the poster. If it weren't for the tattoo on her thigh, Lucia wouldn't have recognized her. Her eyes were bloodshot, her skin damp with night sweats. She was like a wild animal, trembling uncontrollably. The beam from her flashlight wavered, sending scattered Morse code into the night.

"I just want to talk."

"Are you one of them?" Marti asked in a Mexican accent.

"Who?"

"Them." The girl could barely form full sentences. Each word seemed to cost her.

"I'm here to save you," Lucia whispered, pronouncing every word clearly.

"From who?"

"From everyone here. From Father Roderick. From Garcia."

Marti started shaking her head.

"No. They're my friends."

"They're going to hurt you," Lucia pleaded. She was running out of time. They were being too loud—the rest of the homeless camp would have already heard them.

"They can save me," Marti said, staring at the ceiling of the tent as if it were full of stars.

"Save you from what? What's wrong?"

The girl broke down, curling into a ball, rocking back and forth like an egg about to splatter.

"Him. Him. He will find me. He finds everyone who runs away."

"Who? I can help you. But only if you tell me—who are you running from?"

The girl didn't answer. Her body trembled so violently that Lucia thought she was convulsing. Then, she spotted something beside Marti's head—a small plastic bag. She picked it up and emptied it onto the sleeping mat. A lighter. Some cigarettes. A few syringes.

The logo stamped onto them made her stomach drop.

A Spanish galleon.

El Dorado Dust.

The rustling of the plastic bag sent Marti into a frenzy.

"Give them to me!"

She lunged, clawing for the syringes. One rolled under the sleeping bag. She scrambled, tossing everything in the tent.

"Come with me. I can save you," said Lucia.

Marti barely seemed to hear her. The moment her fingers closed around the syringes, her breathing slowed. Her glassy gaze lifted to

Lucia, detached, as if she were somewhere far away.

"Please. I can help you."

She curled into the corner of the tent, clutching the syringes with a desperate grip as she knelt, shaking.

"I'm safe here," she whispered. "He can't find me."

"Who are you running from?"

The girl didn't say anything. She moved her finger so subtly that Lucia mistook it for a tremor in her hands. But then her finger froze as she pointed to something on the floor. It was in the corner of the tent. The playing card lay face up.

It was the card of death.

The skeleton winked at her. Lucia froze now. It couldn't have been Lucia's card—she kept it buried deep in her jeans pocket, buttoned up tight. Instinctively, she reached into her pocket to check, just to be sure. Her hands went numb when she felt it. Her card was still there. She pulled out the identical card and showed it to the girl. Now the girl started to cry.

"He's coming for you. We are dead. Both dead." The girl howled in hysterics.

"They're harming a patient," a voice came from outside.

Suddenly, the tent flap rustled. Lucia spun, taser in hand, ready to strike.

"Lucia," a voice said.

Lucia froze, stopping her thrust of the taser just a few inches from his chest. *How did he know her name?*

She stepped outside the tent, blinking against the glare of a dozen flashlights. A semicircle of figures stood a few feet away, surrounding her. The man in front, taller than the rest, stood with an arched back. She knew he was the leader—the others tracked his every movement, waiting for a command.

"We're not here to hurt you," he said, his voice calm but tense.

"I'm Tom."

She kept the taser raised, her grip tight.

Before she could respond, a bony arm flashed in her periphery, and something rough tightened around her head—a blindfold.

She twisted, swinging the taser wildly.

"Damn it, she got me!" someone yelped.

A boot slammed into her wrist. The taser flew from her grip, her fingers were instantly numb. She was defenseless now.

"Take her to the fire."

THE FIRE

She could hear the fire—the crackle and hiss of dry wood splintering as flames wisped through the crevices. They'd blindfolded her and sat her down on what must've been a tree stump. She felt the fuzz of hot air blowing against her skin, shifting with the wind's sharp turns. On all sides, she was surrounded by laughter. The festive mood unsettled her, a tension in the air—as if everyone were waiting to feast.

Suddenly, a metallic clang echoed against the glass.

"Tonight we celebrate." It was a toast. The background chatter died down as a man continued to speak. "The hurricane may have slowed us, but it won't stop our operation. I want to thank each of you for restoring our facilities so quickly. Without us, our patients would have no other options. They have been abandoned by a city that prefers to profit on their plight, so corrupted by money that even the human soul has a price. Although our resources are limited, we possess something no one else in this city can offer, time. And time is exactly what our patients need most. So I'd like to raise a toast. To saving the city."

The audience erupted into cheers. Tin cups clanked as chants harmonized.

"Save the city!"

"Save the city!"

"Save the city!"

"Now we eat," yelled the man triumphantly. There was more applause. The energy was building. Lucia wriggled her wrists—nothing. No ropes, no restraints. They hadn't bound her.

For a moment, she didn't move. Why were they so confident she wouldn't run?

The laughter continued as she waited for an opportunity to rip off the blindfold.

"Darling, do you want some food?" came a lady's voice.

Lucia cautiously took off the blindfold. In front of her, there was a lady who looked like she had been pretty thirty years ago, holding out a bowl full of sludge.

"It's good stuff," said the lady with a smile, revealing three missing teeth.

"No thank you," said Lucia, confused. She looked around the bonfire. There were about forty homeless people sitting on logs and battered camp chairs as they chatted and laughed. On the far side, there was a man with a tattered chef hat and an enormous pot of stew. He ladled the thick, murky mixture into whatever containers people had—cans, cups, trays. There was no cutlery; people slurped the sludge straight from their containers, ravenously tonguing them clean.

Lucia scanned the crowd, searching for Marti. Nothing. Her gaze darted to the far side of the fire—no Tom either. The laughter, the celebration—it all felt *wrong*. Like she had stepped into a play where everyone knew their lines except her.

No one seemed to notice her, not even the bony man who had blindfolded her. He was smiling, slurping his sludge, treating her like she wasn't even there. Lucia couldn't wait for them to finish eating. From a crouch, she slowly shuffled backward. Only the toothless lady seemed to notice her slipping away.

"It was lovely to meet you, darling. I've heard so many good things about you from your brother," said the woman. *What was going on?* Lucia rose slowly, heart hammering. One step back. Another. Still, no one looked. The laughter, the clinking of tin cups—it continued like she didn't exist. Then she turned and ran. No one called after her. No one followed. That was worse.

Lucia was deep in the encampment. Dozens of tents surrounded her, with plastic bottles littered everywhere and a maze of tent cords. She scanned the horizon for Marti's blue tent, but it was hopeless— she had no idea where it was, not after being blindfolded on the way to the fire. She felt vulnerable without the taser in the dark, especially knowing they had it. She reached into her jeans for her pocketknife. She flicked open the blade, the steel shaking in the air as she ventured deeper into the darkness. Lucia kept scanning for the tent or any sign of the entrance to the tunnels.

"Marti?" she whispered. Nothing. Then she saw a silhouette in the distance. It was a man—he was looking for something. All at once she felt like she was in the moonlight wedding, watching the shadow who lurked in the woods. The shadow seemed to follow her everywhere she went. She steadied her breath. But now, she was the one following the shadow, tracking it from twenty yards back. After a few more steps, the shadow stopped. They turned around. She could see his face—it was Tom. He made eye contact before looking down at the knife.

"Lucia. Please put the knife down. We are friends," he said.

Lucia's hand shook.

"Please, I only want to show you the truth," he said.

A twig snapped behind her.

Before she could react, an arm wrapped around her torso, yanking her off the ground. The impact knocked the knife out of her hands. She tried to scream, but her face was pressed into a hairy chest as someone carried her like a loaf of squished bread. She couldn't move.

The man smothered her with his body, constricting every limb with his big bear hands. He was taking her somewhere—marching.

"Get me some rope," yelled the man. She bit his chest. But nothing happened. There was no sound, not even a frustrated exhale. Only marching. Left, right, left. He knew where he was taking her. He squeezed her tighter. Then ducked. She felt the tree bristle against her back.

"Be still," he said gently as he pinned her against the tree.

"Tie her," Tom said. "Be gentle." The bony man who blindfolded her rushed forward, rope in hand. He dropped to his knees, quickly binding her wrists before securing her to the tree. The big bear man kept her pressed against the trunk. He pushed hard on her collarbone, his breath hot and heavy. Lucia squirmed, but he held her firm. With a burst of defiance, she spat in his face. The glob of spit hit him above the eye. He looked at her, calmly wiping off the spit.

"We only want to help," he said. His lack of anger scared her. If he were angry, at least she knew what she was dealing with. But there was a sickly calmness to the man, a detachment from reality, that was far more terrifying than the most violent scream. The bony man yanked the rope tighter.

"That's tight enough," Tom said. "We'll be back. We have things to show you."

They left. Lucia cursed herself for dropping the pocketknife. She tried to wriggle her arms free, but the rope only cut deeper into her skin. Desperate, her eyes darted across the ground for anything she could use—rocks, sticks, something sharp. But there was nothing. This was how she was going to die, just like her brother. She had to leave a message for her mother—something to make her believe, to let her know she was right. They took him. She wasn't crazy. She wrestled against the rope so hard she could barely breathe. But it was useless. There was no slack, and it just got tighter like a boa constrictor going for the kill. She thought about screaming. But who would hear? *The sea? The wind?*

Instead, she waited.

After a while, a voice spoke from the darkness.

"Lucia? Are you going to play nice now?"

"Yes," she lied.

"We're not here to hurt you. Someone wants to speak with you."

Lucia prepared the saliva in her mouth—the only weapon she had. Just as she was about to spit, she saw Marti's face. She looked less wild now, as if the storm inside her had finally stilled.

"Are you okay?" said Lucia, her hands tied to the tree. "What did they do to you?"

"They are helping me."

The girl crouched under the tree, sitting next to Lucia. She leaned against the base of the magnolia, so the two were side by side.

"I'm sick. They have medicine here," she said in her heavy Spanish accent.

"Who told you to come here?" said Lucia.

"An angel."

"What? An angel?"

"Her name was Maya. She helped me. Because I ran away from them."

"Who is them?"

The girl's expression changed when she mentioned them. The fear was back.

"They gave you the card, didn't they?" Lucia asked. Marti remained silent. Lucia wriggled her bound hands, managing to hook her forefinger into her pocket. She tapped the card free, and it fell to the forest floor. Marti looked at it and began to shake.

"Who is 'they'?" Lucia pressed.

"Mr. Muerte," Marti whispered. "He can make murder look like

Mother Nature."

Lucia's heart pounded as she heard his name spoken by a native Spanish speaker.

"What does he look like?" she asked.

"No one sees him," Marti said, her voice trembling. "But they always talk about him."

"Who talks about him?"

"The men... the ones who work for them." Marti's gaze dropped, her voice faded.

Lucia's stomach churned. She could feel the fear coiling around Marti's words, squeezing tighter.

"Did they kill my brother?"

"Emi tried to save me," she said.

Lucia strained against the rope, wanting nothing more than to shake the answer out of her. "What happened?" she said, each word grinding through clenched teeth.

"He will show you. You will see."

The girl got up from the tree and shuffled away.

"Lucia?" It was Tom.

"We're going to untie you now. We only tied you up for your own safety. But you have to promise me you'll do nothing stupid." Lucia didn't say anything. Tom crouched under the tree, crawling toward her. He held her knife in his hands.

"I'm going to give you this so that you feel safe. Okay?"

Lucia glared at him.

"But you have to promise that you'll listen to us first. We have a lot to show you. And if you run off and do something stupid, you won't be able to get the answers you need."

"Okay," Lucia said. She would wait. He began cutting the rope, his hands so close she could see the veins. She watched until the last thread was cut loose. Finally, she was free. The knife in her hands, she got up.

"This way." He turned his back, giving her another opportunity to run, but he knew the leverage he had over her. Lucia followed him out from under the tree. The bonfire was dying, along with the celebrations. Now, all the homeless around the fire watched her, they had such sorry faces, as if they could apologize with just a stare. The toothless lady gave Lucia a pity smile before quickly looking to the bottom of her empty plate, a sad morsel of potato all that was left.

Tom led Lucia deeper into the camp, the embers becoming a distant glow as they wove silently through the maze of tent cords. Soon it was just the two of them. She flicked open the knife, anxiously.

"Be patient. You haven't given me enough time," he said, sensing the blade. They moved deeper into the dark, the faint murmur of the camp fading behind them. Tom glided through the trees with surprising ease. She thought he was a lumbering oaf, but each step was as soft as hers, despite being five times her size. His back hunched, shoulders curving forward, as if his head were a compass needle, following some unseen magnetic force.

"Here," Tom said, stopping at a depression in the ground. The dense tangle of palmettos told Lucia they were nearing Marti's tent.

Dead leaves had collected in the hollow, masking the edge of something metallic. He brushed them aside, revealing a rusted hatch set in concrete.

"It used to be an old Spanish escape route," he said, fingers tracing the corroded edge. "Connected to all the tunnels under the city. Back then, if they needed to flee to the sea, this was the way. But most of the tunnels collapsed ages ago. Now, it's just a disconnected bunker."

"How'd you find it?" Lucia asked.

"I borrowed a book a while ago, *The Tunnels of St. Augustine*. I was looking for a place to sleep where I wouldn't get robbed. It said that there was an entrance point out here in the forest, well away from everyone else. But I realized the Spanish used magnetic north, not true north, so each location on the map was off by about fifty yards."

The hinges groaned as he heaved it open, and a beam of white light surged into the night sky. The bunker was so brightly lit below that the escaping glow rose like the trunk of a ghostly magnolia.

"After you," he said, gesturing to the ladder.

"You first," Lucia said, still clutching the knife for comfort. Tom didn't argue and climbed down. Lucia paused, thinking of Emi going down the same tunnel. She pictured the skeletal saint of death lurking below, licking the marrow from her lips. *Was she walking into a trap?*

The forest was eerily still, even the frogs seemed to temporarily pause their croaking. If she ran now, no one would stop her. One step back, and she could vanish into the trees. She exhaled sharply.

She had to know.

Lucia swung her legs over the edge and began her descent. The ladder plunged into the earth, each rung like the vertebrae of a vast iron spine, spiraling endlessly downwards.

When her feet finally hit the ground, she turned—and froze.

Rows of hospital beds filled the bunker. Stark white sheets covered still bodies, pulled tight. Six patients lay motionless, IV lines snaking from their arms to silent, gleaming stands. The only confirmation they were alive was the steady beep from the green machines that measured their heart rates.

"Welcome to the program," said Tom, motioning to the refurbished bunker. It had an arched ceiling of exposed brick, extending a dozen feet off the ground. The cobblestone was washed out under the harsh lights, making even the old rock seem surgically sterile.

"Garcia and the church paid for this?" Lucia said, remembering the secret donations in cash to the supposed literacy program.

"Yes, he helped us fund the reconstruction," he said. "Our operation is more expensive than we can afford. Let me show you something."

Tom strolled through the aisles of beds, standing next to the nearest patient's bed. The patient looked unconscious, shifting restlessly in his bed. Lucia recognized his bearded face—the man from the underpass. The one who had pulled a knife on her, jittery, acting like there were slugs beneath his skin.

"Hello, Chris. We've come to check on you."

Chris was murmuring something to himself, but he didn't even notice them. Tom reached in to grab something on the bedside table. It was a mortar and pestle. He passed it to Lucia.

"Take this." She stepped forward cautiously, inspecting the object. It seemed safe to touch. The scent was earthy, with hints of crushed herbs and something rich and fungal, like dried mushroom stalks.

"It's our secret ingredient."

"For what?" asked Lucia.

"To save our patients."

"What are you doing to them?"

"We are helping them overcome their addiction," said Tom. "You met Marti before, she is not ready for treatment. Our patients have to choose this path. Marti is still battling with some demons, the darkness in her past is so strong that only she can make the decision."

"My brother was here?"

"Yes," Tom said, the question clearly made him uncomfortable.

Lucia's gaze flicked over the rows of patients—half-conscious figures, their faces gaunt and hollow. Most looked like they had come from the streets, murmuring in their sleep, tangled in IV lines.

"You didn't save him," she said, her voice low and uncertain now.

"He was the only one we couldn't help," Tom murmured.

"You killed him." Her whole body was shaking.

"We tried to save him," Tom repeated.

Lucia stepped back. She was angry now. The knife shook in her hand.

"Your brother came here because he needed help. He was dying, and we were his only option."

"You killed him."

"No, we were saving him."

Lucia couldn't see Chris's face anymore—only her brother's. Rocking back and forth, murmuring words to himself. He looked so afraid. She squeezed the knife tighter.

"How can I believe anything you say? You helped Garcia and the priest kill Maya." said Lucia, trying to make sense of the rows of hospital beds in the tunnel.

"What?" said Tom, confused. "Garcia and Maya believed in us."

"You're some kind of death cult—you worship it," Lucia said, slowly backing away.

"No. We worship life." Tom held up the mortar and pestle for her to see.

"You think these are just some junkies whose worthless lives you can take to please your god. The mushrooms—is this what you use to euthanize them?"

"No, Lucia. You have no idea what dope does. A life spent on it— that is death. It's a waking nightmare." His words were damning. As if Lucia of all people wouldn't know what addiction did to people, did to Emi. She started to feel her heart hammer in her chest, wanting to run away.

Tom seemed to feel sorry upon seeing this and softened.

"I know why it might seem like that but that's not what we're doing here. It's confronting. But you're just confused. Please listen to me. Look at this closely."

Lucia squinted at the mushroom pulp, staying a few feet away.

"This saved my life," he said, his voice oddly earnest. "I know because I was an addict. Like Emi."

✦

"I remember the first time I saw dope. It's like the memory of an old girlfriend, one that gets sweeter each year that passes. I didn't ask for it but it had a way of finding me. When I first saw it, I thought it would kill me. I liked the idea of that—so I took the syringe and injected myself, hoping to die. But something worse happened.

"I felt amazing. It's difficult to explain, but it was like I was in the womb again. I felt all the promise of being a baby: stem cells, warm milk, and whispers of how strong I'd become. I don't know how long I spent in there, but I never wanted to leave. What came after was the worst feeling of my life—knowing I could never have it again. It took me a while to understand that once you've had everything, you can never live with less. That was the beginning of the end. I lived on the street for the next twenty years, and had an addiction to dope so bad that I never saw my parents again.

"I used to be the golden child. At school, I was captain of the football team, valedictorian, and prom king. My dad would brag about me to strangers on the bus. Every Christmas, the stories were always about me—the time I saved the cousins from creepy Pete, the touchdowns, my long list of girlfriends.

"I wanted to join the Navy when I graduated, taking after my father. He was a frogman in the Vietnam War. I signed the papers with the recruiter who jumped out of his chair when I told him that I wanted to be a Seal. He'd seen me play football. I felt good, I was in perfect shape and it seemed like those days would never end.

"Then there was the accident. I remember it clearly: we were boating in the Everglades, me and the boys. Celebrating just 'cause we'd gotten into Florida State.

"My buddy at the wheel had taken a corner too fast, and the boat flipped. My back got crushed. They hauled me out of the water and rushed me to the hospital. No health insurance and no coverage because I was still two weeks shy of starting my Navy training. I was screwed.

"It was just excruciating. The accident herniated two discs in my spine, pinching nerves. I wanted to cry every time I went up the stairs. My parents remortgaged their house just to cover the cost of the surgery, and it just got worse. The surgeon caused permanent nerve damage near my spine. He said I'd never be able to throw a football again, let alone dive off boats for a living. Everything I'd planned for was gone.

"Still, I could deal with that first year because my friends visited every weekend. I think they felt bad for flipping the boat, seeing me crippled while they got on with their lives. But after enough time passes, people stop feeling sorry. They made other friends from their frats.

"So after I got used to the pain, then there was loneliness. I couldn't pass the time with other people anymore. I started counting sheep during the day to force myself to fall asleep. And while I slept through my life it only got worse. My mother had to bring the food to me on the couch. At that time, my father was starting to get uncomfortable, but he was still patient. At least then I was doing odd jobs here and there. My father insisted I keep working, find something, anything. But I burned through job after job, failing my supervisors with missed shifts and a mind that kept slipping into fog. Meanwhile, the pain kept getting worse, and my painkiller dosage could barely keep up. My doctor refused to prescribe more.

"One time my father took me out in the wheelchair, and I blacked out. I just sort of started doing that at some point. And when I woke up back at home, I just had this feeling of shame, but I didn't know why. My father seemed different because he was openly angry when we were home. It turns out that I'd passed out and pissed myself, like some decrepit old man. When my mother brought the plates to me, he picked them up and smashed them on the floor.

"What the hell do you think you're making him into, Nora?" he yelled at her, like she'd fed something forbidden to a stray dog. It finally seemed to hit him. He realized he wouldn't get the money back for my surgery. I would never be the golden child again. I had come to terms with that myself, honestly, but it must have taken longer for him. I'd always wondered if he was proud of me because of my achievements, but then it hurt to really know for sure. Then my father, seeing all of this, announced that he was ready to give up on me, and he threatened to put me out on the street.

"Then one day, an old buddy of mine came to visit. It had been a few years since I'd seen him, but he was the one who flipped the boat. I think he felt the guiltiest of everyone, he'd made lots of money selling oil bonds, and I hadn't left my parent's couch.

"*I heard you've been having a tough time,*" he said.

"*What makes you think that?*"

"*Your old man.*"

"*He talked about me?*"

"*No, he didn't even mention you. That's why I figured something was wrong. He always used to talk about you.*"

He handed me a little syringe.

"*I use it every now and then. Can help with the pain.*"

"So that was the first time I saw dope."

Lucia's stomach clenched.

"You were an addict?"

"Yes. Lived on the streets since that moment. I like to call this mushroom the *Fountain of Youth*." He picked up the stem from the mortar. "The mushroom gives us our youth back, even if the drugs took it away."

"You give it to these people?" Lucia asked, scanning the rows of patients.

"Yes," Tom replied. "The city is overrun with heroin. We hear their stories every day—our medication is their last hope. But the government would never allow us to treat them with another prohibited substance. Garcia and Maya saw the value in what we do. They helped people like your brother. They knew we could save them from their addictions."

He ground the mushroom further in the mortar. "The mushroom blocks the cravings, it rewires the brain so that the opioid receptors reset, breaking the cycle of dependency without withdrawal."

"But you didn't save my brother," Lucia said.

"I'm sorry. It was too late," Tom said gravely. "He had taken too much—his body was shutting down before we could help. The seizures had already started." He looked down at the mortar. "We tried everything, but his system was too far gone."

"You let him die?"

"No..." Tom's voice was heavy with regret. He hesitated, then reached into his bag. "The only thing that could have saved him was this."

He pulled out a nasal spray and passed it to her. "Naloxone. It blocks opioids completely, shuts them out of the brain like they were never there. But we didn't have any left—we only use it in extreme cases because it doesn't treat the addiction, only the immediate overdose."

Lucia stared at the spray. It was small—too small to carry the weight of a life. But it had. If there had been just one more, her brother might still be alive. Her fingers curled around the nozzle, slipping it into her pocket as if it were a shell to remember him by.

"I'm sorry," Tom exhaled. "Your brother loved you."

"Then why did you lie? Why'd you say you never saw him until he washed up on the shore?" she said in a whisper, as a tear rolled down her cheek.

"We needed to protect the program."

"So you made it look like he killed himself?" said Lucia, the tears gone, as the rage returned. "You dragged his body into the sea and left him for the crabs?"

"We didn't have a choice," he said, unable to look at her.

"You always have a choice," she said, the knife shaking in her hands.

"The police would stop our operation if they knew what happened. They'd take us all away, and we wouldn't be able to gather our medicine."

"You lied." Lucia took a step closer, her vision blurring with rage.

"Look at him," he said. "This boy is being saved as we speak. If the police had known about your brother, they would have shut us down. And everyone who came after him—they'd never stand a chance against the dope."

"What about me?" Lucia whispered. "What about his own mother? You never thought to tell the people who actually loved him?"

"I'm sorry. We had to keep it quiet—for the greater good. Your brother was already gone. We just had to get rid of him. The mushroom leaves no trace after a few days. We let the ocean take him, so when the tides brought him back, there'd be nothing left to find."

"Get rid of him," Lucia said. "Like he was just an inconvenience to you."

"You saw the people around the fire. They've changed. Once, they were addicts—nothing to live for, nothing but dope. They'd sell their own babies for it, and some of them did. But now, they have purpose. They're helping others. Emi was part of that."

Lucia stared at him.

"Everyone said he left me," Lucia said softly.

"He loved you. Your name was the last thing he said."

"But he chose to leave me," Lucia said. "I thought someone killed him because he found something in the tunnels. But everyone else was right."

"No, Lucia, you don't understand. What he discovered did kill him. He uncovered things about this city—truths too heavy to carry sober. Your brother was a sensitive soul. Numbing the pain was the only way he could keep helping others."

"What did he find?" asked Lucia.

"He found what they did to Marti. No one else believed him, but he saw what they did to the girls." Tom paused. "It is the same reason why she is not ready for treatment. Sometimes, the burden of reality weighs too heavily on the sober soul."

"They wanted to kill him?" Lucia asked.

"Yes. They were the ones who gave him the card of death," Tom said.

"Who?"

"The people who got us into this problem in the first place," he said, pulling out a syringe from his pocket.

El Dorado Dust

"The people who sell this," he said, pointing at the syringe.

"The cartel."

SIRENS

A swarm of sirens erupted, their echoes rattling through the bunker.

"They're here," Tom muttered.

"The police?"

"Yes," Tom said. "Did anyone follow you here?"

"No."

"Someone must have known," he said rubbing his neck. "Shit. Marti's still in the tent." His breath stuttered. "We have to get to her before they do."

They bolted for the ladder, hearts hammering in sync with the sirens.

As they emerged into the night, red and blue swirls lit up the forest. Flashlights fired, sending beams shooting into the trees. Distant screams cut through the air. Lucia hesitated, unsure where to go.

"They won't get the medicine if they're admitted to hospital," said Tom as he hastily shut the hatch to the bunker.

"I need to find Marti," Tom said, sprinting back to the bonfire.

The campsite had descended into chaos as people scooped up their supplies and split in different directions. The toothless lady tried to drag a garbage bag of her possessions but the plastic punctured, spilling her socks everywhere. She dropped the bag and ran.

A wall of cops advanced. Lucia could count them by the number of beams of light. There were a dozen flashlights, moving in unison,

247

advancing toward the camp. A dog barked. It sounded like one of those big German shepherds.

"Stay where you are!" came a scream from the distance. Beams of light swept the forest, pinning stragglers in their glare. Everyone from the camp scattered in different directions as flashlights futilely tracked them, the forest awash with weaving beams of light, flickering and darting between the trees like erratic fireflies.

"We'll release the dogs! Stay where you are. That's an order."

Lucia didn't move.

"I think I've found the girl," came a scream. The blinding light rooted her to the spot as she tried to shield her eyes.

"Easy now, Lucia. It's just me." The familiar Alabama drawl cut through the dark as the sheriff stepped into view.

"Hold it right there. We're only here to help."

Lucia was tired of everybody saying that. She remembered the way he made her feel in the station, the threat he made about her investigation. Yet here she was, cornered. The light grew brighter, closing in on her as the sheriff approached.

"He's carrying a girl on his back." Suddenly, all the flashlights shifted focus, converging on one focal point. It was Tom. He had Marti slung over his shoulders as he bolted through the forest. Now all the flashlights locked onto him, merging into the intensity of a single, blinding lighthouse.

"Do you have a clear shot?"

"It's too risky."

"Go! Go! Go!"

The cops broke formation, charging after him. A few stragglers from the camp slipped through their ranks unnoticed, as the officers single-mindedly pursued Tom. For a moment, there was no spotlight on Lucia. It was her opportunity. She slipped behind an oak, flattening herself against the trunk, not daring to let even a finger slip into view. A single flashlight whipped back in her direction, but she couldn't be seen now.

"Now, don't be like that, Lucia. We just wanna take you back to your mama." It was the sheriff. He was the only one who hadn't chased after the boy. He clicked his tongue, his voice dripping with coaxed patience, like a hunter luring a fawn.

"You don't belong out here. These ain't good folks."

There was muffled yelling in the distance. Now the forest was eerily quiet, all the stragglers had run away, and it was just the two of them alone with the owls.

"Just gonna drop you home, that's all." His light got closer, scanning the trees. The softness of his voice sent chills down her spine, making her press herself harder against the trunk, as if she could disappear into it. Her breath quickened, she tried to hold the air in her cheeks, to be completely silent. The sheriff's boots squelched into the mud.

"I think we got off on the wrong foot. Let's work together," he said. "Let's find who killed Maya."

As soon as the words left his mouth, an uncomfortable tingle ran through her body. There was something in his words—a tone, a flicker of something sinister. The cone of light narrowed—he was getting closer.

"C'mon, don't make this harder than it needs to be."

Lucia picked up a rock and held it to her chest.

"I just want to help."

The sheriff was so close now, he was about to pass the oak. One more step, and he'd see her.

"Ain't got all night, Lucia."

Lucia hurled the rock in the distance. It struck a neighboring tree with a sharp crack. The sheriff rushed toward it, his gun unholstered, ready to shoot. He had his back turned, offering her a moment to escape. She flung herself from cover, awkwardly finding her feet as she started to run. He must have heard her, but she didn't dare look back. She broke into a full sprint, darting between the trees and leaping over rocks, her lungs burning with every breath—but she didn't care. All that mattered was escaping the forest.

A gunshot split the air.

The bullet tore past her, splintering into a tree just inches away, sending shards of barky shrapnel flying. She turned around. In the distance, she could see the gun. It was aimed right at her. The sheriff was trying to kill her.

"Contact! Armed suspect," he yelled into the forest. There was no one else around to hear his lies. He fired again. The bullet splintered into the bark, shards flying past Lucia's face. Lucia kept running.

She wove between the trees, trying to avoid his flashlight as he lined her up for another shot. *Run.* The third shot whacked wildly to her left, as she reflexively jumped the other way. She took a few paces to rebalance before she sprinted at full speed. In the distance, Lucia could see the glow of streetlights. She was nearly out of the forest. The gunfire stopped now. She didn't turn around as she made the last dash for the street.

She took her final step out of the forest onto the hard concrete. There wasn't time to relax. In front of her, there were four cop cars parked in the street. Most appeared to be empty, but the one farthest away had someone sitting in the front seat with a radio in his hand. He locked eyes with Lucia, his fingers tangling the radio cord as he pulled it closer to his mouth, muttering something inaudible.

A few seconds later, his door swung open.

"Hey! Are you okay?'"

Lucia looked for somewhere to run.

"I have a blanket for you, if you're cold," he said. Lucia nervously turned around—the sheriff would be coming. She ran.

"Where are you going?" yelled the officer.

She sprinted up the sidewalk. Then she heard the sound of an engine. Lucia was certain a police car would be trailing behind her, but to her surprise, an all-black minivan pulled up next to her. The window rolled down, revealing a middle-aged woman.

"Lucia?" the woman called, her car creeping beside her.

"Who are you?" replied Lucia, between heavy breaths as she continued running.

"Get in the car. You're not safe," said the woman.

Lucia didn't stop.

"I'm a friend of Maya," said the lady.

Lucia snapped her head toward the woman, catching a glimpse of her face. Her teeth were strikingly white, her face perfectly made up, and her butter-blonde hair straightened to perfection. She looked familiar, but Lucia couldn't remember where she recognized her from.

"Please. You're not safe, even with the police."

A siren sounded. Lucia turned over her shoulder and saw that the sheriff had just jumped into one of the patrol cars.

"Fine," said Lucia, as she realized she had no other option. The lady slammed on the brakes, and the minivan screeched to a halt. Lucia opened the door of the passenger seat, and before she had time to put on her seatbelt, the vehicle jolted forward. There was a sticker on the dashboard: Children on Board. She glanced into the back seats, spotting all the telltale signs of kids—crumpled chip packets on the floor, a few picture books jammed into the side pockets, and faint smudges on the leather. *Where was she?*

"I'm going to take you somewhere they won't find us."

"Who are you?" asked Lucia again.

"I'm Mrs. Garcia."

Now Lucia could see it. The teeth were exactly like Javier described, so white that they were almost blinding. She couldn't believe she'd finally met the woman she had heard so much about. She remembered the woman's gossip in the laundry.

That raging political sociopath.

She nervously checked to see if the passenger door was locked. The police car was right behind them. Lucia gulped. Mrs. Garcia's knuckles whitened on the wheel as she floored it. There was a corner ahead, but she didn't stop. Instead, she hit it at speed as the wheels drifted underneath them and burnt rubber smoldered into existence. Not long after, the patrol car took the corner too wide and clipped a postbox. The bull bars crushed it, sending a flurry of envelopes exploding into the air as the car powered forward, still on their tail.

"How'd you know I'd be here?" said Lucia nervously, as she kept as much space as she could between herself and Mrs. Garcia.

"We have friends in the force. And so do they," she said, eyes locked on the rearview mirror. "We heard on the radio that they were going to the forest to find you. They must've been tracking you."

Suddenly, Mrs. Garcia wrenched the wheel, sending the car into a violent skid. That moment was all they needed to slip away.

"We're nearly there."

They tore down suburban streets, ignoring the slow-down signs flashing past. Ahead, Lucia spotted an open garage door with a grandmother standing on the curb. Her house was palatial with creamy colored walls and terracotta tiles. The old woman gestured for them to pull in.

"I have someone I'd like you to meet."

They swung into the driveway, gliding into the open garage. Despite her frail appearance, the old woman moved with surprising agility, quickly shutting the gate behind them just as the garage door began to close, hiding them from the cops.

"Lucia, meet Señora Garcia, Mr. Garcia's mother."

SEÑORA'S SAFE HOUSE

"Come sit down, have some tea. You must be exhausted," said Señora Garcia, ushering them to a room down the corridor. Lucia's head was still spinning. The last thing she expected was tea with an old lady in a room that looked like the inside of a gingerbread house. The walls were quilted together with photo frames, prizes and memorabilia, chronicling Garcia's life from boyhood. A photo of him as a child on a tire swing caught her eye—the same slippery smile, as if he were the guest of honor at the swing's grand opening.

"Please, take a seat, darling," Señora Garcia said. There was a leather chesterfield sofa that reminded Lucia of the waiting room for her doctor. She lowered herself onto the couch. She'd barely had time to process anything since leaving the Anastasia Forest. Emi had been trying to heal himself, but she still didn't understand what happened to Maya.

Now, she sat across from Garcia's mother and wife. Señora Garcia's skin was the color of crushed coffee beans, lined with deep, rich wrinkles—much darker than the pale, porcelain tone of Garcia's wife. The two ladies sat opposite Lucia, perched on the edge of the couch, frowning. Lucia scanned the living room. Every window was intact—except one, where a large crack stretched from the top corner. Lucia traced the light's fractured path through the cracked window. Then she saw a mahogany console with a deep dent in the

corner, as if struck by a bat. Strangely, the space above it was empty—
no photo frame. It was the only spot in the house not plastered with
pictures of her son, as if the photo had been removed—or smashed.
Lucia's gaze locked onto the cracked glass.

"Someone broke in?" asked Lucia.

"Yes, they tried to get in through the window," Señora Garcia
said, noticing Lucia's vacant stare. Then she remembered. That was
Garcia's alibi on the night of Maya's murder. Someone had broken
into the house of Garcia's mother.

"If it weren't for my son, I don't know what they would have done
to me," she said, the porcelain cup wobbling in her hands, as her
voice wobbled too.

"What happened?" asked Lucia.

The old lady took a deep breath.

"Two masked men broke in at night. As soon as I heard the glass
smash, I called my son, he always said to call him before the police.
I thought it was just a robbery, but the men didn't want any of my
jewels. They started to smash my vases with their bats, throwing my
crockery, plate by plate. I was scared out of my mind. My son arrived
just after midnight with a gun. They fled after that."

Lucia saw the fear in the old lady's eyes. She thought back to the
syringe Tom had shown her in the forest. *The Cartel.*

"Where is he—Mr. Garcia?" Lucia said.

They fluttered nervous glances between them.

"It's only fair she meets him," Mrs. Garcia said to Señora Garcia.

"Okay. I'll get him."

Señora Garcia pushed herself up with deliberate effort and hobbled down the corridor. Lucia's stomach dropped. In her mind, she'd
treated him as though he were already gone, a character from a far-
away fable. But now she was about to meet the man she had spent so
long trying to understand. She still didn't know what she believed.

Mrs. Garcia cast a nervous glance at Lucia.

"My husband has not been the same since Maya died. He struggles to talk now. But he is a good man, as good as any that has lived."

Suddenly, Mr. Garcia appeared in the doorway. Towering over his mother, he had to pivot his broad shoulders just to enter the room. Yet his back sagged, his head hung low, as if tethered by an invisible cord pulling him down. Lucia had always pictured him in a crisp suit. Now, he slouched in wrinkled black slacks and a faded sweater.

"Hello, Lucia," he said softly. "I'm pleased to finally meet you."

His voice was tired, his lips curved into a soft, fossilized smile, as if unearthed after centuries, before quickly melting away. She could see the shame in his eyes as he retreated to the couch next to Mrs. Garcia. She had imagined him hiding in some distant country, but now, here he was—a fraction of the man he had been. His wife sat next to him and kissed him on the cheek.

"Thank you for coming, my love."

Garcia took her hand and pressed a gentle kiss to her lips.

Lucia watched, unsettled by the intimacy between them.

"Why did you help me?" she asked, still nervously clutching the sofa, unsure of who could be trusted.

Mrs. Garcia looked at her, lifting her chin high.

"Because we couldn't let them harm you."

The two of them continued to hold hands.

"I knew your brother," said Garcia after a while. "I'm sorry. He was very brave."

Lucia remained silent. Was he baiting her? She glanced at his mother—her soft smile. Surely, she wasn't part of this too?

"Maya tried to help," he said.

"Why did you lie?" Lucia said angrily. "You said nothing after Maya died."

"I can't," Garcia murmured, his voice weighed down by guilt that seemed to paralyze him.

"You saw what they did to her children," Mrs. Garcia continued. "They threatened the same to ours if we spoke. We had no choice," she said softly. She grabbed Garcia's hand, stroking his hair. "Don't worry, darling, I know you wanted to."

Mr. Garcia couldn't speak. He stared at the floor, looking at his reflection in the polished tiles with a frown. The warmth of his legendary charm had melted away, leaving only a cold detachment in its place.

"I thought you loved her," Lucia said, staring at Garcia with his ex-wife on the couch.

Mrs. Garcia gave his hand a reassuring squeeze.

"You must tell her the truth sweetie."

"I never loved Maya," Garcia said after a pause. "And she never loved me."

Lucia stiffened. "What do you mean?"

Garcia exhaled, rubbing his hands together for warmth. "I'll tell you the truth," he said, straightening on the sofa. For the first time, she caught a glimmer of the politician he once was.

Mrs. Garcia looked at him, startled, as if even she wasn't expecting him to speak so openly. But Lucia could see it—the words had been trapped inside him, pressing against his ribs, desperate to escape.

"One Wednesday afternoon, I got a call," Garcia said. "A young man claimed he had information about a missing girl: Marti Cortez."

Lucia leaned forward. His voice had taken on a different weight now, not just the tired murmur of a man unraveling, but the words of a storyteller. He wasn't just telling her. He needed her to understand.

"I'd heard her name before, by then she'd been missing for a few months. I informed the boy that all tips for the investigation should go via the capable hands of our city's police department. But what he said next caught me off guard. The boy told me they couldn't be trusted, he said that there were people implicated in the highest levels of power, and he was personally passed my name by a mutual friend. That friend was Father Roderick, the priest at the Basilica.

"At first I was skeptical. I asked him what information he had—he said Marti had been trafficked by groups using tunnels under the city. He didn't know where she was but he said I had to speak with someone by the name of Maya, she would be able to help me. I asked him why he needed my help, but he kept saying he had things to do—that he couldn't save Marti until he saved himself first. I asked him for Maya's phone number but all he knew was that she resided at the Paradise Motel. I asked him his name.

"It was your brother.

"He didn't sound well—his speech was erratic, almost conspiratorial. At first, I dismissed him as just another crackpot calling to voice his paranoia. A week later, well, I'm sorry, I know it must be a difficult memory. But your brother washed up dead off the shores of St. Augustine. Now I knew I had to follow up. But a name was all I had, so I went to the motel knowing that I would knock on every single door until I found Maya. Naturally, I was aware that my position as the mayor of the city would arouse some suspicions, so I went under the guise of campaigning. I knocked on every single door, introducing myself, carefully listening for their names. An hour later, I found her. She was incredibly polite, but when I told her that I wanted to chat about Marti, she shut the door in my face. She said she didn't want to talk about it. That was when I knew that I was onto something. Someone as courteous as Maya wouldn't lose her composure like that without a reason to hide. Once I had her address—courtesy of some friends in the government—I tracked down her number, but she never returned my calls. A few weeks later, I found myself back at her door, knocking again, hoping she might finally give in. She told me to go away, but her voice wavered—she didn't sound entirely sure of herself.

"Normally, I would've dropped it. But when I spoke to Father Roderick, even he seemed uneasy discussing the girl's disappearance and your brother's death. He was deeply affected and convinced the two were connected. He told me that Emi struggled with drugs, but he was on the path to healing. Around that time, he told me about a program in the forest. He said Maya had helped with the program and knew Emi well.

"So, I returned each day to the motel. If I wanted her to open up, I had to earn her trust. I began sharing the story of my childhood, every detail, hoping my openness would in turn open her door. I wanted her to know I wasn't like the other politicians in this city. I was raised to believe that honor meant more than money—that the truth still mattered. After a few weeks of consistency, she finally opened the door. She was cagey, glancing over both her shoulders before she whispered, "we can't speak here."

"She was reluctant to leave the kids alone, but a friend agreed to look after them. Then we went to a diner nearby. Once we were seated, she began to talk. Maya volunteered at the Basilica, where she provided an English program for disadvantaged youth. That was where she first met your brother. She met a lot of people from the street, hearing their stories, and started to notice a pattern of abuse. There was a group of migrants from Central America who entered the country without documentation, unable to find work. They often ended up homeless, vulnerable to exploitation as organized crime groups preyed on them—many vanishing into thin air. Your brother was an exception, he was a local who still had people who cared for him.

"Emi grew fond of Maya, and the two developed a close relationship. Not long after, he told her about the disappearance of a girl: Marti Cortez. She was from Mexico and couldn't find any work when she arrived. So she started coming to the Basilica programs.

"Emi was distraught. He was convinced she had been taken somewhere by bad people. But no one listened to him. He stopped showing up to the program—he would be gone for long periods of time. Maya was worried about him. He said people were following him and it seemed like he had not been sleeping. With all the drug use, she worried he might be having a psychosis. But then he got a strange card—he said someone called Mr. Muerte was threatening him. They were going to kill him because he was asking questions about Marti.

"He told Maya she'd been taken, that she was being moved all around the city, exploited by men who made her do unspeakable things. The people who took Marti were powerful. Maya had heard their names on the TV. But no one knew where she was.

"I tried to convince Maya that she would be safe to talk about it with me. That I had powerful friends too. But she was still worried. I said it was our moral obligation to find the girl, that she might be shivering in a basement somewhere, praying to the same God as us, the one who keeps our children safe, for now. We both knew there would be more. She looked up at me with heavy eyes. She knew it was the right thing to do, even though it would come at a cost. She saw what happened to Emi and was convinced that it was related. Reluctantly, she agreed. We would try to find out what happened to the girl together, using everything she knew and the resources available to me, but we couldn't involve the police department, there were too many who couldn't be trusted.

"That was the beginning of our fake romance.

"Maya and I realized that for her safety it would be easier to mask our dealings as an affair. That way if anyone was following us they would assume it was a classic case of infidelity as opposed to her providing information."

He paused, his fingers curling against the table. "I'm forever indebted to my wife for her patience during that time."

Lucia glanced at his wife. She sat rigid, her hands folded in her lap, eyes locked on a point just beyond him.

"She knew the truth all along," he continued, his voice quieter now. "She carried herself with unwavering grace, never once confronting me. But…" He hesitated. "It wasn't easy."

His wife's jaw tensed. She still didn't look at him. Garcia held her hand.

"My wife was as resolute in finding Marti as any of us. For months, Maya and I worked side by side, speaking with troubled youths from the church program to piece together a picture of its underbelly and uncover clues about Marti's possible whereabouts. There was more than just her, we were sure of that. We heard of many disappearances—migrant girls whisked away like the wind.

"You see Maya is such a non-judgmental person that she has a way of getting people to talk. People would tell her things, horrible things. Maya gathered the bulk of the evidence against the cartel and its corrupt politicians—the very evidence we planned to use in our case.

"But after a while, the threats arrived. They knew that we were poking around.

"We thought we had enough evidence to pursue a case against them and were preparing to go public. We had the date booked in, Maya and I would go on TV. We decided that if we announced it to the media, it would pressure prosecutors to act. We were confident we had enough evidence to take down some high-profile people. But we were expecting a fight. They had money, and we knew they were going to throw everything at us in court. I just never expected they would do this."

Garcia's voice faded, his words trailing off as he stared at the floor.

"I couldn't save her," he said.

Lucia had spent so long trying to decipher Garcia—was he a coward, a liar, or a man possessed by some evil spirit? But now, hearing the weight in his voice, she realized the truth was simpler. He had tried. And he had lost.

"You couldn't, darling. There was nothing you could do," Mrs. Garcia said, stroking her husband's shoulder.

"But I stayed silent after she died," he said, his voice weighted with guilt.

Mrs. Garcia disappeared through the kitchen door. When she came back, she had something in her hand. It was a book. Instantly, Lucia recognized the cover. It was a copy of *Romeo and Juliet*. Mrs. Garcia flicked through the pages until she reached the last one.

Be careful with the secrets that you sow,
Mr. Muerte.

Drawn in blood were crude stick figures of Mrs. Garcia and their two children.

"You protected our family," she said. "Look at this, you see what these people will do if we speak out."

"I should have said something," Garcia murmured.

"You did the right thing," said Mrs. Garcia, hugging her husband tightly.

The whole time Garcia had been speaking, his mother had a frown on her face.

"I thought the Cuban Revolution was bad—but at least those men believed in something. These men fight for nothing but their own greed," said Señora Garcia.

"So the cartel kidnaps the girls?" Lucia said.

"It's not just the cartel, they work with politicians, the police department, powerful people," he said.

"So they traffic the girls and push drugs, all while operating out of the city?" Lucia asked, her voice heavy with disbelief.

Mrs. Garcia nodded.

"The ones who sell *El Dorado Dust*," Lucia said recalling the dope that killed her brother. "That's why you bought it? Isn't it? You were trying to find the names of the suppliers," Lucia said, finally understanding Garcia's encounter with the pageant queen.

Garcia gave a sheepish nod.

"But there's still one thing I don't understand. Why the wedding?"

Garcia looked uncomfortable now.

"Mamá, can you get me some tea, please?" he said.

"Sure darling."

She waddled to the kitchen as Garcia waited until his mother was out of earshot.

"My mother is a conservative woman—she won't be happy to hear that I bent the rules of the church," he said, leaning closer to Lucia.

"That book planted an idea in her head?" said Lucia, pointing at the copy of *Romeo and Juliet*.

Garcia sighed, the weight of the memory pulling his shoulders down. "It planted an idea in mine. The night before we were supposed to go on TV with our evidence, she came to me. She was terrified. She couldn't stop talking about the kids, about her family, about how they'd all be targets if she went through with it. She knew what would follow. She was haunted by the cost of speaking publicly—the endless legal battles, the witnesses, the threats. It consumed her. She said she couldn't do it—not if it meant putting her children in danger. She wanted me to speak alone on the TV, to keep her name out of it completely. She stressed that there could be no way to trace it back to her."

Lucia tilted her head, confused. "So you thought marriage would protect her?"

Garcia nodded, his voice quiet but steady. "Florida law has spousal privilege—two types, actually. We thought it would protect her.

There's the confidential marital communications privilege," he explained. "It meant the police couldn't force her to testify about anything I told her in private during our marriage. Even if she had evidence, she could claim she only learned about it through our conversations as husband and wife. That would make it inadmissible in court. She believed it would shield her from ever having to take the stand, that way she could protect her children from the aftermath. She thought that if they couldn't force her to testify, the cartel wouldn't see her as a threat—and she and the kids would be safe."

Lucia's voice cracked. "But it didn't keep her safe, did it?"

"No," Garcia replied. "They must have found out we were about to speak."

Suddenly, Señora Garcia came in with a cup of tea.

"Here you go darling."

"But we have to do something," Lucia said, "there could still be girls out there."

"We can't," Mrs. Garcia said, holding Garcia's hand for solidarity.

"Darling, we have helped you but do not come into my house and put the lives of my grandchildren at risk," Señora Garcia interjected in a surprisingly forceful tone.

"I need to show Lucia something," Garcia said. "In private."

Garcia stood up, his full height imposing in a way his slumped shoulders hadn't revealed when he was seated. He drifted down the corridor, glancing back to see if Lucia would follow. She hesitated, glancing at the women on the couch—they wouldn't meet her eyes. Without a word, she followed.

He led her into a small room where an old pedal-powered sewing machine sat by the window. Quilt patches covered every surface, draped over a rocking chair and stacked in neat piles along the cupboards. Against the wall, a headless mannequin stood, dressed in a traditional rumba dress.

"My mother is a keen seamstress," he said, tired, as if any attempt at small talk was painful. Garcia wearily opened a drawer that was hidden by a fold of fabric. Reaching into a box, he pulled out a stack of books. Lucia recognized them instantly—the same ones he had borrowed from the Hidden Lantern.

"The cartel thrives on fear," he said. "The more their name is whispered, the stronger they become. That's why they weave their crimes into myth—it's how religion has ruled for thousands of years."

"Fear is stronger when we don't understand something," Lucia said softly.

"Yes," Garcia replied. He lifted up a *Mexican Symbols of Death* book.

"I've seen those before. That's where this comes from," Lucia said, pulling the card from her pocket.

Garcia turned away as soon as he saw it.

"Yes," he said. "It's the calling card for their assassin."

"Mr. Muerte," Lucia finished.

"Yes. He was tracking your brother down. Emi was snooping about their tunnels trying to find out where they were keeping Marti. He learned things that went on there, things that changed him…"

"There are entrance points, aren't there? Some are closed, but others connect the old buildings together."

"Yes." Garcia exhaled, rubbing his neck. "I need to give you this."

Weary, he reached under a stack of books and pulled out a gun. The indents on the grip fit his palm perfectly.

Lucia stared at it. She had never held one before.

"I don't want it," she said. "I don't want to hurt anybody."

"You'll need it," Garcia said.

Lucia remained still, her mind flashing to Emi—the promise they made as kids: never to kill, not even spiders. But things were different now. The world had already taken so much from them. Did

Emi break his promise? The sheriff said they found him with a gun, crawling around the tunnels.

"I can't," she said finally.

"I get it. I was an idealist too. Why do you think I joined politics?" Garcia said, his voice dry. "The idealistic mayors get voted out in the first term, cast into a career of back-office administration. You know the people I came up with who were the most principled? Their job now is making sure the stationery stays stocked. The only bearing they have on the world is if your pencil is sharp. The ones who got things done were those who'd look the other way when donations arrived on their doorstep without a name but with simple instructions."

He held out the gun. "I tried to do the right thing. Now look at me. Living with my mother like a coward. Take it."

"I can't," said Lucia. "I promised my brother I wouldn't."

Garcia looked disappointed. "Here's my number. If you ever get into trouble, call me." He scribbled his number onto a piece of paper and handed it to Lucia. "And I'll leave the gun in your letterbox if you change your mind," he added. "Look, here's how you use it: first, slide the safety switch to 'off'. Then, press..."

"Thanks," Lucia said.

"They'll come for your loved ones," Garcia said abruptly. "That's how they work."

"But I haven't done anything."

"It doesn't matter," said Garcia. "Now you know, that is enough."

Lucia went silent.

"Who else is there in your life?"

"My mom."

MISSING

It was 10 p.m. when Lucia returned to the Paradise Motel. The night sky was starless, and the neon sign flickered erratically like a satellite spiraling toward Earth. Its light rippled across the pool's surface, creating the illusion of gentle waves. The motel had never felt so still. Every door was shut, every curtain drawn. The only sign of life was a rat scurrying beneath the vending machine. Lucia had never wanted to be a rodent so badly in her life. She had to find her mother but couldn't risk being seen. The police were already looking for her, and the crab was watching. She could feel him through the security camera, tracking the pool. If he saw her, he wouldn't just watch— he'd make the call from his bunker. She needed cover.

Lucia remembered the breaker box on the side of the reception building. She'd seen drunks smashing it on hot days when the AC went out. Keeping to the shadows, she carefully skirted around the building, staying out of the camera's view. She arrived at a green box mounted to the wall. It was locked. Lucia took out her pocketknife and wedged it into the mechanism, trying to pry it open. The blade slipped and slashed her left thumb. Blood swelled in a straight line. Lucia ignored the pain. A few seconds later, the lock popped open, exposing the circuitry for the entire motel.

Outside Lights

She flipped the switch, plunging the motel into darkness. Her timer started now. The crab would head straight for the breaker box to fix it—his priority would be restoring the feed, not watching the cameras. That gave her a small window to slip inside unseen. She rushed toward her room, veiled under the cloak of night. A strange sense of déjà vu crept in—this must have been how the killer felt, sneaking to Maya's room in the dark. The same room as hers.

She climbed the stairs, clutching the rail to guide her. When she reached the second story, the pool was barely visible from the balcony, blending into the night sky—a featureless black void. Lucia felt its pull.

She looked away, anxiously knocking on the door. *Room 201.* No one answered. Maya's killer must have crept up the stairs the same way, syringe in hand. Lucia was starting to see the full picture. While Maya slept, he must have injected her with the dope—a dose lethal within minutes. He would've watched, waiting, as she gargled on her own saliva. Then, slinging her over his shoulder, he carried her down to the pool under the cover of darkness. He would've worn gloves, ensuring he left no prints but making certain hers were all over the plastic tube. Once there, he would've carefully lowered her into the water, making no splash, as gently as placing an injured dove back into a pond.

She could almost see it now. She hesitated, her hand hovering over the door handle. The hinge creaked as the door reluctantly opened. The room was completely empty. Her mother's bed was made. Lucia could hardly breathe. Her mother never went out at night, not since she'd been fired. She had no reason to leave, no place to go. She hurried over, pulling at her mother's sheets and tossing the pillows aside. There had to be something her mother left behind. Turning to the sofa bed, she searched frantically, her hands trembling. Beneath the pillow, she found a note.

"Don't worry, I'll be back later."

There was a smiley face.

Lucia stared at it, her stomach churning. Her mother had even made the beds before leaving—it didn't feel right. The calmness of it all, the note, the tidiness—it felt deliberate, too controlled. It made her think of Carl and Jasmine, the night they died. They hadn't screamed when they were led to the pool to die because no one had heard anything. The autopsy showed the kids fought back as they drowned, but they must have been calm when they walked to the pool at midnight with their killer. Someone they knew. Someone they trusted. He must have returned after disposing of Maya, waking the kids, whispering that it was all just an adventure. They would've gone along, excited, unaware of the darkness ahead, never realizing what was happening until the water bubbled away their screams.

Now history was repeating itself. Someone must've come into the room and taken her mother somewhere.

She rushed back outside. The lights were still off. The crab clearly hadn't made it to the breaker box yet, buying her some more time.

Maybe Javier had seen something.

She knocked on Javier's door, but there was no reply. She didn't have time to wait for him to wake up. She crouched down and used her lock-picking skills to jimmy the door open. It clicked, and she slipped inside. She flicked on the light. The bed was neatly made. Javier was nowhere to be seen. She moved cautiously through the room, it felt like sneaking into a museum, exploring all his decadent furniture without him there. There were his plush red chairs and mahogany coffee table, then the bookshelf. Lucia strolled over to the leather-bound books and scanned the shelf.

Suddenly, a figure appeared at the door—it was the crab. He hadn't turned the lights back on. He hadn't even gone to the breaker box. He must have seen her the whole time, tracking her movements in the dark.

"Lucia."

He stood still in the doorway. His bone white skin a sharp contrast to the black air behind him. The crab stared at her without saying a word. Lucia didn't move. She didn't want to be one step closer. After a long pause, he spoke.

"You're a smart girl."

Her fingers brushed the knife in her pocket.

"You remind me of myself," he said, stepping inside and shutting the door behind him. He wasn't just toying with her. He was flirting.

Lucia's soul quivered. If he wanted to report her, the call would have been made. If the police weren't on their way yet, they soon would be.

"Life doesn't reward smart people," he said. "It punishes us."

He sat down on the edge of Javier's bed. There was a strange energy to him—too at ease, like a man lingering over his drink, waiting for an invitation to be charming. She thought of the diary—the sketches, the fixation on Maya. The way he wrote about her. Now that obsession felt directed at her.

She had to think. If he had been watching, if he had seen everything, then maybe he knew where her mother was.

She had to play along.

Lucia forced herself to stay still. She felt his cursor eyes on her body, clicking. There wasn't anger in him, but something else— something hungrier.

"Take a seat with me," he smiled.

She knew the crab was involved—he had cut the lights the night Maya was murdered. His diary had revealed how he saw himself, not as a man, but something more—something untouchable. Now, a cold dread settled in her gut. If he had been watching everything, if he had seen her mother leave—had he done something to her too?

She swallowed hard. Slowly, she walked over and sat down, leaving as much space between them as possible.

"I've seen you read books by the pool," he said. "You have a taste in books beyond your years." His bony arms repositioned his body a few inches closer.

"You seem smart too," Lucia said, forcing a smile, trying not to grimace at her own lie.

"Smart people recognize their kind," he smiled, tracking her reactions like a scientist observing a lab rat. "Does this room temperature bother you? I perspire at anything above 72 degrees Fahrenheit."

"It's fine," Lucia replied from the edge of the bed. The peppermint gum he'd taken barely masked the foul stench of his breath. She felt herself shake.

"I shouldn't work here," he said after a pause.

"Why are you still here then?" Lucia asked softly, keeping her voice as neutral as she could.

"I have no choice," he said, staring at the floor.

"Everyone has a choice," said Lucia.

He snarled. "Don't be stupid. You don't understand anything about this place."

She couldn't afford to let him shut down now—she had to keep flattering him, keep him talking, whatever it took to get the answers she needed.

"Then I'm lucky I have you," she said, trying to sound eager. "You must understand everything." She kept her hand in her pocket, the only comfort being the cold touch of steel, knowing there was a blade between them.

"Of course I do. Without me this place would fall apart," he said. The anger flushed from his face; he looked almost proud. The room went quiet, as a dog barked in the distance.

"I can imagine. It must be hard when you don't get recognition?" Lucia fawned again. The fawning came easily now, her mind fixed on finding her mother.

"They don't value me, even though I keep so many secrets for them," he said, inching closer to Lucia, his eyes glinting.

"Your secrets could destroy them, but you don't say anything," Lucia said.

"Exactly. I know things that could destroy them all," he boasted. He shuffled even closer. His hot peppermint breath brushed against her exposed skin.

"Why don't you tell someone? It must be hard, someone like you—carrying it all on your own...," Lucia said cautiously. She started to feel herself approaching an imaginary line. Perhaps she needed to pull back a little more.

"No," he shook his head. "They know things about me." The crab plunged his head into his hands, as his spindly fingers ran anxiously through his hair.

"But you're smarter than them," Lucia said.

"Yes, but they try to control me." The crab squinted at the floor as if it were the surface of the sun.

"How?"

"They know things," he said, his voice trailing off. He stayed silent before slowly lifting his head, his eyes narrowing. "Why are you asking me all this?" His eyes were dark now.

"Because... I can see there's something strong about you," said Lucia. "Powerful." She curled her fingers around the blade in her pocket, hoping her compliment would sedate him.

"I am powerful," he said, as if it were an affirmation to himself.

"They trust you to do things. Don't they?"

"Yes," he replied with a sly smile. "They trust me with everything. That's why they put me here, not anyone else."

Lucia thought she had him.

"Did they tell you what they did with my mother?"

His entire demeanor snapped. His smirk vanished, his face hardening like stone.

"What?" he said.

"What did they do to her?"

"They?" whispered the crab. The word drained the color from his face as he paced back and forth, murmuring to himself. He was unraveling.

Suddenly, his hand shot out, grabbing Lucia by the throat.

He squeezed.

The blood drained from her toes, surging to her head. It was dizzying. She tried to reach for the pocketknife, but the lack of oxygen made her hand fall limp to her side. His arms locked her down, and all she could see was the hatred in his eyes.

"You'll ruin everything," he growled. "I'm not losing everything because of a bitch like you."

He was on top of her now, pinning her against the bed. She could barely make out his face anymore, even though he was right above her. His hands clamped tighter around her neck, cutting off her air. She struggled, but he was twice her size. Her lungs screamed, her body growing weaker by the second. With her last remaining strength, she flailed her arms, searching for something—anything— to strike him with.

Her hand hit something metal, sending it crashing to the floor. His grip faltered for a second—just enough for her to drag in a ragged breath. She reached for the knife again, but then his weight shifted.

The pressure moved lower.

A sickening awareness seeped into her body as his breath hovered just over her skin. His fingers pressed down, wandering, testing.

"You are nothing," he whispered, his voice almost gentle.

Lucia thrashed, twisting beneath him, but he pressed down harder, his grip closing around her throat again.

"Don't fight it," he murmured, his breath hot against her ear. "Enjoy it."

The air around her blurred. Her eyelids began to flutter as the darkness closed in. His dry scaly hand on her warm skin made her want to throw up. She thought of Emi, of Maya. Now she understood what they must have felt—the final moments before total blackness. How lonely it was. Her vision blurred again; her eyes began to close.

It will be over soon.

Suddenly, the door flew open. Her vision blurred, but she felt his grip weaken, his weight yanked away. Then—THUMP.

A body hit the floor. Dazed, Lucia looked up. The racy lingerie lady stood over the crab's crumpled body, still gripping the brass desk lamp. Its neck was bent at an angle where it had connected with his skull, the yellowed lampshade hanging askew.

"Are you okay, sweetie?" asked Sara. "I heard struggles from next door."

"I'm fine," said Lucia, the blood slowly returning to her head.

"Let me see if you're okay," she rushed over to Lucia. "Men are disgusting. I wish I could tell you I haven't been there."

"Thanks," Lucia said drowsily.

"I always keep bear spray under my bed in case." Sara looked over at the crab, who had started to stir. "I better call the police."

"No," Lucia said. "Please don't."

"We need a rope or something we can tie him with," Lucia said, rising to her feet.

"Are you crazy?" Sara said. "He needs to be locked up."

"I need to ask him questions."

Sara stared at her for a few seconds, then her crimson lips curled into a knowing smile.

"Oh honey, I get it. Sometimes a girl's gotta handle things herself." She glanced at the crab crawling to his knees.

Lucia grabbed the cord from the landline, yanking it out of its socket. Sara helped her bind his limp arms tightly, pressing him against the wall. He wasn't fully unconscious—just dazed. Once his hands were secured, she propped him up against the wall. He mumbled to himself, eyes half-closed, his head lolling forward. He couldn't move at all.

"Do what you've got to, sweetie," Sara said. "And if anyone asks, I didn't see anything."

Lucia stood over him, shaking. The skin on her neck burned, his thumbprints stamped in raw red. She felt something strange inside, being held down against the bed, as she watched the world fade away. It made her feel so powerless, like in those dreams where you are awake but can't move. She caught her reflection in the bathroom mirror but had to look away. She felt different. His touch clung to her skin like a stain, his fingers branding her thigh with a mark she couldn't wash away.

She looked at the crab on the floor.

She thought of a man like that with her mother—her hair yanked as she was dragged through a tunnel, a voice whispering in her ear to be quiet, whispering worse things. A dark feeling seeped into her soul; a rage so strong it pulsed through her blood. She couldn't control it anymore. There was only one way these men would respect her.

Lucia walked to the kitchen. She filled a large glass of water and marched straight back to the crab, throwing it in his face. The shock of the water jolted him awake, his eyes snapping open instantly.

"What?" he said, disoriented.

Lucia snapped open the knife, pressing the blade against his neck.

"Where is my mom?" she said, hiding her own fear.

"What—" he slurred, still dazed from the blow. His eyes blinked slowly, trying to focus.

"Where did they take my mom?"

"I don't know what you're talking about." His denial ignited a rage within her, all the people who'd lied about Emi. She pulled the blade away from his neck and, in one swift motion, slashed his leg. The wound opened up, blood spilling out in a sudden rush. The cut snapped him back to life, his dazed expression contorting into a grimace of pain. He squirmed, struggling against the phone cord binding his hands.

"Whore."

"Where is my mom?" she said, the adrenaline taking hold.

"I don't know," he spat.

Lucia raised the blade, ready to slash his leg for the second time.

"I told you. I don't know!" he gasped. "They didn't tell me anything this time."

"This time?" Lucia's voice was shaking, eyes fierce. "Like when they told you about Maya?"

He went silent, his lips tight.

"Answer me!" she yelled.

"Yes! Yes," he stammered. "They told me to switch off the lights at midnight, then leave the building. That's all I knew."

"The cartel?"

"Yes," he said, breath coming in short gasps. "They own the motel. They own every building in St. Augustine. It's how they flush the cash from the drug business."

Lucia's grip tightened on the knife, her knuckles white. "What else did they say to you?"

"They told me to watch Garcia and Maya," he said, voice trembling. "They said they were poking into business they shouldn't have."

Lucia paused, her heart pounding in her ears. The room seemed to shrink, the dim light flickered.

"Who killed Maya?"

"I don't know," he stammered. Lucia tightened her grip on the knife, lifting it higher. The crab squirmed, its legs flailing as dark blood dripped onto the carpet.

"They call him Mr. Muerte," he blurted. "But I've never seen him. I've only heard things."

Lucia didn't lower the knife.

"They don't tell me anything. I swear," he gasped. "They just asked me to take notes on all the guests."

The blade gleamed under the light. The crab twitched.

"Did they make you do that for my mother and me."

He went quiet.

"You're not meant to know them. You are both dead now," he said softly.

Lucia slashed him again. The crab screamed.

"Stop! Please!" he cried.

"Where's my mother?" yelled Lucia.

"All I saw was a man in a cowboy hat. She was in her work clothes!"

Lucia rushed to Emi's suitcase to find the book. The man in the cowboy hat—he was the manager from the Casa Monica Hotel.

"Untie me," he yelled. "You don't know what they'll do to you."

She grabbed a t-shirt, rolling it tight before forcing it between his teeth and knotting it behind his head. The fabric muffled his protests as he thrashed weakly against the wall. She rushed back to the suitcase and picked up Emi's copy of the *Tunnels of St. Augustine*, flicking to the map of the various entrance points around the city. She was sure they'd used one of them to smuggle her mother just like they had for Marti.

Emi must have tried to enter the same way.

Then she remembered—the sheriff had said Emi broke into the tunnels, heading for the Casa Monica Hotel with a gun. That's why they locked him in the cellar for a few nights. Maybe he was trying to track the tunnels to their center. Maybe that's where they had imprisoned Marti.

Garcia had said Emi went to the shrine near the woods, searching for the tunnel system. If he was right, there had to be a way to reach the Casa Monica Hotel from an entrance behind the cemetery. But when Lucia had last searched, she found nothing.

Then Tom's words clicked—the Spanish had used magnetic north, meaning most of the locations on the map were off by fifty yards to the right. If she went back, and used a compass to find the magnetic point, she could find the true location. Emi had a compass tucked into his suitcase, she'd never understood the significance of it until now. She picked it up and tore out the map page, folding it carefully before slipping it into her pocket. She had to get to the woods.

But on the way—Señora Garcia's letterbox. The gun.

THE TUNNELS

Midnight consumed the Nombre de Dios Cemetery, the tombstones weakly reflecting the pale moonlight. Lucia stood at her brother's grave, gun in hand, her compass wedged into her pocket.

"I'm sorry no one believed you," she whispered.

She looked ahead into the woods. Just as the bookshop lady had described, a thin mist clung to the trees—the kind that could dissolve someone into a formless vapor. A shrine, too, could turn into no more than a whisper.

The cartel could've used the tunnels from the Matanzas River, where they brought in shipments under the cover of night. From there, they could move things through their underground network, connecting to hidden exit points—abandoned colonial buildings, the basements of old shops—all converging at the heart of the operation: the Casa Monica Hotel.

Lucia scanned the trees with her flashlight, the memory of the bookkeeper's stories guiding her through the woods. The map in her hand was worn at the folds, the compass needle trembling as she traced the route. She was looking for a large oak—that was where the bookshop lady had found the manhole.

She pressed forward, trying not to think about who—or what—might be waiting in the tunnels below.

The compass led her deeper into the woods until she arrived at the exact pinpoint.

Then she saw it. An enormous, gnarled tree stood with the quiet authority of a wise elder in the woods. It had to be the one. She hesitated, scanning the ground around its base before kneeling to brush aside the thick layer of leaves carpeting the earth. Slowly, the edges of a manhole emerged, its rusted metal glinting in the flashlight's beam. She opened the manhole, descending down the ladder. The warm air was replaced by the damp chill of a grimy grotto, as melted wax and damp earth rushed into her nose. Soon her feet touched solid ground. She raised her flashlight, dispelling the shadows.

There she was, lit up like an angel by Lucia's flashlight: *La Santa Muerte.*

The skeleton stood clutching her scythe, while her crystal eyes reflected the light so fiercely that Lucia had to turn away. She lowered the beam so that she could look. The features of her face were exactly like the card. The same skeletal glare that pulled with the force of Jupiter.

Lucia saw something at the shrine's base. There were offerings: extinguished candles, wilted flowers, and old coins. She pictured Emi in the shrine, the card in his pocket, trying to find the entrance to the tunnels.

She scanned the walls, but it seemed like a dead end—just as Garcia had found when he last visited.

She ran her hands along the walls—coquina, compacted coral, and shell. Emi had told her about it when they spoke of the great fires that once swept through the city. After the devastating blaze of 1702, the city rebuilt using coquina for its fire resistance. Its only weakness was water—over time, it eroded, losing small parts of itself every time the sky wept.

They must have built the secret door from another material to prevent the tunnel from flooding when it rained. She scanned the room, but all the walls looked the same.

Then, something behind the statue caught her eye.

Behind *La Santa Muerte*, a tattered curtain swayed from the ceiling. She ripped it down, sending a cloud of dust into the air. A wall stood behind it—not coquina. The stone was smoother, denser. Concrete. She pressed her hands against it, feeling resistance. Then, she pushed harder. A groan of shifting stone rumbled through the shrine.

A damp gust of air rushed out. On the other side lay a fully lit tunnel shaft. The passage was tall enough for Lucia to stand upright, with torches mounted every dozen yards, their flames lighting the path. Little nooks lined the walls, like those in the Basilica—old wine cellars, perhaps. Lucia crept forward. The torches flickered, shadows spilling into every gap, curling into every crevice. She moved between the shadows. Her shoes scuffed the damp stone, the sound echoing through the tunnel's arteries, making her feel even smaller.

She gripped the gun, safety off, just as Garcia had shown her.

A droplet of water struck her nose. She flinched. Her eyes darted upwards, half-expecting a burst pipe. Instead, she saw only moisture pooling on the ceiling. She pressed on, the air thickening with each step. Still, she forced herself forward—the tunnels would lead her to the Casa Monica Hotel.

It felt like she had been walking for miles in a straight line with nothing but the flicker of torches to mark the passage of time. There was a sense of inevitability—she was nearing something. The walls narrowed, and the path bent sharply.

She clung to the sides, the exit behind her fading into the dark. She thought of her mother, whimpering alone somewhere, and something primal ignited inside her. It was the same feeling as when someone called Emi a drug addict, she had snapped, blinded by a fierce, unshakable loyalty. Now, that same fire burned hotter. All she could see was red—a deep, seething anger she hadn't known she was capable of.

As she rounded the corner, a door emerged on her left, half-hidden in the shadows.

It was locked.

Her fingers worked the lock, heart pounding. The latch clicked, and she eased the door open. Inside, she swept her flashlight over hundreds of plastic-wrapped bags, stacked high to the ceiling. Each bag bore the same stamp—the Spanish galleon. Where she once felt sad at seeing this symbol, she now felt a hardening resolve. She was in the right place.

The bags stacked with precision, row after row, the plastic crinkling under the weight of thousands of pounds of dope. The sheer scale of it hit her—this wasn't just a stash, it was a distribution hub, a pipeline running straight through the tunnels beneath the city.

Suddenly, Lucia heard voices. Men were approaching. She quickly shut the door and glanced around. Spotting a stack of dope near the back of the room, she darted toward it. She squeezed herself into the narrow gap between the stack of packages and a stone archway. From this angle, anyone opening the door wouldn't see her at all. She stopped breathing, hoping the voices would go away, but they only got closer. There were at least four of them.

"There's a new batch," a man said. Keys rustled, and the door creaked open. "Why's it unlocked?" His voice was suspicious.

"Must've rusted, the water fucks this place," came another man's voice in a heavy accent.

"Thankfully, we have the tunnels to ourselves," said the first man.

A nervous chuckle followed.

"In all this time, I can't believe you haven't seen how the sausage gets made," the man continued.

"I prefer to eat the sausage, not work in the damn factory," came the slow Alabama drawl. The sheriff.

"Well, you've done important work. We need you to quash another investigation."

"Roger." The sheriff sounded uncomfortable. "But why bring me down here? Y'all know I work better when I ain't seein' things too close."

"We want to show you the product of all your hard work," the boss said smoothly.

The door swung open, and the boss strode in, plucking a packet from a pile near Lucia's head—just inches from where her eyes were. She dropped into a squat.

"Hold this," the boss said, tossing the packet toward the sheriff.

"Ain't see why that's necessary," the sheriff hedged.

"Hold it."

A pause. The plastic crinkled as it changed hands.

"I don't want you to turn a blind eye. I want your eyes wide open," the boss said.

The sheriff was quiet.

"This is just as much your work as it is ours."

"Course," the sheriff muttered. "You know I'll do anything."

"We wanted to show our appreciation for your continued service."

"Don't worry, the money's plenty."

"This is better than money. Take one."

The sheriff chuckled, uneasy. "Money's all I need."

"Take it." The boss's tone sharpened.

The sheriff looked at the bag but didn't reach for it. The boss held it out, waiting. After a beat, the sheriff sighed through his nose and took it, turning it over once in his palm before slipping it into his pocket.

"I'm sure I've got some junkies in the cell who'd know what to do with this." He paused. "That reminds me, been meaning to tell you something."

"Yes?"

"I couldn't get your friend off those charges. The State's breathin' down my neck. He's gotta stand before a judge next week."

The boss said nothing.

"I'm sorry," the sheriff continued. "Over my head."

The boss processed the information.

"What's the judge's name?"

"Giuliani."

The boss smiled.

"That's okay," he said. "We have other ways to solve the problem."

The sheriff hesitated. "You're not gonna mess with a lawman, are ya? I mean, not that I care, but there's a line. Even I can't help you past that."

"We have other ways. Let's just say Giuliani will drop the charges by tomorrow."

The sheriff exhaled, shaking his head with a grin. "You're an impressive bunch. Wish things moved that quick in my department."

"We pay you so that they don't."

They both chuckled.

"C'mon," the boss said, clapping him on the shoulder. "There's something else I'd like to show you."

Footsteps shuffled toward the door. It creaked, then latched shut. She waited a few minutes before she snuck out from her hiding spot. Carefully, she opened the door, peering into the tunnel. The men were gone. She crept deeper, at any moment ready to throw herself into a hiding spot.

The tunnel twisted into sharp, blind corners, letting her see no more than twenty yards ahead. The sound of boots and low murmurs drifted around the bend. Lucia crept forward, she peeked around the corner. The tunnel widened at the end. The men were there, their backs to her, gathered around something she couldn't see.

Dropping to her belly, she started to crawl, the cold grit of the stone scraping her palms. The gun was tucked into the waistband of her jeans. A few yards ahead, there was a dark nook. It was the perfect spot to watch without being seen. She crawled forward, inch by inch, her breath shallow as the earthy moss tickled her nose.

"What in God's name is this?" the sheriff said.

"Our place of worship."

Lucia reached the nook and rose slowly. She leaned forward, just enough to peer around the edge. Now she could see it. There was another *La Santa Muerte*. The four men surrounded it, staring at the skeleton, naked with her scythe. The sheriff stood in his uniform, flanked by three men in suits. Their faces were obscured, but the boss was easy to spot—a cowboy hat perched on his head. The other two stood on either side of him, guns tucked into their belts.

"This some kinda devil worship?" the sheriff said.

"It's not the devil. It's the only saint who listens."

"Look, I don't mind what y'all do otherwise, but this…" He trailed off.

"But what?" the boss said. The sheriff looked away from the statue.

"My wife and I—we're God-fearin' people."

"Have you ever lost someone?" asked the boss.

"Course. Both my parents. Lung cancer."

"And who did you pray to then?"

"God."

"And what did he do for you?" the boss said.

"What could he have done?" replied the sheriff.

The boss smiled faintly. "When a Mexican mother loses her son, you know who she calls on first?"

"God?" the sheriff guessed.

"No. She will call upon *La Santa Muerte*. For a grieving mother knows that death will answer her prayers far quicker than God. And unlike God, death does not judge when she cries for revenge, she understands that death is the only divine justice."

Suddenly, the leader slipped a gold ring off his finger and set it at the base of the shrine. He made the sign of the cross over his body, before he whispered a prayer.

"You pray to her like you pray to God?" the sheriff said disturbed.

"Yes. We all do," the boss replied. "She's the narcosaint. All over the Americas, taxi drivers, beggars, and drug dealers call on her."

"Bible say no other gods?" he muttered.

"It was your people who brought false idols to our continent. Your God met our gods and they had a baby. That's history—the powerful always get to choose the gods of the powerless. And now, we've chosen ours," the boss said, nodding toward *La Santa Muerte*. The sheriff glanced away, his discomfort clear as the others dropped to their knees and prayed.

"Pray with us," the boss said firmly.

The sheriff hesitated.

"Pray with us, sheriff." The boss's gaze grew hot on the sheriff's skin. "We're business partners," he said, finally relaxing a little, like a snake pulling back after a false strike.

"Okay. Guess it's all the same God in the end."

"Exactly."

"What are we praying for?"

"For you to not fuck up again."

"I tried to take care of it," the sheriff muttered, embarrassed.

"And you failed."

"Last time I talked to her, she didn't know a damn thing 'bout this place or the business. That crazy junkie never said a word 'bout you."

"She's spoken with Garcia," said the boss.

"I'll handle Lucia."

THE SECRET LEVEL

When she heard her name, it felt as if the rock crumbled in front of her, leaving her completely exposed. She half expected the skeleton to lift its scythe and point directly at her, betraying her to the men with guns. But instead, the men rose and walked down the tunnel, disappearing around a sharp corner.

"I heard she taped up that dweeb at the Paradise Motel," the sheriff said. "My men radioed it in."

"He's not important," replied the boss. "You've already messed up, we're handling it."

"What'd you do?"

"We have her mother," the boss replied. "Mr. Muerte is with her now."

"She's in the hotel?"

"Yes. He'll wait till the girl arrives."

"How does he know she'll come?"

"He says she's smart. She'll figure it out."

"And then what…?"

"Then there will be another little accident for you to cover up."

Lucia's grip tightened on the gun, rage surging to her fingertips wrapped around the trigger. She would do it. Her mother had given everything for her children, sacrificed her whole life. And now, they wanted to take away the only person Lucia had left—the only one who truly loved her. Her breath came sharp and fast. She thought of the crab, the way he squealed when she dragged the blade across its leg. People only respected her when she drew blood—otherwise, she was just a little girl to be tied down, pressed into the sheets. The rage burned hot inside of her.

She was ready to shoot.

Five bullets in the sheriff's head would do it—the man who let her brother's case rot, who buried Maya's without a second glance.

"Tell me as soon as you find her," said the sheriff, their voices trailed off as they walked further down the tunnel. But she forced herself to wait. If she shot now, she'd never find her mother.

"Of course. But please just enjoy the evening. The hotel's celebrations are just starting. I have some girls for you. Follow me."

The voices died out. Lucia waited a few seconds, before she emerged from her hiding spot. They were gone. Lucia followed the path the men had taken, careful to stay out of earshot. They must've been near the tunnel entrance beneath the Casa Monica Hotel—Lucia had walked miles underground, straight into the heart of the city. She glanced up at the low ceiling, wondering if the hotel sat directly above them.

She kept walking. Soon the tunnel widened into what felt like a vast underground basement. Ahead, a long corridor stretched forward, flanked by rows of numbered doors on either side. It was similar to the refurbished bunker. The hotel had converted the old tunnel into makeshift rooms, using flimsy plywood dividers and lightweight doors, hastily fitted into the stone. *Why were there rooms down here?*

At the far end, she saw an elevator shaft—it must've gone up to the Casa Monica Hotel. Before she could take another step, the elevator lurched to a stop, and the door opened. Quickly, Lucia slipped back around the corner, pressing herself against the wall. Her palm touched the stone—it was smooth, like the secret door she'd found earlier. She leaned her full weight into it. The rock shifted, revealing a hidden passage.

Lucia stepped through and quietly pushed the door back into place. The corridor ahead was brightly lit—sterile and unnatural, a stark contrast to the damp tunnels behind her. She froze. One side of the passage was a glass wall, completely transparent, offering a direct view into the rooms. She could see every detail: the fluffed pillows, the neatly folded towels and the bathrobes draped at the end of the bed. Something felt wrong. Each room was empty, the beds neatly made, as if waiting for someone to arrive.

Then she saw it—a camcorder mounted on a tripod, aimed at the bed. The green recording light, blinking. It was live, capturing everything.

She started to back away from the glass, but as she moved further down the corridor, more rooms came into view—all identical. Each had the same setup: pristine beds, recording camcorders, and blinking green lights.

Lucia's chest tightened. This wasn't just an underground passage, it was a hidden surveillance corridor. Someone had designed it to spy on the rooms, to move unseen behind the glass, recording everything.

Just as she neared the end of the corridor, Lucia's eyes landed on a small television perched on a table. Next to it, a shelf of VHS tapes stretched up to the ceiling. It had to be where they stored the recordings from the camcorders.

She scanned the tapes. They were stacked fastidiously, each one marked with a strip of masking tape. Some she recognized, faces from the TV. Then she saw one she knew: Mick Coates. She remembered his name tag. It was the crab.

She had to know. If Emi was on those tapes, she needed to see for herself.

Balancing on her tiptoes, Lucia reached up and plucked the tape from the top shelf. Her hands trembled as she shoved it into the VHS player beneath the TV. She glanced over her shoulder. The room behind her was still empty. She pressed play. The screen flickered to life, static rippling over an image—the same sterile room she stood before now, eerily unchanged.

A moment later, the crab walked into the frame, alone. Then, a few seconds later, a girl entered. Lucia's breath caught in her throat.

It was Marti. She looked so small, so fragile—no older than fifteen.

Lucia wanted to scream—to reach through the screen and drag Marti to safety. But the footage kept rolling. The crab shuffled closer to Marti on the bed, that look in his eyes—the same one he'd given Lucia. His hand touched Marti's shoulder but it was Lucia's skin that went numb. The footage continued.

Marti stared straight ahead; her face blank. Not a single muscle flinched. Then his hand slid up her leg. Marti must have been paralyzed too, as she stared blankly at the plaster, while he whispered into her ear. Marti wasn't there anymore. She had drifted elsewhere, hiding in a world where his words dissolved into the clouds. Then he leaned in to kiss her, collapsing her world into his—the cheap sheets, white light and peppermint breath. Marti closed her eyes.

Lucia was too angry to cry. She hit the eject button. The tape clicked out, and she stuffed it into her bag, bile rising in her throat, her stomach churning with acid. She turned back to the shelves, hoping it was the only one. But the tapes were stacked high, row after row. Her fingers trembled over another label.

Sheriff Jones.

Her breath quickened; she had to know if there was more. She grabbed the tape and pushed it into the player. The screen flickered to life. The same room. The same bed. This time with the sheriff on the edge of the sheets, undoing his uniform buttons. For a moment, she hoped—prayed—that he'd just fall asleep.

But then the door opened.

Marti walked in.

Now another tear welled in Lucia's eye as she watched Marti sit on the bed, motionless, her eyes vacant. The sheriff leaned in, his lips brushing her neck. Lucia slammed the stop button and yanked the tape out, shoving it into her bag.

Things were starting to make sense. The cartel must have used the tapes to blackmail people. They got footage of them sleeping with underage girls, and then when they needed them to do something they threatened them with the footage. That's how they got the crab to switch off the lights Maya died. They owned him. They owned all the names on the shelf. She shoved the tape into her bag, she would need a few for evidence. She turned sharply, her breath quickening. *Was her mother behind one of these doors?*

She moved quietly down the corridor, the air heavy and still. Each room she passed was empty. But at the last one, she froze. Someone was there. She stopped breathing. It was the sheriff, perched on the edge of the bed, his hands gripping his knees. He wasn't on a screen. He was there. Instinctively, Lucia dropped to the floor. She waited for the glass to smash, for him to fish her out of the shards with his bloody hand. But nothing happened. He couldn't see her. Of course—it was a one-way mirror. She stood up and placed her hand against the glass. Only two feet separated them. He was staring straight ahead, his eyes fixed on hers, as if they were both staring into each other's souls.

He must not have known about the secret passage, or the recording. He looked too content staring at the glass, waiting for his prize. The door opened. A girl walked in. She looked young, her police outfit just a costume—one designed for a different kind of role. Dangling from her hands, were some handcuffs, and a police baton.

The girl didn't smile. She walked to sit on the bed, exactly like Marti had done. Like she'd been told to do exactly that.

Lucia couldn't hide behind the television now. It was really happening. The sheriff slid his arm around the girl, pulling her closer. Lucia glanced down at her gun, feeling its weight in her hand. She gripped it tighter. She didn't trust herself to shoot with the girl so close. She picked up a heavy steel flashlight from the shelf. *That could work.* She wanted nothing more than to smash the glass and end it now, but she couldn't. Not yet. The sheriff was still facing her. If she moved too soon, he'd see her, and it would all be over. She had to wait. She needed him to turn his back.

But each second he got closer to the girl's face. He took the handcuffs off the girl, preparing to tie her down to the bed. He pushed her onto the sheets. Lucia thought of her mother—was she locked in a room just like this, waiting for someone to save her? If she walked away now, she was no better than the men who had turned a blind eye. The sheriff leaned forward to climb onto the bed, his back turned to the secret mirror for just a moment. It was all she needed. Lucia swung the flashlight with the force of her fury.

The mirror shattered into a cascade of glass, shards exploding across the floor. The barrier was gone. Lucia surged forward, gripping the flashlight like a hammer, slamming it against the sheriff's head.

"What the fuck?" he muttered, dazed, trying to turn.

She struck again, harder this time. The impact knocked him off balance. The girl sprang off the bed, her eyes locking onto Lucia in shock. Lucia snatched the handcuffs from the bed. As the sheriff groaned, still dazed, she wrenched his arm up with all her strength and locked his wrist to the steel frame. Before he could react, she looped the other end tightly around the bed frame, yanking it taut. He twisted, trying to pull free, but the angle pinned his arm awkwardly, trapping him in place, unable to move anything but his fingers.

"It's okay," Lucia murmured, steadying her breath. "You're safe now."

The sheriff rolled over and froze. His eyes fixed on the shattered glass; the hidden corridor now lay bare. At its center, the camcorder stood pointed straight at him, its green light, blinking.

The sheriff struggled against his restraints, staring at Lucia in horror.

"You," he said. "The hell you doin' here?"

Then he looked back to the green light.

"What the hell is that?" he muttered, his face twisting in disgust as he pointed at the camera with a flick of his finger.

Lucia jumped off the bed and grabbed his tape from her bag on the floor.

"I know what you did," Lucia said defiantly.

The sheriff's eyes darted to the camcorder, his confusion breaking into panic. "What the hell is this place?" he barked. "They... they film this shit? All of it?"

Lucia didn't answer. She could see it in his face—the slow, sinking realization.

His tone dropped, trembling now. "You need to give me that tape," he said, almost pleading.

"No."

"You don't get it," he stammered. "My little girl—she's nine. You'll ruin her life."

Lucia said nothing as the other girl quivered in the corner of the room.

"Look, we can work somethin' out," he said, his voice quickening. "We take these bastards down together, me an' you. Think about it. You want justice? I'll help you. We'll get the folks who did this to

Maya, we'll find out who killed your brother."

"Where's my mother?"

""I don't know," he insisted. "I don't do that kind of thing, I still got my principles." His pants at his ankles.

Lucia turned to the girl in the corner of the room.

"I've got you," she whispered.

The sheriff exhaled sharply. "Listen to me. My wife an' I—we go to church, we believe in God. I swear, I ain't ever gonna do anything like this again." His voice cracked. "My daughter's name is Anna. She loves horses, wants to be a rider one day. I only took the money to give her a real life."

Lucia looked at the sheriff as he groveled from his back.

"I didn't have a choice," the sheriff said, shifting tactics. "You don't know these people. They'd have put me in the ground if I didn't play along. A man who can make murder look like Mother Nature."

"You always have a choice," Lucia said, her jaw clenched. "And you chose to walk through that door." The words were spewing out of her now at the thought of what he had done to Marti.

"I didn't," he shot back, desperate now. "I had to get my hands dirty, or they'd never trust me. That's how it works. Ain't no way out once you're in."

"You're the sick one," Lucia shot back. She strode over to the sheriff's discarded belt in the corner of the room. Kneeling down, she rifled through his pockets, pulling out a lighter.

"Now don't go doin' anything dumb," the sheriff said, as he watched Lucia pull her gun from her waistband.

"I told you. You always have a choice," Lucia said.

His jaw flexed. "Alright, then. You wanna play it like that? Fine. You got a choice too—destroy that tape, or you take down my whole family. My little girl, you gonna make her pay for my sins?"

Lucia tossed the lighter onto the bed. It landed a few inches away from his fingers.

"The choice is yours," she said.

"What?" he muttered, glancing at the lighter.

"You can protect your daughter from this," Lucia said, her tone flat.

"How?" he stammered, his gaze darting between her and the lighter.

Lucia dropped the VHS tape onto the floor, well out of his reach. His eyes widened as he realized how trapped he was, cuffed tightly to the bed frame, unable to move more than a few inches.

"You have the lighter," Lucia said.

The sheriff flexed his fingers, struggling to curl them around the lighter. It took a few seconds, his movements clumsy, before he finally grasped it.

"Now give me the tape," he demanded desperately.

"I can't do that."

"Then how the hell am I supposed to get rid of it?" he snapped.

She tilted her head, her gaze unflinching. "I told you—we always have a choice. You can burn yourself with it."

The sheriff froze, staring at her in disbelief. "You evil bitch."

"If you don't want to," she said, turning for the door, "I'll take it with me, for everyone to see."

"Why the hell are you doin' this?" he pleaded.

"Stories ripple farther than the truth. Don't you know that? Next time some old creep tries to touch a girl, they'll hear whispers of what happened here. No one will ever know if the sheriff burned alive with his pants around his ankles—or if it was all just a horrible folk tale," Lucia said.

The sheriff sank back onto the bed, his breathing short. The lighter trembled in his fingers as he glanced at the tape, then the pillowcase just inches from his head. To burn the tape, he would have to set fire to the whole room while he was chained to the bed.

Lucia raised the gun. "Make your choice."

"We can still work somethin' out," he said, voice thin.

"This is my deal," she said.

He exhaled, sinking into the bed.

"All I ask is… pass me my cigarette while I decide."

Lucia hesitated. Lucia's hands shook, the gun wavering.

"Please. I can't even move. Just give me that much," he said.

Reluctantly, she turned to his trousers on the floor. She pulled a single cigarette from the crumpled pack and walked back to the bed.

"Put it in my mouth."

Her eyes stayed on his, wary of a sudden lunge. With careful fingers, she wedged the cigarette between his lips.

"Light it."

A lighter rolled from his open palm onto the sheets. She hesitated, then picked it up— the tiny plastic stick somehow heavier than the gun in her other hand. With a flick, a small flame flared into existence. She lit the cigarette, the fire reflecting in her eyes for just a second. He inhaled deeply, letting the smoke slip out of him slowly.

"You're in it now, just like the rest of us." He wasn't gloating, just grim. He blew out another ring of smoke. "Remember. You did this."

"I didn't do anything," Lucia spat.

"You think you can judge me? You have no idea what it takes to run a town like this. There's no stopping evil—I've seen parents put their own babies in a goddamn microwave. You think you can fight that? You can't. You make a deal. Sometimes I have to make sure a kid ends up in foster care 'fore they do something' real bad, even if it means fudging paperwork.

"And these men? If it weren't me, it'd be another cop. That's just how it works. Better it be me—at least I got some decency." He jabbed a finger toward the cameras. "I didn't know they were pullin' this kind of sick shit. But you gotta make deals with the devil to keep the whole town from burnin'.

"And don't act like it's all bad. Since they took over, the gangs stopped killin' each other. Families ain't gettin' caught in the cross-fire no more. You think that's just a coincidence?

"You go upstairs, you'll see. Everyone buys what they sell—always have, always will. We love to cut the hand that feeds us just so we can pretend we don't enjoy the feast. But as long as those bankers keep linin' up their noses, there's always gonna be a place for men like this. And there's always gonna be a need for a pragmatist like me. You can hold onto your ideals all you want. But what's it gonna get you? It ain't gonna bring your brother back from the dead."

He leaned his head forward, pressing the burning cigarette into the sheet. A tiny ember bloomed; a red dot no larger than a coin. But it grew. The cotton curled in on itself, blackening, its edges smoldering into flames. He made his decision.

Lucia shoved the door open and motioned for the girl to follow.

Across the crumpling sheriff, the green light watched, unblinking.

THE HOUSE OF HORRORS

Gun ready, Lucia scanned the corridor. The girl in her police outfit trailed just behind her.

Lucia noticed her eyes—pupils dilated, the same thin beads of sweat clinging to her skin as they had to Marti. Her skin was the same shade too, though the gray smoke muted her tanned face.

Dazed, the girl pointed to a door on the other side of the corridor, closest to the elevator. They crept toward it. The damp stone was replaced by the smell of smoldering cotton as fumes poured into the corridor. Lucia turned. Smoke billowed from under the door where the sheriff was locked inside.

The silence struck her. No crackling flames, no screams. They must have soundproofed the doors. The coquina walls would hold—for now. But she had to move fast. It was only a matter of time before they sent more men.

She pivoted, ready to move on. She had to find her mother. But the girl caught her wrist.

"This is the one," she whispered.

Lucia hesitated.

"Please." Her voice cracked. "My sister's inside."

Lucia gritted her teeth. She was losing time—but she couldn't walk away. She exhaled sharply.

"How many?"

"Ten."

"Any guards?"

"One."

Lucia raised the gun.

"I go in behind you," Lucia said.

The girl hesitated.

"Don't worry, I'll keep you safe," Lucia said.

The girl swallowed hard, then knocked.

"Who is it?" a gruff voice asked.

"Lily."

The door creaked open, and a bearded man filled the frame, his eyes squinting in confusion. Lucia's gun rose to meet his forehead.

"Step back."

"What the—"

"Get on the ground," Lucia growled.

He glared, but the cold barrel on his skin made him lower himself to the floor.

"Do you have more of those handcuffs?" Lucia asked. The girl nodded, disappearing to a closet on the far side of the room. With the guard subdued, Lucia looked around. The room was enormous with five sets of military style bunkbeds. There were girls lying on each, watching her intensely like she was some type of alien. They all had such beautiful sad faces. The kind Lucia had seen in black and white photographs from when people didn't know how to smile. Lucia tried to smile at them, to let them know it would be okay, but it wasn't.

In the corner of the room, she saw a make-up station. There was a large vanity mirror with bulbs around it, and a garment rack filled with racy dresses and costumes. Below it, a box lay partially open, glinting with chains and leather straps. The girl knelt, fingers brushing through the contents, before pulling out a pair of handcuffs.

"Put them on him," Lucia ordered. The girl stepped toward the guard, but as she did, he sprang up, seizing his chance. He grabbed the girl, his arm snapping around her neck like a guillotine. The other girls screamed.

"You'll kill her if you shoot," he warned, dragging the girl in front of him as a human shield. "Put the gun down, and I'll let her go."

The girl's arms were shaking uncontrollably, clattering against his big thighs as he held her in place. Lucia looked in his eyes. She saw nothing behind them. If she dropped the gun, he would kill her.

"Please don't shoot," begged the girl.

Lucia held the gun steady; she breathed in.

"Remember, girl. You'll kill her," the man warned, hoisting her up until her head was level with his own. The girl's face pressed against his, their heads aligned perfectly. Lucia's line of sight blurred—there was no clear shot.

She lowered the gun.

"Good girl."

She'd only dropped her aim slightly—from his head to his exposed ankle. Now it was clear.

The gunshot cracked. The force of it jolted her arm back, pain ricocheting up to her shoulder. The bullet tore through his toe, bone splintering beneath the force. He let out a scream, his grip on the girl slipping just long enough for her to break free.

"Fuck!" he bellowed, lurching forward on one leg.

Her hands shook, fingers slick with sweat as she tried to steady her aim.

Her next shot wasn't as clean—her arm jerked with the recoil, and she almost dropped the gun. But it found its mark. His shoulder snapped backward, jerking his body sideways. His eyes rolled into their sockets.

She aimed again.

The bullet struck his skull. He folded to the ground like a puppet severed from its strings. Silence hung in the gunpowder-laced air as the girls stared in horror. He was dead. Lucia's hands trembled, but she didn't lower the gun. Her chest burned as she saw the camcorder footage on loop in her head. He deserved worse. She stepped over his motionless body, rage fully consuming her, and pointed the gun at his heart.

Now his eyes went hollow like Marti's from the video. He wasn't there—his soul had descended somewhere darker. But so had hers. She looked up; all the girls were hiding behind pillows, staring at her in shock.

She lowered the gun.

"It's okay, he's gone now," Lucia said. She took a step forward, but the girls hid in their beds. Lucia caught a glimpse of herself in the mirror. Blood splattered on her face. She wiped it with her sleeve, but it wouldn't go away. Now her face was just smeared with wild streaks of red.

"You all need to get out of here. They're coming."

The gunshots had been deafening, but the stone tunnels might have muffled the noise before it reached the lobby above. One of the girls got up from her bunk. She had a scar above her right eyebrow. "I'll come." She looked at the man on the floor. "Thank you," she said to Lucia.

Then another girl got down from her bunk.

"I'll come too."

Soon half of them had gotten off their bunks and were ready to leave with Lucia.

"What about the rest of you?" The others didn't move. They shook their heads as they tucked themselves into the sheets.

"They won't come," said the scar-face girl.

"Why?" said Lucia in disbelief. "I'm trying to save them."

"They won't come," a girl with a Russian accent muttered. "They don't want to lose their fix of *El Dorado Dust*."

Lucia watched the girls clutch their bunks, unwilling to let go, even as she tried to pull them toward freedom. She thought of Emi, caught in the same grip of oblivion. They weren't chasing a high—they were trying to numb themselves of reality.

Lucia turned to the door. "We have to go. Now."

No one moved.

She needed to find her mother. She wouldn't have time to lead the girls out of the tunnels. She knelt beside the dead man, patting down his jacket, then his pants pockets. Something hard pressed against the denim. She pulled out a battered Nokia brick phone.

She flipped it open and punched in Garcia's number from the note in her pocket.

"Hello?" Garcia said.

"I need you to meet at the shrine in the woods," Lucia said. "The girls will be waiting for you there."

"Are you okay?" His voice tensed with concern.

"Yes. I'm at the Casa Monica Hotel. They have my mom."

"We'll send someone there too."

"Thanks," Lucia replied. "I have to go." She hung up.

She couldn't wait any longer for the others. Lucia opened the door, and half of the girls followed, the others stayed behind. The fire had grown fiercer. Thick clouds of smoke choked the corridor, causing the girls to cough violently. Lucia's eyes burned as she wiped at them, struggling to see through the haze. The exit was there—she just had to keep moving.

"Follow me."

Lucia sprinted through the smoke, covering her mouth. To move so fast without oxygen made her chest hurt. On the other side, the tunnels lay empty, while the statue of *La Santa Muerte* watched the blaze, seeming to smile. One by one, the girls sprinted through the smoke, emerging on the other side. Lucia took them to the entrance of the passage.

"Go straight down there for a few miles. It will take you to the cemetery. Wait for me in the woods, and I'll have people meet you there."

"Where are you going?"

"I need to go look for my mother."

The girls looked terrified, but the scar-faced girl stepped forward.

"You'll need a mask," she said.

"What?" asked Lucia.

"The hotel is having a masked ball tonight. You'll stick out without one. We have one in the box and a dress you can wear."

"Thank you," said Lucia. "Here. Take these," she passed the girl the bag with the VHS tapes she had stuffed with evidence.

"Take these. The passage door should be open—there's a shelf full of them just around the corner. Grab as many as you can."

The girl nodded.

"Go."

The scar-faced girl took the lead, ushering the girls down the tunnel. Lucia coughed violently. The smoke was becoming unbearable. She flipped the cylinder—one bullet left. She took a deep breath, the burn searing her lungs, then sprinted back through the smoke. She burst into the room. The other girls were still there, unmoved, lying in their beds, eyes fixed blankly on the ceiling.

A large puddle of blood formed around the dead man's body. She turned away, but blood trickled into her field of vision. She felt it on her skin. A sticky ooze that clung to her fingers. She had killed someone. The adrenaline kicked the emotions out of her body, as it thrust her toward the box by the garment rack. She fumbled inside, finally grabbing the bunny mask. She pulled it over her head, the plastic clinging uncomfortably to her face. Then she slipped into a red dress, tightening the straps around her waist. Beneath the fabric, she secured the gun and emptied her pockets into a small pouch strapped to her hip—hidden but within reach.

The other girls barely looked up. They had already stopped hoping.

"You need to get out. There's a fire," she yelled, hoping the girls would move. But they didn't. She scanned the room and spotted a narrow ventilation shaft in the corner, the metal grate barely hanging on. If they could crawl through, it might give them a chance to escape the smoke and heat.

"Through there!" she urged, pointing at the vent. "It might lead to another tunnel—go!"

She couldn't wait to see if they moved. She ran toward the elevator. Frantically, she pressed the button, hiding the gun in her pouch. The elevator stopped; she yanked the shutter and clambered inside. A cloud of smoke followed her in. She pressed the button for the lobby. The blood on her face, concealed beneath the stiff plastic mask.

The doors opened.

THE MASKED BALL

When the elevator doors slid open, Lucia was momentarily disarmed by the opulence of the lobby. A golden honey light oozed into the elevator, casting a warm glow as chandeliers sparkled above. Below, candelabras adorned tables, their candles twinkling, fresh wax pooling at their bases. The lobby was awash in black and gold, suited shadows drifting through the haze, blurring the lines between night and day. It was the masked ball.

Lucia stepped into the lobby, the mask concealing the sheen of blood drying on her skin. A thin trail of smoke clung to her as she emerged, but the room was too raucous for anyone to notice.

Hundreds of masked guests mingled, champagne flutes dangling from their fingers, as precariously as the strings holding their masks in place. The room was a swirl of bodies, guests drifting between groups, conversations flowing like a restless stream—eddying around the most powerful people in the room. It was as if someone had pressed a slow-motion button—Lucia watched as guests cackled in circles, their laughter tilting them off balance. They were drunk. She thought of the girls shivering below, the tunnels lined with dope—fuel for the party's insatiable appetite.

She moved through the raucous crowd, unnoticed, her eyes scanning for her mother. She drifted between the clusters of people like a bubble floating from their flutes.

She couldn't see anyone's eyes; the masks concealed their faces. Men wore jet-black tuxedos, each paired with a unique mask. She'd seen those jawlines on TV—politicians who had railed against corruption, now drinking with the same men they claimed to oppose, their masks doing little to hide the hypocrisy. Others were the golden faces of television, the voices who read the news to her growing up, now foaming at the mouth as they drank themselves into oblivion.

These were the people who persecuted those in the forest trying to help. These were the people who profited off Emi's decline. The mask couldn't stop her scowl, she was shaking with rage.

And then there were the others, their faces completely hidden behind masks like something out of a Greek tragedy. The sight of them sent a jolt through her chest, each one a potential guard from the basement.

She scanned their bodies carefully, searching for any sign of her mother's slender frame.

A large banner near the entrance caught her eye:

The Monica's Charity Ball

"I love your outfit sweetie."

Lucia turned around. A woman stood before her, wearing a red slit dress and a mask that hid her eyes, two plumes of feathers reaching skyward.

"Thanks," Lucia said, startled. Her gaze lingered on the woman's chin—the sharp angles of her bones softened by dimples. She was beautiful.

"Have we met before?" the lady said. "You'll have to forgive me—masks tend to make everything a little more complicated."

"I don't think so," Lucia said.

A moment later, a man appeared at her side.

"This is my husband."

Lucia recognized him by his belly. The way his suit buttons seemed about to pop off. It was the man whose wedding she'd crashed at the Basilica. One of the biggest property developers in the city.

"Nice to meet you," Lucia said.

The man reached out to shake her hand, but as his eyes came up to her face and saw her bunny mask, he froze. He lowered his hand.

"Darling, there's someone you must meet. Victoria Humphrey is here," he said, stiffly.

"The actress?" she said.

"Of course. She'd love to meet you." The man extended his arm for his wife to take, already leading her away.

"It was nice to chat sweetie," the lady said with a smile before disappearing into the crowd. To Lucia's right, a dense mob gathered around a woman—it had to be the actress. To the left, she spotted the familiar square jaw of the local school principal, the one who lectured parents about personal responsibility, the one who hated Emi. He guzzled the remainder of his champagne and snapped his fingers for a refill. Even the servers wore masks. Lucia eyed the waitress approaching him, but she was too tall to be her mother. The principal leaned toward a woman in a purple dress, his head tilted conspicuously toward her chest. Not even the mask could disguise his wandering eyes.

Silver platters of caviar gleamed under the chandeliers, champagne bottles shimmered, and silk dresses twirled like ghosts in the light. She thought of the girls downstairs. Some of these men in tuxedos were in those VHS tapes.

Then, a flash of white caught her eye—a man in a skeleton mask, the kind worn for *Dia de los Muertos*. Her stomach clenched. The world blurred around her as she moved toward him, her hand brushing the gun at her waistband. Surely, Mr. Muerte couldn't be so brazen as to wear the mask of death. As she drew closer, the enormous man turned, moving with an unsettling ease as he reached for finger food. That was when she saw it—the eye tattooed on the back of his skull.

Jonny. The one who had waited for her outside the Basilica booth. He'd been following her. He must have been the one who tipped off the sheriff that she'd gone into the forest. She stopped, trying to merge into a nearby circle of people so he wouldn't recognize her. Jonny decapitated a roll of shrimp sushi with one bite. Suddenly, another man approached him; he was also wearing the skull mask. She scanned the room and realized there were at least half a dozen men in skull masks, all dressed in identical tuxedos.

One of them, on the other side of the lobby, turned and looked at her. The shadows over his eyes were darker than his suit, his pupils so small she couldn't tell if there was anyone behind the mask. Instead of a mouth, the mask featured stitched lines sealing his teeth—a surgical smile that sent shivers down her spine. Yet his gaze pulled at her, just like the card did. The invisible string that she could never sever. *Was it him?*

Suddenly, there was a burst of movement—a man sprinted across the lobby, shoving people aside. Champagne splashed to the floor, and guests gasped as he bumped into them. Someone threw a shrimp at him in protest.

"Shame on you!" another shouted, their words drowned out by the music and drunken chatter. The man stopped when he reached the other men in skull masks and whispered something to them. Within seconds, the group pushed their way through the crowd, as they made their way toward the elevator, yelling for people to get out of the way. They must have heard about the fire. The elevator doors slid open, and they shoved inside, disappearing as it descended to the basement. Then it hit her—the *Dia de los Muertos* masks weren't just costumes. They marked the cartel.

Lucia pushed deeper into the crowd. They may know she was

here—the other girls may have told the man who ran over. She tried to lose herself among the bodies, but then she noticed something unexpected. Another man in a skeleton mask sauntered toward the elevator. He wore a suit identical to all the others. Unlike the rest, he wasn't in a rush. He stood there, waiting calmly for the elevator to arrive. Lucia followed, her heart pounding in her chest. He didn't seem concerned about the fire. He was headed somewhere else. *To her mother?*

Lucia followed him through the crowd. At the elevator, he tapped his foot, waiting. When the bell chimed, he yanked the doors open and paused as though expecting something.

"Are you coming up?" the man rasped, his voice oddly strained.

Lucia was hidden behind a group of people, but his eyes found her immediately. He waited, still and patient, as though he had all the time in the world.

"Yes," she replied nervously, her only comfort being the gun tucked at her waistband.

"Which floor?"

"The fifth," she lied.

The man pressed for the fifth floor—then the top. As soon as she saw the button he pressed, she knew where she had to go. They stood in silence, the elevator doors sliding shut. The silence was earsplittingly loud. The oxygen sucked up by the vacuum of words, as Lucia worried he would hear her heartbeat. The man looked straight ahead at the door; Lucia dared not look at him. Instead, she stared at the floor, trying to steady her breathing. He might know who she was. Maybe he'd already talked to the others.

The man was so close she could smell him, a scent that was inseparable from the hotel itself, a vague air of luxury that said nothing about the man behind the mask. He was old. She could tell by his hands—the way the wrinkles folded over his knuckles, the looseness of his skin. But his body's shape was obscured by the masterful cut of his suit—fabric designed to conceal weight, broaden shoulders, and hide flab.

"I like your mask," he said.

Lucia turned to face him. She couldn't see his expression behind the mask. Lucia said nothing.

"I have seen it somewhere," the man said.

The elevator chimed—the fifth floor. Lucia kept her gaze fixed on the carpet, avoiding his eyes. As she stepped out, his voice stopped her.

"Wait. You dropped something." He motioned to the carpet just outside the elevator. Lucia turned around. The man yanked the elevator shut. She hesitated, then stepped closer, eyes on the carpet.

There it was. The card of death.

MR MUERTE

Lucia yanked the gun from her waistband, aiming at the elevator shaft. But it was too late. The doors inched shut, the elevator taunting her as it lurched upward. She needed to get to the top floor. It was him.

The hotel's fire escape was next to the elevator—she sprinted toward it.

Without thinking, she shoved against the door—it barely budged. She cursed, then threw her weight into it again, nearly stumbling as it swung open. The gun felt heavy in her shaking hands. One bullet left.

She bolted up the stairs, each step a second slipping away. Her panting echoed through the empty stairwell. Three floors left. Her fingers clenched around the gun, slick with sweat.

At the top, she used her back to shove open the door, almost tripping as she swung the gun up. Her arms wobbled from the effort, but there was nothing—just an empty corridor. The royal red carpet stretched to a door, slightly ajar, at the end of the corridor. She walked toward it, passing a few other locked hotel suites.

She kept the gun steady, inching closer to the door, its paneling carved into neat brown squares like a bar of dark chocolate. The silence felt wrong. She hesitated. It had to be a trap. But there was no time—Mr. Muerte could already be inside with her mother. She kicked open the door, ready to shoot.

She froze.

Javier sat perfectly still in the chair, his skull mask resting on the coffee table. His white-gloved hands were neatly folded over his three-piece suit, poised as if he'd been waiting for her.

"Lucia. Please, sit down," he said, his voice calm, his gestures eerily familiar.

She stared at him. The familiar smell of his cologne, soured, as the sandalwood scent splintered her nostrils. It wasn't shock that gripped her—it was a quiet, crushing certainty. The kind that drains all the air from the room. The kindness, the easy smile, the moments she had trusted him—they all curdled in her memory. He was always there, always watching, wearing the face of a friend.

"You're…" She faltered, the pieces falling into place. The pageant queen's death during the hurricane—the killer had to be someone staying at the motel. Someone Maya's children trusted.

She started to shake with rage. A single bullet rattled in the chamber, as she aimed at Mr. Muerte's heart.

"Put the gun down, Lucia," Javier said, even calmer. "That won't save your mother."

"Where is she?" she demanded.

"Please take a seat and lower the gun."

He had his own gun placed on the table just in front of him. He pretended it didn't exist as he spoke with casual ease, like they were catching up over dinner. The luxury room was bathed in the warm glow of the gas fireplace, its flames flickering against the ornate Spanish tile. A crystal chandelier hung overhead, swaying slightly from the draft seeping in through the balcony doors.

"This isn't going to help you find her," he said.

Lucia ripped her mask off. For the first time, Javier seemed unsettled. He saw the blood on her face.

"Alright. I'll tell you where she is. But don't do anything stupid."

He leaned back slightly, his eyes steady on hers. "You'll need a key. And that, my dear, is hidden.'

"Where is she?" Lucia demanded, her whole body shaking.

"You need to play along before I can tell you that."

"Mom? Are you okay," she yelled. "Mom!"

There was no response.

"She won't hear you," Javier said calmly. "She's unconscious."

Lucia leveled the gun at his head.

"She doesn't have long. I suggest you put down the gun."

Javier remained as calm as ever, even with the gun aimed squarely at him. Lucia had no other choice. Slowly, she lowered it onto the table. Without hesitation, Javier rose to his feet, as he effortlessly lunged over the table. He plucked the gun and slid it smoothly into his waistband, as if it had always belonged there.

"She's passed out in the bathtub with the water running. She should have about ten minutes left," he said, glancing at his watch before sitting back down.

"What'd you do to her?" Lucia begged.

Javier pulled out a syringe from his pocket.

"What'd she do to herself is the question."

He placed the *El Dorado Dust* onto the table, his gloves leaving no fingerprints on the tube.

"It's your turn now," he said.

Lucia didn't look away. "This is what you did to Maya."

"It's not personal, Lucia," he said. "Our industry works a little different to most."

"I thought you were her friend," she said, disgusted.

"We were," he said smoothly. "We don't like things to end this way, but warnings were given. Non-compliance has its consequences, even for friends."

"She trusted you with her kids."

"I told you, it's not personal."

"You tried to make me believe in some curse, just so I wouldn't figure out what you were doing."

"I never needed to lie," he said. "You were already seeing exactly what you wanted to see."

"You liar," she spat.

"I'm afraid you need to take some accountability. You were looking to process your brother's grief. It made you susceptible to such stories—ones where the dead can talk."

"You lied to me," she said. "Your daughter didn't die in some car accident. You just wanted me to trust you. You were never a detective."

"I told you, I didn't lie," he said calmly. "I was a detective, and my daughter did die—but not in some accident. The Guadalajara Cartel rigged a bomb in my car while I was investigating their leader, Miguel Gallardo. I barely survived, but my daughter didn't. After that, staying in Mexico wasn't an option. Neither was staying a detective."

"So you joined another cartel to honor her?"

"Do you think that peace honors the dead? An eye for an eye makes the whole world blind, but a soul for a soul, makes the whole world see."

Lucia glanced at the clock on the wall, she was running out of time.

"Where is my mother? She had nothing to do with this. Killing her won't bring back your daughter."

Javier sighed. "I liked you, Lucia. You're brave. But in this business, the only power we have is passed in whispers. Just like it was for thousands of years, everyone learns the consequences of their actions through the oral tradition. Stories are more powerful than laws."

He pulled out the card of death, turning it over slowly between his fingers, tracing its edges with unsettling ease. "Fear is all we have."

"I'm not scared of you," Lucia said.

He shuffled the syringe to the other side of the table.

"Good. Then it's time to play your part in this story."

"Where is she?"

Javier looked at his watch. "She should have about seven minutes." Then he reached into his suit jacket pocket and held up a set of keys, letting them dangle in front of her.

"Your mother has already made her choice. She took a dose so strong, she should be fading by now. Soon, the bathwater will rise to her mouth."

Lucia lunged forward, but Javier yanked the keys back, his gun snapping up in an instant.

"Now, now, be careful," he said, his voice measured. "I'll give you the room number, but you must do something first."

Lucia's breath was ragged. "What?"

"Inject yourself." Javier nodded toward the syringe. "It's preloaded with a dose about five times the lethal amount. You'll have five minutes of pure euphoria—just enough time to enjoy your last moments with your mother. Then, your respiratory system will shut down. You'll slip into unconsciousness, and the world will fade to black."

Lucia studied Javier's face, searching for any flicker of hesitation. There was none.

"This will be one of my more poetic ones," he mused. "I hope you can appreciate the artistry of it. I made sure to sprinkle in a bit of *Romeo and Juliet*—a tragedy in two acts. A mother watches her second child die of an overdose, then chooses to follow, dosing herself into oblivion to be with you in the land of the dead. It's rather beautiful, isn't it?"

"Fuck you," said Lucia.

"Your choice. Spend your last moments with her—or die alone in that chair," he said, nudging the gun toward it.

Lucia picked up the syringe.

"So what do you decide?" he said.

"How long will it take?" she asked, calculating in her head.

"Give or take ten minutes," Javier said smoothly. "But please, enjoy the first five—they will be absolute bliss. I'll let you have them in private."

Lucia took a deep breath, steadying herself.

She knew there was only one way out.

She plunged the syringe into her forearm. The liquid fire and honey flooding her veins all at once—warmth spreading, the world softening at the edges. She closed her eyes and smiled. It felt like floating in a steaming bath, tequila burning warm in her throat, while Emi's voice drifted beside her, rambling about crocodiles. It was the most perfect feeling of her entire life.

Javier smiled. "Good girl. Your mother's in the first room on the left, down the hall."

He tossed the room keys across the table, smirking. "Enjoy. You won't be able to walk in a few minutes—make the most of it."

Lucia rose to her feet. Her joints felt new, the pain in her feet, gone. She was floating through the room. Javier's presence had dissolved, their exchange already slipping away like a flu-induced dream. She tried to recall his words—the instructions, where her mother was— but they drifted from her grasp. Then she pictured herself with her mother and Emi, walking hand in hand along Vilano Beach. *Yes.* That's why she was here. That's what she had to do.

First door on the left.

She opened the door to exit Javier's room, the steel handle buzzing with warm atoms, tickling her hand. She closed it behind her, wobbling into the corridor. The red carpet was so fuzzy she could see every fiber swaying like a cornfield stretching into the horizon.

She needed to focus. *This was all part of the plan.*

The spray was in her pouch—she was sure of it. But her mind was slipping, lulling her toward stillness, like snow pulling a body into its soft embrace with its false promise of warmth.

Focus.

She tapped her pouch to make sure it was still there. The naloxone. She felt it. Tom's words drifted back, light and certain. *The only way to stop an overdose.* Javier could've never known. She yanked off the cap, fingers fumbling, then tilted her head back and pressed the nozzle into her nostril. A sharp burst of liquid shot up, stinging as it coated her sinuses.

She didn't expect it to be so immediate. The warm fuzziness was yanked away as a cold electric charge surged through her body. A metallic aftertaste spread over her tongue, coating her throat in an icy chill that made it hard to breathe.

She dry heaved.

Her knees ground against her joints, tendons feeling on the verge of tearing. Every orifice of her body screamed with a sharp pain.

She needed to get to the room. Her mother had only minutes left before she would drown. The pain brought her to her knees. She crawled toward the door, fumbling with the keys to open it. Her vision was too blurry to see the room, but the sound of running tap water guided her. She crawled to the bathroom and pushed the door handle down.

Her mother was there, the water line dancing dangerously close to her lips, arms slumped over the porcelain edges of the bathtub.

"Mom!" Lucia yelled.

Her mother didn't reply. Lucia looked to her forearm and saw the same injection marks that had been on Emi.

She held the spray, her vision fading in and out of consciousness. The pain was all-consuming.

Focus.

She fumbled with the naloxone, pulling off the cap with trembling fingers. Then she crawled to the bathtub, switching off the tap. The water stilled, lapping dangerously close to her mother's parted lips.

With shaking hands, she pressed the nozzle of the spray into her mother's nostril and administered the dose. Then she lifted her mother's head slightly, watching—waiting—for any sign of movement.

"Come on," Lucia whispered, watching her mother's face for any sign the medicine was working. Her own vision blurred as another wave of pain crashed through her body. She had to stay conscious long enough to make sure her mother was safe.

Her mother's face moved slightly. A scrunch of the eyebrow. Then she started to cough weakly, water dribbling from the corner of her mouth. Lucia supported her head. She couldn't lose her too.

Her mother's eyelids fluttered but didn't open. A low moan escaped her throat. Lucia glanced anxiously at the bathroom door, ears straining for footsteps in the hallway. Javier would come looking for them soon. She still had five minutes.

"Mom, please," Lucia whispered, her voice barely audible over the dripping faucet. Her mother's breathing changed—deeper, more purposeful—but still her eyes remained closed.

Then her mother started to gag.

"Mom? It's okay. Breathe."

Her mother's eyes opened; they made eye contact for the first time. The pain of the Naloxone disappeared, as she felt the warmth of *El Dorado Dust* for a second. Her mother smiled too.

It gave Lucia strength.

"Get up, I will help you."

She hauled her mother out of the bathtub, her clothes sopping wet, as Lucia's shoulder shuddered under the weight. She dragged her out of the bathroom. They had to escape before Javier returned.

But she had one thing to do first.

Lucia propped her mother onto the armchair, steadying her as she slumped forward. Then she wearily marched to the fireplace, identical to the one in Javier's room. Her head was thumping, but her mission was crystal clear. With a quick twist of the knob, she let the gas flow, filling the room with its silent, noxious whispers. It was too slow.

Dropping to her knees, she yanked at the gas supply hose. With a sharp twist, the hose snapped loose—gas hissed out fast, heavy, pooling low.

She had the lighter in her pocket, but she needed to let the room fill first. She checked the clock—four minutes. How would she set the fuse? Then she spotted the microwave. If she could set a delay on something flammable, it would ignite the gas the moment he walked in. Moving quickly, she grabbed a can of cooking spray from the counter, shoved it into the microwave, and set the timer to start in four minutes. The microwave gave a soft beep, then went silent, waiting. She had to move—now.

Throwing her mother's arm over her shoulder, Lucia hauled her up, her own legs screaming in protest as she dragged them toward the door. She yanked it open, stepping into the hall. She pulled her mother toward the elevator shaft, frantically pressing the button. Three minutes. Her mother's left foot dragged on the carpet as Lucia shifted more of her weight onto her shoulder. Step by step, they inched forward until they reached the elevator shaft—an open stretch of corridor leaving them completely exposed. She kept pressing the button, even though the down arrow already glowed.

Moments later, the elevator chimed. Lucia yanked open the metal grate and hurriedly lowered her mother inside before climbing in after her. The metal grate on the door left thin slits—just enough to see through without being seen. She pressed her mother flat onto the floor, then lay down beside her, their bodies hidden in the shadows. Holding her breath, she peered through the gaps, watching the corridor.

The suite door remained shut. Then—movement. Javier stepped out, his pace slowing as he scanned the hallway, his gaze sharp, calculating. Something felt off. He lingered for a beat too long, his eyes narrowing toward the room.

Lucia's body faltered, a wave of weakness crashing over her as the medication pulsed through her veins. Her limbs felt sluggish—but there was no time to collapse. If she lost control now, they were as good as dead.

Then she saw it. He reached into his pocket, fingers fumbling—a cigarette.

Light it.

Suddenly, the elevator lurched downward. Javier's head snapped toward the noise, distracted for just a moment. With a frustrated glance at the moving elevator, he turned back, pulling the cigarette to his mouth. He didn't see them.

There were three long seconds of darkness as the elevator lurched between levels.

Then came the blast.

The whole elevator shook, iron cables rattling like pieces of string. Emergency lights flickered as dust and debris rained through the ventilation grates in the ceiling. A plastic panel tore free, striking Lucia's head with a dull crack. She grimaced. The nausea from the spray swelled in her gut, blending with the sharp, tinny ringing in her ears. She blinked hard, fighting to stay awake as she tightened her grip on her mother. Her mother was fading. Nothing else mattered now—just getting her out. They had to escape.

Suddenly, the elevator stopped, the doors opened to the lobby.

Harsh emergency lights strobed, stripping the room of its golden glow, washing everything in cold, sterile white. Music had vanished—replaced by the urgent scream of the siren. Guests ran in all directions, their masks discarded, faces bare in the stark light.

Lucia seized the moment. The panic gave her cover as she dragged her mother toward the exit, unnoticed in the stampede. She spotted the news anchor from earlier—his wife nowhere in sight as he sprinted for the door, desperate to be the first out.

She scanned for the men in three-piece suits, their *Dia de los Muertos* masks, but they were nowhere to be seen. They must have slipped away through the tunnels.

Her strength was failing. A deep, shuddering chill ran through her, her body on the verge of collapse. Each step was slower than the last. Her arms ached. Her legs burned. But the exit was just ahead—just a few more feet.

She reached the door.

Outside, more sirens wailed in the distance. Guests spilled onto the pavement, hailing limousines and taxis in frantic waves. Then, through the blur of flashing lights, Lucia spotted a familiar car.

Mrs. Garcia's minivan.

She dragged her mother toward it, her vision narrowing at the edges. The door swung open.

Mrs. Garcia leaned forward. "You made it."

Lucia collapsed into the passenger seat, her mother beside her.

Lucia passed out.

FOUNTAIN OF YOUTH

When she woke, an IV drip tugged at her arm. The sterile scent of saline filled the air, but this wasn't a hospital. Her mouth was dry, the kind of dryness that followed a long mosquito-bitten sleep. She blinked against the dim light, her vision adjusting. *The bunker.* Anastasia Forest.

There were girls all around her—dozens of them, the ones she'd helped escape from the hotel, all lying in the beds, sleeping. The girl with the scar lay beside her, curled on her side, her breath rasping softly through her nose.

She searched for her mother. Then she spotted her. Lying on her back, eyes closed. The sporadic beep of a heart monitor punctuated the silence. The faint blip, the only reminder she was alive.

Lucia swung her legs over the bed, drowsiness weighing her down as her feet harshly hit the ground. She could barely stand. She wasn't sure how long she'd been asleep. *Days?*

A lady in scrubs rushed toward her.

"Where are you going, darling?"

"Is my mother okay?"

"Yes," she nodded, quickly checking her vitals. "She's responding slowly, but she's stabilizing."

Lucia exhaled, her body sagging with relief.

"Let me get Garcia. He asked to be called when you woke up," the medic said.

The medic disappeared down the tunnel. Moments later, Garcia emerged, his rumpled collared shirt, sleeves rolled up. He looked exhausted.

"How are you feeling?"

"Okay." Lucia rubbed her temples. "How long have we been down here?"

"A few days. Honestly, I can't believe you even moved after taking that dose of Naloxone. The doctor said it should've knocked you out for at least three days. Yet you managed to carry your mother out of the hotel."

Lucia glanced at her mother, still barely stirring. "Is she okay?"

"She's taking longer to respond to the medication, but she's stable now. The doctor said she was a few minutes from a fatal hypoxia."

Lucia scanned the room, her gaze landing on a familiar face—one of the girls who'd refused to come, clutching a rosary, praying.

"They got out," she murmured.

"Because of you," Garcia said. "They even went back to help convince the others to follow. I still can't believe you found that tunnel entrance in the shrine. I could never figure it out."

"Coquina walls," Lucia mumbled, her mind still hazy. "They trap moisture differently. That's why I knew it wasn't solid."

Garcia nodded, then hesitated. "These girls wouldn't be alive if it weren't for you," he said, voice softer now. "Well—you, Maya, and Emi. They started this."

Lucia swallowed hard.

"What happened after I left?"

Garcia ran a hand over his face. "I still have a few good men in the force. With the sheriff gone, we had enough confidence we could act unimpeded. The girls told us where the dope was stashed in the tunnels. It was the evidence we needed to finally take them down."

He gestured toward the passage. "Come on, I'll show you—it's been all over the news."

Lucia frowned. "There's a TV down here?"

Garcia chuckled. "Yeah. They have a medical room for the staff. I've been holed up there the last few days, watching *MASH* reruns while waiting for you to wake up."

Lucia followed Garcia past rows of sleeping girls. She grazed her fingers across her mother's sheet before continuing to the small room constructed for the medics. A portable Sony TV sat in the corner. Garcia picked up the remote.

"They've been playing the hotel bust on loop."

The TV flickered to life. The same female anchor from the hurricane coverage appeared with helicopter footage of the Casa Monica Hotel behind her.

"Authorities have raided the tunnel system underneath the hotel where they found over 500 pounds of heroin. It is the largest bust in the State's history. The port town operated as the distribution point for the entire East Coast. The Hell's Angels would collect from various exit points to distribute nationwide. Questions are being raised about how historical monuments were used so flagrantly in this criminal enterprise, and how authorities didn't detect such a large operation at the heart of the city."

The footage cut to arrests outside the hotel. Jonny the Giant was forced into a police car, his massive frame barely fitting as the door closed on him. The eye on the back of his skull disappearing behind the tinted glass.

Lucia's jaw tightened, her fingers digging into her palms as she watched.

"Do they know about the tapes?" she asked.

"No," Garcia replied, pointing to a cabinet. "The girls took them when they escaped. We have them here." He reached for one labeled with the crab's real name. "I watched one while you were asleep..."

Lucia said nothing.

"It's half the people in this city. Smith, Edwards—enough evidence to put them away for life."

"No," Lucia said firmly. "It's not your property. It belongs to them." She nodded toward the sleeping girls.

"But we could expose everyone involved. Not just the cartel, but the people in power. It was Maya's..."

"It's their choice what happens with the tapes," Lucia said firmly.

The anchor reappeared with footage of flames engulfing the hotel's top floor.

"The fire that led to this discovery originated from a gas leak. Javier Cortez, 62, died after a mechanical fault in his fireplace led to an explosion in his room. There is nothing left of his body and his room, and he is believed to have died instantly."

A picture showed of him on the TV.

Garcia squinted.

"Hey, isn't that the old man who was friends with Maya from the motel?"

Lucia said nothing.

"Seems strange," he said.

"Maybe he got the card of death too," Lucia said after a long pause, deliberately keeping the identity of Mr. Muerte a secret.

"They must've arrested the cartel's assassin, they got pretty much everyone in there, rounded them at all the tunnel exits," Garcia said. "The deputy will find him. We just need to ask the right questions."

"I'm sure they will," Lucia said, looking at the TV, thinking about the alleged gas leak, as she played with the card of death in her pocket. *Maybe stories were more powerful.*

"You have to promise me something," Lucia said.

"Yes?" Garcia replied.

"You don't tell anyone about these tapes."

Garcia looked uncomfortable.

"Not for any reelection promises or anything," Lucia said.

"Please, I don't want to be the mayor of this city ever again."

A long pause lingered as the machines pulsed with the patients' sleeping heart rates.

"What's going to happen to the girls?" asked Lucia.

"We'll keep them here until we know it's safe. We have a doctor here. You saw the names on those tapes, it's not safe for them till these men are brought to justice. They'll try to keep their secrets."

"They'll be safe here," Lucia said.

"What about you? What are you going to do with yourself after all this?" Garcia asked.

Lucia stared at the tapes in the cupboard silently.

"You know, I think you'd make a great detective," he said.

"I don't want that."

"Why? You practically dismantled their entire operation by yourself."

Lucia paused, glancing back at the beds of girls, thinking of Emi shaking in the sheets.

"What's the point?" she said.

"What do you mean?" asked Garcia surprised.

"Someone's going to take their place. There will always be people in these beds," Lucia said.

"But if you stop the bad guys, you stop this," Garcia said, his voice carrying the energy of his old campaign speeches.

"No," Lucia replied. "It will never stop. It doesn't matter which crime group it is—the bikers will take over the dope trade in a few weeks, and the city will be worse off than before."

"But you have to try," Garcia pressed.

"You don't stop it by cutting off the heads of a hydra."

"Then how do I stop them?" he asked. "The drugs ruin lives."

"They don't," Lucia said.

"What? What about your brother?"

"Drugs didn't kill my brother," she said.

Garcia frowned. "What?"

"People die when they lose control," Lucia said. "When they lose hope."

"But don't they find hope if we try to make things better?"

"You don't get hope by waging a war you can't win."

"Then how do you get hope?"

Lucia met his gaze. "By choosing your own story."

The TV flashed with a breaking news alert, interrupting their conversation.

"In the latest news, police have discovered the body of Father Roderick in the Basilica. It is believed he has taken his own life. The body was tragically discovered when he didn't show up for mass, where parishioners found his two-day-old corpse. An empty bottle of communion wine was found beside him."

"Mr. Muerte?" Garcia said in shock. "The cartel must've done this."

"Or maybe he did it himself?" Lucia said. "Maybe he realized that his silence led to all this suffering, and he couldn't live with that?"

"He was trying to save my children," Garcia said defensively. "He made a vow of silence to me."

"Doesn't make it any easier to live with the consequences."

Garcia went quiet.

There was a rustling from one of the patients' beds.

"We should check on them," Garcia said.

When they entered the room, a girl was standing, swaying slightly on unsteady legs. Her dark hair hung in tangled waves around her hollow face. It was Marti.

"Are you okay?" asked Lucia softly.

The girl shook her head, her eyes glassy with fear.

"Come with us, we'll make you some tea," Garcia said, ushering her to the medic's room.

When they reached the room, Marti froze in the doorway. Her gaze fixed on the countertop where the tape Garcia had pulled out still sat. The label faced upward, the receptionist's name—the crab— scrawled in black marker.

Marti's fingers dug into the doorframe. A small sound escaped her throat—not quite a whimper, not quite a word.

Lucia followed her gaze to the tape, understanding crystallizing within her.

"It's okay," Lucia said, stepping between Marti and the tape. "No one will ever see it. I promise."

Lucia gave Marti a hug while Garcia stood in the corner.

"It's okay," Lucia whispered.

She reached into her pocket, playing with the card of death. The crab would be in his bunker, sipping his tea in that windowless room.

Lucia smiled.

DIA DE LOS MUERTOS

St. Augustine – November 1 – 2004

The Day of the Dead celebrations had arrived at St. Augustine. The plaza had fairy lights twinkling from palm trees with parade banners hanging over street signs. Marigolds shimmered amid a sea of candles, casting pumpkin-orange incantations into the night.

There were dozens of locals dressed in outfits, some in full skeleton suits, others with colorful rebozos flowing inches off the sidewalk. They walked down St. George Street to the steady rhythm of maria- chi trumpets, the procession shuffling lock-step to the music.

Lucia adjusted her mask.

Her pockets were heavy with shells, her hands, carrying a single candle.

She looked up at her mother. It had been over a month since the Casa Monica Hotel, and her face was back to its usual rich coloring, the paleness subsiding with each day of recovery. Her mother smiled. This time it lingered as she reached out to hold Lucia's spare hand.

Lucia was smiling too, though the mask hid it from view.

She looked at the other people in the procession. They were most- ly Mexican: grandmothers with rosaries, fathers with children on shoulders, and widows—all smiling as they carried the memories of their loved ones at the tip of each candle wick. An old lady smiled at her, the same woman who had sold tortillas from a wooden cart near the Basilica when Lucia was small.

Lucia felt him there too, walking behind them, his fingers inter-twined with theirs just like they had done at Vilano Beach. She could hear him whisper, the soft hiss interwoven with the guitar chords.

She turned around. Marti smiled at her. The girls from the hotel basement joined the parade, each holding a candle, their half-skel-eton faces eerily beautiful in the flickering light.

They smiled back at Lucia.

"Mom, we should say hi to Emi now."

"Okay, sweetie," her mother said.

Lucia and her mother broke from the parade that continued to march down Avenida Menendez. They walked to the cemetery, a dozen blocks east of the Castillo de San Marcos.

The candle guided them through the dark streets as they walked in silence that felt like no other before. This one had no weight; it flowed as freely as a stream.

"I'm sorry," said her mother.

"I'm sorry too," Lucia said.

"When the hotel fired me, I never thought..."

"It's okay," Lucia replied.

"I never knew. I should've believed you."

Lucia looked at her mother's face paint. A month ago, she would've never taken her to a Day of the Dead parade. The Catholic Church looks down on 'pagan' symbols. But something in her mother had softened in the last month. She'd stopped reading her Bible every night, and she'd even started whispering Emi's name before she went to sleep.

"It's not your fault."

"I think I felt shame," her mother said. "That I wasn't a good enough. That I couldn't save him."

"You tried. We all did," Lucia said.

"Forgetting him was easier than living with him."

Lucia reached for her hand. "He's still with us."

They walked in silence, weaving through the cemetery until they reached his grave. Lucia knelt, placing the candle at the base of his tombstone, the flame trembling in the night air.

"Mom," she said softly. "I don't want to go to college."

Her mother exhaled, the weight of everything settling in her shoulders.

"I understand," she said. "I guess it's my turn to give you the same bad advice. Follow your heart."

"I want to write stories," Lucia said. "And to stay with you."

Her mother gave a tired, wistful smile. "That's nice."

Lucia's gaze drifted beyond the rows of headstones to a cluster of freshly dug graves at the far end of the cemetery.

"Just a second," she murmured. "There's something I need to see."

She stepped away, moving toward the newest graves, their soil still unsettled. One marker caught her eye.

Rest in Peace
Mick Coates
1970–2004

His name was written just like it had been on the tapes. She reached into her pocket, fingers closing around its sharp edges. She pulled out the card of death. This story had just begun.

She placed it on the tombstone. The signature on the bottom corner.

Mr. Muerte.

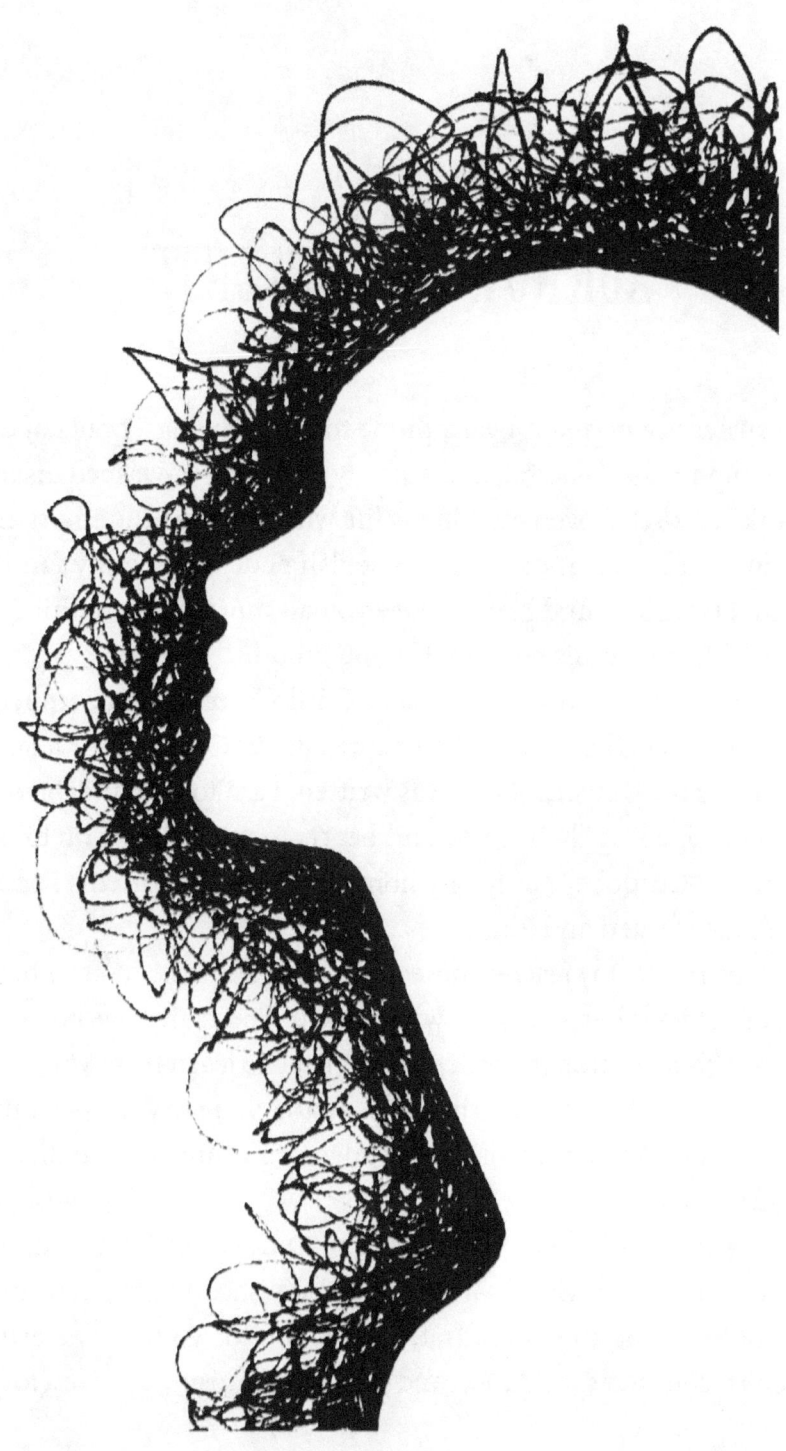

ACKNOWLEDGEMENTS

The writer is a petulant beast, prone to mood swings, bouts of despair, moments of elation, and a steady stream of unwashed dishes. Thank you to the loved ones in my life who provided the emotional support for me to undertake this selfish endeavor. To my family, Mum, Dad, Kelly and Nana, I love you all more than anything in the world. I hope this book makes you proud.

To my other family, mi familia de Córdoba, muchísimas gracias por todo. The Ulla family looked after me in Córdoba for a large portion of the time this book was written. I am forever indebted to them for opening their home and hearts to me. Thank you to my friends in Córdoba, many of whom are ironically villains in this novel: Emi, Marti and Rami.

To my friend, my teacher, my editor—Tom Humphrey—this book would not have been possible without you. You truly have been the greatest collaborator, it has been a privilege to learn from you.

To my other friend, Clarissa Luk, thank you for your beautiful artistic work. You are a world-class talent, and I am grateful that we could work together.

I owe a serious vote of thanks to my publisher, Jessy Wu, the founder of Encour, who must be the first publisher to sign an advance without reading the book first. Thank you for your unwavering support, continued guidance, and eternal optimism. You are a force